KU-541-287

C.J. BOX
LONG RANGE

First published in the UK by Head of Zeus in 2020

Published by arrangement with G. P. Putnam's Sons, an imprint of
Penguin Publishing, a division of Penguin Random House LLC

Copyright © C.J. Box, 2020

The moral right of C.J. Box to be identified
as the author of this work has been asserted in accordance with
the Copyright, Designs and Patents Act of 1988.

All rights reserved. No part of this publication may be
reproduced, stored in a retrieval system, or transmitted in any form or by any means,
electronic, mechanical, photocopying, recording, or otherwise, without the prior permission of both the copyright owner and the above publisher of this book.

This is a work of fiction. All characters, organizations, and events
portrayed in this novel are either products of the author's
imagination or are used fictitiously.

9 7 5 3 1 2 4 6 8

A catalogue record for this book is available from the British Library.

ISBN (HB): 9781788549271
ISBN (XTPB): 9781788549288
ISBN (E): 9781788549264

Printed and bound in the UK by
CPI Group (UK) Ltd, Croydon, CR0 4YY

Head of Zeus Ltd
First Floor East
5–8 Hardwick Street
London EC1R 4RG

WWW.HEADOFZEUS.COM

LONG RANGE

C. J. Box is the winner of the Anthony Award,
Prix Calibre .38 (France), the Macavity Award,
the Gumshoe Award, the Barry Award, and the
Edgar Award. He is also a *New York Times*
bestseller. He lives in Wyoming.

BY C.J. BOX

THE JOE PICKETT NOVELS

Open Season
Savage Run
Winterkill
Trophy Hunt
Out of Range
In Plain Sight
Free Fire
Blood Trail
Below Zero
Nowhere to Run

Cold Wind
Force of Nature
Breaking Point
Stone Cold
Endangered
Off the Grid
Vicious Circle
The Disappeared
Wolf Pack
Long Range

THE STAND-ALONE NOVELS

Blue Heaven
Three Weeks to Say Goodbye
Back of Beyond

SHORT FICTION

Shots Fired: Stories from Joe Pickett Country

THE CASSIE DEWELL NOVELS

The Highway
Badlands
Paradise Valley
The Bitterroots

LONG RANGE

In memory of my parents, Jack and Faye Box,
and to Laurie, always

People should either be caressed or crushed. If you do them minor damage they will get their revenge; but if you cripple them there is nothing they can do. If you need to injure someone, do it in such a way that you do not have to fear their vengeance.

—Niccolò Machiavelli

One must not put a loaded rifle on the stage if no one is thinking of firing it.

—Anton Chekhov, Letter to Alexander Lazarev-Gruzinsky

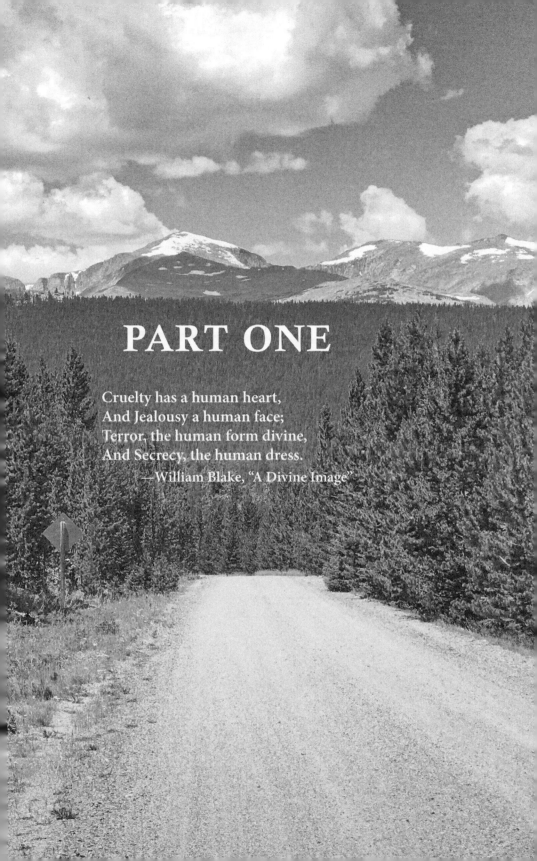

PART ONE

Cruelty has a human heart,
And Jealousy a human face;
Terror, the human form divine,
And Secrecy, the human dress.
—William Blake, "A Divine Image"

ONE

THE SLEEK GOLDEN PROJECTILE EXPLODED INTO THE THIN mountain air at three thousand feet per second. It was long and heavy with a precise pointed tip and a boat-tail design tapering from the back shank, and it twisted at over three hundred and fifty thousand rotations per minute.

Designed by ballistic engineers and weighing one hundred and eighty grains, or slightly less than half an ounce, the bullet was entirely jacketed by a smooth gilding of ninety-five percent copper and five percent zinc, with a wall-thickness variation of near zero. The pointed red ballistic tip of the nose also served as a heat shield. The projectile was engineered to withstand the extreme aerodynamic heating effects produced by the speed of its trajectory.

Inside the jacketed round was a soft lead core. Upon impact and deep penetration, the ballistic tip would drive backward into the lead core and expand the projectile into a mushroom shape in order to create a large wound cavity.

It sliced through the windless evening in absolute silence. But far behind it, two distinct sounds rang out: the report of the shot itself and the sharp *crack* in the air as the bullet broke the sound barrier.

The rocky rise and the sagebrush-encrusted foothills of the Bighorn Mountains receded from view until they blended into the layered landscape.

One second.

The crowns of river cottonwood trees passed far below, as did the lazy S-curves of the Twelve Sleep River. Two distant drift boats hugged the eastern bank as fishers cast to deep pools and holes darker in color than the rest of the river. As if in bas-relief, fishing guides manned the oars and pointed out rising trout for their clients.

Below, a V of geese held in a frozen pattern over the river as they glided toward a field to the south. Above, a red-tailed hawk hovered motionless in a thermal current as it scoured the landscape for rabbits and gophers.

One point five seconds.

A cow moose and her two calves pushed through the willows without stealth or grace to splash into the river ahead, out of view of the angling boats. A river otter slipped into the current without a ripple. Bald eagles on dead branches studied the current below them and didn't look up as the bullet zipped by hundreds of feet above.

The cow moose flinched and raised her head at the sound of the *crack.*

Two seconds.

An ocher spoor of dust trailed a tractor equipped to gather up large round hay bales in an irrigated field on the other side of the river. The dust was infused with the last blast of sunlight from the summit of the western mountains and the combine produced an outsized impression on the bronze terrain.

The backs of Black Angus cattle covered the pasture like cartoon balloons, each animal tethered to its own long shadow.

The red roof of a barn shot by below, and ravens circled the fresh kill of a jackrabbit hit by a motorist on a black ribbon of highway.

Two point five seconds.

Almost imperceptibly, the bullet began to drop and slow and drift slightly to the left, a motion called the aerodynamic jump. Because it was flying east to west through the air, its course was altered slightly by the gravitational force of the rotation of the earth known as the Eötvös effect.

The fourteenth and fifteenth fairways of a golf course scrolled by below, the turf freckled with the gold leaves of fall. A small herd of mule deer grazed on the grass near the clubhouse, unaware that interlopers—white-tailed deer from outside the area—were flanking the mulies in a raid that would play out in minutes.

A large band of pronghorn antelope, their backs lit up by the shaft of light, flowed like liquid across a sagebrush flat on the other side of a service road beyond the golf course.

Three seconds.

A series of expensive homes constructed of gray rocks and heavy dark wood backed up to the fifteenth fairway. Covered lawn furniture and dormant barbecue grills sat on flat-rock patios. Two of the homes were occupied, but only one had lights on.

The home with the lights was dead ahead, and a large plate-glass window illuminated from within formed a yellow rectangle.

Beyond the glass, inside, a small dark man sat behind a dining room table. He was staring intently in the direction of the mule deer. The table was set with a bottle of wine and two glasses, and place settings that glinted in the reflection of an overhead elk-antler chandelier.

The window and the face of the man inside got larger.

Three point five seconds.

The man at the table announced something and gestured with his hand as he did so, accidentally scattering the silverware beside his plate. He leaned to his side to retrieve an errant spoon at the exact second the bullet punched through the glass.

The void left by the man was suddenly filled by the figure of a woman just behind him. She was entering the dining room from the kitchen, carrying a platter of pork chops aloft in both hands.

The top button of her blouse enlarged exponentially and then there was a high impact and an explosion of red and black.

TWO

WYOMING GAME WARDEN JOE PICKETT WAS IN AN UNFA-miliar saddle on the wide back of an unfamiliar horse when the call came for him to return to his Saddlestring District immediately, "if not sooner."

He was eight miles from the trailhead in the Teton Wilderness with three other riders, all on stout mountain quarter horses. Snow had dusted the treeless tops of the Gros Ventre and Teton Ranges during the night and it was cold enough that clouds of condensation haloed their heads.

They'd saddled up in the parking lot of the Forest Service campground before dawn using headlamps to see. The leather of the saddles, reins, and latigos had been stiff with the fall morning cold, and it had taken a full two hours of riding in the light of the sun before the frost in the grass melted away and Joe's tack thawed out enough to be supple.

They'd assembled and left so early for a grim reason: to locate the mauled and likely dead body of a local elk-hunting guide who'd been attacked the evening before by a grizzly bear. Or at least that's what his client, a hunter from Boca Grande, Florida, had claimed.

Joe rode with his twelve-gauge shotgun out of its scabbard and crosswise over the pommel of his saddle. He'd loaded it with alternating rounds of slugs and double-aught buckshot. His bear spray was on his belt and he'd made a point to unhook the safety strap that held the canister tight in its holster.

Over his shoulder was a semiautomatic Smith & Wesson M&P rifle chambered in .308 Winchester with a bipod and red dot scope and a twenty-round magazine. Two of the other riders carried the same weapon because it had recently replaced M14 carbines in the arsenal of the department's newly formed Predator Attack Team— a heavily armed, specially trained SWAT team created for bear incidents—to which Joe had recently been named.

His senses were on high alert for the sight, sound, or smell of a rogue six-hundred-pound bear. To Joe, every noise—whether it was the click of a hoof on a rock or the chatter of a squirrel in the branches of the trees—seemed magnified. He was jumpy and his mouth was dry. The coffee and jerky they'd eaten for breakfast that morning on the drive out to the campground roiled in his stomach.

Although he'd been on many similar horseback expeditions, this one felt oddly different. With all three of his daughters out of the house and Marybeth alone at home, Joe couldn't help but feel he was getting too old for this kind of thing. He did his best to repress the thought and concentrate on the task at hand, although he couldn't deny that he missed his wife and he wished she were closer.

LONG RANGE

———

JOE RODE THIRD in the string of horses, and his mount seemed to be most comfortable in that configuration. There was always a learning curve when it came to riding someone else's horse, and he didn't know the pecking order of the herd or the characteristics of the mount beforehand. Joe wished he were riding Toby, his wife's well-trained horse, or Rojo, his gelding. Even a sure-footed and bomb-proof mule would do.

A Jackson biologist named Eddie Smith, also a member of the Predator Attack Team, rode last on a bay gelding. Like Joe, Smith had a Smith & Wesson M&P semiautomatic rifle chambered in .308 across the pommel of his saddle. The weapon had a twenty-round magazine and a red dot scope. His job was to cover the riders in front of him and to be the first to bail off his horse and confront trouble if it happened.

Joe had had no idea when he'd driven over the mountains to Jackson Hole the previous afternoon that he'd be pressed into helping find the mangled body of a local guide.

Or that he'd be given a gelding named Peaches to do it.

JACKSON HOLE game warden Mike Martin led the search and recovery operation. Martin had been hired by the agency the year before Joe, and Martin was badge number eighteen of fifty in terms of seniority. Joe had badge number nineteen, meaning there were eighteen game wardens with more seniority on the job and thirty-one with less.

Like Joe, Martin had bounced around all over the state of Wyoming in his career. He'd lived in half a dozen state-owned homes—called "stations"—and he'd been responsible for enforcing the Game and Fish regulations in high mountains, arid deserts, and vast sagebrush-covered steppes. Since the districts in Wyoming ranged from two thousand to more than five thousand square miles, Martin had spent a lot of his life in pickup trucks, on ATVs and boats, or on the backs of horses.

Martin had a battered cowboy hat, a thick gunfighter mustache, jowls, and round wire-framed glasses that made him look like a modern-day Teddy Roosevelt. His middle had thickened substantially over the years and strained the buttons of his red uniform shirt, but he was still surprisingly strong and agile and a better horseman than Joe.

Joe and Martin had worked together a few times over the years on cases that spanned both of their districts, and they got along well. Martin was brusque and flinty and proud of how out of step he looked when he was in a room with wealthy, sophisticated Jackson Hole resort elites. He'd become more curmudgeonly and cantankerous by the year, Joe thought. Martin was a fish out of water, a throwback, and it didn't seem to bother him at all.

Joe could tell that Martin was also subtly suspicious of the man riding second and at times side by side with him: the Florida hunter.

"You're sure this is the trail you took going in and coming out?" Martin asked the man, whose name was Julius Talbot. Talbot was dressed in high-tech camo hunting clothing that must have cost more than two thousand dollars from boots to cap. He had prematurely silver hair, a nice tan, pale blue eyes, and a jawline that made him look arrogant, whether he was or not. The only thing that marred his outfit were the floral-like splashes of dark blood on his pants and sleeves from the day before. The blood, he claimed, had come from the guide, not the elk he'd shot.

"I'm pretty sure it is," Talbot said.

"Sure or pretty sure?"

"Sure enough," Talbot said. "And it's not much farther, I don't think."

"Our horses will let us know," Martin said, extending his hand to pat his mount on the neck.

"They didn't yesterday," Talbot said.

Martin grunted in response. When Talbot turned his head away from the game warden, Martin looked over his shoulder at Joe and rolled his eyes. Joe nodded back. He didn't know what to think of Talbot and he had his own doubts that the attack had taken place exactly as he had described it.

Talbot said, "I hope we can get in and out of here fast. I have a meeting in Boca tomorrow I can't miss."

"You might just have to," Martin said without looking at Talbot. Joe could sense the tightness in Martin's tone, as if the man were speaking through clenched teeth. "If what you say is true, there's a dead man up ahead who was working for *you*. He has a wife and three kids at home. You might just have to postpone that meeting of yours."

Julius Talbot sighed. He seemed to Joe to be quite put out by Martin's insistence that he come into the timber with them to point out the site of the attack. It was odd behavior, Joe thought, although not shocking.

In too many instances, out-of-state hunters used to being catered to by underlings in all the other phases of their executive lives expected the same kind of subservient behavior from guides and outfitters in the field.

That wasn't the right way to do things in the Mountain West, where wealth and class didn't mean as much to the locals as it might in other places. The best thing someone could say about a newcomer was that he was a "good guy." Not a rich guy, a *good* one.

Joe found Talbot's attitude as annoying as Martin seemed to.

ALTHOUGH IT WAS in the midst of fall big-game hunting season throughout the state, Joe had agreed to drive over the mountains from his own district to Jackson Hole. He'd slipped away without telling anyone other than Marybeth about it, because he didn't want word to get out to local miscreants in the Saddlestring District that he wouldn't be on patrol.

The call had come to Joe from Rick Ewig, the director of the Wyoming Game and Fish Department in Cheyenne. Ewig worked in the Katelyn Hamm Building, newly named after the game warden who had recently lost her life while on duty. Ewig was a former game warden himself, and he'd asked Joe to meet up with Martin so the two of them could assess the effectiveness of a new piece of technology for finding lost people in the mountains. If the technology worked as well as or better than the FLIR (forward-looking infrared) camera equipment currently used by the Wyoming Civil Air Patrol, Ewig said he might add a couple of the devices to his annual budget request.

Skiers in Jackson Hole were buried every year by avalanches, and hunters frequently became disoriented and lost in the dense alpine terrain. Finding them diverted manpower and resources, so any technology that could speed up searches would save not only money and time—but their very lives. The experimental system known as a Lifeseeker supposedly worked because it could home in on individual cell phones even in remote areas with no cell service—provided the lost person's phone was turned on. A local philanthropist in Jackson had donated one of the $100,000 Lifeseeker boxes to the Teton County Search and Rescue team for which Martin was a liaison.

The plan was for Joe and Martin to fly in a helicopter over the Gros Ventre mountains to see if they could identify people below by the strength of their cell signals. It was densely wooded terrain, and nearly impossible to see through the canopy of pine trees to the ground below. They'd note the GPS coordinates and follow up on the ground later to see if the sightings could be confirmed.

If the Lifeseeker turned out to be a reliable tool in search and rescue efforts, it would likely be incorporated by the Predator Attack Team to pinpoint the location of some human–bear encounters.

When Martin and Joe heard about the bear attack, they were circling the Lifeseeker box on a table in the conference room of the Jackson Game and Fish station, trying to figure out how the dials and display worked. The Teton County sheriff had called to say they were transporting a hunter into town. His guys had picked him up after he'd signaled a passing unit near Turpin Meadow. The hunter, the sheriff said, had a wild story.

MARTIN HAD INTERVIEWED Talbot in the same conference room, and asked Joe to be present during the initial statement.

Talbot claimed that he'd booked a trophy elk hunt months before with a local outfitting company, and that a guide named Jim Trenary had been assigned to him. Trenary seemed like a knowledgeable guide, Talbot thought, and he was pleased to have drawn him. The man seemed pleasant enough and fun-loving, but serious about his job. He made sure Talbot knew that grizzlies were present in significant numbers in the area where they'd be hunting, and that the bears sometimes moved in on elk kills or gut piles to feed. As long as the hunter was cautious and carried bear spray and a firearm at all times, there was little to worry about, Trenary had said. He'd cautioned Talbot never to put himself in danger by walking between a sow grizzly and her cubs.

As Talbot talked, Joe noted that the hunter always referred to Jim Trenary as "my guide" instead of using his given name. It was a revealing tell. It was as if Trenary were simply a tool to get Talbot what he wanted, not an individual.

And the story Talbot told wasn't only wild, Joe thought, it was bizarre.

According to Talbot, they had ridden two horses and trailed a packhorse into the hunting area the day before. Around noon, Trenary pointed out a small herd of elk standing in the shadows of a wall of trees on the side of a mountain meadow. Talbot picked out the largest bull with a set of five-by-six antlers. Trenary used his range finder to determine that the target was one hundred and fifty yards away.

Although it should have been an easy shot, Talbot had missed and the herd had spooked and run away.

The guide and his hunter walked their mounts across the meadow where the elk had been, Talbot said. They were going to follow the churned-up trail of the animals with the hope of finding them again. But before they got close enough to find the tracks, they heard something that sounded like a freight train on the mountain ahead of them. They could hear branches breaking as it crashed through the timber toward them.

"Stand your ground and get out your bear spray," Trenary ordered Julius Talbot. "It might do a false charge, so be ready."

Talbot said he did as he was told.

The grizzly bear flattened a row of willows and came straight at them, Talbot said. It was unbelievably fast and huge, cinnamon in color, with a large hump on its back. It grunted as it ran, and Talbot said he could hear its plate-sized paws thump the ground.

The horses they were holding panicked and bolted, running back in the direction from which they had come. Talbot showed the two game wardens the abrasions in his palm where the reins had been pulled through.

Both the hunter and the guide extended their canisters of bear spray toward the coming grizzly.

"He'll turn," Trenary said.

But he didn't. Both men pulled the triggers of their canisters of bear spray, which should have created large red plumes of noxious pepper spray in front of them. But Talbot had forgotten to pull the pin that would arm his spray, and it didn't fire. Trenary's blast had been shot too soon, before the grizzly was in range, and the bear ducked nimbly to the side of it as the spray hung in the air.

In his peripheral vision, Talbot said he saw the guide throw aside the canister and reach for his holstered .44 Magnum revolver.

According to Talbot, the grizzly hit Trenary before the guide could aim his weapon. The bear struck the guide so hard it knocked him backward off his feet into the grass. The revolver

15

went flying. The bear went straight for the guide's throat and face, furiously slashing with three-inch claws and teeth.

Talbot said he couldn't shoot the grizzly himself because the fury of the attack was so fast and intense that there was no way to get a clean shot without hitting Trenary. Since he'd fouled up his chance to use the bear spray, Talbot said he'd retreated to the other side of the meadow, hoping he could draw the bear away from the guide and get a shot. While he did so, the guide had screamed and fought back the best he could by hitting the bear in the face and kicking up at him.

Then, Talbot said, the bear wheeled and ran back up the hill. He'd moved so fast Talbot couldn't steady the crosshairs of his rifle enough to fire.

Talbot found Trenary mauled, disemboweled, and bleeding profusely. The horses were long gone. But Trenary was still breathing.

Talbot tried to call for help on his phone, but there was no service. So he placed the .44 on the guide's bloody chest so he'd have it handy if the bear came back. Then Talbot started the long hike out to get help. He never caught a glimpse of the horses along the way.

It took four hours to reach the two-lane highway to the south, where he was able to flag down a deputy sheriff and hitch a ride to Jackson.

AFTER JULIUS TALBOT had left the room to get his hand attended to at the medical clinic, Martin had turned to Joe with a doubtful look on his face.

"Did that sound as hinky to you as it did to me?" he'd asked.

Joe nodded.

Martin asked, "Did you notice that he never used Jim's name? Only 'my guide'?"

"I noticed."

"I'll get him to agree to lead us to the location tomorrow," Martin said. "I'd really like you to come along."

Joe didn't respond at first. The Jackson office had more personnel than any other office in the state.

"I know what you're thinking," Martin said, as if reading Joe's mind. "You're wondering why I don't put together a team from here."

"That's what I was wondering."

"Because I trust you and you've been around the block, just like me," Martin said. "In fact, as you know, you're kind of a legend."

Joe felt his face flush hot.

"I'd appreciate your expertise," Martin said. "Besides, I know the folks here. Half of 'em would spend the whole time trying somehow to blame the bear attack on climate change. I want a straightforward assessment from someone I trust. Another set of experienced eyes. I'll ask Eddie Smith to come along with us. He's a good hand."

"What about the Lifeseeker test?" Joe asked.

"We can do both things at once," Martin said. "We'll send up the bird with the equipment while you and me and the wildlife supervisor go into the timber on horseback with Julius Talbot. Maybe the bird will locate Jim Trenary before we do. Maybe not. Either way, it'll be good to have air support if we need to fly him out."

Joe nodded. It made sense. He appreciated the fact that Martin hadn't referred to "the body"—even though the possibility of Trenary lasting through the night in his condition was improbable at best.

They made plans to meet at the office the next morning at four-thirty. Martin had a string of horses assigned to his district. Jackson Hole was considered a "six-horse district" and it had good equine facilities.

"I suppose you want the youngest mustang," Martin asked.

"I do not."

Martin grinned to indicate he'd been kidding.

JOE LISTENED IN as Martin asked Talbot additional questions. In the distance, he heard the sound of the helicopter getting closer.

"Walk me through this again," Martin said to Talbot.

"I've done this three times already."

"Let's do it a fourth time."

Talbot sighed.

"So you take a shot at a bull elk at one hundred fifty yards and you miss."

"Yes," Talbot said with irritation. No hunter liked to talk about when they missed.

"Did you see where your bullet hit?"

"No."

"Did Jim Trenary say anything about where it hit? Like, 'You were way high to the right' or anything like that?"

"No."

Martin said, "I'm just trying to figure things out. I'm wondering if you were way off when you shot and the round went high into the timber where the bear was. Maybe you even hit him and made him mad. Is that possible?"

Talbot scoffed. "That's ridiculous. I might have missed that bull by a few inches, but I didn't shoot that high at a hundred and fifty yards."

"Is it possible there was a ricochet up into the trees? Like maybe you hit a rock?"

"I didn't hear anything like that," Talbot said. His voice was rising with irritation. "I told you what happened. Why do you keep asking me about it?"

"Because," Martin said, "I've worked a dozen or so bear encounters, and I've talked with biologists who've been on the scene of lots more. I've never heard of a grizzly attacking two men without any provocation at all. It just doesn't happen."

"It did this time," Talbot sniffed.

"Is it possible that bear was feeding on a carcass out of your view?" Martin asked. "Maybe he heard the shot and thought you were trying to steal his bounty?"

"I don't know," Talbot said. "We didn't see any carcass."

Martin asked, "Is it possible that you got so excited when you saw those elk that you walked right past a bear cub or two? That maybe you two walked by accident between a mama and her babies? So the mama charged you to protect her little ones?"

Talbot shook his head. "I guess anything is possible. It's pretty dark in that timber. But my guide left me up on the hill while he scouted down below—before he found those elk. I doubt he would have walked past bear cubs twice without noticing them."

Joe noted the "my guide" reference again.

Martin nodded and thought about it. He said, "You might be right. Cubs wouldn't be that far away from mama bear normally."

"Thank you," Talbot said in exasperation, as if the issue were settled.

But it wasn't. Martin asked Talbot, "You say you forgot to thumb off the safety on your bear spray, so it didn't work."

"That's correct. I'd never used one before and I panicked and forgot."

"I understand," Martin said. "At the moment, you were rattled. But when you realized that you hadn't armed the spray, why didn't you flip off the safety and hit the bear with it when it was attacking Jim Trenary? Jim wouldn't have liked it, but I'm sure he'd much rather have bear spray in his eyes than get torn up."

Talbot paused a long time. Then he said, "I'd already dropped the canister by then. I guess I wasn't thinking straight."

"Interesting," Martin said. To Joe, that "interesting" sounded a lot like *You're a fool, then.* In that moment, Joe felt a little embarrassed for Talbot, despite himself.

Joe leaned forward in his saddle. "Mike?"

Martin turned around.

Joe said, "I've talked to a couple of wildlife biologists who are doing a study on grizzly bear behavior. Although they don't have any conclusions yet, one of the things they're studying is if the reason there are more and more bear encounters every year is possibly because the grizzlies are getting more comfortable with humans around in their habitat. And when they hear a shot during elk-hunting season, the bear associates that with easy food. Maybe something like that happened here."

Not said was that the enactment of the endangered species laws in the previous decade had produced a lot more grizzlies in the ecosystem than before. Conservative estimates Joe had read indicated there were more than six hundred in the area. Local outfitters reported that they saw grizzly bears nearly every day out in the field—sometimes as many as five or six. More grizzlies meant more likelihood that there would be human–bear encounters.

"Maybe," Martin said. "But I hope not."

"Why do you hope not?" Talbot asked.

"Because if that's true," Martin said, "it means a total adaptation or change in animal behavior. It means six-hundred-pound predators have lost their fear of man. It means there could be a whole lot of dead people in the future."

"Oh," Talbot said.

"Now," Martin said, "put all those theories aside for the moment. I want you to tell me again the sequence of actions you took yesterday after the bear attacked."

Talbot physically recoiled.

"I've already told you," he said to Martin.

"Tell me again," Martin said. "I'm kind of slow."

BEFORE TALBOT COULD respond, Martin's satellite phone burred. They'd brought it along because there was no cell phone coverage in the area and they thought they might need to communicate with the pilot of the helicopter.

Martin pulled on the reins of his horse and stopped it. The other mounts in the string stopped automatically. Martin dug the sat phone out of his saddlebag and punched it up and listened for a moment.

izei.........aa

Then he handed it toward Joe.

"It's for you," Martin said.

"For me? Who is it?" Joe asked. He tried to tamp down an immediate rush of worst-case scenarios involving Marybeth or their three adult daughters. That seemed to be the only reason why someone would track him down on Mike Martin's satellite phone.

"It's the boss," Martin said.

Joe took the heavy receiver. "Joe Pickett."

"Joe, I'm glad I caught you." It was indeed Rick Ewig, the director.

"I'm in the middle of something," Joe said.

"You'll need to drop it," Ewig said.

"What's up?"

"Your judge up in Twelve Sleep County is on the warpath."

"Judge Hewitt?" Joe asked. Hewitt was short, dark, and twitchy. The judge had a volcanic temper: he carried a handgun under his robes and he'd brandished it several times in his courtroom to maintain order. Every prosecutor and defense lawyer Joe had ever encountered was scared of Judge Hewitt.

"That's him," Ewig said. "He's been on the phone with Governor Allen, and the governor's been on the phone with me. You're being called back immediately. As in right now."

Joe said, "I'm on a horse just a couple of miles from the Teton Wilderness. I'm giving Mike Martin a hand with—"

"Forget that," Ewig said. "Apparently, someone took a shot at the judge last night. He was at home at his dinner table and the bullet missed him by inches and hit his wife."

"Oh no," Joe said. "Sue?" Joe felt his body go cold. It had been less than a year since Twelve Sleep County had been rocked by a massacre on the courthouse steps that had killed the sheriff and seriously wounded the county prosecutor. Now the judge was a target?

"Sue sounds right," Ewig said. "Anyway, she's in critical condition and Judge Hewitt has demanded that all local law enforcement meet with him immediately. He suspects a drive-by shooting and he wants the guy caught. That includes you."

Joe grimaced. "It'll take me four hours just to get back to my truck."

"No it won't," Ewig said.

The volume of the spinning rotors of the helicopter increased in volume as they spoke. Joe understood. Ewig had diverted the helicopter to pick him up.

Joe handed the sat phone back to Martin.

"Gotta go," he said.

Martin shook his head in disgust. His feelings about aggressive top-down management were well known. Martin was old-school: he thought local game wardens should manage their districts as they saw fit with minimal interference from the "suits" in Cheyenne, even though Ewig had once been a game warden himself.

"Can I go with him?" Talbot asked Martin.

"Not a chance," Martin growled.

"I'll be back," Joe said to Martin with a side glance toward Talbot. "I'm really interested to see how this ends."

Julius Talbot looked away.

THREE

AT THE SAME TIME, INSIDE A FALCON MEWS ON THE SAGE-
brush prairie outside of Saddlestring, Nate Romanowski firmly
grasped a pigeon in his left hand and twisted its head with his
right, producing an audible snap. When the bird's body responded
with a last-breath flurry of flapping wings, he held it out at arm's
length until it went still. Then he chopped it up with an ax and fed
it piece by piece to his raptors. It was the fifth pigeon of the morning, and the air was filled with tufts of downy feathers and the
crunching sound of falcons eating the birds, bones and all. The
morning air inside the mews smelled of the metallic odor of fresh
blood and the pungent smell of splashy white bird droppings. The
gullets of the falcons swelled to the size of hens' eggs as they ate,
and Nate made sure all nine of his hooded birds were satiated.

It was the daily circle of life and death for a master falconer.

Nate inspected each bird—two red-tailed hawks, a gyrfalcon,
three prairie falcons, a Swainson's hawk, and two peregrines—to
make sure they were all healthy and fit. One of his prairie falcons

had damaged its left wing the week before during an ill-fated swoop on a prairie dog, but it seemed to be recovering nicely.

He referred to the falcons as his Air Force. They were the instruments of his bird abatement company incorporated as Yarak, Inc. Yarak, Inc. was hired by farmers, ranchers, golf course operators, and industrialists to rid their property of problem birds, many of which were invasive species like starlings. Business was good. To keep up with demand, he knew he needed more birds and possibly an apprentice falconer by the next spring.

Nate washed his hands and the falconry bag that had held the live pigeons under the ice-cold stream of water from a spigot, dried his palms on the fabric of his thighs, and ambled toward the house. He was tall and rangy with long blond hair tied off in a ponytail by a leather falcon jess. He had icy blue eyes and a smile described by most observers as cruel.

The landscape surrounding him was largely scrub in all directions, but it was framed on the east and west by distant blue mountain ranges. There wasn't a single tree for miles—which is how he liked it.

Although the property might have seemed conventionally unattractive to those who took a wrong turn on the gravel county roads and wound up there, Nate appreciated the strategic location of his home. Because it was located in the bottom of a vast natural bowl, the property he'd chosen had the same attributes as frontier-era forts such as Fort Laramie and Fort Bridger: it was impossible to sneak up on it without being seen. Nate had learned the tactic by observing the herd behavior of pronghorn antelope.

He paused before entering the house because he sensed movement. He turned on his porch to see a light-colored plume of dust looking like a comma in the distance. It was from the tires of a large vehicle of some kind. Since he rarely got visitors, he assumed the driver was lost and would turn around long before arriving at his place.

His forty acres contained an aging three-bedroom house, a detached garage, a metal building that served as vehicle storage and a welding shop, and the mews for his Air Force. The land and the buildings—except for the mews, which he'd recently constructed—had formerly belonged to a welder who'd serviced the energy industry until he was arrested for dealing meth on the side. When the welder's property was put up for auction by the feds, Nate was the high bidder. Which meant that, for the first time in his life, he was a homeowner and a landowner. Nate was in the process of transforming the place from a welding-and-meth-friendly outpost to a falcon-and-family-friendly environment.

Because he now had a family. For Nate, who was an outlaw falconer with a Special Forces background and a long list of alleged federal offenses (since dismissed), nothing had caused him more terror than getting married and having a child. He went back and forth trying to decide if it was the best or worst thing he'd ever done. But he leaned toward the former.

NATE WAS A fifty percent owner of Yarak, Inc. His partner in business and life was Liv Brannon, his wife of four months. Liv ran the public side of the company, including marketing, booking jobs, maintaining social media, billing, finance, and compliance.

Liv was a stunning African American woman originally from

Louisiana, and she sat at the computer on her desk in her home office wearing a headset. A Squash Blossoms CD played gently in the background. Cradled in her lap was six-week-old Kestrel, their daughter. Named after a small but feisty falcon, Kestrel opened her eyes when Nate came in the room. Her tiny hand raised up from her blankets and her arm trembled slightly. She didn't yet have the motor control to still her limbs.

Kestrel was a tiny version of her mother and she had Liv's full mouth and long eyelashes. He was devastated by her presence.

Nate placed his index finger in her palm and she gripped it.

Yes, he thought, *the former.*

"Are you still going into town today?" Liv asked him.

"Yes."

"Can you pick up some Pampers on your way home?"

"Pampers?"

"Yes, the ones called 'Swaddlers,'" Liv said. "I'm giving up on the cloth diapers. It's too hard to keep up."

"Swaddlers," Nate repeated.

"You might want to write that down. They're for newborns. The last ones you got were for a six-month-old."

"They were?"

"Yes," Liv said. "I'll save them and use them when she's older. But you need to look at the type."

"I thought diapers were diapers," Nate said.

Liv gave a *They aren't* look and then jabbed a finger toward the screen.

"We got an inquiry from Hamilton, Montana," she said. "A rancher needs to get rid of a barnful of starlings, but it's eight hours away. What should we tell him?"

Before he could answer, Liv said, "Never mind. I think I can pair this job with another job for pigeon abatement in Bozeman."

She waved him away, but he didn't move. Kestrel still gripped his finger. He wouldn't leave until his daughter tired of him. Nate knew deep in his heart it would be like that forever.

"Loren?" Liv called over her shoulder.

Loren Jean Hill emerged from the hallway with a gentle smile on her face. She was barely five feet tall and slight. Loren had answered an online ad Liv had placed for a live-in nanny, and had been the best-natured applicant by far. A redhead in her twenties from South Dakota, where Liv had once lived, Loren had never had children of her own, but she'd grown up wrangling kids in an extended family and she was a wise and knowledgeable caregiver.

Employing Loren meant Liv could continue to work full-time for Yarak from their new home. The bird abatement business and commercial falconry in general was a highly specialized field. Liv and Nate had discussed hiring a general manager from the outside but decided against it. Yarak was too close to their hearts to turn over to an executive. Plus, Nate knew, Liv wanted to continue to be closely involved with the enterprise. She knew, and Nate conceded the point, that left entirely to his own devices, there was a very real probability that people on the outside might be hurt or killed.

Nate had given up on all of that when he'd gone straight and back on the grid. Liv was adamant that he stay there.

"Yes, Liv?" Loren asked.

"Can you please put Kestrel down for a nap?"

Liv turned in her chair and handed the baby to Loren. The nanny gently backed away toward the baby's room so Kestrel's release of Nate's finger wasn't jarring. Nate tried not to show his annoyance.

"Nate's going to get the Swaddlers today," Liv said to Loren.

"Oh, good."

"No more washing cloth diapers."

"I can't argue with that," Loren said.

"Then it's settled," Liv said while turning back to her screen.

Nate beheld his wife, his daughter, and the nanny. He could not believe how his life had changed.

NATE AND LIV turned their heads toward the front door simultaneously as the rumble of a large engine vibrated through the floor of the house. Nate admonished himself for not tracking the progress of the approaching vehicle he'd glimpsed. He'd gotten too wrapped up in Kestrel's gesture to remember.

Going soft, he thought.

"What is *that*?" Liv asked.

Nate strode across the dining room toward the picture window and eased the curtains aside. The massive RV was parked with its diesel engine rumbling less than thirty feet from his house. It was so large it filled the window.

"Someone must be lost," Liv said.

"Maybe."

The engine shut off. Nate could see the form of a man behind the wheel. The man turned to stand up after he'd killed the engine and he was out of sight for a few seconds. It took that long, apparently, for the driver to walk through the behemoth to the side door.

When it opened, it took Nate a few moments to realize who had come. Jeremiah Sandburg looked frail and ten years older than when Nate had last seen him. Sandburg's hair had thinned and grayed and he moved stiffly. He opened the side door of the recreational vehicle and stood within the doorframe as if contemplating whether he wanted to take the long step down to the gravel. Sandburg looked up plaintively toward the house.

"I'll be a minute," Nate said to Liv.

"Do you know who it is?"

Nate said, "Remember that FBI agent who survived the massacre last spring? It's him."

"I thought he'd retired," Liv said.

"I did, too."

Nate tried to fight the feeling of suspicion that always arose in him when he encountered law enforcement officials, especially feds.

"Are you going to invite him in?" Liv asked.

"No."

Nate opened the front door and said to her over his shoulder, "I'll see what he wants."

"Be a gentleman," she cautioned.

"Always," he said through gritted teeth as he stepped outside and closed the door behind him.

Sandburg acknowledged him with a nod of his head. He seemed stuck in the doorframe.

"Nate Romanowski," the man said. "You're a hard man to find."

"That's the idea. What can I do for you?"

Sandburg had short-cropped brown hair, rimless glasses, and a thin face. When Nate had seen him the first time, Sandburg had had a thick barrel chest and the gliding moves of a one-time athlete. Not anymore. His recovery had obviously taken a tremendous physical toll.

Sandburg had been hit four times in an ambush that had killed longtime local sheriff Mike Reed, Sandburg's superior from the FBI, and his partner Don Pollock. He was the only survivor of the attack except for the former county attorney Dulcie Schalk, who had retired to her family ranch. Nothing like it had ever happened in Saddlestring before. Nate kept his distance from town matters and gossip, but the reverberations of the incident still resonated.

Nate didn't know Sandburg well, the way Joe Pickett did. Nate's friend Joe had described the special agent as arrogant, condescending, and more than a little crooked. Sandburg liked to threaten civilians by describing how much trouble they'd be in if he felt they were lying to him—or refused to say what he wanted them to say.

Nate had no idea at all why Sandburg was there.

"IF YOU HAVE a few minutes, I'd like to talk to you," Sandburg said.

"I really don't have much time," Nate said. He didn't mention his mission to buy the right brand of Pampers.

"You'll regret it if we don't," Sandburg said. So far, he was true to form and just as Joe had described him.

"We can do it in here," Sandburg said, meaning inside his recreational vehicle. "I might even have some coffee."

Nate looked the man over. Sandburg looked relieved not to have to step down out of his RV.

"Because of my injuries, it's painful to move around," Sandburg said, as if answering Nate's thoughts. "I notice it's worse out here at high elevation. Everything hurts more."

Nate followed Sandburg into the RV. It took a while for the man to get settled behind a table and Sandburg grunted as he did so. The table was in a dinette booth configuration with one open side. Nate sat opposite Sandburg and looked around. The closets and cupboards were constructed of high-end hardwood and the chairs and sofas were covered in leather. A coffeemaker secured to the kitchen wall smelled of fresh coffee, but Sandburg didn't make a move to get up. Nate assumed he'd either forgotten his offer or, more likely, didn't want to expend the physical effort to serve it. Either way, Nate was fine with it.

"Pretty impressive, isn't it?" Sandburg asked, chinning around the inside of the huge RV. "It's a thirty-nine-foot Entegra Reatta. Satellite TV and Wi-Fi, king bed, fireplace, washer/dryer— everything a man could want. It's like my own private land yacht that sleeps eight people."

Nate nodded. He'd been in high-tech mobile special operations vehicles but never one built solely for luxury.

"Do you want to know how much it cost?" Sandburg asked.

"Not really," Nate said.

"Two hundred ninety-one thousand dollars," Sandburg said. "And that was with a twenty percent discount."

"That's a lot," Nate said.

"Thank you," Sandburg said.

"For what?"

"For paying for all of this."

Nate got it. "You mean the taxpayers," he said.

"Yes. I can't say it was worth it to me completely, since I can hardly get around anymore," Sandburg said. He patted the table and said, "But this was a nice consolation from the settlement I negotiated with the Bureau. My pension takes care of the rest. It's a real chick magnet, as long as you like chicks with blue hair who are sixty-plus. That's what you find at these RV parks I frequent these days."

"Then you're welcome," Nate said. "Not many folks have pensions these days. So what brings you all the way out here?"

Sandburg gave Nate his best cop glare. "You mean besides revisiting the scene of the crime?"

Nate nodded. Although he felt a pang of sympathy for Sandburg's condition, the man's act was wearing thin. He waited him out.

"Abriella Guzman," Sandburg finally said. "The martyr you created."

Nate didn't react outwardly, but he felt the grip of cold tighten in his chest. Abriella Guzman had been a beautiful and charismatic young woman, and the leader of a team of four assassins known as the Wolf Pack. She'd been as cold and ruthless as anyone Nate had ever encountered. The Wolf Pack had been sent north by the Sinaloa cartel and they'd been responsible for the massacre on the courthouse steps, as well as the murder of several others in the area. Nate and Joe had pursued a wounded Abriella into the mountains, where she'd died. He'd willed it to happen and he had no regrets, although he knew Joe still struggled with the circumstances of her demise.

"What do you mean when you say 'martyr'?" Nate asked.

"I did some research on you before I officially left the Bureau,"

33

Sandburg said. "You've had quite the checkered past. You should be buried away in a federal penitentiary instead of running around the countryside in Wyoming, cavorting with the antelopes."

"Pronghorn antelope," Nate corrected. Then: "Those files are supposed to be sealed. I guess a deal with the FBI only goes so far."

Sandburg wagged his eyebrows at that, as if to emphasize his intimate access to "sealed" documents. "I still have lots of friends there," he said.

"Good for you. I have a signed agreement from the Department of Justice agreeing to drop all those charges in exchange for infiltrating a ring of bad guys a few years back. The agreement was witnessed by the governor of Wyoming. I've left all that behind me. I've gone straight, I've got a legitimate business, I'm married, and I have a beautiful little girl inside the house right behind me. If your purpose here is to try to intimidate me, you're wasting your time."

With that, Nate slid sidewise on the leather of the seat and pressed down on the tabletop with his hands to stand up.

"You might want to hear me out," Sandburg said.

"Then get to the point."

"Let me show you something," Sandburg said. He said it with a tone of barely disguised glee.

The man opened a thin laptop, made a few keyboard strokes, and spun the computer around so Nate could see the monitor.

On the screen was a mixture of photographs and graphics from what looked like a crude e-commerce website. In the photos, several of which were blurry, individuals could be seen in staged poses. In one, a dark-skinned Hispanic man held aloft the severed head of a victim by the hair. In another, a group of heavily armed men stood in front of an open grave in a shadowed jungle setting. The lifeless limbs of a pile of victims could be seen jutting from the grave.

Obviously, the photos had been captured off the internet, and they were of Mexican cartel violence, Nate guessed. It was impossible to determine how recent they were.

What stood out when he bent down and looked at the photos, and what they had in common with the rest of the e-commerce offerings, was the image on the simple white T-shirts the killers wore: a stylized graphic of Abriella Guzman. In it, Abriella held a defiant pose with her chin thrust toward the camera. She wore a tight black top, tactical pants with semiautomatic pistol grips sticking out of the side cargo pockets, and high lace-up boots. A stubby Heckler & Koch submachine gun was gripped in her hand and pointed toward the ground. She had a pout on her lips and her big, provocative, dark eyes were trained directly at the photographer.

Abriella was wearing the same clothing Nate recalled her in when he and Joe had chased her down. The photo, he guessed, must have been taken earlier that same day.

The graphic of Abriella reminded Nate of the iconic Che Guevara–in–a–beret image on clothing worn by clueless hipsters and political activists who thought it edgy and cool. Like Che, Abriella had been a stone-cold murderer.

"To the Sinaloa cartel," Sandburg said, "Abriella has become larger than life. They don't care what her real history is or how many innocent people she slaughtered, right? They don't care that she was a psychopath. This image is everywhere: on T-shirts, on posters, on the sides of buildings in Sinaloa. It's even printed on shipments of heroin and fentanyl that have been seized as far north as Maine."

"Where did the photo come from?" Nate asked.

Sandburg shrugged. "It was on Pedro Infante's phone." Infante had been a member of the Wolf Pack and he'd also died that day. "The Bureau digitized it for a press release and the cartel took it and ran with it. No one in the agency thought ahead that it might become a symbol. How do you anticipate these things?"

Nate waited for more.

"Now, listen," Sandburg said as he reached around the computer and clicked on another file. The RV reverberated with a fast, tinny Spanish-language song filled with accordions and tuba squawks.

On the monitor a chubby young man with thin facial hair, a black cowboy hat, and a heavy gold rapper chain carrying an AK-47 pendant gestured wildly at the camera. The lyric-heavy song wasn't entirely unpleasant, but it was certainly not to Nate's taste.

While the performer sang, special-effect machine gun rounds stitched across the screen, as well as red gouts of blood. Crime scene photographs flashed by of mutilated roadside corpses and hooded bodies hung from a bridge. Nate couldn't understand the lyrics, but he noted that the singer wore an Abriella T-shirt under his leather vest and the same image took over the screen at the end of the music video.

"It's called 'The Bloody Ballad of Abriella,'" Sandburg said. "Are you familiar with *narcocorridos*?"

"Yes."

Sandburg continued on as if Nate hadn't answered in the af-firmative. "*Narcocorridos* are folk songs about notorious criminals," he said. "They're officially banned on Mexican radio and television, but that doesn't mean they aren't wildly popular. Drug lords hire songwriters to sing about them, and plenty of gangsters on this side of the border listen to them. The songs get more violent and graphic all the time, just like the cartels get more violent. This one, 'The Bloody Ballad of Abriella,' is the most popular *narcocorrido* in Mexico, SoCal, and Arizona right now."

"Okay," Nate said, waiting for more.

"Do you understand Spanish?" Sandburg asked.

"Some. Not much."

"I know just enough to be dangerous myself, but I asked a buddy of mine in the Bureau to translate a couple of lines I think you'll find interesting."

As Sandburg dug out a piece of paper from his shirt pocket, Nate braced himself.

Sandburg read:

She ventured north into the white gringo mountains and the
   snow
Avenging her people with a goat's horn and fire
She was a deadly angel, our Abriella
Until she was tricked and tracked down by a gringo like
   a dog
Who tore off her beautiful limbs and fed them to his hawks
This is the bloody ballad of our lovely and dangerous
   Abriella.

"They refer to machine guns as 'goats' horns,'" Sandburg said. "Don't ask me why. Anyway, you're famous, and not in a good way.

I think we both know what happens to guys who get this kind of famous within a cartel. They don't last very long. There are known homicides down there where the songwriters of *narcocorridos* themselves get whacked by rival drug lords. But when you're the actual villain in one of them—watch out."

"Where did they get that version of what happened?" Nate asked through gritted teeth. "We both know it wasn't like that."

Sandburg shrugged. "They probably went with the narrative that cast Abriella in the best light and the villain with his hawks in the worst. Who knows? But it's too late to put that genie back in the bottle."

Nate took a long breath and held it.

Sandburg said, "I guess this is what can happen when a guy thinks he's somebody special and he can take justice into his own hands."

Nate said, "Now I get it. I know why you're here. It's not to warn me. It's so you can look me in the eye and tell me I'm a target. Joe said you were a true believer. You're so FBI you shit special agent turds. You think armed feds like yourself should run the world."

Sandburg grinned and confirmed everything Nate had just said by doing so. "They may send another hit team like the Wolf Pack," Sandburg said. "Or they may just send one guy. Or maybe the cartel will just put the word out that there's a big reward for the *pistolero* who brings them your head. It might be like one of those old Western movies where the cocky kid comes to town to knock off the old gunslinger. Who knows?"

He leaned forward on the table and glared at Nate. "All I know is that you had better keep your head on a swivel. You won't know who they send or when they'll show up. But you can count on the fact that they'll want revenge on the man who tricked their Abriella and fed her to his hawks, even if that never happened. They're violent and depraved—but they're also smart. They want to send a message that anyone who fucks with their people gets wiped out. It's good for morale and it's good for business. Fentanyl distribution is a multibillion-dollar industry. They don't want anybody messing that up.

"Oh," Sandburg said, sitting back, "I suppose there have been discussions in DC that the Bureau could put the word out that it didn't actually happen that way. The Sinaloans might even believe it. But when the target is somebody who has embarrassed the Bureau more than once and gamed the system to have a passel of charges dropped, well, that didn't give my friends a lot of incentive to do so."

Nate said nothing.

Sandburg said, "Some of us made it our life's work to nail the drug lords who are pumping that poison into our country. We were getting close to fucking taking them out. But you and your friend Joe had other plans. You went your own way. I lost a partner and my boss, and I can hardly walk because of what you two decided to do."

"We did what was right," Nate said. "Joe doesn't do otherwise, even when he should."

Sandburg waved that away. "Ah, your good friend Joe Pickett," Sandburg spat. "The game warden who does no wrong. Well, I've had plenty of time to think about what happened that day on the courthouse steps and I have my issues with him."

"What issues?" Nate asked.

"I'll keep that to myself. In the meanwhile, you have other

things to worry about. The bad guys might be closer than you think. In fact, they may already be here. I got some gas in Saddlestring before I came out here and all anybody can talk about is that someone took a shot at your judge."

Nate was stunned. "Judge Hewitt?"

"Last night, I guess," Sandburg said. "It sounds like a drive-by to me. Someone took a pop at him and hit his wife."

"I didn't know."

Sandburg tilted his head. "They'll know about that big gun of yours, so they might go after you from a distance like they did him. Your wife and kid are inside the house, right? You might want to shut the curtains and tell them to keep their pretty little heads down."

Nate was across the table and had Sandburg's left ear in his grip so fast that the man couldn't react.

"Go ahead," Sandburg said. "Rip it off. I've read that you do that. Rip the ear off a disabled special agent of the FBI. Show everyone how tough you are."

Nate let go and stood up. He was black with rage. The casual mention of his family had triggered him into an instant state of *yarak*, the Turkish falconry term that describes the perfect condition for hunting and killing prey.

Nate hadn't been in a state of *yarak* for a long time, and he didn't welcome it back.

He said to Sandburg, "Get off my property. You've got thirty seconds."

Sandburg said, "I'm busted up. It might take me a little longer than that."

Nate wheeled and kicked the door open. He knew if he stayed

with Sandburg any longer, anything could happen. He didn't want Liv to look outside and see Sandburg's body parts flying out of the RV.

Outside, he kicked the door shut. He stood there until Sandburg lumbered his way to the cab and started the engine. The big RV slid away.

Sandburg reached his arm out the open driver's-side window and extended his middle finger as a bitter goodbye.

STILL FUMING, NATE strode through his house toward the master bedroom. Liv asked what had happened and he found he couldn't talk to her yet. Kestrel was almost asleep in her crib and he didn't want to scare her back awake.

Nate opened the closet doors and removed the metal lockbox from the top shelf and placed it on the bed. Inside was his five-shot Freedom Arms .454 Casull scoped revolver and its coiled shoulder holster. There were four heavy boxes of cartridges. He hadn't carried, handled, or fired the weapon in months, but it felt comfortable in his hand.

Liv asked, "Nate, are you okay?"

"Not really," he replied.

Nate stepped back out on his porch and scanned the horizon. The dust spoor from Sandburg's RV was still in sight.

OVER TWO MILES away, a man named Orlando Panfile leaned into a spotting scope and adjusted the focus until he could see Nate Romanowski clearly. The falconer had been hidden from his view until he stepped off the front porch of his home and moved into the yard on the side of the structure. Waves of heat wafted through his field of vision, but he made a positive identification of his target. The intel he'd received from his employers turned out to be exactly correct. He could even see the blond ponytail when the man on the porch turned to watch the motor home drive away.

The spotting scope was screwed into the base of a short tripod and hidden within the tough gnarled branches of a sagebrush. Panfile had set it up the night before on the top of a ridge so that his prone body behind it would be out of view from the falconer's compound below in the basin.

When the falconer went back into the house, Panfile wriggled backward until he was far enough down the hill to stand up without being viewed from below. He brushed the dirt and debris from the front of his shirt and pants and started for his camp fifty yards down the hill.

FOUR

THE TWELVE SLEEP RIVER VALLEY OPENED UP BELOW THE helicopter as it cleared the summit of the Bighorn Range. The town of Saddlestring appeared in the distance as a smattering of sparkling debris on either side of the cottonwood-choked river. It looked to Joe like a mighty being had filled a giant cup with houses and low-slung buildings, shaken it like dice, and tossed the contents across on both sides of the banks.

He was always fascinated to see his district from the air since he spent so much time driving and patrolling its back roads, but he wished there were some way he could get the same view without having to be inside a small plane or chopper. Flying terrified him, and it was hard to appreciate the view when he could barely breathe and his heart whumped in his chest.

For the first time, though, he spotted the green metal roof of his new game warden station tucked into a heavily wooded curve of the river. The Picketts had been in the home for less than a year, after his old station had burned to the ground. He was still getting used to it, but he liked the location and he loved being close enough to the river to keep his fly rod strung and ready near the front door.

The palette of fall colors near the river and the multicolored aspen groves in the folds of the mountains made it hard to pick out individual objects. The valley was drunk with color, and Joe had left his shades in his agency pickup in Jackson.

Which was a problem.

He was about to land at the Saddlestring Municipal Airport, but his truck was six hours and three hundred and fifty miles away in Jackson. This wasn't very good planning, although it wasn't unusual when it came to state government.

Joe looked up at his death grip on the overhead strap. He'd been clutching it since he'd lifted off, and his fingers were white with strain. Although the helicopter flight had been smooth and without incident and it was very unlikely that it would suddenly buck in the air and throw him outside through the window, letting go of the strap was something he refused to do.

His phone had a single bar of cell service as it neared Saddlestring and he quickly texted his wife, Marybeth.

Can you please pick me up at the airport? No truck. Long story.

JOE SAW HER driving to the small airport in her white Twelve Sleep County Library van just as the helicopter began to descend. It was the only vehicle on the road.

Touchdown was gentle, but Joe didn't begin to relax until he could hear the rotors decelerate and he was convinced they were on solid ground on the tarmac.

The pilot, a navy vet from Riverton, turned in his seat and

made a thumbs-up, indicating Joe could get out. Joe thanked him for the lift, opened the door, and clamped his hat tightly on his head.

He jogged toward the van in a hunched-over crouch well past the range of the rotor blades so there was absolutely no chance his head would be lopped off by them. He had the .308 in one hand and his shotgun in the other.

As he opened the van door and swung inside, he could hear the engine of the helicopter roar as it lifted off. The pilot planned to fly back to Jackson and resume the search for Jim Trenary. Joe had heard some back-and-forth between the pilot and Mike Martin. While they were in the air, Martin had reported that he thought they were getting close to the location of the grizzly attack.

"Good thing I just got out of a meeting when your text came through," Marybeth said.

"Thank you."

Marybeth was the director of the county library and Joe thought she looked sharp in her dark pantsuit, white blouse, and single strand of pearls. She looked and smelled much better than Mike Martin, Julius Talbot, or Peaches.

The van Marybeth had commandeered also served as the county bookmobile. Joe liked the musty smell of all the books on the shelves in the back.

"I heard about Sue Hewitt," Marybeth said. "It's just bizarre."

Sue Hewitt was on Marybeth's library foundation board and she was very involved in the community. Marybeth had once said that Sue's generosity with her time and money was partly designed to offset the judge's cranky reputation and disposition, and it had worked.

"Have you heard how she's doing?" Joe asked.

"Hanging by a thread," Marybeth said. "They kept her here in the hospital because they were afraid to airlift her to Billings last night. Plus, Judge Hewitt wouldn't let them."

Joe grunted. He'd told Marybeth about the grizzly incident the night before because they talked every night on the phone when he wasn't home, but at the time the news wasn't out about the shooting.

"Does anyone know what happened?" he asked.

Because of her job and her local friends and connections, Marybeth always knew more about what was going on in the valley than Joe did. Since they now had an empty nest, she'd gotten even more involved with activities, fund-raisers, and charity work. Marybeth was plugged in.

She said, "Whoever did it wasn't even close to their house at the time. As you know, the Hewitts live up at the club on the golf course. I've heard some people say they think it was a stray round that just happened to go through the window and hit Sue. That it was some kind of freak occurrence—or a drive-by shooting."

Joe was puzzled. "How can there be a drive-by when there isn't a road?"

The Hewitt home backed up to the eighteen-hole course. There was no road behind them for a long distance, although golf carts likely drove by in the summer when the course was open.

The judge and his wife were rare local members of the Eagle Mountain Club, an old but still very exclusive members-only resort on the eastern flank of the valley. It offered lodging, dining, fishing, and golf primarily. Since most of the members were from out of state, the club was practically vacant in the fall and winter, except for the few members who lived there for the entire year like the Hewitts.

If it was indeed a drive-by shooting, Joe thought, the shooter must have been somewhere on the golf course itself—which was closed. Meaning someone had sneaked onto the property with a weapon and a target in mind. But sneaking onto the Eagle Mountain Club wasn't easy to do. It was surrounded by a high perimeter fence on all sides and the only access was through a gate at the front entrance that required a code or key-card entry. The gatehouse was usually staffed with a guard, who knew each guest by sight. There were cameras and sensors hidden around the exterior fence as well. Anyone who parked outside the club would have left their vehicle on the side of the road near the fence, where it could easily be seen by passersby.

A stray round was just as unlikely, Joe thought, although it wasn't inconceivable. Everybody had guns in Wyoming, and shots were fired—at game animals, predators, targets, whatever—at all times of the day. Bullets traveled much farther than most people realized. The county shooting range was several miles from the club, and stray rounds could easily travel that far and still be lethal upon impact. But the targets at the gun range faced east, and the Eagle Mountain Club was south of the facility. A round that missed the target high—and it would have to be very high to clear the berm backstop—wouldn't land anywhere close to the club.

Odd occurrences and random bullets had happened before, Joe knew. There had been a civil suit recently, north in Casper, where a man watching television had been struck by a .50 round fired two miles away from his home that tore through his wall.

"Any suspects you've heard about?" Joe asked her.

"There's all sorts of speculation," she said. "Judge Hewitt has lots of enemies. But I haven't heard any names."

Joe snorted. The judge did indeed have lots of enemies, including the many criminals he'd sent to jail and prison, as well as most of the lawyers who'd pleaded before his bench. Hewitt didn't suffer fools in his courtroom, and for years he'd humiliated attorneys he considered unprepared or feckless.

Judge Hewitt was brutal when it came to sentencing defendants who were found guilty. He lectured them, called them "pukes," "mouth breathers," and "moral degenerates," and ended many sentencing statements by saying if it were up to him the criminal would be sentenced to hard labor breaking up rocks. If the crime victimized seniors or children, he'd declared from the bench several times that he'd like to take the defendant outside the courtroom and shoot him himself.

An equal opportunity authoritarian in the courtroom, Judge Hewitt had castigated prosecutors and law enforcement officers whom he considered incompetent or derelict in the cases they brought before him. Joe had witnessed both the former county prosecutor and former sheriff get the bark peeled off them by the judge in public. Joe hadn't been immune either, although after calling him a "poor excuse for a game warden" during one trial, Judge Hewitt had invited Joe back to his chambers during the recess. Joe had expected further abuse, but it turned out Hewitt wanted to talk about his upcoming hunt in Texas for feral pigs. He was looking forward to shooting them out of a helicopter with an AK-47.

Most of all, Judge Hewitt was a big-game hunter, and he structured his world around trips to go after exotic prey. He was working on his second North American Sheep Slam now—killing a Dall, desert bighorn, Rocky Mountain bighorn, and Stone sheep. He'd killed a brown bear in Alaska that was still on the record books, and a twelve-hundred-pound Asian water buffalo in northern Australia. Hewitt knew Joe's views about trophy hunters, though, and he steered clear of that subject when they talked about the outdoors.

An alternative weekly newspaper in Jackson Hole had once written a cover story about him titled "'Hanging' Judge Hewitt—the Law East of the Bighorns."

Hewitt had framed the cover and it hung with pride behind his desk in his chambers.

Joe said to Marybeth, "The question isn't who would love to see Judge Hewitt get shot. The question is who wouldn't?"

"Poor Sue," Marybeth said.

Joe told her how the governor had become involved, and that every law enforcement principal in Twelve Sleep County had been ordered to assemble at the courtroom, including him.

"That's unusual," she said. "Why is the governor involved?"

"Beats me," Joe said. "But the request was made to Director Ewig. That's why I'm back here."

"I'll ask around," Marybeth said. "I'll find out the connection between Judge Hewitt and the governor. It's likely to be sordid."

Joe agreed. Just about everything about Governor Colter Allen turned out to be sordid. Joe knew that from past experience, although for the past year Allen had left him alone, for which Joe was grateful.

After a slew of #MeToo allegations had emerged regarding Allen's conduct before being elected, the governor had gone to ground. Like other politicians he no doubt observed, Allen hadn't addressed the charges or really denied them. He'd simply refused to talk about them, and moved on. It was a new political world, Joe had learned. Politicians who were snared in scandal didn't fight back or resign in shame, because there *was* no personal shame. They simply kept going, and it appeared to be working. Talk about recall and impeachment had died down. And for Joe, it meant Governor Allen hadn't bothered him in months—until now.

"Will you be home tonight for dinner?" she asked as she slowed down on Main near the courthouse.

"I don't know, but I hope so."

"How are you going to get your truck back?"

Joe thought about that. "I have no idea."

JOE BOUNDED UP the granite courthouse steps toward the large wooden double doors. He glanced down while he did so and grimaced. Although the blood of the victims had been scrubbed from the steps, the pockmarks from machine gun rounds still scarred the stone. He realized he hadn't been on the steps since it happened, and it jolted him. The photos he'd seen of the crime scene, the four bleeding bodies sprawled on the steps, Sheriff Reed's dead body in the street where his wheelchair had rolled, would always haunt him.

The fact that he could have easily been with them haunted him as well.

He paused on the landing and slowly turned around. He saw where the vehicle with the shooters had been on the street. He remembered the photos of scores of brass casings from the weapons on the asphalt.

Joe tried to shake the images of those photos from his mind. He couldn't.

So he went inside.

STOVEPIPE, THE EX RODEO contestant and stock contractor who'd manned the metal detector in the county building for as long as Joe could remember, stood up from his stool to greet him. He wore his usual black cowboy hat and purple scarf, but his face was ashen.

"Did you hear about Miz Hewitt?" Stovepipe asked.

"I did," Joe said as he emptied his weapons, phone, cuffs, keys, and other metal into a basket. "That's why I'm here."

"It's a terrible, terrible thing," Stovepipe said. "That poor lady."

Stovepipe wiped tears away from his eyes with the tips of his cowboy scarf as he motioned Joe through the machine.

"Are you okay?" Joe asked Stovepipe. "Did Sue . . ."

"No, no," Stovepipe said. "She's still in critical condition. But she's been so kind to me. She brings me cookies and brownies, just to be nice. I've seen her a lot more in the last couple of months and it's just hard to believe that she got shot like that."

"I agree," Joe said. "I think we'll find that shooter."

Joe gathered his gear on the other side. He was allowed to retain his equipment if he wasn't going to court. The security exercise was pointless and it had always been so, but Joe had quit objecting to it because he never got anywhere. Not only that, but the metal detector only worked about half the time.

"I hope you do," Stovepipe said. "But more than that, I hope Sue makes it through all right."

"Me too, Stovepipe."

DUANE PATTERSON WAS loitering in the hallway outside the door to Judge Hewitt's chambers. Patterson looked up when he heard Joe's boots coming down the tile floor.

"I'm glad you finally got here," Patterson said. "I've never seen him so pissed off."

"That's saying something," Joe replied.

Duane Patterson was gaunt and bony with a round baby face and a closetful of suits that didn't really fit him. He'd been the public defender for years and had endured more than his share of courtroom abuse from Judge Hewitt. Despite that, he'd been as surprised as anyone when the judge recommended him to the county commissioners to fill out the term of County Prosecutor Dulcie Schalk after she'd been incapacitated by the shooting on the courthouse steps.

Joe had been impressed how quickly Patterson had adapted to the job. Because he had been on the other side so long, he was experienced in the strategies, rhythms, and occasional tricks played by prosecutors toward defendants and their counsel. He knew which buttons to push, because Dulcie had been pushing his for years.

"Why'd you take so long to get here?" Patterson asked Joe. He was obviously annoyed.

"I was in Jackson Hole."

"I think we could have done this without you, but the judge didn't agree."

"Sorry."

"I'll let him know you're here."

Joe nodded. He opened the door to discover that a state trooper, the chief of police of Saddlestring, and the new county sheriff were impatiently waiting for him as well. Joe removed his hat and nodded at the others.

"About time," the trooper grumbled. "Why we was waiting for a game warden is beyond me."

The highway patrolman's name was Tillis, and Joe recognized him immediately. He'd met him in Jackson a couple of years back, when Tillis had refused to let Joe past the checkpoint of an exclusive gated community even though a crime was taking place.

Tillis was a big man with a square head and a crew cut dashed with silver. His aviator sunglasses hung from his collar and his flat-brimmed hat was on his lap. Tillis, like a few other troopers Joe had encountered, had a territorial bias against game wardens. He assumed Joe and his colleagues spent the bulk of their time hunting and fishing while real peace officers like himself were exposing themselves to drug dealers and other outlaws on the highways. Joe thought of Tillis as a blunt object.

Joe nodded to the state trooper and sat down. There was no point engaging with the man, he thought.

Chief Williamson of the Saddlestring Police Department sprawled on a plastic chair and greeted Joe with a wave of his hand. Williamson had been fired by the city council the year before for overzealously citing tourists for speeding and parking violations, but he'd since been rehired because his replacement had made it a policy to shoot stray dogs in town, not realizing that one of them belonged to the mayor.

The new county sheriff, Brendan Kapelow, sat ramrod-straight in a hard-backed chair with his wide silverbelly Stetson clamped low and hard on his head. His eyes flitted to Joe as he entered but shifted back toward the door where Judge Hewitt would emerge from his back office.

Joe didn't know yet what to think about Sheriff Kapelow, although he hoped his first impressions of him would turn out to be wrong.

Kapelow was in his early thirties, a marine who'd seen combat in Iraq and Afghanistan, who was new to the sheriff's department and had surprised everyone when he decided to run for the office after Sheriff Reed had been gunned down. Reed's senior deputies, Ryan Steck and Justin Woods, had long been thought to be the likely replacements, but the once-close friends had turned on each other when the campaign heated up. They'd accused each other of being lazy and corrupt, and the race had gotten personal and nasty in a way very few Wyoming local elections—except sheriff's elections—ever did. Joe had kept his distance during the campaign season and he'd been disappointed in both Steck and Woods for going after each other, because he liked and respected them both.

Kapelow, an unknown with an impressive background and the cool-eyed demeanor of a mysterious cowboy who had just ridden into town, beat the two deputies primarily because he hadn't slung mud or taken a side. Since the election, Steck and Woods had mended fences and become friends again but found themselves working for a boss they knew very little about.

Which created a natural and obvious problem within the department, Joe noted. Since his election, Kapelow hadn't reached out to the two deputies to smooth things over and welcome them to be a part of his team. He'd chosen to keep them isolated, and rather than speak to them during briefings or over a beer after work, he communicated in terse memos or text messages. Joe had seen a couple of the missives that Woods had showed him on his phone. One had read, *Cut your overtime by forty percent. You're costing me too much money.* Another read, *Iron your uniform and shine your boots. Appearances are important and every member of my staff needs to look sharp at all times. Appearance = Professionalism.*

Sheriff Kapelow, as far as Joe knew, never smiled or joked. He was an imposing physical presence, tall and very fit, and when he spoke it was so softly that listeners had to lean toward him to hear.

He wore his sidearm low on his right hip like a Wild West gunslinger, and his service weapon of choice was a stainless-steel Colt .45 Peacemaker with an ivory grip. He'd made no attempt to get to know Joe, or ingratiate himself into the community. Kapelow seemed to be a blank slate. Locals projected their wants, needs, and observations on him, often unfairly, Joe thought.

The new sheriff was either "strong and silent just like Gary Cooper" or "too full of himself to talk to anyone." He was either "a no-nonsense lawman" or a "humorless stiff."

In the short time he'd been sheriff, there had been no major felonies, cases, or controversies for which Kapelow would have had to prove his competence.

Until now.

Joe deeply missed Sheriff Mike Reed's presence in the room. And he missed Dulcie Schalk's calm and reasonable approach to every situation brought before her. He felt uncomfortable and out of place in this group of law enforcement people.

Because the local sheriff could request backup or assistance from the local game warden at any time, Joe's relationship with them was important. Wyoming game wardens could be asked to help with raids and assaults, or called in to assist with ongoing investigations. Kapelow was the fourth sheriff Joe had worked with in Twelve Sleep County. The first two, Bud Barnum and Kyle McLanahan, had been autocratic and corrupt. Mike Reed had been just the opposite: fair, honest, and straightforward.

Thus far, Kapelow was simply inscrutable.

PATTERSON CAME INTO the room and shut the door behind him. Because there weren't any more open chairs, he moved to the back and leaned against the radiator with his arms folded over his chest. It was a signal that Judge Hewitt was on his way.

Joe noted Patterson's demeanor. The acting county attorney was drained of color and Joe could see that his hands were trembling. Sue Hewitt's injury and the judge's reaction to it seemed to have really shaken him up. Joe thought that even though Patterson dealt with crimes and victims every day, he had likely not experienced anything this personal since the massacre on the courthouse steps.

The door burst open into the chambers and Hewitt stepped in. As always, he was in a hurry. His eyes were red and he had bags under them from lack of sleep.

Joe was used to seeing the judge in his robes, and without them Hewitt looked . . . mortal. He wore casual dark slacks and a rumpled white shirt with an obvious bloodstain on the front of it. He probably hadn't changed his clothes since the night before.

"I just came from the hospital," Hewitt said, standing behind his high-backed swivel chair and placing his hands on the top of it. "Sue is in critical condition and the doctors are talking about an induced coma so her body can maybe recover. It doesn't look good, though."

Hewitt's eyes misted and he looked away. Joe had never seen him like that before, and he felt his own eyes well up. It was a surprising reaction and he hoped the others in the room didn't catch it.

Judge Hewitt recovered and he looked from Tillis to Williamson to Patterson to Kapelow to Joe. He held each of their eyes for a moment.

Then he said, "Someone in this room knows who tried to kill me."

FIVE

The statement hung in the air.

In his peripheral vision, Joe noticed that Chief Williamson had blanched and reached for a bottle of water. Tillis had stiffened and his face reddened. Behind him, Joe heard Patterson gulp. Sheriff Kapelow sat stoic and ramrod-straight, as if the accusation had nothing to do with him.

Joe thought Hewitt had meant something else entirely, and it was borne out when the judge cleared his throat and went on.

"Each one of you has brought a long list of miscreants and offenders into my courtroom over the years," he said. "You've taken the sacred oath and made the case against them and testified to put them away where they belong. No one knows these reprobates better than each of you, not counting their mothers. You've been there during the investigation, the arrest, and the trial. You were likely in the room when they were sentenced, so you know what their reactions were to my judgment of them.

"What I want each of you to do is to reflect on those cases," he said. "Make a list. Write down the names of the pukes who reacted to their punishment by saying they wanted retribution against you, your fellow law enforcement officers, witnesses against them, and especially the judge who sentenced them."

As his request became clearer, Joe noted that Williamson relaxed and Tillis seemed more annoyed. Kapelow was apparently unaffected.

"Duane," Hewitt said to Patterson over Joe's shoulder, "you might be in a really good position to know what threats were made against me, since you defended a number of these pukes. How many told you after sentencing that they'd like to burn down my house or take me out?"

Patterson cleared his throat. "More than a few, Your Honor," he said.

"Write down their names," Hewitt said to him. "See how many are presently in Rawlins at the penitentiary and who might be out wanting to seek revenge. Deliver that list to the sheriff and me by the end of the week."

"Yes, Your Honor," Patterson said weakly.

"Is there a problem with that?" Hewitt asked. His eyes were on the acting county prosecutor.

"No problem, Your Honor," Patterson said. "The list might be longer than you want it to be."

"I don't care," Hewitt shot back. "That comes with the job."

Patterson said, "I've got a lot on my plate right now, sir."

"Not as much as Sue," Hewitt said sharply. "Sue is in the process of dying right now due to a high-powered bullet that entered her left breast and plowed through her lungs."

"Yes, sir," Patterson said with a yelp.

"Kapelow," Hewitt said, focusing on the sheriff sitting in front of him. "This is now the first and only priority of your department. Ask all of your deputies to make lists and start questioning everybody on it who is not currently in jail. Tell all your people to clear their schedules until we have the shooter in custody."

Kapelow nodded so imperceptibly that Joe could barely see it. Joe wondered what the sheriff's reaction would be to being ordered around like that.

"I'll do the same," Williamson said.

Kapelow turned in his chair toward the others in the room. He said, "The club is outside city limits. This shooting is clearly in the sheriff's department jurisdiction. It should all go through us. All of it. We want a well-coordinated investigation and not a bunch of guys tripping over each other with their own personal agendas."

He didn't look over at Williamson when he said it, although it was obviously directed at the chief.

Joe narrowed his eyes at the man. Although it was technically true that the sheriff had jurisdiction over the crime scene, the way he stated it was haughty and unnecessary, Joe thought. He'd aligned himself with Judge Hewitt against the others in the room.

Kapelow turned back to Hewitt. "I've got my guys on the scene out there right now."

"Good," Hewitt said. "Tell them not to disturb anything in my house or there will be hell to pay. I've cleared out for the time being so you can do your work. But when I move back in, there better not be any damage or anything missing."

"Yes, Your Honor."

"Have you determined where the shot was fired from?"

"We think it was from the bunker of the seventh green,"

Kapelow said. "We think someone climbed the fence, trespassed on the property, and lay in wait at dusk. We're combing the area for physical evidence: footprints, the casing, cigarette butts or spent chewing tobacco—anything we can find to help determine the shooter's identity."

Joe was impressed with what Kapelow had done so far.

Hewitt wasn't. "Your 'bunker on the seventh green' theory is outright bullshit," he said. "I sit at my dining room table every night and look out over the golf course and the hills and mountains behind it. From where I sit, I can't even see the sand trap on the seventh fairway. Anybody hiding there could barely see the roof of my house, much less the back window."

Sheriff Kapelow didn't flinch. He said simply, "The investigation is ongoing."

"I hope to hell so," Hewitt said with sarcasm. "Have you determined what kind of rifle or bullet was used?"

"Not yet," Kapelow said. "The preliminary guess from the evidence tech was that it was a .30 caliber or similar."

"Which is just about every bullet and rifle within five hundred miles," Hewitt said. "I hope you can nail it down a hell of a lot better than that."

"We will," Kapelow said.

The man had unerring confidence in his abilities, Joe observed.

Chief Williamson leaned forward, eager to please. "We've got our MRAP gassed up and ready," he told the judge. "Our plan is to move it out onto the golf course so the shooter will have a hell of a surprise in store for him if he decides to come back."

The MRAP was a twenty-ton Mine-Resistant Ambush-

Protected behemoth of military hardware donated by the Pentagon to local police departments throughout the country following the Iraq War. Chief Williamson looked for any excuse to deploy it locally. Helmets, body armor, combat boots, and camouflage uniforms were also provided.

"That's one of the dumbest fucking ideas I've ever heard," Judge Hewitt said to Williamson. "If you drive that thing out onto my golf course and tear up the grass, I'll take a shot at it myself."

Williamson slumped back in his chair, completely deflated.

"Instead of jumping in your tank," Hewitt said to the chief, "make a list just like the others and then go out and talk to people. Let us know who you've brought before me that wants a piece of me. Can you do that?"

"Yes, sir," Williamson said while looking at his boots.

Trooper Tillis said, "Your Honor, I'm not sure I can help you here. I didn't get assigned to the highways around here until a couple of months ago. I was over in Jackson before that. I've only testified in your court a couple of times and both of those offenders are still in jail. If you want a list of past offenders who have it out for you, you'll need to talk to the guys who were stationed here before me."

Tillis gathered himself up in his chair as if preparing to leave, but a twin-laser stare from Hewitt froze him to his seat.

Judge Hewitt said, "So your contribution to the homicidal targeting of a judge and the possible murder of his wife is to tell *me* to go talk to some troopers who were around here before? While Sue is clinging to the last thread of her life in a hospital?"

"W-well—" Tillis stammered, but Hewitt cut him off.

"*You* go talk to them," Hewitt said. "Go through their arrest records for the past few years. Make a list of suspects and then go *interview* those suspects. Pretend you're an officer of the law instead of a glorified traffic cop. Do you think you can do that, Tillis?"

The trooper mumbled, "Yes, Your Honor," his entire head flushing red.

Hewitt nodded his satisfaction. Then he turned to Joe.

"Pickett," he said. "The list you are going to make is unique in my way of thinking. The violators you bring before me are mainly hunters and other types who are well versed in high-powered rifles. They also tend to be independent and sneaky—not the typical meth head or wannabe gangbanger Duane would defend or prosecute."

Joe nodded in agreement. He looked at the side of Kapelow's head and asked, "Has it been determined that the bullet was fired from a rifle and not a handgun?"

"Pretty much," the sheriff responded softly.

Hewitt said, "It was from a rifle. I'll bet you any amount of money that it was from a high-powered rifle. A pistol shooter would have had to have been much closer to my house and I would have seen him out there. It was a rifle."

Joe said, "Some handguns have a lot of range and accuracy. My buddy Nate Romanowski has a single-action revolver he can shoot accurately at several hundred yards."

"Maybe it was *him*," Williamson offered.

"It wasn't Nate," Joe scoffed. "He doesn't operate that way."

"And he wouldn't have missed and hit my wife," Hewitt said. "I would guess you'll be able to follow up on my request in short order?"

"Yup, Your Honor," Joe said.

Already, Joe had come up with several names of suspects. As he and Marybeth had discussed, the judge had a lot of enemies.

First on the list was Dallas Cates, or one of Cates's associates. Although Joe had helped put Cates into prison two years ago, Dallas had an almost legitimate beef with the judge. Hewitt, Joe, Dulcie Schalk, and Sheriff Reed—they'd all bent the rules to put Dallas Cates away. Cates had vowed retribution. But as far as Joe knew, Dallas Cates was in the midst of serving five to seven years in the Wyoming State Penitentiary. Despite that, the ex–rodeo star was charismatic and convincing enough that he might try to reach beyond jail to someone who would take a shot at the judge.

Joe planned to start there.

There were others. Ron Connelly, aka the Mad Archer from Baggs, had been thrown the book by Judge Hewitt, with maximum sentences for wanton destruction of wildlife, assault, and animal cruelty. He'd targeted Joe's half-Corgi, half-Labrador dog, Tube, with an arrow. The Mad Archer had been overcharged and oversentenced, though. Judge Hewitt clearly hadn't liked him and said as much during sentencing.

Although his weapon of choice was his compound bow, Joe could conceive of the Mad Archer taking up a rifle and plotting his revenge.

There was also Dennis Sun, the millionaire rancher and film producer who had purchased a large ranch on the eastern slope of the Bighorns. Sun was used to having his own way, and he'd long decided that Wyoming Game and Fish Department rules and regulations hampered his style. When he wanted a new set of antlers for one of his many guest cottages, he'd kill a mule deer buck or bull elk despite the hunting season dates or hunting licenses required. Joe had caught Sun poaching on his own ranch and had arrested him.

Although Sun had hired celebrity lawyer Marcus Hand, it was assumed he would get a slap on the wrist and sent home. But it hadn't worked out that way, for two reasons. The first was Judge Hewitt's visceral hatred toward Hand in his courtroom. The second was because the record bull elk in velvet that Sun had poached was one Hewitt had scouted himself and had planned to harvest for his own game room, although legally.

Dennis Sun had been sentenced to multiple hunting violations; his airplane, helicopter, ATVs, and rifles all seized, and his hunting and fishing privileges revoked for life. He'd also been sentenced to six months in the county jail, although Hand had appealed and won and Sun had gotten off with time served. Even so, Sun had vocally attacked Judge Hewitt as he was led from the courtroom in handcuffs. The story had been prominent in both *Variety* and *The Hollywood Reporter* and Sun had claimed that Joe and Hewitt had combined to adversely affect his livelihood.

Sun, Joe guessed, had money and connections to hire someone to take a shot at the judge.

And that was just the start of Joe's list.

"OKAY, THEN," HEWITT SAID, stepping out from behind the chair he'd used like a combination of podium and shield. "We have our assignments. As for me, I plan to spend my hours overseeing this investigation whenever I'm not at Sue's side at the hospital. You have your jobs," he said to the room. "Do I make myself clear?"

Joe looked around and wished he had more confidence in what would happen next.

He thought the lists, once compiled, would be a good place to start. But what Hewitt hadn't mentioned was the possibility that the shooter wouldn't be on any of them. Over his career, the judge had angered defense lawyers, witnesses, law enforcement officers, and some of his own staff. Hewitt didn't seem to consider that someone other than a criminal he'd sentenced could have pulled the trigger. He also hadn't seemed to entertain the possibility that it really was a stray shot that hadn't been intended to hit him or his wife.

Before exiting through his private door, Hewitt turned back to the room and said over his shoulder, "Gentlemen, please don't make this a clusterfuck. Can you do that?"

Everyone mumbled their assurances.

When Hewitt's door closed, Patterson was the first to speak.

"Lord help us," he said to no one and to everyone.

"JOE, DO YOU have a minute?" Duane Patterson asked once all of the others were gone and only he and Joe remained.

"Yup."

Joe noticed the perspiration beading on the prosecutor's forehead and on his neck above his collar. He leaned into Joe and said, "Have you ever seen the judge like this before?"

Joe shrugged. "I've seen him angry, but not like this."

"He's *manic*," Patterson said, his eyes wide.

"I'd probably be, too, if someone took a shot at me and hit Marybeth," Joe said. The image of what he'd just described sent a shiver down his spine.

"He's asking the impossible," Patterson said. "He's putting it all on us to find the shooter."

"Maybe we'll do just that," Joe said.

"But that's not what I *do*," Patterson said. "I'm a prosecutor. I'm not a detective." He seemed panicked.

"Just do your best," Joe encouraged him.

"My best won't be good enough for him," Patterson said. "He'll ride me until I break down. I know him. I know how relentless he can be."

Joe nodded.

Patterson continued. "He's powerful. He's got his fingers into everything, and he can pull strings you don't even know he has. How do you think he was able to assemble all of us in his office in a moment's notice just now? He went straight to the governor and the governor danced.

"I've got this job because Judge Hewitt recommended me and made his case to the county commissioners," Patterson said. "He could just as easily take them aside and suggest they hire a new county prosecutor if he thinks I didn't do enough to find the shooter. I could see that happening."

Joe agreed, but didn't say so. He changed the subject. "How well do you get along with our new sheriff?"

Patterson frowned. "Our relationship is nonexistent," he said. "I can't figure him out. He keeps his cards so close to the vest they're like a skin graft. No one knows what he's thinking, including his deputies. He makes it a point not to talk with me, even about important matters. Instead, he sends memos."

"I've heard about that," Joe said.

"I want to think he's some kind of oddball investigative genius," Patterson said. "Like he's our own Columbo or something. But so far, I just can't read him."

Joe acknowledged him but said nothing.

"This will be his test," Patterson said. "After this, maybe we'll know if he's good at his job. But in the meanwhile, *we* have to contend with the judge. It's a nightmare. I can't ever recall someone taking a shot at a sitting judge in Wyoming, can you?"

"No."

"And Sue," Patterson said. "Poor Sue. She didn't deserve this. She's the only person who makes Judge Hewitt halfway tolerable because she's the only one who can keep him in check. If she goes . . ."

"I know," Joe said.

"We're all screwed," Patterson said.

"Then let's find the shooter," Joe said while fitting on his hat to go.

JOE PAUSED OUTSIDE Judge Hewitt's office door before going to the lobby. He could hear the man sobbing inside.

For a second, Joe considered opening the door and trying to console the man. He thought better of it, though. Maybe Judge Hewitt needed privacy to break down and cry.

Joe's heart went out to him.

Then he remembered he didn't have his truck outside. Again he called Marybeth, and asked her if he could get a ride to the highway department building on the outskirts of town.

While he waited for his wife, Joe fished his notebook out of his pocket and opened it to a fresh page.

Under the header *Suspects*, he wrote down:

Dallas Cates (and associates)
The Mad Archer
Dennis Sun

SIX

THE EAGLE MOUNTAIN CLUB WAS SPRAWLED OUT ON A vast sagebrush-covered bench overlooking the Twelve Sleep River Valley. Within the perimeter fencing it was an oasis of grass, mature trees, ponds, and manicured fairways bordered by club facilities and private homes. With the short but intense summer season over, an air of exhaustion hung over it and it reminded Joe of a big-game animal that had been run to the point of extreme fatigue and had bedded down.

He'd wrangled a beat-up two-wheel-drive GMC pickup from the Wyoming Department of Transportation fleet and had negotiated a deal where he could "rent" the vehicle for a day or two until he could reunite with his own truck. The WYDOT supervisor didn't like the arrangement because of the paperwork that would be involved to get reimbursed by the Game and Fish Department, but in the end, he capitulated because the truck wasn't being used by any of his people anyway.

The supervisor did point out that Joe's reputation for the loss of and damage to state property was well known and that he hoped and expected to see the pickup returned in one piece. Joe had promised nothing.

The vehicle was dingy white in color with the WYDOT logo—ironically similar to the triangular slow-moving-vehicle symbol—on both doors. There was an amber rotating light on the roof, rusted shovels in the bed, and a fast-food wrapper covering the passenger-side floorboard. The windshield was cracked and the gas gauge never wavered from one-quarter full.

Joe was grateful to have it, though, and he found as he drove through town toward the club that unlike his own distinctive green pickup, no one gave it a second look as he passed by. Everyone, it seemed, was interested to find out where the game warden was headed. No one cared about a highway department guy. The .308 rifle and shotgun he'd brought with him from Jackson and hadn't yet had a chance to store away were muzzle-down on the floorboard next to him.

HE THOUGHT ABOUT the weapons when he saw that a sheriff's department SUV was parked crosswise in front of the entrance gate to the Eagle Mountain Club. Not that he'd think to brandish them, but he hoped the deputy who manned the gate wouldn't see them inside the cab and overreact.

Fortunately, Joe recognized the deputy to be Justin Woods, one of the losing sheriff's candidates. Woods climbed out of his vehicle and held his left hand out palm-up while gripping his sidearm with his right.

C. J. BOX

Joe rolled to a stop and instinctively reached for the toggle switch to power down the window, but it wasn't there. Instead, he had to crank it down by its handle the old-fashioned way.

"I didn't recognize you in this truck," Woods said to Joe with a puzzled smile. "Are you sneaking around all undercover?"

"My truck is in Jackson," Joe said. Then: "Long story."

"What can I do for you?" Woods asked.

"I'm here to look at the crime scene at Judge Hewitt's place."

"No can do. I'm sorry, but I can't let you in. If I did, the sheriff would have my head."

"Seriously?" Joe asked.

"Seriously. He said no one was to access this property except for department personnel."

"Even if Judge Hewitt personally ordered me to investigate the shooting?" Joe asked, even though he was pretty sure what the answer would be.

"No one gets in through the gate," Woods said, shaking his head. He drew his cell phone out of his jacket and showed the screen to Joe. It was a text message from Kapelow that read exactly those seven words: *No one gets in through the gate.*

"Okay," Joe said. "I don't want to get you in trouble."

"Thank you. You don't know what it's like in the department these days."

"I'm starting to get a better idea," Joe said as he put the transmission into reverse and started to back away.

"You gave up easy," Woods said, puzzled. Then he grinned and nodded as he figured out Joe's intentions. "Oh . . ."

Joe winked at him and gave him the thumbs-up.

LONG RANGE

———

THE OLD RANCH bridge that crossed the river and accessed the Eagle Mountain Club from the other side was three miles from the gate. The bridge was used by service vehicles and employees of the club in the summer so they wouldn't have to be observed by members who didn't like to see traffic.

Just like many of the members didn't know of the existence of the bridge, Joe had guessed that the new sheriff didn't, either. Woods's text had said nothing about a bridge, after all. Technically, he wasn't defying Deputy Woods's orders.

Joe slowed on the bridge and looked out his window. There was a fine deep pool underneath and the warm spurt in the afternoon had encouraged a hatch of insects. Good-sized brown and rainbow trout slid up from the depths and sipped Trico flies on the surface, then pistoned back from where they'd originated.

Despite the circumstances of his visit to the club, and despite the fact that Joe's fly rod and flies were in his pickup in the parking area of the trailhead at Turpin Meadow in Jackson, no matter where he was or how much he was in a hurry, he always paused to observe rising trout.

It drove Marybeth crazy.

THE MAINTENANCE FACILITY for the club grounds was hidden beneath the bluffs that looked out over the river and the valley so members and residents couldn't see it. It was a long-weathered metal building surrounded by huge river cottonwoods and flanked by utility vehicles, earth-moving equipment, the cage-cab ATV used to pick up driving-range golf balls, and a long line of drift boats covered for the winter and stowed away.

Joe stopped and got out adjacent to the open garage door that led to the maintenance supervisor's office inside. He entered the dark building and looked around. Unlike the immaculately decorated homes and club facilities up on the bench, the maintenance facility had the blue-collar ambience of an auto shop: grease-stained floors, benches cluttered with tools and parts, the hum of an ancient radio playing classic rock, the smell of spilled diesel fuel, and a ubiquitous Snap-on Tools calendar featuring a blond model in a hard hat and a yellow bikini.

"Hello?" he called out.

There was a dull *thump* from underneath a utility pickup to Joe's left. Joe turned at the sound and saw a pair of legs writhing from beneath the truck.

Darin Westby, the maintenance supervisor, rolled out on a creeper, wincing and rubbing a red welt on his forehead. When his eyes focused, he said, "Joe?"

"Yup. I'm sorry I startled you."

"I banged my head a good one," Westby said. "I didn't hear you roll up and I didn't expect any company today."

"Really?" Joe asked. He wondered if sheriff's department personnel had been by the shop but hadn't noticed Westby underneath the pickup.

Westby sat up on his creeper and Joe extended his hand to help him to his feet. Westby was a tall man with lengthy arms and legs and oversized hands that looked like paddles attached to his wrists. He'd been the center for the Casper College basketball team before he wrecked his knee, and he'd started as a seasonal golf course groomer and had risen until he was now the maintenance supervisor for the entire Eagle Mountain Club. He'd married a local girl and they had two young children who already looked destined to star in basketball. Joe knew Westby to be a hard worker whose passion, aside from his family, was hunting sage grouse and mourning doves with his two golden retrievers.

The month before, on the nationwide mid-September opening day of dove season, Joe had encountered Westby in a wild-bean field in the breaklands. Although Westby had a bird license and conservation stamp, he'd forgotten to obtain a federal Migratory Bird Harvest Information Program (HIP) stamp. It was a technical violation that could have resulted in a citation, but Joe had given the man a pass and suggested he obtain a HIP stamp at his earliest convenience.

Joe hoped Westby remembered that favor.

"Why should I have expected visitors?" he asked.

Joe said, "I would have thought the cops would be crawling all over this place because of the shooting. Are you saying you haven't seen them?"

Westby wiped grease from his hands with a soiled red rag and shook his head. "You're the first guy I've seen today."

"You know about Sue Hewitt, though."

"Of course I do," Westby said. "She's a really nice woman and I feel terrible about her getting shot. It's such a crazy thing to have happened here at the club."

"So the sheriff's department hasn't questioned you?"

"Nope. Not that I'd have much to tell them," Westby said. "I had to run to Casper yesterday to pick up a new blade for the snowplow. I was gone when it happened. I didn't get back until eight-thirty last night and I went straight home. You can check that out with my wife if you want to. I didn't hear about the shooting until my wife told me she read about it on Facebook this morning."

Joe nodded. Because the weekly Saddlestring *Roundup* newspaper wouldn't come out until Wednesday, that's how locals kept abreast of breaking news, he knew.

"Did you see any suspicious people around the club before you left?" Joe asked. "You know, maybe someone driving slowly on one of the perimeter roads?"

Westby thought about it. "No."

"What about in the last week? Like maybe scouting the grounds?"

"It's been really quiet since the club closed for the season," he said. "The only thing I can remember is there were a couple of out-of-state antelope hunters I found standing outside the fence on the west side. This was last week. They said they'd wounded a buck that crawled under the fence and they wanted to come in and get it. I let them in and we found the buck dead on the ninth fairway. They started to field dress it right there and I told 'em, 'Nope, that's not a good idea.' Can you imagine that—leaving a gut pile on the fairway?"

Westby related the story of how he helped the hunters load their gut pile into their truck and drive it out of there. He confirmed for Joe that the two hunters didn't learn the code to the front gate, and hadn't done anything suspicious while he was with them. He agreed to email Joe their names and plate number.

"Another thing," Joe said. "Is there a record of everyone who went in and out of the club in the last week? Especially last night?"

"Sure," Westby said. "We've got CCTV at the gate and if someone entered using their transponder there's a printout at the front office. Are you suggesting a member might have done it?"

"I'm not suggesting anything," Joe said. "I'm just trying to cover all the bases."

"Talk to Judy in the office," Westby said. "She can get you the printout and copies of the video."

"I'm sure the sheriff already has," Joe said. Even though he wasn't sure about that at all since they hadn't even been to the shop to question Westby, who was one of the few permanent employees on the grounds.

"Anything else you can think of?" Joe asked.

"Not really," Westby said. But he hesitated when he said it.

"What?"

Westby pursed his lips. "It's club policy not to gossip about the members, you know. And it's a good policy, because they pay our salaries."

"But?" Joe asked, urging him on.

"Judge Hewitt is not exactly the most popular man around here. I know of a dozen members who just plain don't like him. I've always gotten on with him fine, but I know he can be really can-tankerous."

"True," Joe said.

"Sue's great, though," Westby said. "She's always kind and nice to everyone here. We all love her. It's too bad she got shot and not . . ." He caught himself and turned red. Westby said, "I didn't mean to say it like that at all."

"I believe you," Joe said.

"Judge Hewitt is crabby, but it's hard to believe a member took a shot at him for it," Westby said. "Most of our members are type

A executives from around the country. They have strong opinions about everything under the sun and they're used to getting their way. But taking a shot at another member? Nah. They'd just sue him instead."

Joe agreed and gave Westby his card so the supervisor could have his email address to send the names of the hunters.

"Oh," Joe said, "I have a favor to ask."

"Shoot." Then, realizing the double meaning of the word given the circumstances, Westby reddened further and said, "That's probably the wrong thing to say as well."

"Don't worry about it. Could I borrow one of your ATVs? I don't want to drive my truck out on the golf course."

"Sure you can," Westby said while looking over Joe's shoulder at the WYDOT pickup parked outside. "I wouldn't want to drive that thing *anywhere.*"

While Westby went to the attached garage to pull the Polaris Ranger around for Joe to use, Joe opened his notebook again. Well underneath the list of three suspects he wrote: *Second Tier.*

Then he wrote: *Club member? Ask Judy.*

Then: *Darin Westby: Check Casper alibi.*

Then: *Out-of-state antelope hunters.*

Joe fully expected to cross Westby's name off the page in the coming hours. His story about not being in town and picking up a part in Casper—which was a four-hour round trip—would be easy enough to verify.

As for the hunters, Joe could use the database of the Game and Fish Department to cross-check their names and verify that they'd drawn the antelope hunting area. Since the computerized drawing had been held months before and there was no guarantee to applicant hunters of successfully obtaining a license, it made little sense that assassins would use that procedure for gaining access to the area.

Joe expected he would cross their names off his list of suspects as well.

HE DROVE THE RANGER up the dirt service road to the bench and turned onto the smooth asphalt drive that accessed the outer circle of fine but empty homes. He glanced over at the houses as he passed them and tried to guess how much they'd cost to build. Most had five or six bedrooms and bathrooms and oversized garages to house several vehicles plus personal golf carts. In the first quarter-circle of the drive, the homes faced the golf course. In the second quarter-circle, as the road turned, the houses had been built so the views and access to the course were in the back.

That's where the Hewitts lived, in a low, sprawling McMansion with a driveway flanked by perfectly spaced mature cottonwood trees flush with fall colors. Joe had never been to the judge's house before, but it was obvious because of the number of sheriff's department SUVs in the driveway and the single deputy—Ryan Steck, the other losing candidate for sheriff—who stood in the middle of the road to turn away any oncoming vehicles.

Steck turned toward him with a stern expression on his baby face and his right hand resting on the grip of his sidearm, but when he recognized Joe, his face and posture relaxed.

Joe pulled up alongside him.

"Sheriff inside?" Joe asked.

"He is," Steck said. "He's supervising Gary Norwood's crew."

Gary Norwood was the crime scene forensics investigator shared by three northern Wyoming counties. He had a part-time assistant. Although the square mileage of the combined counties was just slightly smaller than the state of Massachusetts, only one CSI was necessary and there were weeks when Norwood complained they had nothing to do.

They did now, Joe thought.

"Have you figured anything out yet?" Joe asked Steck.

"Not that I'm aware of." Steck shrugged. "I'm pretty sure I'd be the last to know."

Joe grimaced.

"Yeah," Steck said. "It's like that. It's like working for the Finks."

"Do you mean the *Sphinx*?"

"Yeah, that guy. The one who just stares ahead and never talks."

"Gotcha," Joe said. "I need to go see him. I'm supposed to share information with you guys."

"*Information?*" Steck said theatrically. "You mean you've got some?"

"Some."

"That's more than I've got. I'm just supposed to stand here and keep people away from the scene while the boss does his work."

Joe asked, "Aren't you and Justin the lead investigators for the department?"

"Not anymore," Steck said. "We've been busted back to patrol. There are no lead investigators anymore. Sheriff Kapelow assumed our duties. He's the *only* chief investigator now."

"I guess he has his reasons," Joe said. Although he sympathized with both Woods and Steck over their demotions, he was in no position to get involved with an interdepartmental reorganization or to clearly take sides.

"It's almost like he doesn't trust us," Steck said with barely disguised sarcasm. "Is the Game and Fish Department hiring these days?"

"Nope," Joe said. "We still have a freeze on."

"Let me know if it thaws," Steck said. "And if it does, tell me before you tell Justin, okay?"

Joe smiled and said, "Will do." Then: "I'm going to park here for a minute while I go inside."

"Don't expect to be welcome in there," Steck said. "And if the boss asks, I did everything I could to stop you, short of pulling my weapon."

THE HEAVY DOUBLE front entrance doors of the Hewitt home were unlocked, and Joe stepped inside and closed them behind him. He found himself in an anteroom with gray stone tile and dark wood paneling. Coats and jackets of every weight hung from hooks inside, and lined neatly on the floor beneath them were men's and women's shoes ranging from Columbia fishing sandals to golf shoes to Sorel Pac boots for winter.

The hallway was festooned with trophy big-game mounts and carved fish. Joe noted not only a display featuring Wyoming's own Cutt-Slam of native trout including the Bonneville cutthroat, Yellowstone cutthroat, Colorado River cutthroat, and Snake River fine-spotted cutthroat, but Judge Hewitt's prized display of the North American Wild Sheep Grand Slam. An eight-foot-tall full-size Alaskan brown bear mount stood at the end of the hallway as if to scare away visitors.

Although Joe wasn't good at guessing the price of real estate, he knew the Hewitt home was worth millions, as were all the other Eagle Mountain Club residences. A multimillion-dollar home and extensive domestic and international trophy-hunting excursions couldn't have been underwritten by Hewitt's compensation as a county judge. So either Hewitt had a fortune behind him or— more likely—the wealth came from Sue. Joe made a mental note to find out. Great wealth often birthed great resentment and envy, often within extended families. Joe had experienced that situation before among area ranch scions. That angle was one he hadn't thought about before and he wondered if it might open a whole new can of worms.

Joe could hear the murmur of voices coming from the back side of the house. On the way to the source, he passed several bedrooms, a home office, and a trophy room packed with more dead creatures from around the world.

"Sheriff Kapelow?" he called out.

"Back here, Joe," Gary Norwood responded.

Joe walked around the bear, saw the kitchen to his left, and paused on the threshold of the dining room when Kapelow said, "*Stop where you are.*"

Joe did.

The sheriff stood facing Joe with his hands on his hips. Norwood and his evidence tech were on their hands and knees near the kitchen table wearing surgical masks and nitrile gloves. Norwood looked up and nodded a greeting to Joe. The forensics investigators were placing numbered cardboard tents on the perimeter of a large dried pool of blood on the hardwood.

"Don't contaminate the crime scene," Kapelow said.

"I didn't intend to," Joe replied.

"How did you even get in here?" the sheriff asked. His cadence was choppy and flat and he displayed no emotion.

"I took the back way," Joe said.

"There's a back way?" Kapelow asked, looking to Norwood.

Norwood shrugged. "Must be," he said. "Joe said he took it."

Kapelow said, "My explicit orders were to keep everyone away from the crime scene until it was investigated and secure. We haven't even photographed it yet."

"Don't blame your men," Joe said. "I bigfooted my way in."

Joe looked over the sheriff's shoulder into the room. He could see the large kitchen table, which was set with two empty place settings and a three-quarters-full bottle of wine. A mottled pile of food was on the floor to the left of the table next to a platter broken into white shards. The chair in which the judge had sat the night before was pushed back, and the large plate-glass window that spanned most of the back wall had a neat bullet hole in the center of it laced with a spiderweb of cracks in the glass.

"What are you hoping to find in here?" Joe asked. "It's obvious where the bullet came from."

He noted in his peripheral vision that Norwood looked away in response so Kapelow wouldn't see him grin. Joe guessed that the sheriff had been an overbearing presence in the room and he hadn't let Norwood simply do his job without interference.

"Solving a crime is as much about ruling things out as anything else," Kapelow said. "It's imperative that we corroborate everything the judge told us. In a panic situation like what he and Sue went through, memories can sometimes be less than accurate."

Joe had no idea what that meant. "Do you suspect that something happened in here other than what Judge Hewitt told us?"

Kapelow narrowed his eyes and didn't respond. There was an uncomfortable silence.

Finally, the sheriff said to Joe, "I'd appreciate it if you let me conduct this investigation without interference or second-guessing. I thought I'd made that clear."

"You did," Joe said. "I'm here to help."

"You aren't."

Joe let that sit. Then he said, "I talked to the maintenance supervisor. His name is Darin Westby. He said he wasn't on the property yesterday, but he suggested a few leads we should talk to. I thought maybe you'd like me to share that information with you since you're in charge of the investigation and you have the manpower, and I'm just me."

Kapelow didn't react in any way. After a long half minute, he said, "Write it up and email it to my office. We'll follow up."

Joe moaned. "I could just tell you—"

"Write your report and forward it to my office," Kapelow said, cutting in. He thrust out his jaw and said, "I don't know how things were done around here in the past, but an investigation is a process. It's linear. It starts by ruling things out and then proceeding in the proper direction and not everywhere at once. We gather and then evaluate hard evidence and don't run around due to speculation. Too many inputs and it goes off track. I understand that you're trying to offer assistance, but it needs to be done in a methodical way."

It was the longest Joe had heard Kapelow speak.

"I'll write it up," Joe said through gritted teeth.

"Thank you." Kapelow turned his back to Joe and said, "That will be all."

Joe bristled. It went against his grain to be dismissed like that. He said, "I drove an ATV up here, so I could go down on the property and take a look. Maybe I can help figure out where the shooter set up."

Kapelow didn't move except for slightly turning his head. He said, "I've got the rest of my men and most of the PD down there on the golf course doing an inch-by-inch grid search. We've only got a half hour of daylight left and I can't let you disturb their search."

"So it's a no?" Joe asked, even though he knew the answer.

"It's a no."

"Have they found anything?"

"Not yet. So I can't risk you driving around down there like a maniac. You could run right over the depression in the grass where the shooter set up."

Despite himself, Joe saw the logic in it. And there was no doubt Kapelow was in charge.

"Do you mind if I come in and look out the window?" Joe asked. "I'll steer clear of the blood on the floor."

Kapelow said, "Are you some kind of expert in trajectory and ballistics?"

"Nope," Joe said. "But I've spent my career out in the field doing investigations of big-game hunters and poachers. I've done hundreds of field necropsies of animals that were shot and left to die. I've developed some pretty good instincts where a shot came from and from how far away based on the angle of impact and how deep the slug penetrated a carcass."

Before Kapelow could object, Norwood said to him, "He knows his stuff, Sheriff."

"This is much different from finding a dead deer," Kapelow said to Norwood.

"With all due respect, sir," Norwood responded, "meat is meat and bone is bone. I know that sounds crass, given what happened to Sue Hewitt, but . . ." He trailed off.

Joe appreciated the support. "What can it hurt?" he asked the sheriff rhetorically.

"I already told you," Kapelow said. "Too many inputs."

Meaning, Joe knew, the sheriff didn't welcome any opinions except his own.

"You've got a minute in this room," Kapelow said to Joe. "Then please exit the crime scene and let us do our work."

Joe nodded, then stepped into the dining room and skirted around the area where Norwood and his assistant were working. He gave them a ridiculously wide berth. Joe could feel the sheriff's eyes on his back.

He walked into the space between the dining table and the window and looked out at the golf course. The dusk sun was at its most intense and it lit up the golden leaves of the trees so that they looked almost neon. The crowns of the trees against the horizon looked like upside-down clouds. He could see several Saddlestring PD officers walking slowly between the trunks in their grid search.

The bullet hole in the glass was almost squarely in the center of the bottom third of the window.

Joe turned around toward the table. He pointed at the empty place setting and the chair behind it.

"Judge Hewitt was sitting there," he said. Then he sidestepped so that Hewitt's chair was directly at his back. "That means the angle of the bullet wasn't dead-on center. It came from the south-east."

Which meant, he figured, that the shooter hadn't been on the fairways or bunkers within sight straight east. That's where the searchers were.

Unfortunately, the ground sloped from left to right. A grassy berm obscured the line of trees until all that could be seen of them were the very tops.

"I doubt the shooter climbed to the top of those trees to gain a clear shot," he said as much to himself as to Kapelow and Norwood. "Otherwise, he'd be holding on to the top branches for dear life and trying to aim a rifle at the same time. But if he was lying prone on the top of that berm . . . Maybe."

Joe bent over so he could peer through the hole itself. He could see the top of the rise, but at a downward angle.

From where he was, he turned his head and imagined where Sue Hewitt had been next to the table. The line was off. If the shooter had fired from the top of the berm, he would have been aiming up and the bullet would have hit the top of the west wall or even the ceiling.

"That doesn't work," Joe mumbled to himself.

"What doesn't work?" Kapelow asked.

Joe explained his reasoning. He said, "You might want your

guys to do a grid search of the berm down there, but I'd bet they won't find anything."

"We're losing our light," Kapelow said.

"Do it tonight," Joe said. "Sometimes you can see more by flashlight, especially when you keep the beam low along the top of the grass. If the shooter was there, you'll see a shadowed depression that would be hard to see in daylight."

Kapelow grunted as if indulging a crank. Joe ignored the sheriff's reaction.

Joe placed his hands on his thighs and slowly lowered himself while concentrating on the view through the bullet hole. The berm passed out of view, then the crowns of the trees. The hole filled with the mottled gray of a distant sagebrush-covered hillside.

He kept lowering his point of view. The hillside got murky with shadow and distance. Then it topped out. Behind the apex of the hill was the dark blue of the distant Bighorn Mountains.

He raised up again, studying the top of the hill. Then he turned his head again to visualize where Judge Hewitt had been sitting.

Joe's knees popped as he stood up to full height. He pointed at the distant sagebrush foothill.

"I think it came from there," he said, pointing.

Kapelow scoffed. "That's insane. It isn't even on the property and it must be a mile away."

Joe nodded. That's what he'd guessed as well.

"What a waste of our precious light and time," Kapelow declared. Then: "Thank you for your effort, Mr. Pickett. We can take it from here."

"Sheriff . . ."

"That will be all," Kapelow said.

Joe turned again and watched the last slice of evening sun glide over the top of the sagebrush hill. Within minutes, he knew, it would blend into the view of the mountains until it couldn't be seen at all.

Joe said, "Sheriff . . ."

"That will be all."

Joe sighed and retraced his path through the dining room. Sheriff Kapelow didn't even watch.

On his way out, Joe clamped on his hat in the hallway and said, "Sheriff . . ."

"That will be all."

Joe bit his tongue, turned on his heel, and strode down the hallway toward the door. It was either that or punch Twelve Sleep County's new sheriff in the mouth.

BEFORE RETURNING THE RANGER to the maintenance shed for his WYDOT pickup, Joe walked around the outside of the house to cool down. He reminded himself that it was the sheriff's investigation to conduct, not his. It had been a very long day and his nerves were frazzled.

While he debated with himself if he should share his concerns about Kapelow's methods with Judge Hewitt, Joe found himself on the side of the house where he could see the golf course. There wasn't much light left in the evening, and the ongoing search already looked like something out of a Hollywood premiere.

Dozens of deputies and town cops walked the grass in individual grid patterns with their flashlights bathing the turf in front of them. Joe wondered how long Kapelow would allow the search to go on before calling it a night.

Joe's gaze lifted from the golf course and trees to the sagebrush-covered hills in the distance. They were nearly out of view in the gloom and they were a very long distance away: beyond the grounds of the club, beyond an irrigated hayfield of a ranch, over the river. He wished he had his range finder (which was in his pickup in Jackson) to get an accurate estimate of the distance, but he guessed the top of the hills were over fifteen hundred yards away.

That was three times what a typical long-distance shot would be on a big-game animal, he knew.

Still, though . . .

SEVEN

ON THE FOURTEEN-MILE JOURNEY FROM THE EAGLE Mountain Club to his state-owned game warden station and house on the east bank of the river, Joe called dispatch in Cheyenne on his cell phone. He'd gotten used to using the Bluetooth system inside the cab of his pickup and it felt odd to talk with the phone pressed to his face like he used to have to do.

"This is GS-19," he said. "Can you patch me through to GS-18? I don't know whether he's still in the field on his sat phone or back in town."

"Have you tried him on your radio?" the dispatcher asked. She sounded young and a little put out by Joe's request.

"I don't have my radio," Joe said. "I don't have my truck. It's a long story."

The dispatcher paused. "Stand by," she said. The music playing on hold was Lil Nas X and Billy Ray Cyrus doing "Old Town Road." Joe wondered who at headquarters had made *that* choice. The only reason he recognized it was because his oldest daughter,

Sheridan, had blasted out the country/rap hybrid the last time she'd visited.

I'm gonna take my horse to the old town road
I'm gonna ride till I can't no more . . .

Joe grimaced until Mike Martin came on the line.

"How's it going?" Joe asked.

"Complicated," Martin said. The connection was poor and Martin sounded bone-tired. "We found Jim Trenary's body, which is something I won't soon forget. Two bears, a yearling and his mama, were there in the meadow when we found him. They weren't feeding on the body, though. It was like they were guarding it."

"That's just strange," Joe said.

"You're telling me," Martin said. Joe could imagine him shaking his head while he said it. "Both bears took off when we got there, but I don't think they went far. Now we're kind of at an impasse. It's too dark to land a chopper and go home tonight, so we're just going to dry camp here on the edge of the crime scene and hope the bears don't sneak up on us."

"I'm sorry I couldn't help more," Joe said as he cruised down Main Street in Saddlestring and out the other side.

"It's gonna be a long night," Martin said. "We can't determine yet if the killer was the yearling or the mama bear."

"Is it possible there was a third bear you never saw?" Joe asked.

"It's possible, but unlikely," Martin said. "I thought about that myself. But both bears were aggressive and territorial when we found them. They fit the profile."

It was as if he were talking about a gangbanger, Joe thought.

"That's why I could still use another set of eyes, if you can shake free of whatever it is the boss asked you to do," Martin said.

"Does Talbot's story check out?" Joe asked.

"Well, not really." He said it in a breezy way that was discordant to the tone of their previous conversation.

"Is he standing right there?" Joe asked.

"Yes, that's the situation, Joe." Then: "Our crime scene guy will be with us tomorrow. We didn't get a chance to investigate the scene after we located the body. There's plenty of evidence scattered around. I hate to leave Jim's body out there, but I don't see where I've got a choice."

"Got it," Joe said. He knew Martin was conveying that there were questions about what had happened based on the scene and the evidence, but that he couldn't talk about them in front of Talbot.

"The chopper will be here first thing tomorrow," Martin said. "Mr. Talbot will be boarding it so he can fly back to Florida."

"I figured he would."

"No doubt about it," Martin said, as if addressing something else entirely.

"My pickup is over there at the trailhead," Joe said. "Do you know of anyone who might be headed over the mountains in my direction?"

"I'll ask around," Martin said.

"The key fob is under the rear bumper."

Joe had learned not to take his vehicle keys with him into the field. It was too easy to lose them or damage them while on horseback.

"When we get down from here, I'll grab it and take it with me,"

Martin said. "I'll let you know about getting your truck back to you. But if that doesn't work out, you might have to come get it."

"That may be a couple of days," Joe sighed. "It's complicated over here as well."

"We'll have to have a long sit-down and swap stories," Martin said.

"Yup."

JOE TURNED OFF the state highway into a thick bank of trees and willows on a two-track that led to his home. After so many years of living at the old place on Bighorn Road, he still felt like he needed to pinch himself when he pulled up to the ten-year-old, three-bedroom, two-bath house next to the river.

In addition to the structure itself, there was a barn and corrals for their horses, a shed for his departmental ATV and drift boat, and a two-car garage. The irony of finally being assigned living quarters with twice the floorspace—now that their three daughters had left the nest—didn't escape him. And that he could grab his fly rod and walk to the river for a few evening casts seemed too good to be true.

For the past week, a big cow moose had stood in the middle of the two-track when he returned home in the evening. She was old, with snow-white legs and a white snout and she'd glare at him with an uncomprehending squint until he stopped his pickup. Then she'd amble into the timber with the grace of a charging line-backer. But the moose wasn't there this evening.

The house was lit up from within and the porch light was on. Marybeth's van was parked in the garage and Joe was surprised to see Nate Romanowski's Yarak, Inc. utility transport nosed into the space between the house and the shed. He smiled wryly.

Joe and Marybeth were still adjusting to a house without daughters in it now that Lucy was a freshman at the University of Wyoming. The situation was both thrilling and terrifying at the same time, and it depended on the circumstances. It was a tougher adjustment for Marybeth, he thought, but he certainly missed his girls as well. For over twenty years, he'd return each night to the "House of Feelings," no matter what actual structure it was. Now it was just Joe and Marybeth.

They found themselves getting on each other's nerves at times since there weren't any daughters around to buffer a disagreement or distract them from it altogether. It had been so long since the original empty house, he thought, that it was more effort than he'd anticipated for him and Marybeth to return to the balance they'd once had before starting a family. But things were certainly trending the right way. They were getting used to it.

They found themselves getting closer, reconnecting, having more conversations, and getting to know each other again.

Well, he smiled, it was just Joe and Marybeth—and now *Nate*, apparently, since his car was there.

The garage was too nice for the WYDOT pickup, so Joe parked outside and climbed out. Daisy, his yellow Labrador, had heard him pull in and her blocky head parted the curtains of the picture window. He could hear her heavy barks when she realized it was an unfamiliar vehicle. He was glad he'd left her home for his brief sojourn to Jackson, or he'd be without both his pickup and his dog.

Joe carried the weapons he'd had with him into the mudroom and propped them in the corner. He was tired of carrying them from place to place all day. He kicked off his boots, placed his cowboy hat crown-down on a shelf, replaced it with a King Ropes cap, and hung his jacket on a peg. Daisy bounded into the room and he cradled her head in his hands and rubbed her ears while she shimmied in place. She was happy to see him and he felt just the same.

"Joe?" Marybeth called out.

"Yup."

"What are you doing?"

"Saying hi to Daisy."

Marybeth sighed loudly. "Maybe you two should get a room. Meanwhile, we've got guests."

"I see that," he said.

"You need to light the grill," she said. "We're all getting very hungry."

He heard them talking as he walked down the hallway toward the dining room. Both walls of the hall were covered with photos of their daughters and the entire family at every stage of their lives together. Marybeth had been working on framing and hanging the collection since September. Often, he stopped to study the photos and reminisce.

Sheridan, twenty-three, was tiring of her job as head wrangler on an exclusive guest ranch resort near Saratoga, Wyoming. She said she was restless and getting ready for the next stage of her life, once she could figure out what that would be. Joe and Marybeth had been more than a little surprised that their oldest daughter was having a tough time deciding what to do next. She'd always been the most decisive, always had everything planned out and organized. Her detour from college graduation to the Silver Creek

Ranch had been complicated by her attraction to a fellow wrangler named Lance Ramsey, but they'd recently broken up for good, although both still worked on the ranch.

In a discussion the month before with Marybeth, Sheridan had compared her time at Silver Creek to the long European break that some kids took between college and graduate school. She'd mentioned possible future degree pursuits of wildlife and resource management or a law degree. Joe had blanched at the words "graduate school."

April, twenty-one, was in her last year at Northwest Community College in Powell. Although she'd been by far the most challenging of the girls to raise and live with—April had a storied past and was the most mercurial and unpredictable—she seemed to be clear-eyed when it came to what she wanted to do with her life.

It had come as a mild shock to Joe and Marybeth when April had announced that she wanted to devote her life to "putting pukes away where they belong." "Pukes," to April, meant criminals. She wanted a career in law enforcement. April had always been quick to judge and quicker to condemn and demand retribution, but an assault several years before had sharpened her worldview. The world, to her, was black and white and without nuance. Joe hoped she would become a cop and not a bounty hunter, although he'd be happy with something in between. Her aim, she said, was to become an intern in a law enforcement agency or a private investigations firm the coming summer so she could learn on the job.

Lucy, nineteen, was in Laramie. She was as beautiful and popular as ever and had adapted easily to college life. A bit too *easily*, Marybeth had observed, and she admonished her youngest to keep her grades up and maybe dial down her very active social life. Lucy was still seeing Justin Hill, although Marybeth sensed a cooling off between them without being told about it.

Lucy had grown into her role as the central communications and emotional hub of the entire family. She was the only one who kept in frequent contact with her siblings and her parents, and she made it a point of being there for anyone at any time. She even texted Joe to see how his day was going, and Joe found himself responding to her on an adult-to-adult basis, which was both satisfying and vaguely unsettling. Lucy was wise beyond her years.

The one thing in common with all of their daughters, Joe noted, was that they were their own people, they were doing well, and they were no longer home.

They were missed.

MARYBETH WAS IN the act of pouring red wine into glasses for Liv and herself when Joe entered the dining room. His wife cradled baby Kestrel in her other arm while she did it. The baby was content.

The name Kestrel had been chosen, Nate had explained, because a kestrel was the smallest species of falcon but was also known for its tenacity and willfulness.

"You haven't lost a step," Joe said to Marybeth.

"Holding this baby makes me want one of our own," she responded. When Joe froze, she said, "I mean a grandbaby."

Liv said to Marybeth, "You can come over and hold her as much as you want, you know."

"Maybe I will," Marybeth said.

Nate raised a glass of Wyoming Whiskey to Joe, paused, and said, *"Hey."*

"Hey," Joe said back.

"Why don't you get the grill started and then come back and tell us what's going on with the shooting," Marybeth said to Joe. She nodded toward a platter of raw elk steaks on the counter that had been brushed with olive oil and were already seasoned with salt and pepper.

Joe nodded his agreement while he held out a glass toward Nate, who splashed bourbon into it. Joe was exhausted from the long day and he cautioned himself about drinking too much alcohol. He'd need to be sharp in the morning.

"You look like you need it," Nate said.

"Yup."

Like the situation in their now-empty nest, the relationship between the Picketts and the Romanowskis had taken a decidedly unpredictable turn in the past year. Where once it had been Joe, Marybeth, and their young daughters with the violent and mysterious falconer hovering just out of the frame, now it was wildly different.

Nate was now the father of a little one, and Liv was a working mother who'd married later in life and had brought a wonderful baby girl into the world. Nate sometimes seemed to Joe to be like a samurai warrior who'd exchanged his sword and ancient code for a clip-on tie and a nine-to-five job selling women's shoes.

But he was still Nate, and Joe was still Joe, and they'd shared too many experiences and tragedies together over the years to change that.

"I'll give you a hand," Nate said to Joe.

"You don't have to."

"It wasn't a question."

Joe saw something in the set of Nate's mouth that concerned him. Something was eating at his friend.

"I'll grab the platter and you grab the bottle and let's go outside," Joe said.

NATE STOOD IN silence surveying the trees, glimpses of the river through the brush, and the distant mountains while Joe sipped on his drink and waited for the coals to get hot. Joe was familiar with Nate's long silences, and he was used to Nate observing things in a common landscape that Joe didn't see. Nate regarded the terrain with the singular concentration of a falcon looking for a meal.

"You've got a beaver thinking of starting a dam right at the mouth of the channel that runs through your place," Nate said. "I saw him swimming upstream along the bank with a test stick. You'll have to keep your eye on him or he might build one next spring and flood your property."

"A *test stick*?" Joe asked.

"That's how they scout out a new location for future planning," Nate said with mild derision. "I'm surprised you don't know about that, being a game warden and all."

Joe snorted. But he assumed Nate was correct. After all, Nate was the only person he'd ever known to sit naked in a tree for hours and study animal, fish, and bird behavior as if he were a charter member of the ecosystem.

"We're just about there," Joe said, nodding toward the coals in the grill. The secret to good elk steaks was to sear them on a very hot surface to lock in the juices since there was practically no fat in the meat.

"Are these from the cow elk you got last year?" Nate asked.

"Yup. Backstraps."

"Nothing better."

Joe looked up. "I assume you didn't come by tonight to talk about beavers and backstraps."

Nate nodded. He asked, "What's Sheridan up to these days?"

The question came from out of the blue, even though Nate and Sheridan had history. Nate, in his role of master falconer, had long ago taken her on as his apprentice. The relationship had gone dormant after Sheridan went to college.

"I think she's trying to decide," Joe said. "Why?"

"Our business is growing. I need someone reliable to help out."

"Are you asking me permission?" Joe asked. "As you know, Sheridan has a mind of her own. Maybe you should ask *her*."

"Maybe I should," Nate said. He turned back to studying the river.

Joe considered the possibility of Sheridan joining Yarak, Inc. He didn't know what he thought about it. It would be good to have her around again and it was good Nate respected her falconry chops enough to consider her, but Joe had sometimes fantasized about his oldest daughter following in *his* footsteps. They'd even discussed it a few times when Sheridan accompanied him on ride-alongs when she was younger. She'd always liked being outdoors and "saving animals," as she put it.

"Is that all?" Joe asked after several minutes. Having a conversation with his friend was filled with starts and stops.

"Do you remember Jeremiah Sandburg?" Nate asked.

"Yup. I wouldn't mind never seeing him again."

"He dropped by the house this morning in his new motor home," Nate said.

"He was here?"

"And he had a warning for me."

Nate told Joe about his conversation with the ex–FBI special agent. As he did, Joe felt a shiver up his back.

As he lay the steaks on the red-hot grill he said, "Is it just you they're coming after? I was there, too, at the time."

"I know that and you know that," Nate said. "But they aren't singing *narcocorridos* about Joe Pickett."

"I suppose that's a good thing for me," Joe said. "But what are we going to do about it?"

"Keep our heads on a swivel," Nate said. "It won't be the first time someone has come after me. But it's the first time I had a wife and a little angel to protect. It makes everything three times more complicated."

Joe agreed as he flipped the steaks. They had perfect grill marks on them.

"I'd be lying if I didn't say I was worried," Nate said.

Joe had never heard Nate utter anything like that. It shook him and he didn't know how to respond.

"I know you've got a lot going on with the shooting and all," Nate said. "But I may need some help. You may hear of someone coming into the area that I don't. Or you may run into someone who could be working for the Sinaloans. I guess I'm asking you to keep your eyes open and ears turned on."

"Of course I'll do that," Joe said. "Does Liv know?"

"Not yet."

"You should tell her," Joe said. "That's one thing I've learned over the years. Don't keep secrets. I'll help you however I can, but Liv is smart and tough, she's your best ally."

"Better than you?" Nate asked. He seemed genuinely interested in the answer.

"Better than me," Joe said. "Don't get me wrong—I'll do whatever I can, of course. You can count on me. But if it weren't for Marybeth's involvement over the years, I'd be washed-up, homeless, or dead. You've got to trust her with everything, Nate. She's smart and clever and she'd do absolutely anything necessary to protect Kestrel."

Nate thought it over while Joe moved the meat from the grill to the platter. Finally, he said, "I'm going to set up a range and teach her how to shoot."

"That's a good start."

"If something happened to her or my little girl . . ."

"I know," Joe said. "Believe me, I know."

"This is hard sometimes," Nate said.

"It is, but it's worth it."

Nate did something he'd rarely ever done. He reached over and gripped Joe's shoulder and squeezed it.

"I've got a question for you," Joe said. "Don't you have experience with military snipers in the field?"

Nate nodded that he did. Joe didn't know the particulars and Nate hadn't shared them, but he was aware his friend had been in hot spots all over the world with a team of special operators.

"Do you have some time to look over a location with me tomorrow?"

"Yes."

"Great," Joe said. "Let's eat."

JOE OUTLINED THE FACTS as he knew them about Sue Hewitt's shooting at dinner, although Nate was much more interested in hearing about the bear attack. He found the circumstances as puzzling and discordant as Joe and Mike Martin had. So the conversation had been steered away from the local crime.

Not so Marybeth. She wanted details and he recapped his day from landing at the Saddlestring airport to climbing into bed.

"Do you have a prime suspect?" she asked him.

"No. There are people I want to talk to. And I want to figure out where the shot was fired. That'll help us home in on the weapon itself."

"What does our new sheriff think?" she asked.

Joe shook his head. "Either Kapelow is some kind of brilliant detective with his own special powers and a theory of his own, or he's absolutely clueless and he's mucking up the investigation before it can get started. I can't decide which, but I'm leaning toward the latter."

"I hope you're wrong," she said.

"Yeah—me too. Judge Hewitt will blow a gasket if we don't find the shooter. Or he'll decide to take matters into his own hands."

Marybeth nodded in agreement. She said, "I heard this evening that Sue's chances aren't good. But she's strong. I hope she pulls through."

"I hope we find the guy," Joe said. "And I think we have to find him fast. The longer it takes, the less chance we have, unless someone comes forward."

JOE SAT UP in bed with the table light on until Marybeth finished scrubbing her face in the bathroom and emerged in her nightie and slippers. Even without makeup she looked fresh and beautiful, he thought. She'd been going for early-morning swims at the high school and her limbs were toned.

She slid in next to him with a novel about singing crawdads, but she hadn't yet opened it.

"I'm surprised you're still up after the day you've had," she said to him. "Didn't you say you were up at three-thirty?"

"Yup."

"You need to get some rest."

He sighed. "I've got so much on my plate right now I feel paralyzed."

There was the grizzly bear attack in the Teton Wilderness, Sue Hewitt's shooting, and now the possible revenge of the Sinaloa cartel on his friend Nate. He told Marybeth about Nate's meeting with Jeremiah Sandburg, the ex–FBI special agent and the threat he'd gleefully warned Nate about.

Afterward, she said, "Liv said he was acting strangely after the motor home left."

"Nate *always* acts strangely," Joe said. "But that's why."

"Do you think the threat is legitimate?"

"Nate does."

"I'll put some feelers out in town," she said. "If anyone suspicious shows up I'll make sure you know about it."

"That would be good," Joe said. Because the library was the community center of sorts, Marybeth had access to people and information that would fly under law enforcement's radar, he knew.

Locals operated and communicated in entirely different lanes than the law enforcement community. It wasn't unusual, for example, to find out later that locals knew who the perpetrators of crimes were long before that perp's name ever came up during the investigation. That was due to gossip, social media, and one-on-one interaction within the valley that cops weren't involved in.

Sheriff Reed had made an effort to bridge the divide with locals by having coffee every morning with the city fathers at the Burg-O-Pardner restaurant or simply rolling his chair down the sidewalks in town and making small talk with his constituents. Because of Joe's job and the locals he encountered in the field, he was hooked into the blood, fins, and feathers crowd. But overall, Marybeth took the pulse of the *entire* community daily in and around the library.

Not only that, she said, she'd spend as much time as she could doing research on the deep web cartel sites she'd discovered and social media posts that might unwittingly give them a leg up on who might be coming and when.

"You'd think they'd stay off the internet," she said. "But they don't. They think because you can't google them, they're invisible, but if you know the specific IP addresses, you can access the cartel sites. People just can't help themselves—they talk too much. Even criminals."

Marybeth said she could monitor suspicious guests checking in at local hotels and motels as well.

"How?" Joe asked.

"It's the month of our annual book sale," she said. "We put collection boxes all over town for people to drop off used books. That includes the lobbies of all the accommodations, since visitors often leave books they've read or they want to be rid of. I usually assign that job to one of our library foundation volunteers, but this year I could do it myself. I can ask the front desk people if they have any interesting guests."

Joe whistled. He was impressed with her, as always. Marybeth had a manner about her that made people want to talk to her. And if the cartel hit man had the same look and characteristics as the members of the Wolf Pack who had ventured to Twelve Sleep County six months before, they'd stand out among the tourists, hunters, and fly fishermen who stayed at the hotel properties.

"Now *I* won't be able to sleep," she lamented. "I'll worry about Nate and Liv and especially Kestrel. That little girl of theirs took me back. I want another one around this house someday. Do you think it'll be Sheridan, April, or Lucy first?"

"I try not think about that," Joe said.

"Don't you want to be Grandpa Joe?"

He moaned and rubbed his eyes. It was too much for him to think about right now. But he kind of liked the idea, now that he thought about it . . .

———

IT WAS THREE-THIRTY in the morning—again—when Joe awoke to Marybeth's prodding him. He'd been sleeping hard and he was momentarily confused.

"Your phone," she said.

He fumbled for it on the bed stand as it skittered along the surface. It took a few seconds for him to focus on the name on the screen.

DUANE PATTERSON

Joe punched him up and said, "This better be good."

Patterson was out of breath as if he'd been running. He said, "It isn't good. It isn't good at all."

"So what's up?"

"I was driving home and someone took a shot at me in my car. Right through the windshield."

"What?"

"They missed," Patterson said. "But I've got glass in my hair and my eyes. I think my head is bleeding."

"Did you see who it was?"

"Hell no," Patterson said angrily. "It was too dark to see any-thing at all. But I'm so shaky I don't think I can drive."

"Where are you?" Joe asked, throwing the blankets aside and leaping up. The bedroom floor was cold on his bare feet.

Patterson said he was on Four Mile Road and Highway 78 in the borrow ditch on the side of the road.

"Stay where you are," Joe said. "I'm on my way."

"What if he's still out there?"

"Stay low."

"Hell, I'm on the floor of my car. If I got any lower, I'd be underneath it."

"Did you call the sheriff?" Joe asked as he stepped into his Wranglers and reached for his uniform shirt in the closet.

"Why would I call *him*?" Patterson said with heat borne of panic.

"I'll let him know," Joe said.

As he buttoned up, Marybeth asked from the dark, "Was that Duane? Is he okay?"

"Someone took a shot at him," Joe said. "I'm going out there."

"Please be careful."

"Always am."

"No, actually, you never are," she said. "But now we know."

Joe paused within the doorframe. "Now we know what?" he asked.

"That this is a courthouse thing," she said. "Someone is going after the prosecutor and the judge. At least that narrows it down from all the other speculation out there. And it also means the shooter is still in the area."

Joe agreed. "He's missed his target twice now. I doubt he'll miss again."

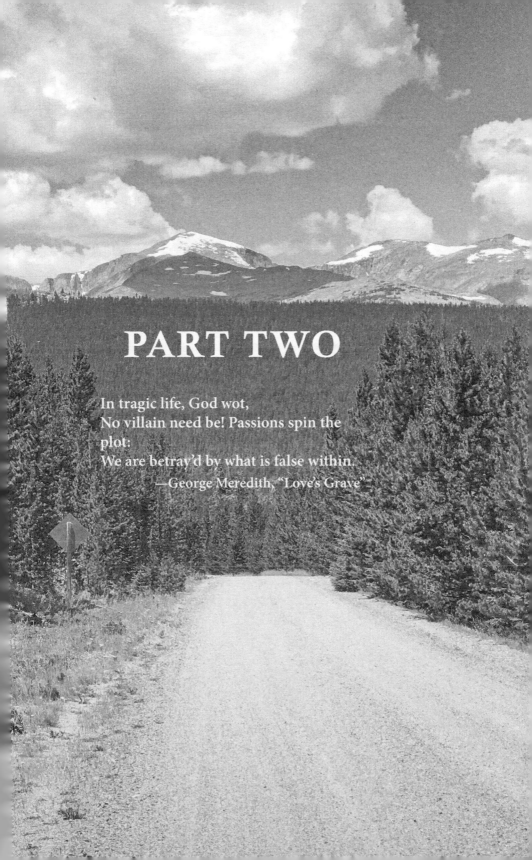

PART TWO

In tragic life, God wot,
No villain need be! Passions spin the
plot:
We are betray'd by what is false within.
　　　　—George Meredith, "Love's Grave"

EIGHT

EARLY THE SAME MORNING, CANDY CROSWELL STIRRED in bed when she heard a sound from down the hallway in the dark. She was on her side and she flattened the side of her down pillow to get a look at the clock that glowed dull blue across the room. Four-ten in the morning. She sighed and dropped her head back down.

He was as considerate as he could be when he came home so late. Tom never turned a light on when he came into the bedroom, and he didn't talk. Often, he'd use one of the hall bathrooms to change out of his clothes so the rustling wouldn't disturb her. Then he'd slip into the huge soft bed like an alligator entering the bayou—without a ripple.

She was a light sleeper, and she always woke up despite his efforts not to disturb her. But she didn't hold it against him. He tried. She'd been with men who wouldn't even think of being so considerate.

Some nights Tom wouldn't come straight to bed. He'd tell her later that he was too wound up, that his shift had been stressful and chaotic, and that it took him an hour or so and a couple of strong drinks at his wet bar to relax. When she heard the clink of ice in a glass, she knew it had been one of those nights.

She sighed again, but softly, so there would be no way he could possibly hear it.

Because after a single-malt scotch or two, Tom often became amorous. She thought of it as a stress reliever for him, like the drinks. She doubted he thought of it the same way.

Sometimes, he'd inadvertently bang his knee into the bed frame as he got close. Or when he threw the sheets back, he'd bend back the comforter only and climb in between it and the top sheet where he couldn't touch her. Which meant he'd have to climb out clumsily, sort out the covers, and come back to bed.

Then he'd start nuzzling her, pressing his erection against her thigh. He'd tell her she was sexy and warm and that he needed her.

If he insisted, she'd comply. It wasn't romantic, but it was necessary. Like most of the men she'd been with, Tom had simple needs. In fact, despite his advanced education, his responsibilities, and his position within the community, it was *very* simple to keep him happy.

Which, for Candy, was a very small price to pay to live in a five-bedroom country house on fifteen acres with horses to ride and no incentive or need to work outside the home herself. They'd gone on fifteen- and twenty-one-day boutique river cruises in Europe and she'd seen Broadway shows in New York City. When they hosted a party, they hired a caterer. And the cleaning crew showed up twice a week to make sure the home was a showplace.

He'd told her more than once that he enjoyed spending money on her and there was plenty more where that came from. She didn't object, of course.

Of course.

SHE HEARD THE SOUND of ice again just as she started to doze back to sleep. Then his footfalls in the hallway to the bathroom. Then a flush of the toilet and the sound of him washing his hands.

He was naked when he snuggled up to her. Her back was to him and he threw a leg over hers and burrowed into her. His left hand cupped her left breast, and she moved her arm so he'd have better access. She feigned a happy, sleepy moan and turned over to him. Although he'd brushed his teeth, she could taste single-malt scotch on his tongue.

Tom was more energetic and aggressive than usual, if clumsier. It took him longer than she was used to and she chalked it up to the alcohol, which had likely dulled his nerve endings. More than once she got the impression that he was exorcising something from his system, as if transferring it to her, where it would dissipate. Which wasn't a very nice thing to think about, actually.

Finally, he shivered and rolled to his back. Within minutes, he was snoring.

She lay still, wide-awake. She waited for his breath to become rhythmic.

Then, with the grace of a cat, she slid out of bed. There was no going back to sleep for Candy; she knew she wasn't wired for it. Once she was up, she was up. And she could always take a long nap in the late afternoon after he'd dressed and gone back to work. Two glasses of wine followed by a long, leisurely nap.

It was such a small price to pay.

CANDY CROSWELL PADDED across the bedroom and closed the door to her walk-in closet behind her. She turned on the light and looked at herself in the full-length mirror. Her nightgown was gone, balled up somewhere near the foot of the bed.

She was redheaded, lithe, long-legged, and in good shape for her age. There was a constellation of freckles on her shoulders and back, but Tom said he liked them. Everybody told her she looked hot, but the one whose opinion mattered the most was Tom.

He was the reason she didn't eat carbohydrates, though she loved bread and pasta. He liked to run his hands over her body as if checking for fat pockets or other anomalies. She purred as he did it and acted as though she didn't realize what he was doing.

Candy wriggled into a pair of yoga pants and a tight spandex top. She turned slowly in front of the mirror and looked at herself from every angle. She wished her thighs were slimmer, but that had always been a problem. Fortunately, he'd never pointed that out.

This, by far, was the best situation she'd ever had, and she was determined not to lose it. During the evening, after her nap and when Tom was gone, she'd walk through all of the rooms with a glass of wine and pinch herself.

Like Tom, she'd been married before, but in her case it was twice. The first time she'd lived in a double-wide trailer outside of Williston, North Dakota, which was quite unlike the failing dairy farm she'd grown up on in southern Nebraska. She'd never been as cold or as lonely as she had been in North Dakota. Although Brent made good wages in the Bakken oil fields, the money never went as far as it should have, given the inflated prices of everything during the energy boom and Brent's penchant for wasting it. Brent never saw the incongruity of driving his new yellow Corvette home and parking it in a snowdrift by the side of the trailer at night. She did, though.

Her second husband, Nicolas, worked as a financial planner in Bismarck when she met him and he wore a tie and drove an SUV and he urged her to order another glass of wine when they had lunch together to discuss a plan that would result in Candy and Brent's fiscal stability. Brent hadn't thought the meeting was necessary, but Candy knew it was. He feared she'd try to put him on a budget.

But the actual result of the lunch, once Candy realized how handsome and charming Nicolas came across, was: *Goodbye, Brent.*

UNFORTUNATELY, THOUGH, NICOLAS turned out to be a very unhappy man. What he really wanted—and he confessed to her six months after her divorce to Brent was final and they had married—was to go off the grid and "get back to nature." Nicolas revealed to Candy that he'd been born a hundred and fifty years too late and he craved a simpler and more basic existence that actually meant something tangible. He wanted to kill and catch their food and make love to her under the warm hides of big-game animals he'd shot and tanned himself. He wanted to be one with the earth, and he was sure it would fill up his heart.

They'd moved from North Dakota to Alaska, which was even

colder. The log cabin he built for them was on the bank of the Chatanika River thirty-five miles north of Fairbanks. The first fall, Nicolas grew out his beard and killed a moose and a caribou, and caught salmon and Arctic graylings in the river. He talked for hours about writing a book about his journey back to the simple life, but he never started it. Candy drove the snowmobile an hour each way to the post office to retrieve the parcels of fashionable clothing that Stitch Fix sent every month. They were too impractical to wear—but she kept them all.

While Nicolas was on a two-week bear hunt with some neighbors, Candy strapped all of her Stitch Fix boxes onto the back of a sled and towed it behind the snowmobile to Fairbanks, where she used a stash of cash and Nicolas's credit card to buy a used minivan. Then she motored south for forty-one hours and over two thousand miles until she collapsed from exhaustion at a resort near Whitefish, Montana, where she slept for two days straight.

Candy had no idea she was one of the few non-attendees of a national conference at the resort when she dressed in her best Stitch Fix cocktail dress and went to the bar that night. But that's when she met Tom, who was recently divorced and lonely and attending the professional event from northern Wyoming.

She thought a lot about that double-wide trailer and that drafty log cabin when she walked through Tom's home with her glass of wine.

CANDY GRABBED A plastic bottle of Vitamin Water from the refrigerator and selected a jacket from the back closet because it was getting colder every night as fall came. Her state-of-the-art yoga studio was located a hundred yards from the house in the loft of the sprawling horse barn. It had been completed the previous summer, but she'd yet to teach any classes in it.

There were two reasons for that. The first was she didn't know many locals and she had no network to get the word out. Her target clientele were women like her, of a certain age, who had free time during the day to drive out to the property. She didn't want super athletic young things who would show her up and create a judgmental environment for her clients.

Candy knew there was a way to find those kind of women—she didn't want any men, either—and she'd recently learned about the members of the Eagle Mountain Club and considered it a target-rich environment. Unfortunately, by the time she'd settled on a word-of-mouth marketing campaign among the older female spouses of the club, it was fall, and they'd left the place.

The other reason was she enjoyed having the studio all to herself. Tom had never pressured her about opening it up to strangers, and until that happened, she felt no reason to do so.

To avoid the hassle of keying the password into the alarm system for the front door, Candy left the house through the four-car garage. There was an illuminated pathway outside from the side garage door to the barn and her studio.

Tom's new gunmetal-gray Ford Raptor pickup was parked next to her Mercedes. Tom loved his pickup, and he'd explained to her that it cost $53,000—as much as a luxury car—but that because it was a pickup it didn't raise as many eyebrows among the locals as a Mercedes or BMW would have. Candy herself didn't mind being seen in the Mercedes that Tom had passed along to her. In fact, she reveled in it.

As she walked between her car and Tom's truck, she noticed the pickup was covered with a thin layer of road dust and the tires were discolored by dried mud. This was out of character for Tom, who kept his vehicle immaculately clean.

She paused and peered over the bed well into the back. In the bed of his pickup were several sandbags and two gearboxes, plus a canvas duffel bag. She didn't open any of them.

Candy was puzzled. She cast a glance at the door from the mudroom on the off-chance that Tom would open it and see her snooping, but he wasn't there. Then she opened the truck's rear door.

On the floor mats was a pair of lace-up hunting boots next to crumpled coveralls. Under the backseat on the floorboards was a stout oblong aluminum case that spanned the width of the cab. She recognized it as an expensive rifle case. Nicolas had had one for his prized big-game hunting rifle.

However, she couldn't recall seeing this case before, although she knew Tom, like so many others in the area, enjoyed target shooting. He was also a big-game hunter and had several fine elk heads in the great room to show for it.

So when, she wondered, had he taken a break from his shift and gone to the range to blow off steam? Even if he hadn't, she thought, he'd obviously taken the Raptor off-road recently. That he hadn't mentioned either bugged her, and she made a mental note to ask him about it later. She'd do it in a gentle way that was not accusatory, because the last thing she wanted was for Tom to think of her as controlling or hectoring. He'd mentioned that those qualities had annoyed him greatly in his first wife.

Instead, she'd say that she'd learned to shoot in Alaska and she enjoyed it almost as much as she enjoyed four-wheeling. Perhaps Tom would like a couple's date at the range?

It was so easy.

Then she fitted in her earbuds, launched her carefully curated playlist called *Yoga Sounds*, and went outside toward her studio sanctuary.

NINE

JOE ASKED NATE, "IF YOU WERE A MILITARY SNIPER WITH
a designated target, where would you set up to take that shot?"

"Are you sure it was from this side of the river?" Nate asked
back.

"No, not at all. But these foothills can be seen very clearly from
the picture window of the Hewitt home, and the angle seems right,
even though the sheriff dismissed the idea."

Nate nodded that he understood.

They were rumbling along a rough two-track on the other side
of the river in the WYDOT pickup. The path led to nowhere, but
it paralleled the river and it was used primarily by fly fishermen.
Across the river was a vast, flat, irrigated hayfield and beyond it
was the green smudge of the Eagle Mountain Club.

It was a sunny and cool fall morning with no clouds. A slight
breeze in the treetops along the river dislodged errant yellow leaves,
which floated down and carpeted the old road or became small
rafts in the current. Fall in the Rockies brought the widest swings
in temperature at high elevations, with thirty-degree mornings

climbing to the upper sixties or low seventies by midafternoon. Everyone dressed in layers and they were constantly stripping off clothing or adding it back on. Joe had started the morning with his uniform shirt, wool vest, and windproof outer shell. The shell was now discarded and crumpled on the seat between them. Nate wore a heavy hooded sweatshirt with YARAK, INC. printed over one breast.

Joe had noted there was still plenty of law enforcement activity on the faraway golf course. Tiny commandeered golf carts moved in and out of the trees driven by cops completing their assigned grid searches. He wondered if Sheriff Kapelow had kept them at it the entire night, and he hoped not. And he doubted they'd found anything of significance, because there had been very little chatter on the mutual aid band from his handheld radio.

Nate didn't answer the question Joe posed for a while. He'd rolled down the passenger-side window and stuck his head out of it so his blond hair blew back behind him. He studied the terrain on their right and measured it against the club on their left, looking for angles and locations.

"Daisy does the same thing," Joe said. "She likes to stick her head out the window like that."

Nate scowled, but didn't respond.

Then, pointing up a steep hill on the side of the road, he said, "Here."

The sagebrush-covered hills undulated from the riverbank all the way to the base of the mountains. The one Nate indicated rose the highest and, Joe assumed, afforded the greatest view of the river valley and the golf course in the distance.

"I don't see a road to the top," Nate said.

"If there was, I doubt this truck would make it," Joe grumbled as he stopped and killed the engine. "We'll need to hike."

He climbed out and stretched and he could hear and feel his spine pop like muffled fireworks. His knees ached. He felt all of his fifty years.

Joe threw a daypack filled with a spare evidence kit over his back and cinched it tight for the climb.

HE'D BEGUN THE DAY five hours before at Duane Patterson's Toyota 4Runner on the side of Four Mile Road. The county prosecutor had still been huddled on the floorboards when Joe arrived and shined his flashlight inside. Bits of glass in Patterson's hair sparkled like diamonds. Duane was relieved to see him and he smiled grimly. There were trickles of blood on his face from cuts in his scalp, but he seemed okay.

Within minutes, Deputies Woods and Steck arrived in their SUVs, grateful for being released from their posts at the golf course. There were no other vehicles on the road or in the area, although Patterson said he thought he heard one start up and drive off right after his windshield exploded and he was on the floor. He hadn't looked up to get a description of the car.

Patterson said that he often worked very late at the courthouse and that he took Four Mile Road to clear his head before returning to his small apartment downtown. He said he had no idea how the shooter knew when he'd arrive, but he guessed the rifleman had tracked his movements and set up to wait. At the moment the bullet had shattered the glass, he'd been fiddling with the radio dial, trying to find the all-night sports talk station he sometimes picked up on this stretch of road. If he hadn't been bent over awkwardly to the right, the bullet would have likely hit him square in the face.

Steck helped Patterson into his vehicle and transported him to the Twelve Sleep County Memorial Hospital for observation. Joe and Woods remained on the scene until dawn, keeping a watchful eye out for the shooter if he decided to double back, which he didn't do.

It was obvious to both of them how the incident had taken place. The stretch of Four Mile Road that Patterson had been driving on was a three-mile straightaway that led to the T-junction that was Highway 78. On the other side of the highway was a thick stand of cottonwoods approximately two hundred yards away, which were the only trees in sight. The shooter had obviously parked in the trees to set up, and had waited for Patterson to drive down the road toward him.

It was a miracle that the shooter had missed and Patterson was still alive. The bullet had punched through the windshield directly above the steering wheel. The shooter had assumed he'd hit his target when Patterson careened off the road into the ditch. Why the gunman hadn't followed up to make sure Patterson was dead was a mystery, Joe thought. Perhaps he'd been afraid of being seen by a passerby, or he had been so confident in his shot that he'd deemed it unnecessary.

Woods reported that Sheriff Kapelow and forensics tech Norwood were on their way and that the sheriff had warned Joe and Woods not to enter the trees and risk fouling the crime scene. No doubt, Joe thought, Kapelow's hope was to find footprints, used food wrappers, or a spent casing.

Joe used that unnecessary warning as his excuse to drive away and leave Woods to deal with his boss.

HALFWAY UP THE HILLSIDE, Joe paused to get his breath back and to turn and look at the Eagle Mountain Club. In the distance, the line of homes including the Hewitt home was no more than a pale band set against the green of the grounds. He couldn't make out individual structures, and the band undulated slightly in the heat waves as the temperature rose. Joe shook his backpack off and stuffed his vest into it for the rest of the way.

Nate had a sophisticated range finder around his neck and his weapon in a shoulder holster. Joe had found a spare set of binoculars in his office and brought them along as well.

"From here," Nate said as he peered through his range finder, "we're just short of a mile. Sixteen hundred yards, to be exact."

"That's a long way," Joe said.

"It is. But it's doable," Nate said.

"Seriously?"

Nate nodded. "It's right at the edge of the envelope for a special operator with the right weapon, but it's a shot he would take."

"I can't even see the Hewitt house clearly from here."

"I think that was the idea," Nate said. "If you can't see him, he can't see *you*. Every man can be a sniper these days."

THE WORLD OF long-range shooting wasn't unfamiliar to Joe, because it had become an integral aspect of his job as a game warden in an incredibly short period of time. He couldn't recall a technical revolution in big-game hunting happening as quickly, and he likened it to when repeating arms had been introduced to the American West or when modern gunpowder had replaced black powder over a hundred years before he was born.

He still cringed when he encountered a hunter in possession of such a technically advanced weapon.

Before the last ten years, a six-hundred- to eight-hundred-yard shot had been considered extreme and ill-advised. Ethical hunters rarely even tried one because the possibility of wounding an animal that far away made it more difficult to finish it off or track it if it ran away. Most hunters didn't even pull the trigger if the game was over two hundred yards away.

High-tech laser range finders like the one Nate carried had changed everything. Knowing the exact distance of the target made ultra-long shots possible, because the shooter could adjust his aim to account for all of the factors—wind, temperature, atmospheric pressure, incline/decline—that would affect the shot. There were now rifle scopes that were computers in and of themselves and they enabled the shooter to dispense with a subsequent laser range finder. Scopes were now range finders and ballistic calculators.

In addition to precision optics, carbon fiber–wrapped barrels were lighter and stiffer and they cut down on vibration. Bad rifle ergonomics had been replaced by perfectly sculpted composite stocks. Bad steel triggers had been replaced by foolproof titanium. Specially engineered ammunition resulted in rounds that were more powerful, more accurate, and more consistent. Copper alloy–jacketed bullets with ballistic tips emerged from muzzles at over three hundred thousand rotations per minute.

As Nate had said, any man could now be a sniper. The average-

Joe hunter could own a technologically advanced and engineered rifle that was beyond anything a military sniper had possessed twenty years before.

All it took was money.

Joe had seen rifles that cost the hunters carrying them over six thousand dollars for the rifle and scope. And he'd met an elk hunter who bragged that his weapon was custom-made for him for nearly twenty thousand.

Most of the ultra-long-range rifles Joe had seen in hunting camps were chambered for .300 Winchester Magnum, .338 Lapua, 7mm Magnum, or 6.5 Creedmoor Magnum cartridges. All of the rounds were close enough to the .30 caliber bullet that hit Sue Hewitt that Sheriff Kapelow's determination of the projectile was all but useless.

Factory or aftermarket suppressors mounted on the muzzles reduced recoil and muted the decibel level of the shot itself from 160 dB down to 120 dB. It was still loud—Joe scoffed when he saw a silencer used in a movie or television show that was whisper-soft—but it resulted in a *crack* that was below the 140 dB threshold that could result in hearing loss.

NATE WAS BREATHING hard as they approached the top of the hill. Because they'd had to skirt gnarled sagebrush all the way up, their route had been half-again more taxing than walking straight up the rise. Joe caught up with him and they summited the ridge side by side.

The folds of the terrain opened up before them all the way to the mountains. A herd of twenty pronghorn antelope had strategically selected the top of the ridge, where it was flat to mill around. The height afforded them clear views in every direction. When Joe and Nate appeared on the western rim, the herd scattered. The flat was littered with pronghorn excrement in pellet piles, and churned-up dirt where the animals had prepared the ground.

Nate paused on the top and turned on his heel.

"Yep, this is where they set up," he said.

Joe walked cautiously along the rim, and within ten steps he found where the shooter had been. A slight depression that butted up against the lip of the ridge was long enough for a man to lie prone. Several flat rocks had been stacked on the end of it in the direction of the club, and a small ball cactus had been kicked loose to the side so the shooter wouldn't have to make contact with it on the ground. The dried yellow grass was crushed in the hollow and he could make out two oblong depressions in the dirt where the toes of two boots had dug in.

Joe backed off a few feet and let his pack drop to the ground. As he did, Nate joined him.

"That's where he shot from," Nate said. "He used those rocks as a gun rest to elevate his aim, although he probably brought along some sandbags to further stabilize the rifle. He might have used a bipod."

Joe agreed. He dropped to a knee so he could dig into his day-pack for a bundle of wire flag markers. After determining the exact coordinates and photographing the crime scene—both accomplished with his phone—he'd mark it off with the flags so the very busy crime scene tech could find it.

Joe wasn't really surprised that Nate had located the spot so quickly. His past experience certainly helped, but Nate also had a very rare ability: he was an intuitive shooter who didn't need technology and optics to make a shot—even with his .454 revolver. Like the birds he flew, Nate interpreted variables for an accurate shot without instrumentation, and he rarely missed, even at a tremendous distance. When Joe asked how, Nate couldn't explain his abilities other than to say that he could "see" wind speed and atmospheric pressure as long as he didn't think too long and hard about it. Like a peregrine falcon who zeroed in on prey thousands of feet above the surface and tucked in its wings to begin a bullet-like drop, Nate said he had to make split-second decisions based on what he referred to as "informed instinct."

"I'm not surprised there isn't a spent casing on the ground," Joe said. "The guy only fired once, so there was no need to eject it."

"Either that, or his spotter picked it up," Nate mused.

Joe froze. "Spotter?"

Nate nodded. "It's just about impossible for most shooters to make a shot like this without a spotter. Even the best. That was my role on the team. The spotter is just as important as the guy who pulls the trigger, if not more so."

"Really?"

"Sometimes I did it without a range finder," Nate said.

"I'm not surprised."

"But in reality, and on the battlefield, the spotter determines everything," Nate said. "He's the one with the laser optics and the computer readings. The shooter programs in what the spotter tells him. We're talking wind speed—crosswinds, updrafts, downdrafts—settings, distance. Adjustments need to be made on the scope depending on the atmospheric pressure—how thick the air is. It's the difference between shooting through water versus motor oil."

Joe shook his head. "I never even considered two people."

"Very few if any snipers could make this shot by themselves, and I doubt that's what happened here."

Joe placed the last of his flags in the ground. He removed his hat to wipe the sweat from his forehead.

Joe asked, "How long does it usually take for a high-tech range finder to determine the distance and all the variables for the shot?"

"On average, fifteen seconds."

The distant Eagle Mountain Club undulated in waves of heat from the valley floor.

"Neither Sheriff Kapelow nor Judge Hewitt are going to like hearing this," Joe said.

Then: "This changes everything."

KAPELOW DIDN'T PICK UP and Joe's call to him went straight to voicemail.

Looking out across the river valley at the Eagle Mountain Club, he said, "Sheriff, I think we're looking for two suspects, not one. The shooter is in possession of an advanced long-range rifle. I'm standing twenty feet away from where I think the shot was fired and the location is secured for you and Norwood. We haven't disturbed a thing and there may be tracks or forensic evidence up here. The GPS coordinates are . . ."

After reading off the numbers he signed off and called Deputy Steck.

"I'm trying to find the sheriff," he explained.

Steck said Kapelow had left the Hewitt home to meet with Judge Hewitt at the hospital and brief him on their progress thus far.

"What progress?" Joe asked.

Steck sighed, then proceeded with a faux reverence for Kapelow that Joe picked up right away. "My boss has a theory now that we've gone over the entire golf course inch by inch and found nothing. He thinks the bullet that hit Miz Sue was a stray round. 'A million-to-one coincidence with a tragic ending,' as he put it. He spent twenty minutes on the internet this morning googling 'victim struck by stray bullet,' and he announced that he got over a million hits. He printed off a few of the articles to take to the judge to show him how often it happens."

"Seriously?"

"I was there. I watched him at the computer," Steck said. "Most of the news stories were about urban drive-bys, but the boss found a couple where a stray bullet came from nowhere and hit somebody."

Joe didn't know how to respond.

"Are you sure the Game and Fish Department isn't hiring?" Steck asked.

"Sorry."

"But you'll let me know if an opening comes up, right? Before you tell Justin?"

"Sure," Joe sighed.

"Because if I stay in this loony bin much longer, I'm gonna eat my gun."

"Don't do it," Joe said. "We need you around."

"Sheriff Kapelow doesn't," Steck groused.

Joe told Steck about finding the location where the shot had been fired.

After a long pause, Steck asked, "How far away was it?"

"At least sixteen hundred yards."

"Jesus. Who are we dealing with here?"

Joe looked up to see that Nate was following the conversation. His friend rolled his eyes, as if confirming that his long-standing opinion of law enforcement bureaucracies was once again being confirmed.

"We're looking for a shooter *and* a spotter," Joe said. "Two suspects, not one."

"Oh, man. Who's going to tell the judge?"

"I will," Joe said. "I'm headed to the hospital as soon as I get off this hill."

"I'd like to see the sheriff's face when you tell him," Steck said with a chuckle.

TEN

BUT THE SHERIFF WAS NOT AT THE TWELVE SLEEP COUNTY Hospital when Joe arrived after dropping Nate at his van. There were a half-dozen cars in the parking lot, but no departmental SUV.

Kapelow had been there, though. Joe noted his name just before his own on the visitor registry. He'd missed him by five minutes.

As he walked down the hallway to the small ICU, Joe checked his phone to see if Kapelow had called him back. There was a "Call me when you can" message from Marybeth, but nothing from the sheriff.

He paused outside a door with the name *Hewitt* written on a whiteboard and speed-dialed Marybeth at the library.

She said, "Given what's going on right now, what is the worst thing that could possibly happen?"

"Did someone take a shot at you?"

"Worse than that," Marybeth said. "My mother is waiting for me at our house."

Joe felt a wave of revulsion and fear wash over him.

"Missy is here? *Why?*"

He knew it sounded like a plea to the heavens.

"I don't know, but it can't be good."

"I thought she was still traveling the world."

"So did I," Marybeth said. "But apparently she's back."

"You're right," Joe said. "That is the worst thing I can think of. But her timing is still true to form."

"It's one of her special gifts," Marybeth said with a bitter sigh. "I'll head out there and see what she wants. Maybe I can convince her to leave before you get home."

"That would be nice."

Missy Vankueren Hand had been married six times, most recently to the infamous defense attorney Marcus Hand of Jackson Hole. Each husband—with the exception of Hand—had been wealthier and more influential than the previous one, a strategy she referred to as "trading up." Hand was more of a lateral move because he'd served as her defense attorney when she'd feared prison for the murder of husband number five, wealthy rancher Earl Alden. Not only would Hand defend her, but as her spouse, he wouldn't be forced to testify against her in court. So she solved two problems at the same time.

Missy had not only disapproved of her daughter's wedding to Joe Pickett; she'd relentlessly tried to sabotage the marriage ever since. Joe thought of her as his nemesis and he still marveled at how Marybeth had turned out to be the opposite of everything her mother stood for. Although Missy had recently turned seventy— Joe was sure of that because they'd received a postcard from her from Venice where she'd written in a flowery scrawl that *Seventy is the new forty-five*—his mother-in-law had somehow maintained her tiny hourglass figure, heart-shaped porcelain face, and the ability to melt the hearts and morals of new wealthy husbands while simultaneously gutting the men she'd left behind.

His mother-in-law was now independently wealthy because she'd sold the ranch that had been passed along to her and she could afford to pick up and travel the world whenever the mood struck her or the law closed in.

And now, Joe moaned to himself, she was back.

He slid the phone into his pocket and closed his eyes for a moment. Then he remembered why he was there.

JUDGE HEWITT SAT unshaven and disheveled in a hard-backed chair at the bedside of his wife, Sue, who was both unconscious and looked to be sprouting tubes and wires from her body beneath her sheet. Her head was turned to the side, facing the judge, but her face was obscured by a cloudy oxygen mask. A bank of monitors blinked and clicked behind her headboard.

Hewitt's eyes were red-rimmed when they rose to meet Joe's.

"What now?" he asked sharply. "First that idiot Kapelow and now you."

Joe removed his hat and nodded. Although Judge Hewitt's greeting had been less than friendly, Joe chalked at least some of it up to the judge being viewed in a very vulnerable and intimate state. Judge Hewitt was used to looking down on others from his bench while wearing a black robe that served as a kind of force field. Now here he was in rumpled clothing grasping the hand of his wife who couldn't squeeze back. Joe felt for him.

"How is she doing?" he asked softly.

Hewitt started to speak, then caught himself and looked away. Sue was obviously not improving, but he couldn't come up with the words without breaking down.

"She's opened her eyes and looked at me a couple of times," Hewitt said. "I thought she was here with me and I started to talk to her. Then she slipped away. I can't say for certain she even heard what I said."

"I'm sorry," Joe said. "We'll pray for her."

"Do that," Hewitt said. "I'm doing all I can. I've threatened to cite Him for contempt if He doesn't bring her back to me."

His attempt at dark humor—and the reminder that he was still a judge—made Joe wince.

"This is a terrible thing," Hewitt said while stroking Sue's hand. "I can't help but think how much I wasn't there for her over the years. I was selfish—either on the bench or chasing after trophies all over the world. She had to resent it, but she rarely complained. It must have been very lonely for her.

"Now this has happened. I've sworn to God that if she makes it through, I'll change. I'll be different. I'll listen to her when she yammers on and I'll be there for her the way she's been there for me. I swear it."

Joe was taken aback. Judge Hewitt had never spoken to him with such intimacy or regret before.

"She always wanted to go on a European trip," Hewitt said. "I told her we would—someday. But I used my time off for me—always thinking we'd go later after I retired. Now . . . Now I realize that time may never come."

His eyes filled with tears and Joe had to steel himself not to look away.

"If she gets through this, we're going to Europe, which I hate. They're so smug over there that they don't know their time is up. But I can put those feelings aside for a few weeks for Sue. And I hope I have the opportunity to do just that."

"I can't imagine how you feel," Joe said.

"I have a long bucket list of species I have always intended to kill," Hewitt said. "I'm about seventy-five percent through the list. But those remaining creatures mean nothing to me at this moment. Right now, I want just two things."

He turned to Sue as if she could hear him. He said, "I want you to get through this."

Then he turned to Joe. "And I want retribution for what happened to her."

Joe gulped.

Hewitt gently lay Sue's hand down on the mattress and released it, then he turned and grasped a sheaf of papers from a bedside table and shook them at Joe.

"This is what Kapelow brought me," he said angrily. "Newspaper stories from around the country where people were struck by stray rounds fired from miles away. He thinks this proves something in Sue's case. He's a mental midget like I've rarely encountered. The only people worse are the moron voters of Twelve Sleep County who elected him sheriff."

Joe didn't want to remind Hewitt that those same morons had elected the judge time and time again.

Hewitt said, "I reiterated to him that every hour that goes by without real progress in the case is an hour lost that we'll never get back, and he's spending his time printing off garbage stories and running around like a chicken with its head cut off.

"It's really very simple. So simple even an idiot can get it. Someone tried to kill me and they hit my wife. Why is that such a difficult thing for the sheriff to grasp?" Hewitt asked Joe.

"There's some news on that front," Joe said.

As he detailed his trip up the hill that morning, he showed Judge Hewitt the photos he'd taken on his phone. Hewitt grasped the significance instantly.

He said, "So we're looking for a man of means with a motive to kill me who can afford a weapon like that—and his minion."

Joe nodded, although he wasn't ready to call the spotter a minion yet.

"That should narrow things down," the judge said as he handed Joe's phone back.

"Yup."

"Give me a minute to think about it." The judge sat back in his chair and rubbed his chin. Joe had seen the gesture many times in court just prior to his making a ruling.

Hewitt dropped his hand to his lap and looked up. "I think I know who it might have been."

Joe raised his eyebrows while he waited for a name. But he noticed that the judge's attention had strayed to something behind him.

Joe turned to see that Dr. Arthur had paused just inside the door. He was standing there in his white coat, reading a display on an iPad.

Dr. Arthur was in his midthirties and he was trim and fit, with thinning rust-colored hair. He'd come to Saddlestring from a critical care hospital in eastern Montana, and was the pride of the hospital foundation's recruiting committee, who had issued a press release about how, prior to coming to Wyoming, Arthur had done stints in Arkansas, Texas, Louisiana, and Mississippi. Joe didn't know him well, but he'd met him a couple of times in the last year at community events Marybeth had wanted to attend. He seemed competent and Joe hadn't heard disparaging things about him— the last emergency room doctor had been accused of unnecessary pelvic exams on young women who'd arrived at the ER with broken arms or legs.

Medical doctors in small isolated communities like Saddlestring were recently regarded as a kind of royalty, Joe knew. It was difficult to convince doctors to forgo the security and structure of narrowly defined specialties in large urban environments and move to rural locations where they were obligated to work more hours for less pay and become general practitioners. Dr. Arthur was an exception, and his reputation had apparently spread to the point that people made appointments with him from hundreds of miles away. Rumors were already circulating that he was such a fine doctor that he'd soon be lured elsewhere and Twelve Sleep County would once again have to begin the search for a new one.

"Am I interrupting something?" Dr. Arthur asked Joe and Judge Hewitt.

"You're the doctor," Hewitt said. "I think you're allowed to enter a hospital room.

"Did you bring me good news?" Hewitt asked Arthur. His tone had returned to its usual intimidating cadence.

"I wish I could say yes," Arthur said while keeping his eyes on his tablet. It was obvious to Joe that Dr. Arthur was cowed by Judge Hewitt and didn't want to meet his withering glare.

"Then what is it?" Hewitt demanded.

"As you know, we removed all of the remaining bullet fragments and repaired what internal damage that we could, but her heartbeat is weak and irregular," Arthur said. "We may need to increase her oxygen."

"Then do it, for God's sake," Hewitt snapped. "What are you waiting for?"

"I'll order it right away," Arthur said.

Hewitt asked, "Did you FedEx the bullet fragments to the state lab like I asked?"

Dr. Arthur said he had.

Joe was puzzled. "Just fragments?" he asked them. "Not an intact slug?"

Arthur nodded.

"Why do you ask?" Hewitt demanded of Joe.

"I do a lot of necropsies on big-game animals," Joe said. "I realize that's different, but a bullet does the same damage to a deer or elk that it would to a human. It mushrooms on impact and burrows through flesh and organs. Sometimes it hits a bone and deflects its angle. But I've rarely seen a bullet disintegrate within a carcass. Sometimes I find it whole after digging around, but it's usually caught just under the hide after passing through the body. The hide is tough and elastic and the round is out of energy by the time it gets there and gets trapped."

Dr. Arthur shrugged. "I haven't operated on a lot of gunshot wounds in my career, but I can tell you that this bullet fragmented."

"Why would that happen?" Hewitt asked Joe and the doctor.

Arthur shrugged again. "Maybe it was a unique round. Maybe it was designed to fragment."

"I've never heard of such a thing," Hewitt said.

"Neither have I," Joe agreed. Then he asked the doctor, "Was there enough of the bullet left to identify the caliber?"

"I don't know what to tell you," Arthur said. "Maybe it could be pieced back together by an expert, but that's out of my field."

"Damn," Hewitt said. "Another impediment to the investigation." Then to Dr. Arthur, "Thank you. Now get that oxygen going."

Dr. Arthur spun on his heel quickly and exited the room. Joe guessed it was unusual for the doctor to be ordered around like that by a patient or the spouse of a patient.

"I've heard good things about him, but he may turn out to be an incompetent quack," Hewitt said sotto voce to Joe. "I may have to airlift Sue to Billings for decent care before that man kills her."

Judge Hewitt paused to reconsider his words. He said, "At the same time, I don't want to be the one to run him off. He might actually know what he's doing, unlike our sheriff."

Then: "I seem to be surrounded by incompetent fools."

Then: "Dennis Sun. He's rich enough to have one of those ultra-long-distance rifles and I know he thinks he's quite the marksman. Plus, he's got a crew of assistants around him at all times and one of them could be his spotter. He's had a bug up his ass for me after I took away his hunting privileges. So go talk to that son of a bitch, and if he doesn't have a good alibi you need to string him up."

Joe winced. It made at least some sense to talk to the movie producer, and he was on his list of suspects. But string him up?

"Don't tell the sheriff what you're doing," Hewitt said. "He'd just figure out a way to throw a wrench in it. Let's keep him out of this."

LONG RANGE

———

County Attorney Duane Patterson was in an observation room down the hall from the ICU and Joe poked his head in as he passed by. Dr. Arthur was in there as well. The two of them were in the midst of an animated but hushed conversation while Arthur probed through Patterson's scalp with his fingers, no doubt checking the wounds from the glass. Patterson sat on top of a recliner bed in the clothes Joe had seen him in that morning.

Joe heard the doctor emphasize the words "oxygen" and "asshole" and Patterson glared at him while he spoke. Joe thought it was unprofessional for Arthur to discuss his other cases with a patient, if that was in fact what he was doing.

"Now *I'm* interrupting," Joe said to them.

They stopped speaking abruptly and Arthur quickly said, "Just making my rounds."

Joe had assumed that.

"I'm trying to convince him to release me," Patterson said to Joe. "There's no reason for me to be in here taking up a perfectly good bed."

"How's he doing?" Joe asked the doctor.

"Cranky," Arthur said. "But not as cranky as the last one."

"Welcome to my world," Patterson said. Then, to Dr. Arthur, "So can I go?" He seemed unduly angry, Joe thought.

Arthur probed through Patterson's hair thoroughly but gently. He said, "There are a couple more slivers we'll need to take out. But after that I see no reason to keep you here."

Patterson sighed impatiently. Something Dr. Arthur had said or done had obviously set him off. Joe was curious what it was.

"Do you need a ride to your house?" Joe asked Patterson. He intended to brief the prosecutor on both the sheriff's theory and the discovery on the hill.

"My office, maybe," Patterson said. "I've got a ton of work to do."

"I'll give him a lift," Arthur said to Joe. "My shift's just about over."

Joe thought it was a kind and personal gesture.

"*After* we increase Sue Hewitt's oxygen, of course," Arthur said with a wan smile.

Patterson said to Arthur, "I wish you'd spend more time with Sue than on me. I'm fine."

"First things first, Mr. Patterson," Arthur said. "I can handle more than one patient at a time. That's what I do here."

Joe clamped on his hat and told Patterson, "I'll catch up with you later."

He made a note to himself to remember to ask the prosecutor what his problem with the doctor had been.

ELEVEN

Dennis Sun lived with his third and much younger wife on a five-thousand-acre ranch outside of Winchester and it took Joe twenty minutes to get there. He took the exit off the interstate, cruised through the small town, and noted that no one on the street took a second look at him in his beat-up WYDOT pickup. He felt like he was operating undercover.

Sun had purchased the ranch ten years before after the worldwide success of an action-thriller starring Bruce Willis. The movie had been the high mark of Sun's career and subsequent films had been panned by critics and avoided by American audiences, but, Joe had heard, they did well enough in Asia that Sun continued to work. Joe hadn't seen any of the movies, although Sun had premiered the last two—a fantasy about a Genghis Khan–type conqueror and a space thriller set on the rings of Jupiter—in Saddlestring for area audiences.

The producer was short and compact with darting eyes. He used different accents at different times, depending on which country he'd visited last. He was an eccentric who wore scarves even in the warmest weather, but he was embraced by the local art community because he was the only Hollywood figure most of them had ever met and he lived part-time in Twelve Sleep County. Sun raised beefalo on his ranch—a hybrid of bison and Hereford cattle—and he had a small herd of large exotic draft horses that had been left over from the Genghis Khan movie. Joe knew about the unusual mix of livestock because the beefalos had flattened a barbed-wire fence and frightened a grazing elk herd, and someone had called the Game and Fish Department to shoo them back. Sun had been on location somewhere in Eastern Europe at the time.

Dennis Sun had done extensive construction at his ranch head-quarters when he was flush with cash and converted one outbuild-ing into a private screening facility and another into an editing studio. A large hangar on the property had stored his airplane and helicopter until Judge Hewitt ordered them seized for his poaching crimes.

Until Joe had arrested the man for killing deer and elk on his ranch two years before, he hadn't met him in person. Sun had been apoplectic when Joe handed him the citations. He couldn't believe that it was possible to be arrested for harvesting big game on his own property, and although Sun was a well-known and outspoken progressive in his politics who gave large contributions to big-city socialist candidates, he'd accused Joe and the state of Wyoming of acting like "anti–private property totalitarians."

Joe had explained that in Wyoming the wildlife belonged to the state, not the landowner. As he did so, he thought he sounded just like an anti–private property totalitarian.

Joe was sure that Sun wouldn't be excited to see him again.

———

HE DROVE HIS PICKUP to a stop under an elk-antler archway and a locked gate that served as the entrance to Sun's ranch. Joe pulled to the side, got out, and picked up a weathered telephone receiver mounted on the inside of a stout post.

After thirty seconds, someone picked up the other end.

"Sun Ranch headquarters," said a bored young male voice.

"I'm Wyoming game warden Joe Pickett and I'd like to talk with Mr. Sun, if he's around."

"Who?"

Joe repeated it.

"Hold on. He's out back." The phone was dropped with a *clunk*.

Five minutes later, the man came back on. "He says you can go piss up a rope."

"Look," Joe said, "I'm not here to arrest him for another violation. I just want to talk to him."

"Do you have a warrant to come on the property?"

"No, I don't. But I do know a judge who would sign one in a heartbeat if I called him. Mr. Sun knows exactly who I'm talking about."

"Hold on."

Again, another long wait. Then: "Mr. Sun says to stay where you are until I can come pick you up and escort you on the property. He also said to tell you that he plans to videotape your conversation with him so you can't lie about it later."

"I don't lie," Joe said, offended.

"Stay where you are and leave your weapons in your vehicle," the man said before he hung up the phone.

Joe sighed, shook his head, and unbuckled his holster. He thought that if Dennis Sun knew what a poor shot he was, he wouldn't have even asked that he leave his .40 Glock behind.

TEN MINUTES LATER, as Joe leaned back against the grille of the pickup with his arms folded, a new-model full-size SUV appeared from a bank of aspen trees a half mile away. It approached at a faster speed than the dirt entrance road warranted, and when it skidded to a stop on the other side of the gate, a roll of dust washed over Joe so he had to close his eyes.

There were two profiles behind the tinted-glass windshield, and neither appeared to be Sun.

The passenger jumped out and punched numbers into a keypad that opened the gate. He was in his midtwenties, deeply tanned, thin and angular, with tight black jeans and a man bun. He did *not* look like a ranch hand.

After the gate was open, Joe introduced himself and extended his hand.

The man looked at it and said, "I'm Renaldo Bloom. I'm Mr. Sun's personal assistant. You're supposed to get in the car and we'll drive you to him."

"I've never met an actual personal assistant before," Joe said.

Bloom shot a withering glance to Joe and gestured toward the SUV.

Joe got in, closed the door, and sat back. The vehicle was much nicer and cleaner than Joe's borrowed pickup and it smelled of leather upholstery and Bloom's body spray. The driver was around the same age as Bloom, but he hadn't introduced himself or turned around.

"Are you the personal assistant's personal assistant?" Joe asked the driver.

"He's a team member," Bloom answered for him.

"How big is the team?"

"Please," Bloom implored. "Just sit back and enjoy the ride. Mr. Sun is waiting for you."

Joe nodded.

They drove across the meadow into the aspen grove and out the other side. Joe noted a small herd of beefalos grazing near the tree line toward the mountains. The creatures were leaner than cows, dark brown in color, with dangerous-looking horns.

As they neared the ranch headquarters, he observed a long narrow chute-like clearing that stretched from a set of tables and bench rests into the distance. Metal tree-like devices were set up at intervals down the length of the chute until they were too distant to see.

"That looks like a long-distance shooting range," Joe said, "with targets set up every hundred yards. How far does it go?"

"How would I know?"

"You're the assistant."

"I work for Mr. Sun in other ways," Bloom sniffed.

"Did all of the members of the team attend the same hospitality training seminar you did?" Joe asked.

Bloom pretended he hadn't heard Joe's question.

"So Mr. Sun is a long-range shooter?" Joe asked.

"Mr. Sun has a lot of abilities," Bloom said. "You'll have to ask him what he does."

"What does he shoot?"

"I have absolutely no idea. I don't care for guns and I've never touched one."

"You live in the wrong place," Joe said.

Bloom sighed. He was obviously annoyed with Joe's comments and questions.

The driver slowed after he entered the headquarters complex and pulled in next to an identical SUV in a parking lot on the side of the main house.

Sun's home was a rambling two-story Victorian structure with gables and a low sloping roof that extended to cover a large screened-in porch. The outside was original to the rancher who had owned the property and built it in the 1940s, but the antennae and satellite dishes mounted on the side revealed it to be surreptitiously high-tech. Joe admired Sun for keeping the exteriors of the home and outbuildings authentic while gutting and modernizing the interiors.

"Follow me," Bloom said to Joe.

As he climbed out, Joe saw Dennis Sun standing on the porch behind the screen. He wore a flowing white puffy shirt, a long scarf, and a battered straw cowboy hat. Behind his left shoulder was an attractive woman with long straight dark hair. She rocked a very young baby in her arms.

Bloom opened the screen door to the porch for Joe and gestured that he should go inside.

"Hello, Mr. Sun. I'm Joe Pickett. I'm with the Game and Fish Department."

"I remember you," Sun said without a smile.

"I'm Becky Barber," the woman said. "Or Becky Barber *Sun*, if you prefer."

"My wife," Sun said. "And my sweet little daughter, Emma."

"I'm pleased to meet you both," Joe said.

Becky Barber Sun looked oddly familiar to Joe, although he was sure he hadn't met her before. She had a square jaw, lush mouth, and wide-spaced hazel eyes. Her skin was white and flawless.

"Let's go inside," Becky said to Sun. "It's a little breezy out here for the baby."

Sun looked squarely at Joe while he apparently contemplated inviting him inside his home. Then he said, "Please, come join us."

Joe followed. When Sun gestured toward a hard-backed chair just inside the doorway, Joe removed his hat and placed it crown-down in his lap.

Sun walked behind a large glass coffee table, but didn't sit down on the couch behind it. Instead, he turned on a small digital video recorder mounted on a tripod and aimed it squarely at Joe. A tiny red light on the face of the device indicated it was recording.

"This is for my protection," Sun said. "It's not that I don't trust you. It's that I don't trust authority. I hope you understand."

"Sort of," Joe replied. He shifted uncomfortably in his chair. He was very aware of being taped. Joe didn't object, though. He had nothing to hide and he'd triggered his own digital audio recorder in his breast pocket before climbing into Sun's SUV with Renaldo Bloom.

Becky moved to an overstuffed chair next to the fireplace. Above her was a movie poster featuring a very familiar raven-haired bombshell actress named Vera Dayton. Joe recognized her from several movies he'd seen in his twenties.

"Is that . . . ?" he asked.

"My mother," Becky said. "Emma's grandmother. Dennis and I met on the set of *Savage Beauties*, where my mom was the star. Mom doesn't like to be referred to as a grandmother."

"I have a mother-in-law like that," Joe said. He'd never heard of *Savage Beauties* and he hoped she wouldn't ask him if he'd seen it.

Unfortunately, the exchange reminded him of who awaited him at his house when he went home.

Sun observed the exchange with barely disguised boredom.

Joe looked up at him and said, "I guess you know why I'm here."

It was a line he'd used countless times to open up conversations with suspects, potential witnesses, and perpetrators he had dead to rights. The opening had led to a litany of results including confessions, lies, and sometimes an open door to crimes Joe knew nothing about and hadn't associated with the person he'd asked.

Dennis Sun stifled a smile, and said, "Yes, in fact I do. You have no idea what you're looking for and you're asking me an open-ended question to see if I'm gullible enough to confess to something about which you have no idea."

"Dennis, that's rude," Becky said to him.

Joe knew that his face had flushed and he'd looked away from Sun.

"Exactly," Sun said to him. "Your response is a tell. It's proof that I hit the target."

"You did," Joe admitted.

Sun said, "You need to understand that you're dealing with a man who has spent his entire life observing and manipulating the feelings and reactions of other people, primarily actors, to obtain a certain end. Every look, every facial tic, every emotion can be seen on the face and from the eyes.

"I've spent the best years of my life dealing with sharks and deviants in the business—people who love you one minute and then sever your femoral artery with a bowie knife the next. So forgive my caution. If you thought you could come here and bait me into admitting something, you've come to the wrong place and you're dealing with the wrong man."

"I'm here for a reason," Joe said. But he felt humiliated.

"Are you here to arrest me for doing something on my own land again?" Sun asked.

"No."

"Are you here to ask me if I know anything about the shooting of Judge Hewitt's wife by mistake?" Sun said.

Before Joe could confirm it, Sun said, "Ah. I thought someone might wonder about that. As soon as I heard about it, I suspected I might get a visit from local law enforcement, although to be honest I expected a cop or the local sheriff. After all, it's well known the judge and I have an adversarial relationship."

Joe said, "You were overheard saying you'd like to kill him."

"Heat of the moment," Sun said with a dismissive wave. "But do you want to know why it wasn't me?"

"Yes."

"Because I wouldn't have missed," Sun said with a triumphant smile.

"Dennis!" Becky said again. "I'm taking Emma out of the room. She can't hear you talking like this."

"She's four months old, for God's sake," Sun said to Becky with an upward roll of his eyes. "She understands nothing and will remember nothing of this."

"You don't give her enough credit," Becky Barber huffed as she gathered up Emma and stormed out of the room.

"Tell her," Sun said to Joe. His voice rose and he shouted, "A four-month-old baby comprehends nothing."

Joe nodded reluctantly that he agreed with the producer.

"You've had children who are now grown," Sun said. "You know. As have I—five of them scattered around the world. Children are both resilient and oblivious to any stimuli up to a certain age. They certainly don't understand actual words—just tones. Becky doesn't know this yet. Emma's her first, and of course being her first means Emma is an exceptionally bright and perceptive child who is wise beyond her months on earth and cognizant of everything going on around her. According to Becky, Emma is the smartest baby on God's green earth, you know. And Becky is the only woman to have ever given birth."

Joe wasn't sure how to respond.

"Can I tell you something?" Sun asked.

"Sure."

"My unsolicited advice to you is to never marry someone younger than your oldest daughter."

"That's not likely to happen," Joe said.

"Good. Because it isn't as fun as it looks," Sun said. "Now, if we're done here, I've got a motion picture to edit and I'm sure you have many important things to do."

Joe said, "I saw your range outside."

"Yes, and?" Sun asked, arching his eyebrows comically.

"You're a long-distance shooter?"

"You know I am," Sun said. "You and Judge Hewitt confiscated several of my best rifles, if you'll recall."

"I do," Joe said.

"Since then I've managed to acquire two new ones," Sun said. "I've a wonderful Gunwerks Verdict in .338 Lapua and a Cobalt Kinetics BAMF XL Overwatch PRS in 6.5 Creedmoor. The Gunwerks rifle was accurate at fourteen hundred yards straight out of the box."

"So a sixteen-hundred-yard shot is within your range," Joe said.

"Obviously. And farther than that if wind conditions and atmospheric pressure are favorable."

Which echoed what Nate had said that morning, Joe thought.

"Look," Sun said, "there's no law against having an interest in premium precision rifles or acquiring them. I got interested in them shooting *Assassin's Castle* in Bulgaria several years ago and I've kept up with the technology. Becky absolutely hates my interest in weapons. Hates it. She'd rather I take up painting landscapes. By the way, did you see *Assassin's—*"

"No," Joe answered quickly.

Sun grunted. "Not many people did, I'm afraid. It was about a dozen international hit men and women invited to a mysterious castle by a supposed employer. None of them knew the others would be there. Only, instead of hiring them for a job, the overseer created a scenario in which the assassins were set up to take each other out one by one until only one was left standing. I won't give away the ending in case you'd like to rent it. But it involved a lot of high-velocity long-range headshots."

"Anyway," Sun said, "I ended up with several of the rifles we used after the filming. Those are the ones you stole from me. So in order to keep up with the sport, I needed to buy new ones."

"Who is your spotter?" Joe asked. "Not Renaldo?"

"God, no," Sun said with a laugh. "The only thing Renaldo can spot are emerging fashion trends. No, when I shoot on my range, I invite David Gilbert out to the house."

"I know him," Joe said. Gilbert was a local insurance broker in Winchester and Joe had interviewed him several years before. Gilbert's reputation as an honest businessman and/or ethical sportsman was spotty at best. There was no doubt, though, that Gilbert lived for the outdoors and considered his small business solely as a means of financing his adventures.

"I didn't realize Gilbert was a long-distance guy as well," Joe said.

"He is. We trade roles spotting for each other."

"There are a lot more of you people around here than I realized," Joe confessed.

"Alas," Sun said, "every man can be a sniper these days."

Joe recalled that Nate had used the exact same words.

"There's something esoteric and darkly fascinating involved with it," Sun said. "Hitting a target so far away that it can't even see you fills a man with a sense of lethality and power that's hard to describe. And once you do the math and unleash that bullet, you actually have time to think about taking it back—but you can't. It's either on target or it isn't. The target is dead before the sound of the shot even gets there."

"Where were you two nights ago?" Joe asked.

Sun paused and considered the question. "Just like that, huh?" he asked. "No building up to it or slipping it in there?"

"No."

Sun sighed. "I was flying back from a production in Tunisia. Commercial."

"Tunisia?" Joe said.

"Yes. Unfortunately, most of my motion pictures are now filmed overseas where I can get financing. The Hollywood elites shun me these days because they consider me too right-wing for their tastes, which is ridiculous and unfounded. My newfound interest in special firearms and choosing to live here in a flyover state only bolsters their view of me, I'm afraid. It doesn't matter if it isn't true. The fact is they don't want me in their club anymore."

"When did you get back here?" Joe asked.

"I didn't get back until *very* late last night. I had to take a puddle jumper from Denver to Billings and Renaldo picked me up and drove me home. I didn't get in bed until four-thirty."

Joe nodded.

Sun walked over to a large closet, opened it, and fished a thick envelope from the inside breast pocket of a rumpled safari coat. He handed the folder to Joe. Inside were boarding passes and used airline tickets from flights from Tunis to Munich to Chicago to Denver to Billings. They were all in Sun's name and they'd been used the day before.

"You can check the manifest of the airlines and talk to Renaldo to confirm all of that," Sun said with a tired wave. Then, flaring and gesturing wildly to Joe, "I got home that late because my private aircraft—that I used to keep on call to fetch me when I landed stateside—*got confiscated by fascists because I harvested game animals on my own ranch*."

"I know that's a sore spot with you," Joe said.

"Do you think?" Sun said with sarcasm.

"We'll check it out," Joe said, "but it sounds like you're in the clear for this."

"While you're checking, talk to David," Sun said. "He'll verify that we haven't shot together in the last couple of weeks while I was away."

As he said it, Becky Barber brought Emma back into the great room.

She asked, "Is everything okay?"

Joe said, "Yup."

"Of course it is," Sun said to Joe. "Because if it were me, Sue Hewitt would be fine and her husband would be on a slab in your local morgue."

"*Dennis!*" Becky hissed.

"I don't like Judge Hewitt," Sun said. "He's a tyrant and a bully. But I didn't shoot at him. I have enough problems as it is around here."

At that, Becky burst into tears and left the room again with Emma.

"Postpartum depression," Sun said to Joe while ushering him from his chair toward the door. "Anything seems to trigger it. And she worries that *my* words will psychologically injure the baby. What about her mother dissolving into an emotional pool of goo at the drop of a hat? What about that?"

"Thank you for your time, Mr. Sun," Joe said on the porch. He clamped on his hat to go.

"So when do I get back the stuff you seized from me?" Sun asked.

"That's not my call," Joe said. "Judge Hewitt is the one who decides those things."

"And he's a little distracted right now, isn't he?" Sun said without empathy. Then: "Renaldo, take Mr. Pickett back to his chariot."

TWELVE

An hour later, in a narrow arroyo that cut a sharp gash from the timbered mountains to the basin below, Orlando Panfile bent over a small white gas Polaris Optifuel stove and lit the flame with a wooden match. It took and hissed and he waved his bare hand over the top of it to verify that it was working. Then he balanced an aluminum pot on the top of the stove's assembly and poured three inches of water into it from a plastic gallon jug.

While the water heated, Panfile opened the small Yeti cooler that also served as a makeshift stool and dug out three hard-frozen chiles rellenos that had been prepared by his wife, Luna. They were stuffed with chiles from their garden that had been charred and peeled, *queso asedero* cheese, and coated with a crisp egg-and-flour breading recipe that had been passed down in Luna's family for generations. Each was lovingly wrapped in yellow paper and foil. Each wrap was sealed with a red heart valentine sticker, which made him smile.

When the water finally boiled—he was reminded how long it took at this high altitude—he slid the rellenos one by one beneath the surface and the water instantly stopped rolling. Frozen ziplock bags containing seasoned rice and green chiles were placed into the pot as well. When the water started boiling again, he'd heat his food for five additional minutes and then unfurl the rellenos, dump the rice onto the tin plate next to them, and cover everything with the spicy sauce. It would be as close as he could get to being at his home with his family—his plump wife, Luna; daughters Adriana, Julieta, Ximena; and sons Gabriel and Orlandolito.

Although Luna had prepared, frozen, and packed enough rellenos and other home-cooked food to last him two weeks, Panfile had stared hard at a cottontail rabbit earlier in the day before he decided to pass it up. Fresh *conejo en adobo* would be a welcome change of pace.

Perhaps tomorrow.

HE WAS PLEASED with the location of his camp. He'd found a deep den beneath an overhang within the arroyo where he could store his goods and equipment and have enough room for his sleeping bag. There was a trickle of fresh spring water in the ditch below that he used for washing his face and cleaning his cooking gear. If it rained hard and a flash flood roared down the cut, he was camped high enough on the side of the draw that his gear wouldn't be washed away.

His den couldn't be spotted from the air, and it wouldn't be stumbled upon by anyone other than perhaps a hiker or trekker walking directly up the draw. That was unlikely, he'd determined, because there was no public access to the foothills from either above or below. Even then, the camouflage mesh material he'd strung across the opening of his den disguised it so well that he'd walked by it a couple of times himself and not realized where he was.

The Toyota Land Cruiser he'd driven up from New Mexico was two miles away and above him, deep in the timber and covered by camouflage netting. If it were discovered, the authorities would learn that the license plates had been stolen years before in El Paso, Texas, and the VIN was bogus.

He'd left no paper trail on his journey north. No hotel room stays, no gasoline purchases except with cash. Orlando varied his look prior to and during every interaction he had with the public on the way north. In a gym bag at the foot of his sleeping pad were an array of wigs and press-on facial hair that he'd alternated three times a day until he got to his destination. He couldn't be tracked electronically because he didn't have a GPS device or cell phone.

The satellite phone they'd given him was turned on for no more than ten minutes at 9:30 p.m. During that period, they could call him with updates or fresh intel. That was the only way and time he could be reached. He'd yet to initiate a call of his own, and his habit was not to do so until his assignment was completed. They trusted him completely and he'd never given them a reason not to.

It was the same with Luna. She trusted him and she knew he always came back.

ORLANDO PANFILE WAS short, stocky, and dark with small stubby fingers and an oversized shaved head. One of his friends had nicknamed him El Puño, The Fist, because they said he looked like one walking around on two legs. He didn't like to be called that, although he knew it was used when his back was turned. He was forty-six years old and he'd grown up fending for himself and living off the land.

Camping by himself for weeks on end, even so far away from his home, meant nothing to him. It reminded him of the months he'd spent alone as a teenager high in the Sierra Madre Occidental range after the corrupt local cops and the *federales* had surrounded his boyhood home in El Pozo, twenty minutes northeast of Culiacán, the capital of Sinaloa.

Orlando's father was a farmer and his crops were marijuana and poppies for the buyers from the cartel. Both crops would be packaged or refined and sent north where the market for them was. All of the locals had switched to those cash crops. Like their neighbors, the Panfiles didn't consider themselves to be part of a criminal enterprise. They considered themselves to be what they were: farmers.

Nevertheless, the authorities had slaughtered his mother, father, and uncle as well as his younger brothers and his only sister in a hail of gunfire.

It was well known in the state at the time that the police were conducting raids on farmers in the area. The cops were doing it because they were associated with competing cartels, not because they were enforcing existing drug laws. After the local farmers were wiped out, new growers affiliated with the competing cartels were moved in to replace them.

Somehow during the firefight—and he still thought about it almost daily—Orlando had hurled himself out a back window and had run away, covering his head with his arms as if he were being attacked by swarming bees, not bullets. One brother had followed him, but he went down with a headshot.

Rounds had snapped through the air all around Orlando but, miracle of miracles, he wasn't hit. He kept running until he was beyond their fields into the tangled brush and then he climbed, vanishing from the assailants into the mountains that rose six thousand feet. They searched for him for days and he saw them coming, but he hid and continued to go up. He climbed so far that the nights were cold and the pines, oaks, and firs gave way to grasslands on the mountaintops.

He ate nothing but roots and tubers for the first five days. Although he caught glimpses of mountain lions, badgers, coyotes, gray foxes, and white-tailed deer, he didn't find meat until he stumbled on a fresh ring-tailed cat that had been killed by an eagle. He skinned the carcass, then roasted and smoked the flesh while the eagle circled through the sky above him.

Orlando had climbed so high that when he reached the top of the mountains, he could view the Sea of Cortez to the west and the state of Durango to the east. He'd eventually found an unoccupied, well-hidden cabin probably used by drug smugglers and he'd broken into it and stolen tools, clothing, binoculars, a tarp, and a bedroll. He'd been disappointed that there weren't any weapons to take. Orlando didn't stay long, though, because he knew that if the smugglers caught him, they would kill him as quickly and easily as the cops and *federales* would.

Orlando now thought of those months in the Sierra Madre Occidental as his real education. Living alone in the mountains taught him to be patient, resourceful, and tough. He learned how to catch rabbits with snares and he once dropped from a tree onto the back of a deer and slit its throat. Mountain lions stalked him at night, although none ever attacked. Regardless, he knew it was kill or be killed, and Orlando turned into an apex predator.

Once, while he was tracking a deer with a bow and arrow he'd made himself, he heard low talking and the footfalls of men in the bush. He flattened himself against the root pan of a downed pine tree when they got close. There were two of them: wiry, well-armed bounty hunters. Orlando never found out if they'd been sent by the police or the smugglers, and it didn't matter. He shot an arrow through the temple of the first man, who'd dropped straight down and died before he hit the ground. While the second man bent over the first, trying to figure out what had happened, Orlando charged him from behind with his knife and sliced through both of his femoral arteries on the backs of his thighs, then retreated into the forest until the bounty hunter bled out. Before the second man died, he fired bullets wildly in the direction Orlando had run. Rounds smacked into tree trunks and cut down pine branches. Orlando waited him out while lying flat on his belly in the pine needle loam.

ALTHOUGH HE MOURNED his family and lamented the situation he was in, Orlando had been determined not only to survive but to come out the other side as a man to be feared. With the weapons and ammunition he'd taken from the two dead bounty hunters— a goat's horn AK-47, a semiautomatic twelve-gauge shotgun, a 9mm pistol, and a .357 revolver—Orlando eventually hiked down from the mountains and slept for a few weeks in the burned-out home of his family in El Pozo while he plotted his revenge on the men who had wiped them out.

By the end of the year, by the time Orlando had turned twenty, he'd killed thirteen of the men who had ordered and participated in the raid. Seven of them died at the same time when the local police station exploded after a package bomb addressed to the chief of police was delivered.

The rest of them were killed one by one using the stealth, patience, and ruthlessness he'd learned in the mountains.

Orlando wasn't garish or showy in his methodology. He didn't humiliate his targets ahead of time or mutilate their bodies afterward. He didn't hang the dead men for public display, or pin notes to their clothing to trumpet his revenge. He also varied his technique based on the target and the circumstances.

Two he shot point-blank in the face while they sat napping in their patrol car. A *federale* had his throat slit while sitting on a barstool at the local cantina. Another was garroted on his day off while he was bent over weeding his vegetable garden.

The local commander of the *federales* who served as liaison to the national army and who had likely approved the raid on the Panfile farm, was strangled to death in his bed by Orlando's bare hands.

It wasn't long before word spread about what had happened in and around El Pozo. Orlando had become a man to be feared. When the bosses of the cartel asked him to join them on an official level, Orlando shrugged and agreed. His enemies already considered him a member of the Sinaloans as it was.

He'd become known as El Puño, The Fist.

DESPITE HIS RAPID rise in the structure of the cartel, Orlando never succumbed to the temptations all around him. He didn't drink alcohol or use the products they distributed, he wasn't needlessly cruel, he didn't lust for power, and he never cheated on his wife, whom he loved with all of his heart. During raids and operations, El Puño never panicked, never lost his cool, and never inflicted more damage or pain than absolutely necessary.

He preached to others that patience and strategy were more important than ruthlessness or bloodlust. He was never in a hurry as he surveilled and observed the habits of his targets. He almost always refused to go after the families of their enemies, although he knew there were plenty of thugs who would and did. Orlando was an apex predator with nothing to prove to anyone.

When he was promoted to the exalted position of head of security for the entire organization, he tried to teach those same virtues to the hundreds of soldiers they sent him for training and instruction. With just a few exceptions, he failed. The men they sent learned his techniques, but they were largely hotheaded, bloodthirsty, and sloppy. He couldn't train that out of them.

There were a few exceptions. Pedro "Peter" Infante had been one of them. Infante had headed up the Wolf Pack of four assassins. Despite Infante's skill and caution, his entire team had been wiped out. It was the first time that had happened within the organization.

And as far as Panfile was concerned, it would be the last time as well. He'd come north with three other handpicked men, but he'd left them at a cartel-affiliated motel property in Roswell, New Mexico. He'd told the men to wait there until they heard from him.

The three weren't happy about being left behind, but they did as they were told. They wouldn't be there when Panfile returned, he knew. They'd get bored waiting and go back home. The three men were well trained by him, and they were efficient and ruthless killers. But for this assignment, he knew he couldn't fully trust them and he couldn't afford any mistakes. Plus, this was personal.

It was personal because Orlando's protégé, the best of them all and the most famous, had been Abriella Guzman.

Abriella, who'd been brutally murdered six months before, not far from where Orlando Panfile made his camp.

Abriella, his beautiful and charismatic student, who had been taken from the world by a gringo falconer who lived less than three miles away.

Abriella was the one protégé who could make him abandon his principles about not harming families because she'd been slaughtered before she could ever have one of her own.

AFTER HIS MEAL, Orlando washed his dishes in the small creek and propped them in a sagebrush to air-dry. Then he walked up the hill and dropped to his hands and knees to approach the spotting scope.

He'd inadvertently timed it just right. This was the period in the afternoon when the family went to town for grocery shopping or doctor's visits. He watched as the falconer stood by while his wife buckled their baby into her car seat. Both adults climbed into the white van with lettering on its side, and they drove away.

Americans treated their babies like eggs, he thought. All five of his children had grown up happy and healthy without ever once being strapped into a car seat.

He waited until the car was out of sight and then another fifteen minutes to make sure they didn't forget something and come back.

Orlando went to his den and fitted a curly black wig on his head and used adhesive to apply a thick beard to his face. He checked his appearance in a hand mirror and approved of what he saw.

Then, with a pistol in the back waistband of his trousers and a long, thin skinning knife up his sleeve, he began the long hike down the draw toward the falconer's home.

THIRTEEN

Between Winchester and Saddlestring, Joe took a ranch road exit off the highway and drove deep into the breaklands, a unique geological feature that existed between the Twelve Sleep River Valley and the Bighorn Mountains for several hundred square miles. The breaklands consisted of knife-like draws that ran in zigzags offset by flat-top buttes and two-track dirt roads that often went nowhere. Although it was very difficult terrain, deer and antelope hunters ventured into it during the hunting seasons because the harsh landscape provided refuge to wily big-game animals. Plus, ranchers rarely grazed cattle there because they were too difficult to locate when it was time to round them up.

The destination he had in mind was the highest point in the area: a grassy plateau he often used as his perch. He'd parked there many times over the years and had used the high ground to set up his window-mounted spotting scope. On a clear day, and most days were clear, the view was incredible. From his perch he could see the smudge of Winchester to the northwest all the way to the outskirts of Saddlestring to the south and the tree-lined curves of the river that threaded through the floor of the valley.

Joe noted a couple of vehicles in the area by spoors of dust in the distance. They were likely road hunters who drove slowly and hoped they'd blunder into something. He didn't mind it that hunters could see him up there watching them. It was a good reminder to them that he was on the job.

But Joe chose to drive to his perch for different reasons than checking on hunters. One was that because of the altitude and openness, his perch had excellent cell phone service. The other was that it delayed his arrival home, where Missy would be.

HE OPENED HIS NOTEBOOK and placed it next to him on the front seat. Daisy lifted her blocky Labrador head from the cushion to watch him before sighing and settling back to sleep with her snout between her paws.

Joe reviewed his notes from the previous thirty-six hours. There were plenty of items to follow up on, and he couldn't assume that Sheriff Kapelow would beat him to it. As far as Joe was concerned, he was on his own in the investigation.

First, he confirmed with United Airlines at the Billings airport that Dennis Sun had, in fact, arrived the night before after a long international flight. The producer was well known among the employees of the airline because he was memorable and a frequent flier.

Then he placed a call to Sarah Vieth, the public relations liaison for the Department of Corrections at the Wyoming State Penitentiary for men in Rawlins. When she answered, it was obvious she was eating a late lunch at her desk at the same time.

"Hello, Joe Pickett," she said. Her desk phone obviously had caller ID.

"Hello, Sarah. Is this a good time?"

"It's always a good time for you," she said while chewing something.

Vieth had worked in the administrative offices of ex-governor Rulon, and Joe knew her from there. When Rulon had been replaced by Colter Allen, Sarah had seen the writing on the wall and managed to be transferred to Rawlins before Allen's inauguration. She was competent, generally cheerful, and she'd thrown herself into her new job.

Sarah Vieth was tall, thin, and fit. She was married to her partner, Vanessa, an artist who had moved with her to Rawlins. Vanessa created trout out of wire, and Marybeth had bought one for their living room.

"I'm wondering about the status of two of your guests at your establishment," Joe said. "Specifically, Ron Connelly and Dallas Cates."

While there were over seven hundred inmates at the state prison, Joe kept a mental inventory of nearly every man he'd helped put there. It wasn't as many people as the average cop, sheriff, or prosecutor, because most game violations were misdemeanors, but those who were in Rawlins were the worst of the worst in Joe's world. For that reason, he kept aware of when specific inmates were scheduled for parole hearings or when they were likely to be released back into the public. Ron Connelly and Dallas Cates were of special interest to him. Especially Dallas Cates.

"Is there a specific reason you're asking?" Vieth said.

"Yup. You've probably heard that someone took a shot at Judge Hewitt up here and hit his wife instead. We're tracking down the status and whereabouts of everyone who publicly threatened the judge with retaliation to see if we can place them here at the time. If nothing else, we can clear them off our list of suspects. Those two are on my list."

"Well," Vieth said, "neither has been released. If that were to happen, I'd make sure to give you a heads-up."

"Thank you."

"I did see your name when I reviewed their files," she said.

"I hope they said nice things."

"They didn't," Vieth said with a chuckle. "I make it a point to read the files on all of the high-level offenders—all the guys in C and E buildings. I want to know who we've got here and, believe me, we've got some bad dudes. I try to meet with all of them at one time or another. The prison psychologist and I tag-team it. We started with the white and orange shirts and we're about halfway through the blue and red shirts in A and B pods."

Joe knew from visiting the pen that inmates in blue and red were in the A and B pods and they were well behaved, generally harmless to others, and in for nonviolent crimes. The inmates confined to the C and E pods were a different matter and they wore orange or white clothes. Orange meant the prisoner was considered dangerous or unstable, and white meant death row.

"So, Ron Connelly, aka the Mad Archer . . ." she said. Joe could hear her tapping on a keyboard.

"You can finish your lunch first if you want," Joe offered.

"That's okay," she said with a smile in her voice. "Vanessa packed me a salad, so I don't mind pushing it aside.

"So Ron is an Okie, as you know. He was a rough guy and he had a whole list of write-ups the first year he was here. He was reprimanded for assault, stealing phone minutes from other inmates, and thievery. But in the last year he's really straightened up. He claims he finally found God, and both the psychologist and I believe him. There's a recommendation in his file that he be moved from C to B in the next few weeks."

Joe said, "He used to like to kill and maim animals by shooting them full of arrows and leaving them to die."

"Yeah, I know. But his sheet has been absolutely clean for a year and he's organized a Bible-study group in C pod. He's got a parole hearing scheduled for December, so maybe that's what actually inspired him, but I think he's sincere."

"That's interesting," Joe said. "I hope you're right. Is there anything in his record that would make you believe he still has it out for the judge? Or that he's got people on the outside who would kill for him?"

"No," Vieth said with clarity. "He's kind of a loner. He doesn't seem to have a network like that at all. His only friends on the inside are the guys in his Bible-study group. And he rarely gets visitors, so I don't know who he'd conspire with to go after a judge."

"He can make phone calls, though," Joe said.

"Yes, and we monitor them. He talks to his mother in Tulsa every week or so, but he's never had a conversation with her that we've flagged. It's all very mundane."

"What about social media?" Joe asked.

"Our policy is that blue and red shirts have limited access to the internet on a time-reserved basis. We have filters on what they can see and they're not allowed to post anything. Ron's still orange, so he doesn't get access at all. I just don't think Ron is your shooter, Joe."

"What about Dallas?" Joe asked.

Vieth whistled, and said, "Here's an example of two inmates going in opposite directions when it comes to behavior and reha- bilitation. Dallas is a piece of work, as you know. He's been moved from red to orange recently, and he's cooling his heels in E pod because he assaulted a couple of guys. He stomped one of them bad enough, the guy had to be airlifted to a hospital in Denver."

Joe felt a chill go through him. E pod was where the most dan- gerous inmates were sent. Dallas Cates was tough, violent, and a keen manipulator of other men. He'd surrounded himself with gullible hangers-on during his days as a rodeo star. If he'd recently become more unstable, that wasn't good news for anyone.

"Dallas is one of the leaders of the WOODS," Vieth said.

"What's that?" Joe asked.

"Whites Only One Day Soon," she answered. "Our very own white power gang."

"Oh no."

"Yeah, we've got 'em. We've also got the Hispanic La Familia, the black Brothers in Arms, and the Native American Warrior Chiefs. Believe me, we keep a really close eye on them. Dallas jumped a couple of the Warrior Chiefs. That's what got him in trouble.

"Rodeo cowboys versus Indians," Vieth said. "Welcome to the New Wild West."

"Man," Joe said. "I was hoping he'd see the light and come around."

"He's got plenty of time to think about it in isolation," Vieth said. "You'd be surprised to see him now. You might not even recognize him with his shaved head and prison tats."

"I never want to completely give up on an inmate turning the corner," Vieth said, "but I'd say Dallas Cates is as close to a no-hoper as you can get. He belongs here. He's the kind of guy who reminds me why we have prisons. I fear the day that he gets out."

"So do I," Joe said.

"You should," Vieth said darkly. "Your name is mentioned several times in his file. He vows that he's going to come after you, the prosecutor, and the judge."

Joe paused. He asked, "Do you think Dallas has connections on the outside who could pull a trigger on Judge Hewitt?"

"Impossible to say," Vieth said with a heavy sigh. "The WOODS are a fairly new gang here. We don't know how well established they are beyond the prison walls. But I suppose it's possible you've got a member or two up in your county."

"We're looking for a team of two," Joe said.

"That really complicates things, doesn't it?" she asked rhetorically. "This thing happened with your judge was just a couple of days ago, right?"

"Yup."

"Dallas has been in isolation for a month and a half. No visitors, no phone calls. He couldn't have given the order recently, is what I'm saying. If he's the guy behind the shooting he would have had to set it in motion back in August or September before he was confined to E pod."

Joe thought about it. Although he couldn't rule Dallas out completely, the timeline of when Cates went into solitary and when the shootings took place in Twelve Sleep County were a real problem. Would a shooter—even if he was sympathetic to Dallas's new ideology and under his influence—wait forty-five days to do Cates's bidding? Without even checking in with the man? Would a team of two men?

"It doesn't really work," Joe said to Vieth. "I can't scratch him out completely, but he goes a lot farther down the list, based on what you've told me."

"I'll talk to him," she said. "Dallas likes to talk because he really does think he can charm anyone who'll listen to him. I'll play along, but I'll be very subtle. I think between the psychologist and me, we'll be able to tell if Dallas knows anything at all about the shooting. He wouldn't admit it outright if he did, but there might be a tell when we talk to him."

"Please let me know when you do," Joe said.

"I'll get right on it," she promised.

"Thank you, Sarah."

"You bet, Joe. We can't have our guests putting out hits on sitting judges—or their wives."

THE TALK WITH Sarah Vieth prompted Joe to make another call to check on someone he hadn't considered earlier: Dallas's mother, Brenda Cates.

Brenda was also in prison, but across the state in Lusk at the Wyoming Women's Center. Brenda was a quadriplegic incarcerated for life for kidnapping and murder, and she'd almost maimed

Joe a few years before with her high-tech wheelchair when he went to question her. Dallas was a chip off the old block when it came to Brenda.

Whereas Joe doubted Dallas had been behind the sophisticated shooting at the Hewitt home, Brenda was mean and diabolical enough to have arranged for something like that to happen. She'd once had a stash of money that she'd used to hire people to get jobs done, and although the account had been seized, it was possible she had more funds squirreled away somewhere to pay off an assassin.

The warden of the Women's Center, Martha Gray, took Joe's call. After catching each other up on their families and the weather, Joe asked, "So how is Brenda doing?"

"Not well," Gray said. "She's in Stage Five."

"Meaning what?" Joe asked.

"There are five stages of isolation in East Wing," Gray said. "One being the most lenient and five being the most severe. Brenda is the sole occupant of the Stage Five ward."

"Like mother like son," Joe said. "What did she do to deserve that?"

"Oh, she's so clever," Gray said. "You know—you've met her several times. She looks and acts like everybody's sweet old grandma. After you were here and she attacked you in that wheelchair, I foolishly thought that she was getting old enough and sick enough that the fight had gone out of her. We put her back into the general population and she was a model prisoner. After a year, since she miraculously regained the use of her hands, she got a job in the kitchen because whatever else you say about Brenda, she *can* cook."

Joe waited for the rest of the story.

Gray said, "Of course, that lasted until one of our girls disrespected her in the dinner line, as Brenda put it. So Brenda bribed one of the girls who works in our Aquaculture building to smuggle out some items for her. At the next meal, the girl who disrespected Brenda started choking horribly and grabbing at her throat. It seems Brenda had put a handful of fishhooks into her stew. They nearly killed that poor dumb girl."

"Yikes," Joe said, inadvertently reaching up and touching his own throat.

"So Brenda got moved back to the East Wing," Gray said. "She's had no communication with the outside world and there are no visitors allowed. We know she figured out how to thwart us before, but believe me, she can't do that this time. We took away her fancy chair, too. She's absolutely miserable, but at least she's not a threat to our COs and other girls. And I'm not falling for her sweet grandma act ever again."

"Yikes," Joe said again.

"I'm two weeks away from retirement," Gray said. "I have good people here, but I won't miss this place for a minute."

JOE REVIEWED HIS NOTES further and then confirmed that Darin Westby had indeed picked up a new snowplow at the implement dealer in Casper on the day of the shooting. Joe spoke to the salesman who had helped Westby load the item at three in the afternoon and saw him drive away after that. There was no way Westby could have been back to Saddlestring and the club by the time the shooting happened.

That left two groups of suspects on his list. He checked with headquarters in Cheyenne on the two antelope hunters from Greeley. As he guessed, their names were in the database because they'd been drawn for the specific hunting area that bordered the Eagle Mountain Club. They hadn't given bogus names or address details to Westby when he met them. It was incomprehensible to Joe that if the men were anything other than what they claimed to be, it made no sense to try to gain access to Judge Hewitt in such a convoluted way. The deadline for the antelope tags had taken place May 31—five months prior to the shooting. Especially when their odds of drawing the antelope tag in the first place weren't assured.

The last item to check off in his notebook was: *Club member? Ask Judy.*

Judy ran the administrative office for the club and she was a full-time employee. Joe didn't know her well enough to call and interview her, he thought. That needed to be done in person.

But, as Westby had mentioned, a club member targeting Judge Hewitt was unlikely. *Two* members teaming up to make an extreme long-distance shot bordered on the unbelievable.

Joe's list of suspects was all but cleared. That meant the shooters had a motivation that wasn't likely related to Game and Fish violations, he thought. Because Duane Patterson had been targeted as well, Joe theorized the assailants likely came from a pool of individuals who had been involved with both Patterson as a public defender and later prosecutor and Hewitt as the presiding judge. The combination of the two of them could include scores of cases over the years, Joe guessed.

He'd need to talk to the judge again. Patterson and Hewitt needed to get together and come up with a list of suspects they both knew and had interacted with in some way. Perhaps, Joe thought, the shooters were in plain sight.

Just then, a text message from Marybeth appeared on the screen of his phone.

Where are you?

It was accompanied by an emoji with steam coming out of its ears.

Joe typed back: *On my way.* He didn't do emojis.

To Daisy, he said, "Why couldn't you be the kind of dog that bit people if they came to our house?"

Daisy sighed and closed her eyes.

FOURTEEN

CANDY CROSWELL GLIDED THROUGH THE BIG HOUSE WITH a glass of wine in her hand and the playlist she'd titled *Chillax*, for chilling and relaxing, on the internal sound system. She played it loud—Sade, Jai Wolf, Chet Porter, Nujabes, J Dilla—and she swayed to the rhythms and caught glimpses of her reflection in mirrors and glass-covered bookshelves as she did so. She looked happy, she thought, and she was. The tunes coursing through the home gave it an aura of high-tech élan, and Candy reveled in it. Tom had once surprised her when he arrived home unexpectedly while she was dancing alone to *Chillax* and he'd been delighted with her tasteful and obscure taste in music, he'd said. So cool, he'd said.

Honestly, she hadn't curated or assembled the playlist herself, although Tom didn't know that. She wasn't that sophisticated, and she'd taken herself out of years of hot-take pop culture by diverting to North Dakota and Alaska for all of those years. Candy had downloaded the playlist to her phone from a yoga instructor who'd taught at the resort in Whitefish where she'd met Tom. Candy was unfamiliar with most of the music and nearly all of the artists, but she was trying hard to appreciate and understand the tunes. It was fun playing the role of the cool girl, and the wine helped.

One would think, Candy mused, that being alone in a big house day after day would be boring. And it was, at times. But Candy knew boring. Boring was a double-wide trailer in Williston or a one-room log cabin in Alaska.

AS SHE REFILLED her glass and before she set out on a second hip-swaying tour of the residence, she recalled the odd conversation she'd had with Tom before he'd gone to work an hour and a half before. He'd been at the breakfast bar filling a thermos with the strong coffee that he always took with him to keep him alert during his shift.

She had said, "You know, I noticed you had your target rifle in your pickup this morning."

"I didn't know you spied on me," he had said coldly.

His reaction surprised her. She hadn't seen that look in his eyes before: a startled mixture of anger and panic. He was instantly very tense.

"I wasn't spying, Tom," she said with a warm grin designed to defuse the situation. "I was going out to the studio to work out. Your equipment was in the back of your truck in plain sight."

"What about it?" he asked.

"Don't get so defensive, honey," she cooed. "I wasn't giving you a hard time about anything. I just wanted to say, for the record, that I'd love to go shooting with you sometime. I got to be a pretty good shot up in Alaska. I might surprise you."

His expression softened considerably as she talked. She noticed that his shoulders relaxed.

"Really," she said. "It might be fun."

Then he had grinned. "You continue to surprise me," he said.

"That's good, isn't it?"

"Yes, that's good," he said. "It's just hard to picture you with a high-powered rifle in your hands. But I kind of like the idea. You'd look pretty hot."

She laughed and batted her eyes at him in a theatrical way.

He said, "Maybe tonight you could . . ." And he didn't finish his sentence. She could tell he wanted to ask her to do some play-acting, something he'd asked her to do before, although he'd seemed ashamed of it at the time. Candy had obliged. Once, she'd dressed up as a French maid. Another time it was a candy striper. Both outfits had really revved him up.

"I could, what?" she asked.

Tom shot out his sleeve and checked his watch. He said, "I've got to get going. Maybe I'll text you while I'm on shift."

"Do that," she said, pretending she was eager to take up the challenge, which she wasn't. "Just give me enough time to, you know, get ready."

Costumes were hard to come by in Saddlestring. Her previous outfits had been cobbled together from items she found at the thrift store. The women clerks there didn't make eye contact with her as she paid for them, which was a reminder that nothing was private in a small town. But dressing up as an armed temptress? That wasn't a problem. Camo tube top, bikini bottom, knee-high hunting boots . . .

"I'll be in touch," he said as he carried his coffee away.

Her smile had faded the minute he walked out the door to get in his pickup. What remained was the afterimage of his face when she mentioned the rifle.

If he didn't want her to know he was going to the range on his breaks, why would he leave his rifle in his pickup in plain view?

Then she had a thought that chilled her for a moment. What if Tom was taking someone else to the range? What if there was another woman?

CANDY TRIED NOT to let that suspicion eat at her. She didn't want to taint the wonderful situation she had with Tom. She didn't want to be the jealous or suspicious lover. Candy couldn't abide women like that, and she knew Tom felt the same way. His ex, after all, had been one.

So although she was almost entirely able to convince herself that Tom wasn't straying—why would he when he had *her* at home?— there was still that jarring moment when he'd revealed something from inside him. She knew Tom had secrets, and he wasn't a man who liked to share much. His past before he'd divorced and moved to Wyoming was unclear to her. He said he preferred to live in the present.

Which was fine with her, but it didn't really explain what he'd been doing with his rifle and shooting gear, did it?

Candy knew that often there was one thing that could turn a relationship sour if it wasn't resolved. From that moment on, everything could go downhill. The assumption was that it would all have to do with lying, but she knew better. That one thing was sometimes too much honesty. That one thing could be when one person in a relationship revealed something very personal that turned the other one off. With Brent, the one thing had been that ridiculous yellow Corvette. With Nicolas, it was when he'd announced he was going bear hunting with his buddies for two weeks without discussing it with her beforehand.

She hoped with Tom that the one thing wasn't her discovery of his rifle in his pickup truck. She vowed to herself to not let it be. But as she danced through the rooms of the house and into Tom's book-lined den, she realized she was looking at his possessions with a keener eye than she ever had before, although she didn't know what she was looking for.

Most of the books on his shelves were dry and uninteresting to her, but they were obviously of professional interest to him. There were lots of college textbooks and very few novels. There was a section on big-game hunting and firearms, but she was used to that.

Candy rarely spent much time in his study. Frankly, neither did Tom. It consisted of floor-to-ceiling books that she'd never seen him read, an overstuffed chair and lamp, and a small antique desk she'd never seen him occupy. There were two stacks of papers on the desk and a legal pad with no writing on the pages. One stack was of opened and unopened bills. The second stack, which was nearly an inch deep, appeared to be of personal checks made out to Tom but not yet cashed. She thumbed through them and was struck by the fact that nearly every one was for five thousand dollars.

The desk had a single drawer in it where he stored an array of pencils and pens. She got the sense from the room that Tom wanted to say he had a study, but he never really used it for anything.

As she strolled by the desk, she reached out and opened the drawer and then quickly closed it again in embarrassment. She looked around the room to see if there were any cameras watching her, but she saw none and she hadn't noticed any other security cameras on the interior or exterior of the house.

Occasionally, Tom came back to his home for something he'd forgotten during his shift, but when she parted the curtain and looked out the window, she didn't see his pickup.

She asked herself: So what was she doing? Was she really spying on him as he had accused her of?

Nevertheless, she reopened the drawer and did a quick inventory of the items in it. There were, in fact, only pencils, pens, and paper clips.

Then she thought: Where would a man hide something he didn't want found?

IN THE GARAGE, she looked out the window of the door to once again make sure Tom wasn't driving up the road to surprise her. The road was clear.

She turned toward Tom's workbench and tools in the front of the garage. She'd only ventured there once before and that was to borrow a screwdriver to open plastic clamshell packaging containing cosmetics.

Men hid things among their tools, she'd learned from experience. Brent used to hide bags of weed and pornographic DVDs in the bottom of his toolbox. The DVDs were old, from before Brent met Candy, but they must have held sentimental value to him. She didn't mind that he hid the weed there because if he was ever arrested for possession, she could plausibly deny she knew anything about it. So she'd never said a word about her discovery to him.

Nicolas hid cigarettes in his workbench. He'd made a point to confess to her that he'd once been a two-packs-a-day man but that he'd quit cold turkey back in North Dakota. But she knew he still sneaked cigarettes when he was outside because she could smell smoke on his heavy clothing when he came in.

Like everything else in Tom's life, his workbench and tools were organized and fastidious. He'd used a black marker to outline the shape of hand tools he hung on the pegboard backstop so they could be returned to their proper place. In his big red rolling toolbox, one drawer was devoted to wrenches, another to screwdrivers, another to dozens of trays of screws, nails, washers, and other things Candy didn't know the names of.

It was in that catchall drawer, in the back, that she found the cell phone.

She knew Tom had his iPhone with him. She'd seen him snatch it up from the breakfast bar and place it in his pocket. The phone she'd found was new and she'd never seen him with it before.

Candy looked around again before she drew it out. She now recognized it as a design knockoff of an iPhone or Samsung Galaxy and she recalled seeing something similar in the prepaid phone section at the local Walmart. She was familiar with prepaid burner phones because that's how she'd communicated with Nicolas before her divorce from Brent had become final. Brent had been a snoop who knew the password to her regular phone. She didn't want her soon-to-be ex-husband to read the text threads she was running with Nicolas at the time because they had very little to do with financial planning.

Although she knew deep down that what she was about to do

might really impact her relationship with Tom and the way she might think about him going forward, she couldn't help herself and she powered up the phone. The display required a seven-digit password to open.

Candy tried 1-2-3-4-5-6-7 and nothing happened, so she reversed the sequence to the same result.

Then she entered Tom's home landline telephone number. Why? Because that's what *she* used on her burner when she was cheating on Brent.

It opened up.

Candy spent the next several minutes navigating around the icons. There were no names or numbers in the contacts. The call history was blank. There were no suspicious apps and the history on the web browser revealed only preloaded sites. She felt both immense relief and shame at the same time. Tom obviously didn't even use the phone, much less to communicate with his secret mistress. She was ashamed of herself for suspecting him.

Then she opened the text message app. There was one text thread with another number, but there wasn't a name attached to it. The person Tom was communicating with was designated 307-362-5545. So, a Wyoming prefix.

She scrolled back to when the text conversation began, which was dated a week before.

#5545: This is a test.
TOM: Got it.
#5545: Great. We can't talk about anything that might be overheard, so keep the phone handy.
TOM: Will do.

And that was it until it resumed with #5545 several days later.

#5545: We need to do that thing we discussed.

TOM: Tonight?

#5545: Tonight.

TOM: What time?

#5545: Let's meet at 16:00.

TOM: I can be there.

#5545: Lock and load. Tell no one.

TOM: Of course.

Then, the next night:

#5545: I hate myself for what happened.

TOM: You'll get over it.

#5545: Have you?

TOM: Trying to move on.

#5545: I'm sick about it.

TOM: Does anyone suspect anything?

#5545: No. And they won't if we keep our heads down.

TOM: Good.

#5545: There's that one more thing.

TOM: Then it's over?

#5545: Almost.

TOM: WTF?

#5545: We need to do it tonight.

TOM: The time and place we discussed?

#5545: Exactly.

TOM: You had better be there.

#5545: Oh, I will. And if I get delayed, I'll text you.

TOM: No deal. This is for you, not me. If you're not there, that's
   it. You can't ask again.

That was all there was on the phone. There had been no subsequent conversation.

Candy closed her eyes and felt the tears stream hot down her
face. She was distraught.

It was obvious what she'd discovered, she thought. Tom and a
woman had bought prepaid phones to communicate with each
other. They'd made a date because they needed to "do that thing
we discussed." Meaning they'd talked about it before. Candy
guessed it was a workplace romance.

That also explained the rifle and the gear. Tom had put them
in his pickup to give him an excuse for why he'd left work if anyone asked. The woman probably had a similar ruse up her sleeve.
She wondered where they met up. Which hotel? Or did Tom go to
her house?

She decided right then and there she wouldn't confront Tom
about it. Tom and his fling obviously had second thoughts about
what had happened. She'd even admitted she hated herself, which
told Candy the woman was married. Tom wasn't, of course, but
Tom and Candy's relationship was still undefined. Sure, she'd
moved into his home with him, but he'd never pledged monogamy.

And from what she could tell, it might be over and done. The
woman wanted Tom more than he wanted her. She must have
something on him, Candy thought.

Candy also thought she could live with it. The texting and the tryst weren't a deal breaker. She hadn't been so innocent or faithful herself in the past.

It was the "almost" that distressed her the most. The bitch wanted one more thing. Candy could easily guess what it was. She appreciated Tom's reluctance to give it to her and his statement that she couldn't ask again. Maybe, Candy thought, Tom had made his choice. And his choice was *her*.

Candy powered off the phone and placed it back exactly where she'd found it.

Then she finished her glass of wine in three big gulps and went inside to pour some more.

FIFTEEN

THE COW MOOSE WAS ONCE AGAIN STRADDLING THE PATH to his house and Joe slowed his WYDOT pickup to a full stop. The moose squinted in his headlights and looked dully at him through the windshield. Perhaps, Joe thought, she was still flummoxed by the battered yellow truck and didn't know what to make of it yet.

Then, slowly, she ambled away into the trees and he continued on.

On the slow curve to his home, he winced and felt the air go out of him. A gleaming pearl-colored 4 × 4 Range Rover was parked in his usual spot. It had county twenty-two license plates, which meant Teton County.

It was a new vehicle, but it meant one thing: Missy was there.

He fought against an urge to slam on the brakes, shift into reverse, and back away. Instead, though, he rolled on and parked next to the Range Rover. As he did, Daisy stirred and sat up. It was dinnertime.

Joe's phone burred in his breast pocket and he drew it out. Anything, he thought, to delay the inevitable. The display read MIKE MARTIN.

"Hey, buddy," Joe said. "Please tell me you're driving my truck over here."

"Tomorrow," Martin said. "I think I can shake free in the afternoon. Eddie needs to pick up a box of tranquilizer darts for a problem bear in Cody—so he can drive his truck and then take me back."

"Thank you," Joe said with relief. "I really appreciate it. I owe you dinner and drinks."

"You'll owe me more than that," Martin said with characteristic gruffness. "But that'll be good. I'll be able to catch you up on our grizzly case. It's getting more and more interesting."

Joe wanted to know more, but he looked up to see Marybeth glaring at him through the front window. She had her hands on her hips and he knew what that meant. She was impatient for him to come in. Marybeth didn't like spending any more time with Missy than Joe did. Thus the emoji she'd sent him with steam coming out of its ears.

"I'm anxious to hear about it," Joe said and punched off.

"Come on," he said to Daisy as he opened his door. "Remember to growl and bite her if I give you the signal."

Instead, his dog bounded for the door with her tail wagging back and forth like a metronome.

AS HE ENTERED the house, Missy looked up at Joe from their high-backed wicker chair in the living room. Her mouth pursed with contempt, but then instantaneously returned to a well-practiced half smile that was equal parts amusement and disdain. Her lacquered fingernails wrapped around the stem of a wineglass that rested on the arm of the chair.

She wore a high-collared jacket that looked Scandinavian, a soft turtleneck sweater, shiny black slacks, and knee-length high-heeled boots. Her heart-shaped face looked sculpted out of flawless ivory with the exception of an almost invisible web of wrinkles around the corners of her mouth. Missy, Joe thought, was remarkably age-less, although he had seen her once or twice without makeup where she *almost* looked her age.

She said, "I bet you thought I'd never get back."

"A man can dream," Joe said. What he'd dreamed about was her cruise ship hitting an iceberg. Or the vessel being boarded by murderous Somali pirates.

Missy didn't respond to him. She seemed distracted, although when Daisy padded up to her with her tail wagging, Missy froze the Labrador in her tracks with a withering *Don't come any closer* glare. Daisy turned away in mid-stride and sulked past Marybeth toward the kitchen.

Marybeth watched the exchange between her mother and Joe with caution. He noted that there were no place settings on the table or any food warming up on the stove. That was a positive sign, he thought. Marybeth had made no preparations for dinner and therefore there was no reason for Missy to stay. The wine was no surprise. His wife probably needed it to get through the evening.

Marybeth said to Joe, "I was catching Mom up on what the girls are doing. Somehow, she didn't realize they were all out of the house."

"Imagine that," Joe said.

Joe wagered that Missy, if put on the spot, would be unable to say how old Sheridan, April, or Lucy was. She'd never really kept track of her growing granddaughters, although for a few years she'd sent Lucy a card on her birthday because she'd thought, erroneously, that their youngest daughter was the most like *her*. Sheridan and April had been onto Missy's act and therefore hadn't been gifted with her attention.

"One minute they're babies," Missy said wistfully, "and the next minute they're grown."

"Not really," Marybeth said.

Again, there was no pushback from Missy. To Joe, that was uncharacteristic of his mother-in-law.

"So," Joe asked as he passed by Missy, bound for the bourbon in the pantry, "what brings you here?"

"I really can't say," she replied.

He paused. "You mean you don't know?"

"She means she won't tell us," Marybeth said. "I've asked. She's being inscrutable."

"I have my reasons," Missy sniffed. She changed the subject by looking around the house. "This house is so empty and cold without the girls in it. I find it ironic that they moved you to a nicer and larger place once the girls were gone."

"It wasn't like that," Marybeth said to her mother. "I told you what happened."

"Oh, yes, your house was burned down," Missy said with a roll of her eyes, like she didn't really believe it.

Joe flushed with anger and embarrassment as he poured himself a drink over ice. Missy had a way of putting things that made him feel embarrassed for the life they lived. And he noted that she referred to his daughters as "the girls" because she couldn't bear to call them her granddaughters. That would suggest she was old enough to be a grandmother, which she was.

"So you were out driving around and just decided to drop by?" Joe asked her.

Missy turned in her chair to look at him. She said, "I suppose I could have come over here and gotten my business done and not called at all. But I wanted to see the girls and my only daughter. I've been out of the country for a long time and I missed them."

He squinted at her. Was she getting soft and sentimental? Was he too hard on her, given her age? Then he thought: *Naw.*

"What business could you possibly do in Saddlestring that you couldn't get done in Jackson Hole?" Joe asked.

Missy and Marcus Hand lived in an exclusive gated community north of Jackson. They had access to private aircraft and amenities few others in the state could even imagine.

Missy took a thoughtful sip of wine and looked out at a middle distance between Joe and Marybeth. She said, "I had no choice but to cut my trip short and return. In my case, it happened in the Venetian lagoon. Marcus told me to continue on, but I just couldn't."

She paused dramatically, then said, "Sometimes real life just intrudes."

Joe had no idea what that meant. Intrudes on *what?*

Perhaps, he thought, the feds were closing in on her. Maybe the IRS, SEC, or FBI? All three agencies likely still had her in their sights.

"Let me guess," Joe said. "You needed to come back in order to destroy evidence."

Marybeth had to turn her head away so she wouldn't be caught giggling at that. But Missy simply scoffed. "Joe, when you reach my station in life and you're married to a man who is an absolute titan in the legal profession, there are certain things you no longer need to worry about. That's why we pay lawyers, accountants, and politicians such ridiculous amounts—so we're insulated from all of that."

"So what's the occasion of your visit?" Joe asked. "Are you hatching another plot to get me fired?"

"I have no idea what you're talking about," she said.

"Right," he said. Two years before, Missy had used her influence with Governor Allen to set Joe up in a situation where he'd fail spectacularly and therefore lose his job. Apparently, she'd thought that when it happened, Marybeth would come to her senses and move on.

There was no need to point out to her that he, and they, were doing better than ever with a new home, a new truck, and a raise in salary. It seemed petty to do so, although he had no doubt that if she had pulled off her scheme, she would have rubbed his nose in it.

Missy tucked a stray hair behind her ear and said, "It's about Marcus. He's been diagnosed with pancreatic cancer."

Marybeth gasped and covered her mouth with her hand. It was very much to his wife's credit, Joe thought, that despite what her mother was and all the things she'd done, her first reaction was empathy. Marybeth was the precise opposite of Missy.

"You didn't know?" Joe asked Marybeth. She shook her head.

"My daughter has a much firmer grasp on what this news means than you do, Joe," Missy said with distaste.

Joe looked to Marybeth for an explanation, but before she

spoke, Missy provided it in a schoolmarm tone, since he was obviously not smart enough to understand.

"Pancreatic cancer is a death sentence ninety-five percent of the time," Missy said. "Most people who have it die within three years. With the exception of small-cell lung cancer, it's the worst cancer you can get. That's because the tumor releases cancer cells that infect other organs even if the tumor has been surgically removed."

"I'm sorry to hear that," Joe said.

"We're so sorry," Marybeth added.

Missy thrust her chin out defiantly and looked at them both. "Oh, I'm not going to let him die. He's not going to get off as easy as *that*."

"What are you talking about?" Marybeth asked.

"I'm going to save his life," Missy said. "He's really going to owe me."

Joe and Marybeth exchanged a puzzled glance.

"Despite what Marcus told me, I had to come back here," Missy said. "Marcus was all ready to give up. But one of the many things I learned abroad is that we tend to look at sicknesses and diseases from the perspective of our own health industry. We don't know what else is out there in the world. There are creative ways to treat even the worst diseases—we just have to find them and embrace them."

Missy launched herself up and walked over to the kitchen counter to refill her wineglass. As she did so, she said, "He's too sick to travel internationally right now to where the clinical trials are taking place. But that doesn't mean he has no options. I told him to leave it up to me. I told him I'd save his life and that's what I'm going to do."

Joe was shocked to realize that he found himself admiring her will and tenacity. It was an uncomfortable feeling. Until that moment, he hadn't known Missy could have such deep feelings for anyone in her life as she apparently did for Marcus Hand. When he looked over at Marybeth, he could see she had tears in her eyes as well.

"There are experimental treatments for pancreatic cancer," Missy said. "I've read all about them. They might not yet be approved in this country, but they exist."

"Where?" Marybeth asked.

"The treatments are being done in France and the Netherlands," Missy said.

Joe was flummoxed. "We only have one doctor," he said. "Dr. Arthur isn't known for special cancer treatments."

"Who said it has to be a doctor?" Missy asked with a mad gleam in her eye.

"Mom, what are you talking about?" Marybeth asked.

"No," Missy said. "I can't tell you any more or I void the deal I made. I'm sworn to secrecy." Then she wheeled and set the glass down hard on the counter without drinking from it.

"I knew I shouldn't have come here," she declared. "I knew I should have just gotten my business done and not said a word about it to either of you."

She strode toward the front door and snatched her purse from the wicker chair in mid-stride.

Joe watched her go until Marybeth said, "I'm really worried about her frame of mind. Don't let her leave like this."

He sighed and followed Missy. He caught up with her as she

was opening the door to her Range Rover. She paused and didn't climb in, but she refused to look over at him.

"Your daughter would like you to come back. She has some questions," Joe said.

"She does?" Missy said with sarcasm. "Or do the two of you want to make more jokes at my expense? Don't think I didn't hear them."

"We didn't know about Marcus," Joe said.

The interior lights from her car were harsh and they made her look older and much frailer than in the house. They also reflected on moisture in her eyes. He'd never seen her cry before and he felt very uncharacteristic mixed emotions as far as Missy was concerned.

She said, "You know, when you two got married I was heartsick. I was depressed and disappointed. You know that, don't you?"

Joe rolled his eyes and said, "But you always kept so quiet about it."

Missy ignored him. She said, "I had such high hopes for my daughter. She had such promise. Everything I did, I did for her— to make her life better. I wanted to open doors for her that had always been closed to me. She was my first priority, but she didn't get it then and I'm afraid she still doesn't understand what I went through to provide her opportunities and connections. I thought I'd showed her the way, but she refused to give me credit or follow my example. When you two got together I thought she deserved so much better than a state-owned shack to live in and a paycheck-to-paycheck existence with an unimpressive state employee."

Joe didn't say, *I agree with that*. But he agreed. He always had. And he'd heard it all before.

She continued on in a soft cadence that had the tone and rhythm of a dramatic reading, he thought. She said, "That was a long time ago. Before you had children together and raised them well. I'll give you credit for that, although I think you poisoned them against me. Now the girls have grown up and moved away. I'll reconcile with them someday. And despite all the odds, you two are still together. And after all these years, you know what?"

"What?"

She looked over at him and, despite the tears, her eyes were ice-cold. "I was right all along."

With that, Missy slid into her car, slammed the door, and backed away without another glance.

Joe stood for a moment and watched her taillights strobe red through the timber. He hoped the cow moose would startle her on the road and she'd swerve headlong into a tree.

Then he tossed his drink in the gravel and went back inside.

"SHE'S LOST IT," Marybeth said over omelets later. "My guard is always up when she's around and I've learned always to be looking for her scheme or long con, but this time I have to admit that she got to me. She cares about Marcus in a way that's almost human, and she's willing to put herself out for him. That's a very unfamiliar place for her to be. I almost feel sorry for her."

"Don't go overboard," Joe said. "She's still Missy. You should have heard her goodbye speech to me."

"I'm afraid she's getting feebleminded," Marybeth continued, as if he hadn't spoken. "She's falling for some kind of scam where some mystery person claims he can help cure Marcus's cancer. It's just crazy. If there was somebody around here making those kinds of claims, we'd know who they were."

Joe agreed with a grunt. When Marybeth was on a single-minded roll, he knew better than to interrupt.

"There are times in my life when I've absolutely hated her," Marybeth said. "I felt bad about it because you shouldn't hate your own mother. But if it wasn't hate, it was shame and disgust. And the way she's treated our daughters! What kind of grandmother is like that?"

Joe shrugged.

"For the first time I can remember, I actually felt for her tonight," she said. "My heart went out to her for being so fierce and determined. She thinks she can help Marcus beat this disease and she's blind to any other possibility. Maybe for once she's realizing she can't scheme her way out of it."

"Sometimes real life just intrudes," Joe said, repeating Missy's own words.

"Please, Joe. Don't mock her when she's down," Marybeth said.

"Sorry." But he wasn't sure he really was.

"I'm going to spend some time figuring out who is scamming her and put a stop to it," Marybeth said. "Whoever it is shouldn't be taking advantage of desperate people, even if it is my horrible mother.

"I'm going to text the girls," Marybeth said, pushing her plate aside and reaching for her phone. "They need to know what's going on. Plus, I really miss them."

"I do, too," Joe said. This he absolutely meant.

———

JOE'S PHONE LIT UP at 5:00 a.m. and he rolled over in bed and squinted at the screen.

"Who is it?" Marybeth asked.

"Duane," Joe said, instantly awake. He swung his feet out from under the covers and padded into the hallway.

"What's up?" he asked.

"Things are happening," Patterson said in a rush of words. "The sheriff got a tip about the shooter. We have a suspect."

"How do you know about this?" Joe asked.

Patterson sighed. "Judge Hewitt asked me to be in his chambers a half hour ago to meet with Kapelow and to approve a search warrant."

"Who is it?" Joe asked, furiously rubbing sleep from his eyes. "Do we know him?"

Patterson paused a beat, then said, "I'm afraid so. And you're not going to like it."

SIXTEEN

NATE ROMANOWSKI SPUN A FALCONRY LURE THROUGH the predawn air in ever-growing circles by playing out a few feet of line with each rotation. The lure was made of a severed duck wing that he'd fashioned himself and weighted with lead shot clamped to the base of its primary feathers. It whistled through the still morning like a scythe.

The sun was about to shoulder its way over the summit of the eastern mountains and the grass was wet with sequin-like sparkles of melting frost. In the distance, a bank of fog rose from the contours of the Twelve Sleep River.

The activity with the lure was designed to attract the attention of a young peregrine falcon he'd released to the sky a few minutes before. The falcon had risen so quickly on the waves of a thermal current that it could barely be seen against the light pink belly of a cumulus cloud.

As the lure extended into wider circles, Nate kept his eyes on the peregrine. The falcon was not only the fastest raptor in the natural world, capable of speeds over two hundred miles per hour, but its advanced binocular vision enabled it to literally see the individual feathers of the distant lure in mid-flight. The circling lure looked enough like flying wild prey to become a target.

The exercise was one of the many preliminary steps to training a falcon to eventually join the Yarak, Inc. Air Force. The peregrine was learning quickly to come to the lure and Nate estimated it would take another few months before the bird connected with him in that special way that confirmed it was tuned in to his activities and movements on the ground. Once that happened, that almost mystical bond they formed between falcon and falconer, the peregrine could take its place with the older and more experienced birds. Either that, or it could simply fly away, never to be seen again. That sometimes happened as well.

"Nate, you've got a call," Liv shouted from the front porch of their house. "It's Joe."

Nate glanced over to see her cradling Kestrel with Loren Jean Hill hovering next to her.

"I'll call him back," Nate replied.

"He says it's urgent."

Nate frowned while he whipped the lure in a circle. Joe didn't use words like "urgent" unless something was . . . urgent.

"Okay," Nate said. "I'll be right there as soon as I can bring her in. He'll understand."

There was no way to suspend the training and resume it later without running the risk of losing visual and elemental contact with the peregrine, so Nate vastly sped up the pace of the exercise. He continued to loop the lure around him, but he shortened the length of line with every rotation. The peregrine obviously tracked the change and that prompted it to tuck its wings and begin a harrowing dive toward Nate and the lure.

In his peripheral vision, Nate saw Liv hand Kestrel off to Loren so the nanny could take the baby back into the warm house from the early fall chill of the morning. Liv stood huddled on the porch in her robe, watching him bring in the falcon.

The peregrine dropped like a missile and closed the gap on the lure in seconds. Just before the falcon could smack the lure with its balled-up talons, Nate jerked the wing to him out of the path of the attack. The peregrine recovered quickly and shot its wings out to break the momentum of the dive. When it landed a few yards from Nate's boots, he bent over it, slid a tooled leather hood over the head of the peregrine, and loosely wrapped jesses from the falcon's talons around his gloved hand.

He carried the falcon aloft on his fist as he walked over to Liv and reached for the phone. While he did, he was distracted by the fact that he would soon have more capable falcons than he could reasonably fly himself. He needed another falconer on staff he could trust as Yarak, Inc. grew. That Joe had called reminded him that he had the perfect apprentice in mind . . .

"Nate," Joe said, "I shouldn't be calling, but I wanted to give you a heads-up . . ."

As he listened to Joe, he heard the whine of oncoming engines from the direction of the state highway. So had Liv. He followed her line of sight and he turned to see three sheriff's department SUVs speeding toward him on the gravel road. The lead vehicle had its lights flashing. The two vehicles behind it were close and partly obscured by the cloud of dust kicked up by the lead car.

"I see them now," Nate said before Joe could continue. "Three sheriff cars led by Barney Fife himself, I suspect. What's this all about?"

"You'll find out soon enough, I'm afraid. The sheriff thinks you were involved in the shootings," Joe said.

"What did you just say?" Nate asked. He could feel Liv's searching eyes on the side of his face.

Joe repeated it, followed by "I'm on my way out there now."

Nate didn't hear it. Instead, he narrowed his eyes on the coming convoy. The aggressive approach by the sheriff's department set him instantly on edge. How *dare* they raid his home where his wife and child lived?

A fury rose in him from a dark place that had been previously dormant. Usually, his ire was aimed at macho federal agents who threw their weight around because they knew they wouldn't be held accountable for their actions. It had been months since he felt the internal surge of righteous anger that would inevitably lead to violence. A familiar coldness overtook him and his entire focus became two things: the threat and how to deal with it. In falconry terms, it was the first stage of *yarak*.

He assessed the situation.

His weapon lay coiled in a shoulder holster on a porch bench within easy reach. There was a bend in the road about a hundred yards from his house where, at the speed they were coming, all three units would line up like ducks in a shooting gallery. With his .454 and a rest to aim from, he knew he could take out the lead driver first and work his way back one by one.

"Nate?" Joe said with a note of panic. "Nate, don't do anything stupid. Just sit tight. You've got your wife and baby there . . ."

At the same time, Nate felt Liv's hand grip his arm. She was cautioning him to stay still and keep his anger in check.

Without disconnecting the call, Nate handed the phone back to Liv and he turned to face the law enforcement vehicles as they roared into his yard.

"NATE ROMANOWSKI," the sheriff called out as he emerged from his GMC with his hand gripped on his holstered weapon, "I need you to come down off of that porch right now for me. Keep your hands where I can see them and move slow and easy."

To Liv, the sheriff said, "Miss, please step away to the side."

The commands were singular in purpose, Nate thought. If Kapelow started firing his gun at Nate, he didn't want to hit Liv as well.

"Do as he says, babe," Nate said.

Liv stepped to the side and crossed her arms in front of her. She glared at Sheriff Kapelow with intensity.

The two other vehicles pulled up on either side of Sheriff Kapelow's rig and Deputies Woods and Steck got out and took positions behind their open driver's-side doors. Woods had a Glock pistol drawn and Steck held a pump-action shotgun. Nate looked from one to the other and noted the pained expressions on their faces. It appeared to him they didn't want to be there and they didn't like what they'd been ordered to do. He noted that Woods kept his finger out of the trigger guard of his handgun and that Steck kept the shotgun muzzle pointed at the sky and he hadn't racked a shell into the receiver.

"I ordered you to come down off that porch," Kapelow said. "I need you to do it *now*." His fingers were white on the grip of his weapon and veins bulged in his neck and temple. His feet were set into a shooter's stance and he was definitely prepared to draw and fire. Nate recognized the look in the man's eye of equal parts fear and exhilaration. Kapelow *wanted* him to make a wrong move.

"I'm coming down," Nate said softly. "But this is stupid. You don't need this show of force. You could have called me and I'd have come in to talk to you."

Kapelow said, "Come down the stairs and take three steps toward me. No more than three."

Nate sighed, but he did as he was told.

"Now place your hands on your head and turn around."

"Sheriff, is this really necessary?" Liv asked from where she'd retreated on the end of the porch. Her voice was strained with anger. "We're citizens and business owners in this county. He's done nothing wrong. We've done nothing wrong. We have our baby in the house and if you start shooting—"

"There'll be no need for that if your husband will obey my commands," Kapelow said without looking up at her. He ordered Deputy Woods to pat down Nate for weapons and cuff him.

"You don't have to do this," Nate said through clenched teeth. "My weapon is in plain sight up on the porch. I don't have one on me." But he reached up and laced his fingers together on top of his hair. Then he turned around so his back was to the sheriff. He glanced up at Liv. She was furious. He loved to look at her when she was furious.

"You have no right to be here," Liv said to Kapelow, her eyes flashing. "You're way out of line to come here and start giving orders like jackbooted thugs. This is America. This is *Wyoming*. You don't know what you're doing."

"Please shut up or we'll arrest you for interference and you'll both come in," Kapelow said to her, and Nate felt a red balloon of rage float over his eyes.

Liv shouted to Steck and Woods, "Guys, you know us. We know you. Why are you helping this man?"

"They work for me," Kapelow said to Liv. "One more word from you and you'll be detained along with your husband." Then to Nate: "On your knees."

Nate briefly closed his eyes. When he opened them, he said, "No. I'll cooperate with you, but I won't get on my knees. And don't threaten my wife again." He said it calmly and coldly.

"I can search him and cuff him while he's standing up," Woods said to Kapelow. "It's okay. He'll comply."

"I gave him an order," Kapelow said. To Woods, he said, "I gave you one, too."

Woods demurred. "Boss . . ."

Nate saw Liv's eyes get big as she fixed on something taking place over his shoulder. Before she could call out to warn him or he could react, Nate was hit in the back of the neck by twin steel-needle probes followed by thousands of volts in an internal explosion of electrical current.

His eyes involuntarily rolled back in his head and he felt his knees give way, but he somehow staggered to his left and stayed on his feet. Nate's arms flopped lifelessly at his sides. His entire body surged with pain and his mouth filled with a metallic taste. He'd been tased before, but during special ops training he knew it was coming. This was much worse—and more debilitating—because he hadn't anticipated it. He tried to regain his balance, when he was hit *again* in the small of his back and he lost all control of his muscles.

Nate pitched forward like a severed tree and he fell face-first into the dirt. Spangles of red and orange burst in front of his eyes. His limbs twitched and he could hear gurgling sounds from his throat, but he couldn't stop them. He also couldn't raise his head or move his eyes.

From above him through a painful fog, he heard Deputy Woods say, "Jesus, boss, you didn't have to empty both barrels."

"I did when he wouldn't go down," Kapelow said defiantly. "We know what this man is capable of. I couldn't risk it."

Nate heard the *thump-thump-thump* of footfalls as Liv ran down the porch stairs toward him.

"Get back. Stay away from him," Kapelow ordered her.

Then a grunting exhalation of air as Woods scooped her up and held her in place.

"He won't forget this," Liv cried. "*I* won't forget this."

"Cuff him and get him up," Kapelow said to Deputy Steck.

Nate heard the handcuffs ratchet tight on his wrists but he couldn't yet feel them. He couldn't feel anything. Then he was rolled to his back and pushed into a sitting position. His head flopped forward and his eyes rested on a tangle of thin wires that were attached to the embedded probes in his neck and in the small of his back. The wires stretched from the probes through the air to a large squared-off black and yellow Taser the sheriff held in his left hand. Kapelow's service pistol was drawn and in his right.

"If you give me any more trouble," Kapelow said to Nate while brandishing the Taser, "I'll give you another jolt."

It wasn't necessary. Nate lost consciousness and slumped over into the grass.

SOMEONE WAS SQUATTED down beside him when Nate opened his eyes a few minutes later. It took a moment for him to focus and realize the person next to him was Joe. Nate turned his head: he was sitting down with his wrists bound behind him and his back against the muddy front tire of Sheriff Kapelow's SUV.

"Where's Liv and the baby?" Nate asked. His voice was a croak.

"Inside," Joe said. "They're okay. Steck went in there to try and calm her down and to give her the search warrant for your property. As you can guess, Liv is not a happy woman right now."

"I'm glad you made it," Nate said.

"Me too, but it looks like I was a little late."

"I would say so," Nate said. Then he groaned. "Every muscle in my body aches."

"You'll recover soon enough, but it looks like you might have broken your nose when you went down. That'll take longer."

That's why his voice sounded unnatural, Nate realized. His nose was plugged with broken bone and cartilage and coagulated blood.

Joe said, "He zapped you with a Taser X2, which has two sets of probes."

"I'm aware of that. Are the probes out of me?"

"I removed them. He fired both sets into you. That's fifty thousand volts per shot. What did you do to provoke him?"

"I wouldn't go down on my knees. He shot me when my back was turned."

Joe whistled and shook his head. "That's not exactly procedure."

"No shit. Do you know what this is all about?"

Joe nodded. "A little, but the sheriff deliberately kept me in the dark. I guess he was afraid I'd tip you off."

"You did."

"And I'd do it again," Joe said. He watched as Deputy Steck emerged from Nate's house and walked across the yard to join his colleagues. Steck shook his head as if he were in the process of denying to himself he was there.

"So take these handcuffs off of me," Nate said to Joe.

"I can't, Nate. I already asked Kapelow and he said no."

"Why do you listen to him?" Nate asked.

"Unfortunately, he's in command of the scene."

"What are they doing over there in my mews?" Nate asked as he chinned toward his falcon enclosure.

Sheriff Kapelow directed Deputies Steck and Woods to search within the structure. They were looking under the eaves and peering between the floorboards of the shack. The hooded falcons inside were upset with the activity and several screeched.

Nate said, "If they hurt or release any of our birds, I'll have to kill them all. Of course, I'm already going to kill the sheriff. He's a dangerous idiot and he made Liv upset."

Joe said, "Nate, don't talk like that. You forget I'm law enforcement."

Nate ignored him. "So that means I'll have to kill the sheriff twice. After they bury him, I'll dig him up and do it again."

"Nate, please . . ."

"What are they looking for, anyway?" Nate asked.

"The long-distance rifle that was used to shoot at Judge Hewitt and Duane Patterson," Joe said. "Apparently someone called the sheriff's office and told them it was stashed away out here on your property."

Nate squinted in thought. "Sandburg, I'll bet," he said. "I could see that guy doing something like that. He likes to use law enforcement procedures to screw people over."

"I could see that," Joe agreed. "But I have to ask. You don't have any high-tech rifles, do you?"

"Don't need 'em," Nate said. "I've got my low-tech weapon and it does the job."

"Is that it?"

"Of course not," Nate said. "I've got a .17 HMR for varmints, a couple of .22s, a twelve-gauge over-under for pheasants and quail, a 6.8mm Ranch Rifle for deer and antelope, and my 7mm Magnum for elk hunting. And I just bought Liv a little .38 revolver to defend herself and the baby."

By Wyoming standards, Joe knew, it was a surprisingly small arsenal. Guns to locals were like hand tools. Each had a specific purpose. Except for the .454 Casull revolver, of course. That was for taking down people in the most definitive way possible.

"AM I BEING charged for something?" Nate asked Joe.

"Resisting arrest and interfering with an investigation," Joe said. "I heard that over the radio before I got here."

"That's bogus," Nate said. "But not attempted murder?"

"Not yet," Joe said with gravity. His phone chirped and he

checked an incoming text on his cell phone. After he read it, he told Nate, "Liv told Marybeth what happened and she's already flown into action. She's on the phone with Kink Beran."

"Who?"

"Ken 'Kink' Beran. He's a defense attorney out of Cheyenne. He's in the same law firm as Governor Rulon, but Beran specializes in criminal defense law. With the exception of Marcus Hand, he's the best in the state. He's agreed to represent you, so you're in good hands. Rulon might get involved as well, considering you two know each other."

"I hate lawyers," Nate said. "Nearly as much as I hate politicians."

"Everyone does until you need one," Joe said. "Man, my wife works fast. She doesn't want to see you cooling your heels in the county jail, I guess."

Nate and Joe had skirted around the fact that Marybeth had had maybe a little more than just a soft spot for Nate in the past. But they'd never discussed it.

"Oh good," Nate said, nodding over Joe's shoulder. "Here comes Barney Fife."

Sheriff Kapelow left his deputies and walked toward them across the gravel yard. As he got close, he reached back and once again gripped his sidearm.

"I don't know what he thinks I'll do to him like this," Nate groused.

"Sheriff," Joe said as he stood up and his knees popped, "I'm no lawyer myself, but I know you've either got to charge this man or let him go. I'd suggest cutting him loose."

Kapelow nodded at Joe and said, "Of course you would."

"Somebody fed you some bad information," Joe said to the sheriff. "Plus, I think you're looking at a situation where you used unnecessary force."

"I'm not worried about that," Kapelow said. He pointed at Nate on the ground. "This friend of yours has a long-standing animus toward authority and members of law enforcement in particular."

"Just the bad ones," Nate interjected.

Kapelow ignored him and continued. "He's had federal charges made against him, and there are rumors that he had something to do with the disappearance of a Twelve Sleep County sheriff who was here before me. He was also a member of a special ops sniper team, so he's a skilled assassin. When we find that rifle and he's charged with the attempted murder of a county judge and the county prosecutor, I don't really think the manner of his arrest will matter all that much. Do you?"

"W-well, when you put it like that . . ." Joe stammered.

Nate coughed up some blood and spit it to the side. He asked, "You know what really makes me mad about all this?"

Both Kapelow and Joe turned to hear him.

"I used to operate with my own set of rules before I came back on the grid," Nate said. "I put all that behind me and went legit. I started a business and a family. I kept my head down and I've operated within *your* rules."

He said it to both of them. Only Joe winced.

"And now look at me," he said. "I'm chained up on my own property and I'm accused of things I never did. My wife can see me like this through the window and it's humiliating. It makes me wonder if it made sense to come back."

Nate read Joe well enough to know that his friend wanted to

argue with him about what he'd just said. But he didn't want to do it in front of Sheriff Kapelow.

At that moment, Deputy Steck shouted from the mews.

"Boss! Come look at this."

"What is it?" Kapelow asked.

Nate watched as the deputy pulled a long parcel from beneath the floorboards of the shack. It was wrapped in a blanket.

When it was unfurled, Steck held up the heavy high-tech rifle with its massive scope. He opened the bolt and sniffed it. "It's been recently fired," he said.

"Well, what do you know?" Kapelow said with a grin. Then to Nate: "I don't know how you thought you'd get away with it."

Nate shook his head and said, "I've never seen that weapon in my life. Somebody planted it there."

"I'm calling Marybeth," Joe said while raising his phone to his ear. "I'll see how fast Kink Beran and Rulon can get here."

OVER TWO MILES AWAY, Orlando Panfile watched the activities at the Romanowski falconry compound with great interest through his spotting scope.

PART THREE

So full of artless jealousy is guilt,
It spills itself in fearing to be spilt.
—William Shakespeare, Hamlet

SEVENTEEN

Two hours later, Joe sat across the table from Marybeth in the Twelve Sleep County Library conference room with the doors closed and the blinds drawn. Marybeth's phone was on the table between them.

"How did you get this?" he asked her.

"Let's just say friends in the sheriff's department," she replied.

Marybeth opened a voice memo she'd received via email on her phone and turned the volume up.

An oddly distorted deep male voice said, "The guy you're looking for in the shooting of Sue Hewitt and Duane Patterson is named Nate Romanowski. He's a local and you can look him up. The rifle he used in both shootings is stashed on his property where he keeps his falcons."

There was a long pause and Joe could hear the caller struggling for breath. Then he continued.

"Don't bother trying to trace this call or identify me. Consider me just a helpful witness who wants to stay anonymous. I won't admit to making this call and I won't testify to how I know all of this. This guy has been operating in plain sight under your noses the whole time. He's a killer. If you don't believe me, just look him up. I want nothing to do with him. But once you've found the gun, you shouldn't need me anyway."

"Please play it again," Joe asked. He listened as carefully as he could.

"I don't recognize the voice at all," Joe said. "The guy sounds drunk or on something."

"I think neither," Marybeth said. "He's using some kind of voice-altering software. There are apps available and they're really easy to download to your phone."

"Man," Joe said, sitting back. "This whole thing went from zero to a hundred really fast."

"You don't think Nate had anything to do with it, do you?" Marybeth asked him.

"Nope."

But despite Joe's certainty, there was an intrusive kernel of doubt. Although he'd had a long friendship with Nate and they'd been in so many situations together, Nate had always been unpredictable and eccentric in his own way. Not only had Nate sat naked on branches observing wildlife, he'd also spent hours submerged in the river to "experience what it was like to be a fish." And there was no doubt Nate was capable of taking violent action when he felt it warranted. Nate was known for ripping the ears off of men he was angry with. His friend had a clearly defined sense of justice that had very little to do with the actual law. Nate hadn't ever hesitated to punish those he thought were guilty. But that was in the past, Joe thought.

Even then, when Nate was off the grid and operating at times like a rogue vigilante, he hadn't been sneaky or subtle about his actions. It wasn't his style to hide in the shadows and ambush someone. Nate wanted his target to know who had come after him and why.

And that was before Liv, Kestrel, and Yarak, Inc.

It was also before the long-range sniper rifle was discovered on Nate's property.

"So who do you think left that message?" Marybeth asked Joe. She had absolutely no doubt about Nate's innocence, which was no surprise.

"Nate suspects Jeremiah Sandburg," Joe said. "The ex-FBI guy who paid him a visit."

"Maybe," Marybeth said with a doubtful shrug. "I suspect someone local, though. The caller assumes the sheriff's department is familiar with Nate and where he lives. And he was right."

Joe nodded. He thought, *Good point.*

He said, "If we can find the caller, I think we'll find the real shooter. Does the sheriff's department have any way of tracing the call?"

"Yes, but it's no help," she said. "The call was placed from an untraceable burner phone using a local cell tower. No doubt the burner's been disposed of by now."

"That's interesting," Joe said. "It shows some real planning by whoever made the call.

"The other big question," he continued, "is when the rifle was planted. That's a tough one. Nate is usually at work during the day, but Liv has stayed close to home since the baby came. If Nate and Liv go somewhere together, their nanny is home with Kestrel. Whoever planted the rifle knew enough about all of their habits that he used a short window of time when all of them were gone or distracted to hide the weapon. Either that, or he managed to come on the property during the night without anyone hearing him. Since it's just been a couple of days since Sue got shot, he must have done it during the last forty-eight hours."

Marybeth nodded while Joe talked. She was obviously trying to find an angle or explanation.

"We need to talk to Liv and Nate and figure that out," Joe said.

She agreed.

Then she asked, "How was he doing when the sheriff put him in his truck?"

"Stoic," Joe said.

"What about Liv?"

"Liv is tough," Joe said. "Like you."

"I made the offer that she could bring Kestrel to our house and stay with us until this blows over," Marybeth said. "She says she's fine for now. She'd got Loren to help her with the baby and she wants to keep the business going. But she knows she can stay with us."

"That's good."

"Kink Beran had a court appearance this morning in Cheyenne and then he'll drive north and be up here by five tonight," Marybeth said.

"Will Rulon be with him?" Joe asked.

"I hope so," she said. "I really hope so."

BEFORE JOE HAD returned to town from Nate's residence, he'd had a chance to examine the rifle the deputies found before it was tagged to be used as evidence and examined by Gary Norwood. It was a Gunwerks Magnus 7mm long-range Magnum with a sophisticated Nightforce scope. The rifle cost well over ten thousand dollars and it was in very good shape.

He'd explained to Deputy Woods that long-range rifles weren't Nate's weapon of choice and that he had no doubt someone had planted the gun. Woods made sure Sheriff Kapelow didn't overhear him say he agreed with Joe, but it didn't look good for Nate.

It looked worse when Deputy Steck located a box of long-range 147-grain cartridges in a plastic bag that had been hidden under falcon excrement in the mews. There were two rounds missing from the box.

The range finder Nate had brought along when he and Joe climbed the hill was found in his panel van and tagged as well.

Before Nate was taken away, Joe had approached Sheriff Kapelow and said, "It's my understanding that it takes two men to pull off a shot like the one that hit Sue Hewitt. You'd need a spotter *and* a shooter."

Kapelow looked over with an annoyed expression. "What's your point?"

"So who is the spotter?" Joe asked.

"Maybe your friend will tell us."

Joe scoffed.

The sheriff said, "Maybe one of his outlaw falcon buddies showed up. Those people are a tight bunch from what I understand. And they all have the same attitude toward law enforcement."

"Not all of them," Joe said. But having met several of Nate's circle of falconers, he had to partially agree with Kapelow.

"How do you know so much about long-distance shooting?" the sheriff asked Joe with barely disguised suspicion.

"I'm a game warden, remember?"

"Were you in the military?"

"No," Joe said. It was something he'd always felt guilty about. Since Kapelow *had* served, it was a cudgel he was quick to use.

"Where did you learn about sniper teams?"

"Nate," Joe confessed.

"Well, isn't that interesting?" the sheriff asked.

"That was in the process of determining where the shooter set up," Joe explained. "Do you really think Nate would lead me to the location if he had anything to do with it?"

Kapelow looked away from Joe with a smug look on his face. His mind was made up.

"Sheriff," Joe said. "If you'll recall, you dismissed the possibility of a long-range shot."

Kapelow turned away as if he hadn't heard the question.

Joe was still steaming about the exchange when he'd arrived at the library.

MARYBETH SLIPPED HER PHONE into her purse and asked, "Were you invited to the press conference?"

"What?" Joe asked.

He learned from her that Sheriff Kapelow had called a press conference to begin in fifteen minutes at the county building.

"Should we go?" Joe asked her.

"Of course," she said.

———

THE TWELVE SLEEP County Building was only two blocks away from the library, so they walked there. The day had warmed up considerably and the mountains towered clear and blue in three directions. It was a perfect fall day, Joe thought. Except for the reason they were together.

"Has Kapelow ever had a press conference before?" Marybeth asked. Her heels clicked on the sidewalk.

"Not since he's been elected," Joe said. "This is probably a big day for him."

"Obviously," she said with a roll of her eyes.

"HERE FOR THE SHERIFF'S shindig?" Stovepipe asked them as he lumbered to his feet from behind the metal detector.

"Yup," Joe said as he once again dumped all of his electronics and hardware into a tub.

"Don't bother," Stovepipe whispered. "It's busted again."

Joe nodded and retrieved his items.

"I have pepper spray in my purse," Marybeth confessed to Stovepipe.

"Keep it in there," he said. "Just don't spray nobody."

THE BRIEFING ROOM in the sheriff's department had been hastily rearranged for the event, Joe noted. A podium used by the town council had been wheeled to the front of the room and a microphone was set up. Empty folding chairs flanked the podium and more had been set up for reporters and interested citizens. The table that was usually in the center of the room had been shoved to the far wall to accommodate the guests.

Joe and Marybeth took seats in the back row. It was a very small crowd. He recognized reporters from the Casper *Star-Tribune*, K-TWO radio, the Billings *Gazette*, and a twentysomething from the local Saddlestring *Roundup*. A skeletal-looking man with long wispy hair set up his digital recorder on the podium. He wore a name badge identifying himself as representing a statewide web news service Joe had never heard of.

The *Roundup* reporter, whom Marybeth knew from when she used to intern at the library, saw them sitting in the back and approached them.

"Hello, Mrs. Pickett," the former intern said.

"Alyssa, this is my husband, Joe. Joe, Alyssa. She's been working at the *Roundup* for what, nine months?"

"A year," Alyssa said. She was redhaired and Sheridan's age. Alyssa had a camera with a long lens looped around her neck and she grasped an open reporter's notebook.

"Did you see what happened outside?" Alyssa asked Marybeth.

"No, we just got here."

"Look," Alyssa said, and she turned the camera around so both Joe and Marybeth could see the digital screen. Alyssa scrolled through a series of photos: Nate arriving in the sheriff's SUV, Nate climbing out of the vehicle with his hands cuffed and with a contemptuous expression on his face, Nate walking up the courthouse steps flanked by Deputies Steck and Woods with Sheriff Kapelow leading the way, Nate passing close by Alyssa and her camera with his chin held high.

"It's a perp walk," Alyssa said. "That's what a couple of the reporters called it. It's my first, and I got some really good pictures, don't you think?"

Joe could imagine them on the front page of the paper.

"The sheriff didn't have to do that," he said to Marybeth.

"Poor Liv," she replied.

AT 10:00 A.M. SHARP, the back door to the room opened and Sheriff Kapelow blew through it with a stern look on his face. Joe noted Kapelow had changed into an unrumpled uniform and he wore a flawless silverbelly cowboy hat with the brim folded so sharply it looked like it could draw blood. He looked serious and professional, Joe thought.

Behind him, Judge Hewitt, Duane Patterson, and Deputies Woods and Steck came out. The judge and the prosecutor flanked Kapelow on one side and the deputies on the other. No doubt, Joe thought, Kapelow had instructed them where to stand when they entered the room for maximum photographic impact. He was surprised the judge had agreed to the choreography.

"Greetings, ladies and gentlemen of the press," Kapelow read from a statement he'd placed on the podium. "I'm here to announce a significant development in our investigation regarding the attempted murders of two of our county law enforcement officials, namely Judge Hewitt and prosecutor Duane Patterson. I'd ask that you hold your questions until the end of the briefing."

Joe looked up at the assemblage and was confused by what he saw. Judge Hewitt looked red-eyed and hollowed out, and he bent over slightly at the waist as if recovering from a gut punch. He had none of the swagger Joe was used to. Patterson looked even worse. The county prosecutor averted his eyes from the press when he wasn't clamping them tightly, as if to stave off a breakdown. He swayed slightly as he stood, as if he were a reed in the wind.

"What's *wrong* with them?" Marybeth whispered to Joe.

He shook his head. "I don't know."

"This morning," Kapelow continued, "a suspect was apprehended here in Twelve Sleep County by my team and a very specific rifle was found on the suspect's property. The weapon is being tested to confirm that it was used in the shootings and it will be later sent to the state crime lab in Cheyenne to verify our findings.

"The suspect is an on-and-off resident of the county who has long been a person of interest in this and other crimes," Kapelow said.

"Bullshit," Marybeth hissed.

"I'm not at liberty at this time to provide a name for the suspect until he's been formally charged," Kapelow said. "You'll know when that happens."

Kapelow looked up from his statement and turned to his deputies. "At this time, I'd like to publicly thank the dedicated members of my department for their hard work and long hours . . ."

He went on for a while and Joe tuned out. Kapelow was performing a dance that irritated Joe whenever it took place: the over-the-top press conference where the actual case took a backseat to self-congratulatory speeches by the law enforcement officials who were present. After several minutes of thanking his deputies and staff and "support from the police department," Kapelow looked up from his notes and directly at Joe.

He said, "We have a suspect in custody because we did excellent by-the-book police work. It's unfortunate that our efforts were hampered by others who questioned our every move and interfered with our investigation."

With that, several of the reporters turned in their seats and looked over their shoulders at Joe, who'd been singled out. He felt his face get hot.

"At this point in the proceedings," Kapelow said, "I'd like to turn the briefing over to Dr. Arthur from the hospital. He's present to announce another significant development in the case."

It took Joe a moment to recover from the sheriff's accusations so he didn't get the gist of the doctor's first words. All he knew was that Kapelow had stepped aside the podium and his place had been taken by Arthur.

The importance of Dr. Arthur's message didn't hit home until Joe felt Marybeth's hand grip his knee.

". . . about an hour ago," Arthur continued, "Sue Hewitt succumbed to her injuries . . . We did all we could."

"My God," Marybeth whispered to Joe. She looked at him with tear-filled eyes. "Poor Sue . . ."

Joe was confused. He glanced to Dr. Arthur's side. Judge Hewitt was covering his face with his hands. Apparently, he'd been trying to hold himself together, but Arthur's announcement made it all very real to him. Duane Patterson had turned so his back was to the room. His shoulders shook as he cried silently to himself.

That explained their demeanor, Joe thought. The news overtook him and the implications of it were clear.

"If you haven't figured it out yet," Sheriff Kapelow said to the room, after gently shouldering the doctor from the podium, "instead of attempted murder, our suspect will now be charged with murder in the first degree of Sue Hewitt."

"I'm heartsick," Marybeth said to Joe. "I thought she was recovering."

"I thought she was, too," Joe said. He recalled Arthur's talk of the bullet splintering inside and how unusual that was. He wondered if the judge was lamenting his decision to keep her close and not have her airlifted to Billings or Denver. And he wondered why Patterson seemed to be so overcome by the sudden turn of events.

Then something hit him. Two revelations at once.

The first was that he suddenly knew what motivated Sheriff Kapelow, and that answer put everything that had happened into perspective.

The second was something Stovepipe had said.

EIGHTEEN

It was an hour after the press conference had taken place in town and Candy Croswell was flustered.

She'd read the sheriff's announcement on Facebook and at the time it had filled her with immense relief. They had a suspect in custody. The knot in her stomach about Tom was finally starting to unclench. It wasn't until that moment when she read about the man in custody that she acknowledged her growing suspicions about Tom had likely been wrong. It was a huge burden off her shoulders. She rewarded herself with a third glass of wine.

But her joy and relief were short-lived when the annoying woman driving a pearl-colored Range Rover showed up and demanded to speak to Tom. Candy now regretted opening the door and letting the woman into the house.

"Call him," the annoying older woman demanded of Candy. "Tell him Missy Hand is here to see him with a five thousand dollar check, as agreed. We have business."

"Missy Hand?" Candy asked. She'd never heard the name before.

"He knows who I am," Missy said with a sniff.

"*I* don't," Candy said.

Missy responded with a wave of her hand. "That doesn't really matter, does it? I'm not here to see you. He's expecting me."

"He is? He didn't say anything to me about it."

"Imagine that," Missy said with a roll of her eyes.

Missy Hand was direct, determined, and dismissive. She knew what she wanted—whatever it was—and she was there to get it, Candy thought.

Through the peephole in the door, Missy had looked small and frail but well put together. Her clothes were fashionable and they fit perfectly, so she obviously wasn't a transient or door-to-door salesperson. The Range Rover had Wyoming plates, but it was from a different county—number twenty-two. Candy was not yet familiar with the confusing numerical designations of various Wyoming counties. She assumed the woman was lost and that she needed directions somewhere.

But what did she want?

Candy asked her.

"Are you his wife or something?" Missy asked.

"No."

"Then it doesn't concern you. He never even mentioned you when I talked with him and you have no standing as far as I'm concerned. Anyone can shack up, believe me."

Candy was speechless.

"I need to talk to him now," Missy said. "I can't wait around all day. Call him. I'm sure you can do that without messing up your nails. Call him and tell him I'm here."

Without waiting for an invitation, Missy walked across the living room and poured the last of Candy's wine into a glass. Missy lifted the glass and looked at it from below as if confirming from another angle that it was less than barely one-quarter full.

"You could have saved some for me," she said.

"I don't even know you," Candy replied. She wanted to sound angrier, but the woman unnerved her. Missy acted as if she belonged there and Candy was the interloper.

"You do have a phone, don't you?" Missy asked her.

"Look, lady . . ."

"Call me Mrs. Hand."

"Look, please, Mrs. Hand," Candy pleaded, "he'll be home later tonight. Leave me your number and I'll ask him to get in touch with you and you can figure it out from there."

Missy simply shook her head no. "Where do you keep your wine?" she asked.

Candy didn't reply, but she'd inadvertently cast a glance toward Tom's under-the-counter wine storage. Missy caught it and opened the glass door. She chose a very expensive 2004 Joseph Phelps Insignia Cabernet that Candy knew Tom had been saving for a special occasion.

"There are other bottles to choose from," Candy said.

"There are," Missy said as she nudged the door closed with her knee. "But I choose this one."

She was the type of woman, Candy thought, who did what she wanted and expected others to comply. It was incongruous how tiny she was physically. A stiff wind might blow her over. Candy was a head taller and fit. Candy knew that if it came down to it, she could throw Missy out the front door without much of a problem. Missy was an example of an outdated kind of beauty that was all about sublime and delicate slimness. The thought of putting her hands on the woman, though, was simply inconceivable.

Missy expertly removed the cork from the cabernet using the German precision tool Candy often struggled with. Then Missy tossed the last of the wine she'd poured earlier into the sink as if it were bilge water. After rinsing her glass clean, Missy poured a full glass of the cabernet and tasted it. She closed her eyes as she did so and smiled.

"It's good."

"It was a special bottle."

"And this," Missy said, while raising her glass toward Candy, "is a special occasion."

"What special occasion?"

"I'm here to save my husband's life."

"What?"

"My," Missy said, "you're cute. But you're dim, aren't you?"

"Please," Candy said, "tell me what you want with him."

"Call your boyfriend," Missy said. "Tell him I want to talk with him."

"And if I don't?" Candy asked.

"You'll wish you did," Missy said with pursed lips, as if the very thought of the potential consequences was distasteful even to her.

TOM WAS OUT OF BREATH when he answered his cell phone. He was also clearly angry.

"How many times have I told you not to call me at work?" he asked.

"I know, I know. I'm sorry," Candy said. "But there's a situation here at the house. This older woman showed up here and she absolutely demands to talk with you."

Tom said, "Who is she?"

Candy turned away from Missy, who was listening carefully from her perch at the breakfast bar. She lowered her voice and said, "She says her name is Missy Hand and that you're expecting her."

"Oh."

"She says she absolutely won't go away until she talks to you. She says the two of you have business of some kind."

He hesitated. She imagined him stopping in mid-stride and thinking it over. Tom was always in a hurry, rushing from place to place. That he didn't immediately deny knowing Missy or why she was there surprised Candy.

Finally, Tom said, "I completely forgot she was coming over today. There has been so much going on . . ."

"You knew she was going to show up here?" Candy asked, hurt. "And you didn't tell me?"

"I didn't know where we'd meet," Tom said. "But never mind that. I didn't expect her to just show up at my house."

My house, Tom had said. Not *our* house. Not even *the* house.

"Give me the phone," Missy said to Candy. She'd slipped off her stool and was right behind her.

"Tell her I'll call her tonight," Tom said.

"I tried. She says she has to talk with you and she's not leaving until she does."

"I'm probably not leaving even then," Missy said with a light laugh. "I don't know where you got *that*."

"Tom, what is this all about?" Candy asked. She was exasperated. "Why does this woman just show up here like this?"

Tom didn't reply.

In Candy's ear, Missy said, "This woman? *This woman?* I'd be offended if I didn't think you were just a run-of-the-mill yoga floozy."

That was more than Candy could take. She was now just as angry with Tom as she was with Missy. They'd put her in the middle of . . . something.

"Here," Candy said, thrusting the phone to Missy.

When Missy took it, Candy stormed across the room and stood behind the breakfast bar as if guarding it.

She listened as Missy said, "Did you forget about me? I'm not really accustomed to being forgotten."

Candy could hear Tom stammering something. He was obviously apologizing. As he did, Missy half listened and topped off her glass. Then she opened her small purse with one hand and drew out a dainty card. It looked like the kind of stationery wealthy old people sent thank-you notes on, Candy thought.

Missy said to Tom, "Do I need to go over the list with you again or do you have it on you?"

When Tom apparently asked her to remind him, Missy said, "Forgive me if I mispronounce some of the names. You people exist in a world of your own with your own special language. But here we go: oxaliplatin, leucovorin, irinotecan, and 5-fluorouracil. Do you need me to repeat that?"

Candy had no idea what she was talking about. She'd never heard any of the terms used before.

After a long pause, Missy said, "And you're sure you have them all?"

When Tom replied, Missy nodded her head and said, "Good.

That's wonderful. I'll wait for you here and, yes, I've got your fee. You said cash and that's what I brought. Money is really the last thing I'm worried about right now."

Then, after listening for thirty seconds, Missy turned to Candy and said, "He wants to talk to you."

CANDY WAS TREMBLING with anger when she raised the phone to her mouth.

"*What?*"

"I'll explain all this later," he said. "Don't get all worked up. Just calm down."

"I'm calm," she said through clenched teeth.

"You don't look calm to me," Missy said from across the room.

Candy turned away from her again. She said, "Tom, I don't know what's going on and I'm stuck right in the middle. You're obviously keeping secrets from me. First there's a rifle case in your truck, then . . ." She almost mentioned the cell phone, but she caught herself. "This strange woman just shows up and I'm supposed to entertain her. What other things aren't you telling me?"

He didn't respond.

She said, "My imagination kind of ran away from me when I saw that. I mean, there's these shootings in the area, you know? I was starting to think . . ."

"Think what?" The question was hostile and she immediately backed down.

"Well, until that press conference today, I was starting to wonder, you know . . ."

"It's not like that," he said. "Not at all. Look, I'll explain every-thing after she leaves tonight. Trust me on this."

"Trust you?" Candy said, her voice rising. She disconnected the call and tossed the phone aside. She'd never hung up on him before.

Candy felt a sense of déjà vu. This was Brent's Corvette and Nicolas's bear hunting trip all over again. The end was in sight.

From behind her, Missy said, "If you can't trust your doctor, who can you trust?"

CANDY ASKED MISSY, "So those names you read over the phone—they're drugs, aren't they?"

Missy took a sip. "Good guess."

"So Tom's your drug dealer?"

Missy chuckled with a deep-throated laugh that was disarming. "Drug dealer? I never thought I'd have a drug dealer. But it isn't like that. My husband—I'm old-fashioned that way—is very sick with pancreatic cancer. He's likely to die from it. All the traditional treatments the doctors over in Jackson have put him on aren't working. He's currently on gemcitabine."

"I don't know anything about pancreatic cancer," Candy said, trying not to let the *I'm old-fashioned that way* dig bother her.

Missy poured herself another glass of the Cab she'd opened and offered some to Candy. Candy's first inclination was to demur—it was Tom's special wine, after all—then she said, "Fuck it," and held out her glass.

Missy filled it and said, "Pancreatic cancer is sinister. Gemcitabine is a drug that's supposed to stop the spread of cancer after the tumor is gone, and that's what Marcus is taking now. That's the go-to drug and it's what the doctors know about. Unfortunately, the survival rate with it is thirty percent. *Thirty percent.* I won't stand for it.

"It's not the only treatment, however," Missy said. "I found out about an experimental treatment that's being done in Europe that raises the survival rate to forty-two percent. It hasn't been approved by our Food and Drug Administration to be administered here yet. It may be in a few years, but I can't wait."

Candy was puzzled. She said, "Tom is going to help you with an experimental treatment?"

"I wish," Missy said. "But he refused. The furthest he'd go is to provide the four drugs for a kind of chemotherapy cocktail. Those were the drugs I ordered from him."

"I had no idea," Candy said. "I don't know whether to say good for Tom, or Tom is a drug dealer."

"Both, actually," Missy said. "I got his name from a couple of people in the know in my social circle in Jackson."

Candy absorbed the information. "Are you telling me Tom sells drugs to your friends?"

"He does," Missy said. "And to be honest, most of them are prescription opioids. You'd be surprised how many upstanding citizens are addicted. People you'd never suspect. But they all love your Tom!"

Candy thought about the stack of checks she'd found on Tom's desk. She sat down on the couch. Another secret exposed.

"Don't worry," Missy said, misreading her reaction. "I won't try to administer the chemo cocktail myself. If you get the dosages wrong, it's toxic. Lucky for me, I met a doctor in France who is willing to come here and assist. He's smitten with me, I'm afraid."

Candy looked up at Missy and didn't know how to respond.

"Let's make a nice dinner together and wait for Tom to get back," Missy said. "I assume you have some food around here."

Candy shrugged. She watched as Missy rummaged through the refrigerator and pantry.

"I take it you don't cook," Missy said.

"Not well, although I used to cook for my husband. Both husbands, actually."

Missy paused and her assessment of Candy was clinical.

"So you've been married?" she asked.

"Twice."

"Did they leave you or did you leave them?"

"I left."

"I see," Missy said with approval. "At least you got that part right. But it's easy for me to see that you've got trouble brewing with Tom."

Candy nodded.

"Come on over here," Missy said while slicing through the plastic on a package of angel hair pasta. "We'll make a nice dinner together and drink more good wine and wait for Tom to get back with my package."

"Make dinner together?" Candy asked.

"Sure. Since we're both stuck here for a while, let's make the best of it," Missy said. Then: "I know about men like Tom. I know about *men*. They're amazingly simple creatures and I fear you think they're more complicated than they are. I could tell that when you asked him about his secrets, as if it were his duty to tell them to you."

"You don't understand," Candy said.

"Oh, I understand," Missy said, gesturing around the house with the point of her knife. "This is a wonderful house. Tom has built a lucrative practice with his legitimate work and his special job on the side taking care of people like me. And you're just shuffling around here hoping he'll take pity on you and include you in all that he has. This is what *you* don't understand."

Candy drained her wine. Her head was fuzzy. "What do you mean?" she asked.

"Come on over," Missy said. "Maybe you'll learn something. God knows my daughter never did."

NINETEEN

JOE AND MARYBETH DID SOMETHING THEY RARELY DID: they sat together in a bar, namely the Stockman's, with its knotty-pine interior, black-and-white rodeo photos, and private high-backed booths. They were there for two reasons. The first was that it was the place defense attorney Kink Beran had said he'd meet them after his initial consultation with his new client, Nate Romanowski. The second was that with all of their daughters out of the house, it was something they could do again.

Joe ordered a draft beer and Marybeth a glass of red wine.

Joe had spent the afternoon after the press conference in the field, checking hunters for valid licenses and habitat stamps. It had been a good day for big mule deer bucks, and he inspected the camps of several groups of out-of-state hunters to make sure the carcasses were properly hung and cooled. He'd been offered beers and whiskey at a couple of the camps—hunters generally wanted to be on the good side of local game wardens—but he'd declined, as he always did. Joe did allow Daisy to gobble up some dog treats a Michigan hunter offered her, though.

He'd performed his duties by rote because he was distracted the entire time by the events of the morning. Joe didn't like checking hunters and camps while distracted because he wanted to observe them in minute detail and pay close attention to what hunters did and said to him. If they were a little too accommodating, it might mean they were hiding something. If the hunters were surly, it might mean there was trouble in the camp that might result in later violence or they had an animus toward law enforcement in general.

After visiting the too-accommodating camps, Joe often left but parked somewhere where he could remain in visual range. On a few occasions, he'd observed the friendly sportsmen walk from their camp to where they had poached game animals hidden away in the trees. Or, in one instance, the summoning of a prostitute they'd picked up in Denver along the way.

With the surly camps, Joe noted the license plates on the vehicles and called them in to dispatch. This procedure sometimes revealed men who had outstanding warrants or were wanted in different states for nongame crimes.

But he'd detected neither circumstance on his afternoon patrol. The hunters he'd met were friendly but not too friendly, and they all seemed to be serious and ethical sportsmen.

Joe was grateful for that because he could barely concentrate on what he was doing.

Meanwhile, Marybeth had returned to work after the press conference to complete the last of her staff evaluations. She kept in communication with Liv and the defense attorney, and monitored social media to find out that Sheriff Brendan Kapelow and his statement to the press was trending everywhere.

JOE SAID TO Marybeth, "I figured out something today about our new sheriff."

Marybeth raised her eyebrows to urge him on.

"He's very ambitious," Joe said. "He's using Nate's arrest to raise his profile in the state. I hadn't seen that in him before and I hadn't seen it coming. I knew there was something behind his odd demeanor and his need to control everything around him, but now I think I get it. Kapelow is using the Twelve Sleep County Sheriff's office as a stepping-stone to bigger and better things."

"That's a very interesting observation," Marybeth said.

"Think about it and tell me if you think I'm off base," Joe said. "But I noticed how Kapelow orchestrated that perp walk of Nate and how he organized the press conference in record time. Those aren't things that just come naturally to a new sheriff. That leads me to believe he's been preparing for both of those events for quite a while and he was finally able to pull the trigger. None of this is about finding Sue's killer—or about Nate. It's about finally having a case sexy enough to get attention. It's all about being seen as a crusading sheriff in the media."

Joe continued. "It was obvious he didn't know what he was doing when he was leading the investigation. I thought for a while maybe he had a unique approach to law enforcement or something. But now I see he was just marking time looking busy until something hit him right in the face. In this case, it was an anonymous tip he could jump on. Nate's just collateral damage."

"And the real killer is still out there somewhere," Marybeth said.

"Correct. I think Kapelow probably measured the conference room to figure out where the folding chairs should be, and he's practiced walking into that room like he owned the place.

"No," Joe said, "this isn't about solving the crime. This is about higher office. I know this sounds cynical, but Kapelow is more a politician than a cop."

She thought it over and nodded. "Military vet, tough-as-nails, law-and-order sheriff. He's got it all if you don't dig into it too much. That's a pretty fine résumé."

Joe nodded. "He's probably looking at the political landscape just like he measured that conference room. He might be going for state senator, head of DCI, or even governor someday."

"What happens when it all blows up in his face?" Marybeth asked. "Assuming, of course, that Nate is cleared."

Joe shrugged. He said, "I've worked with enough politicians over the years to know that some of them survive no matter what, especially if they don't hold themselves accountable for anything and they have no shame."

"It sounds like you're talking about Governor Allen," she said.

"He's one of 'em," Joe said. "But now we've got one closer to home. And I'm guessing that since his name and face are going to be broadcast all over the state, he won't be trying particularly hard to find out if there's really another shooter. I think his mind is closed to that possibility."

"So it's up to us," Marybeth said.

"It might be."

"We've done it before," she said, lifting her glass for a toast. Joe clinked his mug against it.

"So where do we start?" she asked.

"That's the second thing that came to me today at the end of that press conference," Joe said. He recounted Judge Hewitt's monologue to him at Sue's bedside, how the judge had committed to spending more time with his wife if she survived. That he was always either working or gone on exotic hunting or fishing trips.

"I believe he was sincere," Joe said. "I can't imagine how much pain he's in right now."

Marybeth wiped a tear away. The story had touched her.

"But here's the thing," Joe said. "The day after her shooting, I went to the courthouse for the meeting with the other cops in Judge Hewitt's office. Stovepipe was shocked by what had happened to her. He called her 'Miz Hewitt.' Stovepipe said Sue had been coming to the courthouse regularly the last few months and bringing him treats when she did. He said he really liked her."

Marybeth frowned. "That doesn't really square with what the judge told you. Do you think he was misleading you about how they'd drifted apart?"

Joe shook his head. "No, I think he was telling the truth."

"Then why was Sue visiting him so often at the courthouse?" Marybeth asked. "Why didn't she just call if she needed to talk to him?"

"That's what I'm wondering," Joe said. "But who says she was there to see the judge?"

"*What?*" Marybeth asked. Then she realized what Joe was driving at. She stood up and surveyed the bar to make sure there were no customers in adjoining booths who could overhear them. Satisfied, she sat back down and leaned across the table toward Joe.

She spoke in a low voice. "Are you suggesting she was seeing someone else in the building?"

"I'm just speculating," he said.

"Who could it be and could that person be connected to what happened?"

"I don't know," he said. "It could be someone in the sheriff's office, or anyone. A lot of lawyers come through those doors. And it might even be someone in the jail where Nate is now."

Joe could see her mind working. She said, "I can see a scenario where after years of neglect Sue fell for someone who actually paid attention to her. She was an attractive and interesting woman, after all. What if she had something going on right under her husband's nose?"

"That's what I'm wondering."

Marybeth quickly jumped ahead. "Then we've got a motive that hasn't been considered in this case. And maybe we've been looking at what happened all wrong. Is Sue the type of woman who would plot with her lover to get rid of her husband?"

"Not likely," Joe said. "Not from what I've heard about her."

"Love makes some women do crazy things," Marybeth said. "The Wyoming Women's Center is full of them."

"True," Joe said. In his visits there, nearly all of the women were incarcerated because of drugs or relationships gone wrong, or both. "But if it was that kind of plot, would Sue want to be standing right behind her husband when he got shot? I don't see it."

"You're right," Marybeth said. "But what if she'd broken up with her lover and he wanted revenge? Or he wanted Judge Hewitt out of the picture so he could take another run at her? Or what if *Sue was the target all along*?"

Joe thought about it and shook his head. "I don't see how that works. She would never have been hit if the judge hadn't ducked at exactly the right second. There's no shooter alive who could have anticipated that happening. The bullet was literally already in the air when Judge Hewitt leaned away."

"I'm sure you're right," Marybeth said. "But now you've got me thinking of everything that happened in a different way."

"Me too," Joe said.

"So how do we find out who she was meeting at the county building?" she asked. "It doesn't *have* to be for romantic reasons, I guess."

Joe explained that, in addition to a closed-circuit camera mounted above Stovepipe's metal detector, every person entering and exiting the building had to register their name and reason for being there in a logbook. Stovepipe kept his logs in three-ring binders.

"I've signed in dozens of times," Joe said.

"But we know she went there," Marybeth said. "How does knowing the exact days help us?"

"That's what I've been thinking about all afternoon, and this is where you come in," Joe said. "You're a county employee. You have access to the county-wide Google calendar for everybody and everything, right?"

"Right."

"So if we check Sue's visits against the calendar for, what, the last six months? Maybe you can find a pattern to what was going on and who was in the building at the times she showed up. Maybe something will jump out at you."

She sat back and a slow grin took over her face. "I see what you're thinking," she said. "So how do we get the logbooks?"

"I'll figure that out," Joe said.

She shook her head and whistled. "This is getting interesting," she said. "Do you think it'll help Nate?"

"Maybe," Joe said. "I hope so. But what I really hope is that it helps us get closer to the shooter. I know if we learn something, the sheriff won't even listen, but I'll go over his head to Duane or even the judge if we've got a new suspect."

"The judge may not want to hear who his wife was visiting," Marybeth warned.

"You're right," Joe said. "I'll loop Duane in, though. But not until we've got something solid."

"Oh," Marybeth said, raising a finger in the air. "I did some research and found out where Sue got her fortune before Judge Hewitt married her."

"Where?"

"Her grandfather founded Castle Arms in Connecticut. He was a gunmaker. He later sold the company to Remington and now they make long-range rifles."

"Interesting."

"And ironic if the rifle that eventually killed her was a Remington," Marybeth said. "And another thing: I figured out the connection between the judge and Governor Allen."

"Let me guess . . ."

"The judge was a major contributor to Allen's campaign," she said. "There's also some speculation that our judge has been advising the gov through many of his legal issues."

"Ah," Joe said.

The waitress appeared and she asked if they wanted a second drink.

"I don't," Joe said. "I've got things to do."

251

Marybeth ordered a club soda. She said she'd wait until Kink Beran arrived.

WHEN JOE ENTERED the lobby of the courthouse, Stovepipe was kicked back in his chair with his cowboy boots up on his desk and his hat brim pulled down over his eyes. His mouth was agape and he was napping. It was five minutes before six by the ancient clock on the wall. The public parts of the county building were locked up at six, although the sheriff's department had a 24/7 entrance in the back of the building.

Joe's boots clopped along the stone floor, but apparently not loud enough to wake Stovepipe.

"Hey, buddy," Joe said gently as he took in the security camera mounted over the doorway that led to the courtroom.

Stovepipe awoke with a start and he made an "*Unnngh*" sound. The old rodeo cowboy swung his feet down and peered at Joe though sleepy eyes.

"Didn't hear you come in," he said. "Nobody ever comes in this late."

"Sorry," Joe said.

"Did you hear about Sue?"

"I did."

"Bless her heart," Stovepipe said sadly. "I thought she was going to make it."

"We all did."

"My heart hurts for her," Stovepipe said.

Joe nodded in agreement.

Stovepipe reached over and hit a button that activated the metal detector. "Coming through?" he asked.

"Nope," Joe said. "I was just wondering about the camera up there. Do you know how long they keep the digital files of who comes and goes through the lobby?"

Stovepipe cocked his head, puzzled. "Why do you want to know that?"

"It's for an ongoing investigation," Joe said. "It might not mean anything at all."

"Well, I just don't know what to tell you," Stovepipe said. "Manning this security checkpoint is about as much modern technology as I can absorb."

"Even though it doesn't work?"

"Shhhhh," Stovepipe said, raising a finger to his lips. "Somebody will hear you."

"About the files," Joe said.

"Right. Well, I can go back and ask. I think Norm the IT guy would know that answer. But, you know, some of these county guys start leaking out of the building early."

"Would you mind finding out if he's still in?"

Stovepipe glanced at the wall clock. "Sure, I'll check. Otherwise you'll need to come back tomorrow. Or I guess I can call him at home."

"Thank you," Joe said.

He felt guilty for making the man get up and walk into the back of the building in search of Norm. Stovepipe had a bad hip and knee from an old bull-riding injury. His progress to the administration section in the back was painfully slow.

When he was gone, Joe stepped behind the metal detector into Stovepipe's area where the current logbook of visitors was in plain view near Stovepipe's chair. Each page was lined and included the name, time of entry, time of exit, and purpose of visit for everyone who came through the lobby.

Joe didn't think he had time to review the pages in the three-ring binder. Instead, he photographed the top sheet with his cell phone and turned the page back and shot the next one. He repeated it until he'd covered eight months of records. Joe was grateful the traffic in the courthouse was sparse enough that he could document that much time and that there had been no major trials with lots of people coming and going. He noted Sue Hewitt's name several times as he raced through the pages, but he knew he'd likely missed other times she'd signed in.

When he heard Stovepipe's voice and another coming toward the lobby in the hallway, he flipped all the log sheets back to the current one and returned to where he'd been standing on the other side of Stovepipe's alcove. Stovepipe appeared with Norm, who was a heavy guy wearing a short-sleeve shirt and a lanyard that extended to his belt buckle.

"Forty-eight hours," the old cowboy said as he shuffled back to his desk. "Norm says the files are kept for forty-eight hours and then deleted or something. Some kind of technical jargon."

"I keep asking to update the system so we have more storage capacity on it," Norm said. "Nobody pays any attention to me."

"Forty-eight hours of memory is not very long," Joe lamented.

"Talk to the county commissioners," Norm said. Then he glanced at his wristwatch to suggest that it was time for him to go home for the night.

Stovepipe shrugged. He had no opinion on the matter.

"Is there something in particular you're looking for?" Stovepipe asked after Norm had retreated to the bowels of the building.

"Whatever it was, it happened more than forty-eight hours ago," Joe said.

"Sorry," Stovepipe said as he gathered up his jacket and lunch box. "I guess it's close enough for government work."

"Isn't that always the case," Joe said.

"Come on," Stovepipe said, "I'll walk you out. They're locking all the doors. We don't want to get trapped in this hellhole for the night."

"Is Duane Patterson in his office, by any chance?" Joe asked.

"He's always in his office," Stovepipe said.

"I need to see him. Don't worry, I'll go out through the back."

"Suit yourself," the old man said. "And have a great night."

"You too."

"Too damned bad about Sue," Stovepipe said as he pushed through the front doors.

JOE BYPASSED the metal detector after Stovepipe was gone and entered the hallway that led to the courtroom. He paused and forwarded the series of photos he'd taken to Marybeth's email account.

LIGHT SPILLED on the floor from the county attorney's office when Joe turned the corner. The door was open and Joe peered inside without entering. The receptionist's desk was empty, but behind it he could see Patterson sitting motionless at his desk behind an interior window. The county attorney could be seen in side profile. He was staring at the wall with his hands resting on his desktop.

Joe paused. It was probably not the best time to bother him. Patterson looked to be deep in thought or in some kind of coma.

That's when Patterson turned his head and caught Joe peeking in. The county attorney looked lost and forlorn. Pitiful, even.

"Do you have a minute?" Joe asked, knowing his words probably couldn't be heard through the glass.

Patterson motioned weakly for him to enter and then dropped his hand back to the desk.

"How are you doing?" Joe asked as he sat down across from Patterson.

"You know, Joe," Patterson sighed, "it's the shits."

"You're taking things hard," Joe said.

Patterson leaned back in his chair. "I deal with criminals and victims all day long. I think I do a pretty good job. But that's at a distance, you know? I don't really know these people. They're *cases*. So when something happens this close to home, when it happens to people you actually know, it's different. Does that make sense?"

Joe nodded that it did and said, "Not to mention that somebody took a shot at you as well."

"That, too," Patterson said, almost as an afterthought. Joe found that an unusual response. Barely avoiding a bullet in the face would deeply affect most people, Joe thought. Including himself.

"Maybe you ought to go home," Joe said. "It's been a rough day."

"Why?" Patterson asked.

Unlike Joe, Patterson didn't have anyone to go home to. Joe had been to his apartment over the hardware store on Main Street just once, to watch a Wyoming Cowboys football game. The Cowboys had lost, and Joe had found himself looking at the walls within the apartment. There was nothing on them except a few old posters that had probably been in Patterson's college dorm room. That was one reason, Joe always assumed, that the man spent so much time at the office. The courthouse was his home, in a way, whether he was the public defender or now the prosecutor. This was Patterson's world, and it had been violently disrupted.

"He actually broke down and cried," Patterson said.

"Judge Hewitt?"

Patterson nodded. "He put his head on my shoulder and cried." As he said it, Patterson reached up and touched his collar with the tips of his fingers, as if feeling for dried tears.

"This may not be a good time," Joe said, "but I'm following a lead that may exonerate my friend Nate."

Patterson reacted with alarm, but that was replaced quickly with a dispassionate professionalism. "What kind of lead?"

"Nate didn't do this," Joe said. "I'm starting from that premise. So who did?"

"Don't let your loyalty blind you," Patterson cautioned.

"I'm not. I'm just here to let you know that as far as I'm concerned, the investigation isn't over."

"Do you want to clue me in on where you're headed?"

"Not yet," Joe said, "but I'll keep you apprised. I want to keep this on the up-and-up. It's not right to brief the prosecutor on my suspicions without facts backing them up."

"Dudley Do-Right until the end," Patterson said. "You do know that I have to prosecute this case, don't you?"

"I know you have to do your job," Joe said. "That's why I'm telling you this in confidence. I don't plan to tell the sheriff until I have to."

"Wise decision," Patterson said.

"And I don't want to bother the judge right now."

"Good, because he's a mess."

"But if I find solid evidence of Nate's innocence, I'll turn it over to you and Nate's lawyer," Joe said. "You'll have to make the call then if you want to continue."

"I'll make that call if I have to."

Joe held out his hand because he didn't know what else to do. When Patterson grasped it, Joe said, "I know this has been tough. Get some rest."

"I will."

"Go home. Have a drink."

"Maybe I will."

As Joe stood up and put on his hat, Patterson asked, "Who knows about this?"

Joe said, "Nobody." He chose to keep Marybeth out of it.

Patterson nodded.

"I'll be in touch," Joe said.

He avoided the sheriff's department on his way out and he used a utility door to exit the building. Sheriff Kapelow's unit was still in the lot, parked in its designated space right up front.

TWENTY

LESS THAN FIFTY FEET FROM WHERE JOE LEFT THE COUNTY building, in a small room built of lime-green-painted cinder blocks and a stained tile ceiling, Nate met his defense lawyer for the first time.

Nate sat at a scarred table with shackles on his ankles and handcuffs on his wrists. He wore an oversized orange one-piece coverall with TSCJ—Twelve Sleep County Jail—stenciled across the shoulders. They'd taken his boots and given him a fifteen-year-old pair of cracked Crocs for his feet.

After Nate heard a key in the lock of the interrogation room door, the lawyer blew into the room and extended his hand. The man was tall and sandy-haired with a ruddy complexion and wide-spaced eyes. He wore an open sports jacket and a string tie over jeans and pointy-toe cowboy boots. His demeanor was rushed but friendly and there was no doubt he commanded the room.

"Kink Beran," the lawyer said to Nate. "I drove a long way to meet you and now we're going to set about getting you out of here and getting the charges dropped."

Nate tried to raise his hand, but a chain tethered at his ankles to his cuffs prevented it. Beran wheeled on the heels of his caiman cowboy boots and erupted at Deputy Woods, who was in the process of closing the door.

"Unlock my client this instant," he bellowed. His tone was high and grating like a chain saw. "*This fucking instant.*"

Woods was taken aback. "I'm not sure I can—"

"You can, oh you can," Beran said. "In fact, if you don't produce the keys, I'm bringing proceedings against you and everybody else in this department. I need to consult with my client and you have him bound up like he's Charles Manson."

"I'll see what I can do," Woods said, cowed. He backed away and closed the door.

Beran leaned over the table so close to Nate that Nate could breathe in his aftershave lotion.

"That was just for show," Beran whispered. "And so is *this*."

With that, he strode across the room and his hand shot out and thumped the mirrored glass that dominated the east wall.

"Clear the observation room," he shouted directly into the mirror. "There'll be no spying. Do you think this is my first rodeo?"

Then he turned to the closed-circuit camera that was mounted high in the corner near the ceiling and he approached it with a sneer. "The same goes for you, Sheriff," he said. "Turn it off and make better use of your time. Maybe hold another press conference or something."

With that, he winked at Nate and sat down.

"They've been put on notice," Beran said. "You'd be dismayed to find out how many local yokels listen in on attorney-client meetings. It happens all the time."

"What happens now?" Nate asked.

"As tough as this is going to sound to you, you need to have patience. We've both got all the time in the world. So we'll wait for the deputy to unlock you." He opened his briefcase and placed a fresh yellow legal pad on the tabletop. "Then we'll start the process to get you the hell out of here."

Nate said, "I was hoping Governor Rulon would show up."

Beran winced at that. "He handles civil law in our firm. I do criminal. I'll keep him apprised of the case, because he has a very keen interest in it, as you might have guessed. But Rulon would be the first to tell you that a criminal courtroom is not where he shines. In fact, Rulon's best work is done behind the scenes. I can't even recall the last time he was before a judge. Criminal defense is my bag at the firm. At times I might scare you and I'll sure as hell cost you a fortune," Beran said, "but you're in good hands."

"I'd better be," Nate replied.

The door opened again and Woods came in with the keys. Nate said nothing as the deputy opened the locks on his ankles and wrists.

"Sorry," the deputy whispered as he did it. "Boss's orders."

Nate nodded.

When Woods retreated and closed the door again, Beran used a low whisper to say, "I met Sheriff Kapelow before I came in here. He's a piece of work. He's all full of himself now that he thinks he's caught the killer."

Beran said the word "killer" with derision.

"There's nothing worse than a small-time sheriff who's full of himself," Beran added. "Except maybe a judge who thinks he's God."

"We've got 'em both," Nate said.

"Yes, and it poses a bit of a procedural issue," Beran said, leaning in, in case someone was listening to their conversation. "In fact, we've got problems on top of problems with this situation."

Nate responded by raising his eyebrows.

"First," Beran said, "you'll have to spend at least tonight in jail, I'm afraid. There's nothing anyone can do about it."

"I don't like jail," Nate said. "I found out in federal custody that I'm not built for it."

"I heard you were some kind of nature boy," Beran said. "But nobody likes jail except creeps."

"I'll do anything to keep out of a cage," Nate said. "I've done all the time I'm ever going to do and it doesn't suit me."

Beran shrugged. "I'm sorry, but there's nothing I can do. Like I said, we've got problems on top of problems. Tomorrow should be your preliminary hearing where bail is set and we could get you out of here, but Judge Hewitt isn't returning calls and the court has postponed any hearings of any kind for the rest of the week while he mourns."

Nate nodded. He'd anticipated that hurdle.

"Even if he does come back to the bench," Beran said, "we're talking about a judge presiding over a procedural hearing where the accused is there for killing his *wife*. Even Judge Hewitt will have to recuse himself in this case, which means we need to go before another judge. It might take days to find one who will hear the case, and we might encounter even more delays, because judges tend to protect their own. No Wyoming judge wants to be the one who frees the alleged killer of Judge Hewitt's wife."

"How long are we talking about?" Nate asked.

"I don't know," Beran said. "These are special circumstances. I'm already seeking a bond hearing date to get you out on your own recognizance until we can get a new judge or a new venue, but there's nobody to rule on the motion."

Nate scowled.

"I'm going to get with the county prosecutor as soon as I can," Beran said. "I don't know him, but I've heard he's reasonable. My hope is that we can bypass Judge Hewitt and hold the preliminary in front of another judge, maybe Judge Hartsook-Carver over in Shell County. If I ask her, she'll take a pass, believe me. But if Duane Patterson asks her, she might consider it. I left a message at Patterson's office and I hope he calls me back first thing tomorrow."

Nate said, "I need to get out however I can."

"Of course you do," Beran said.

"It's not just that I don't like jail. It's that someone has threatened my family. It's totally unrelated to this idiotic case. But I need to protect them."

Nate briefed Beran on what ex-FBI agent Sandburg had told him. While he did, Beran doodled idly on his legal pad. Whether he did it consciously or not, he drew a skull and crossbones.

When Nate was through, Beran said, "That's good information to know. We can use that to bolster our motion to get you out of here until trial—if there is a trial."

"Do what you can," Nate said. "Or I might have to get out of here on my own."

"Please don't say that," Beran cautioned in a whisper. He chinned toward the camera and the two-way mirror.

"I'm not kidding," Nate said. "I'm not a fan of our legal system. It can be a stacked deck. I've seen too many unaccountable bureaucrats use it to frame innocent people and ruin lives."

"That's why I'm here," Beran said. "To cut 'em off at the pass. So let me do my best. My best is really, really good. We can start by you not explaining how much you dislike and distrust officers of the court. That could be construed by the prosecution as a motive in this case."

"I didn't kill Sue Hewitt," Nate said. "And I didn't take a shot at Duane Patterson."

"You don't have to tell me that," Beran said.

"Yes, I do."

"Don't do it again."

Nate shrugged. "I'll tell anybody and everybody. That's why I need to get out of here."

"Please," Beran pleaded. "Let me do my job."

Nate said, "You've got a couple of days. After that, all bets are off."

Beran took a deep breath in an effort not to respond. Then he folded the doodled-upon page back to a fresh one. He said, "Let's start at the beginning. Where were you the night Sue Hewitt was shot?"

"At home with my family. You can check that out with Liv."

"Oh, we will. And we'll confirm it using your cell phone GPS log. Were there others besides your wife who can verify your whereabouts?"

"Loren Jean Hill, our nanny."

"Good, that's good," Beran said. "Our hope here is to destroy the prosecution's case before it ever gets legs. Our goal is to have the charges dismissed at the preliminary hearing—wherever it is."

Then: "Where were you the night somebody took a shot at the prosecutor?"

"Same place," Nate said. "I'm a family man."

"Very good," Beran said, scribbling. While he did, Nate could hear the attorney's cell phone vibrate.

"They didn't take your phone?" Nate asked.

"Not this one," Beran said with a wink. He reached down and hiked his pant leg up and drew the phone out of the shaft of his boot.

"Speaking of Rulon," Beran said. Then: "Excuse me, I have to take this."

"Tell him howdy," Nate said.

He waited while the two lawyers talked. Beran paced the room and became more and more animated the more he heard. Beran said, "Um-hmmm, Um-hmmm" several times and grinned while he did it. Then he said, "Spell it for me."

Nate watched as Beran scratched out two words on the pad.

"You're sure about this?" Beran asked Rulon. After hearing an affirmative response, Beran said, "I owe you one, Spencer."

BERAN SAT DOWN across from Nate with a sloppy smile on his face. After sliding the illicit phone back into his boot top and covering it with his pant leg, he said, "Governor Rulon sends his regards."

Nate acknowledged them.

"He also said the firm received a call this evening from a man claiming he could exonerate you in this case."

"Go on," Nate said.

"Rulon talked to the witness personally. He said the man had a very heavy accent," Beran said. "But according to the witness, he saw someone come to your house when you and your wife were away and plant the rifle in your birdhouse."

"It's called a mews," Nate said.

"Whatever. That doesn't matter. What matters is this witness saw the gun being hidden. And there's more." With that, Beran's eyes got large and his grin even larger. "The witness says the vehicle that came to your house was a white SUV with an insignia on the front doors. He's pretty sure it was a Twelve Sleep County vehicle."

Nate sat back, a little stunned. "Like a sheriff's department unit?" he asked.

"That's what it sounds like," Beran said.

"When did this happen?"

"The witness said he saw it happen yesterday afternoon."

"That's when Liv, Kestrel, and I went to town," Nate said. "Somehow, the sheriff knew when to plant the gun. But how could he? And how is it this witness saw what happened? We live in an isolated location. Where was this guy, anyway?"

"First things first," Beran said. "We don't need to know that now. But what a development! If our witness is credible, there's no way the charges will stand."

Nate shook his head, trying to make sense of what he'd just been told.

He asked, "Does the witness have a name?"

Beran looked at his pad. "Orlando Panfile," he said. "Odd name, I know."

"I've never heard of him," Nate said. "Where did he come from?"

"Apparently he's an undocumented migrant," Beran said. "He was camping up in the forest somewhere where he could see your property."

"What?"

"I've told you all I know," Beran said. "Rulon is coaxing Panfile to appear and swear out an affidavit. If anyone can convince the guy to show up, it's Rulon. But don't worry. We'll get the charges dropped as soon as we can get a hearing. It's just a matter of time."

"Which is what I don't have," Nate said.

TWENTY-ONE

AN HOUR AND A HALF LATER, JOE SAT IN HIS BORROWED vehicle in the parking lot of the DOT building outside of town, waiting for Mike Martin to show up to deliver his pickup. Martin had texted from Winchester to report his ETA. Joe was grateful to Martin for driving it over. He'd parked under one of the overhead pole lights so the Jackson game warden could see him.

"We're getting our truck back, girl," he told Daisy. "Are you excited?"

Daisy sighed.

"I am," he said. "I'll feel whole again."

Because his pickup was also his mobile office on wheels and all of his outdoor clothing, equipment, paperwork, communications gear, and weapons had been taken away, it felt to Joe that he'd been unbalanced since the Hewitt case commenced. His pickup was his suit of armor, and without it he felt vulnerable to outside forces.

He kept his eyes on the dark two-lane highway. He expected to see two pairs of headlights any minute, one set from his own pickup with Martin at the wheel and the second set from biologist Eddie Smith's rig. After dropping off Joe's truck, Martin would climb in with Smith and continue on to Gillette, where another biologist had a box of tranquilizer darts for them he could spare.

It was taking Martin longer than it should have, Joe thought. He checked his phone to see if there were any additional messages. There weren't. He texted Marybeth to tell her he'd be later than he thought he'd be.

She responded with:

That's fine. I'm learning some VERY interesting things from the logs you sent. Bring a pizza.

AFTER TWELVE MORE minutes of listening to the local AM station play faux country song after faux country song, Joe lifted his phone to call Martin to check on his progress. As he did, two vehicles appeared, slowed, and made the turn from the highway to the DOT facility. He recognized their profiles as they passed under the first pole light as Game and Fish units with light bars, gearboxes, and the familiar pronghorn antelope insignia on the front door.

Joe placed the keys to his borrowed truck in the ashtray, confident that no one in their right mind would want to steal it. He climbed out and was instantly bathed in headlights. Joe squinted and waved hello.

Martin was indeed driving Joe's pickup and he slowed to a stop. Eddie Smith parked behind him.

"Did you decide to stop along the way for a beer?" Joe asked

Martin when the other game warden opened his door and climbed out.

"I wish," Martin said. "But the reason we're late is way weirder than that. Come over here so I can show you something."

Joe frowned and approached his own vehicle. Martin held back on the side of the open driver's-side door.

"I stopped at the rest area just out of Winchester so I could take a leak and Eddie could catch up with me," Martin said. "Do you know it?"

"Sure," Joe said. The rest area was a DOT facility built into a saddle slope from the Bighorns and it was about a quarter of a mile from the highway. High wooded mountains surrounded it on three sides. Joe used to stop there until he discovered . . .

"The toilet was broke," Martin said, as if finishing Joe's thought. "I decided to just pee right there in the parking lot. You know how that goes. Then I realized if someone drove by, they'd see a Wyoming game warden exposing himself in a rest stop parking lot with my wanger out for all to see. Hell, knowing my luck they'd report me to the governor. So I started to walk over and do my business in the trees on the side of the building."

"Okay," Joe said. He'd used the same trees.

"That's when I heard a thump behind me," Martin continued. "It came from where I'd just stood."

"A thump?"

"Take a look," Martin said, indicating the door panel just below the window.

Joe did and saw the neat bullet hole. Then he walked around the open door and touched the interior metal where the round had left a puckered and expanded exit hole.

"It went clear through the cab and it's embedded somewhere inside the passenger door," Martin said. "It didn't go clean through it. But if I'd been standing there a couple of seconds longer, or I was sitting in that cab at the time, I'd be a dead man."

"That's when I pulled in," Eddie Smith said. "I found Mike here hunkered down behind the bed of your truck sneaking a peek up over the bed wall. His pants were still open."

"I zipped up right then and there," Martin said irritably to Smith. He obviously didn't appreciate the extra detail.

"Whoever it was didn't take another shot," Martin said to Joe. "We scoped the mountain to the east where it must have come from, but we didn't see anyone."

Smith said, "It had to come from up there, but where the thick timber is, it's short of a thousand yards from the rest area. Whoever did it made a hell of a shot."

"But you didn't hear it?" Joe asked, feeling the skin crawl on his chest.

"Must have used a suppressor," Martin said. "When I think back on it, I might have heard a crack up in the trees, like a branch breaking. I can't swear to it and I didn't associate it with a gunshot at the time. It seemed like a second or two before I heard the thump. At the time, I was busy getting ready to get rid of some coffee."

"Then it got dark," Smith said. "We didn't want to hike up that mountain in the dark to see if we could find a shooter. We were both kind of confused by everything that happened. Mike thought it might have been a stray round from somewhere, but we just don't know."

Martin said, "Maybe someone over here doesn't like game wardens."

Joe nodded. A cold knot formed in his stomach.

"Anyway," Martin said with a clearing sigh, "here's your truck. Except for a bullet wound, it's just fine."

"I'm glad nobody got hurt," Joe said.

Smith chuckled and said, "Even if he's not driving it at the time, Joe's truck gets damaged. The streak continues. It's a hell of a thing."

MARTIN, SMITH, AND JOE rested on their elbows on three different sides of the truck bed with their hands dangling inside. Joe leaned on the driver's side, Martin was directly opposite, and Smith took the tailgate. Joe thought about how many conversations he'd had with other game wardens adopting the same posture over the years. It was as if the open bed of the pickup were a kind of neutral conversation zone.

Martin caught Joe up on the grizzly bear investigation. He spoke in a world-weary tone Joe associated with longtime law enforcement officers who thought they'd seen it all but could still be unpleasantly surprised by how screwed up things turned out.

"I told you we located Jim Trenary's body right where Julius Talbot said it would be," Martin said. "The next morning, the sow grizzly and her yearling cub came back and we found them patrolling the site. The sow saw us coming from a long way and came right at us. She didn't even hesitate. Her very obvious purpose was to run us off."

Martin stopped speaking and Joe waited. Martin had trouble telling the story for a moment and Joe caught a glint of moisture in his eyes.

Martin cleared his throat and composed himself. "It was one of the worst things I've been involved in. We took out that sow as she charged us. We must have hit her a dozen times with .308 rounds before she tumbled and dropped hard. I know I hit her at least five times and she reacted like I was shooting blanks. But she was dead before she hit the ground. It was like she was possessed with super-human, *superbear*, strength.

"Her yearling saw the whole thing and he went kind of crazy. He started bellowing and crying over his dead mother. It was awful because sometimes he sounded just like a human wailing. Then he stopped and looked at us with absolute rage in his eyes. We had to kill him as well, because at the time we didn't know if Jim's killer was the sow or the yearling, and that orphaned bear wasn't running away. He was intent on doing the same suicide charge his mother did."

"Man," Joe said.

"Trenary's body was torn up but not fed on," Martin said. "It was like the bears were hoarding it for later. I've never seen anything like it. Who knows what those bears were thinking?"

"So Talbot told the truth?" Joe asked.

"He told *part* of the truth," Martin said. "Just like we thought. But he's sticking to his story.

"Turns out we were able to pretty much establish what really happened by footprints and the evidence we found," Martin said. "By the time we got it all sorted out, Talbot was being transported back to Jackson so he could make his flight. We couldn't hold him, although we asked him politely to stick around. He refused."

"So what did you determine?" Joe asked.

Martin shook his head. "What we found was that it looked like the grizzly charged them just like Talbot said. Unprovoked. But we

273

found Talbot's canister of bear spray *underneath* Jim's body. We think Talbot didn't stand there fumbling with his spray like he told us. Instead, he jumped behind Jim just as the bear charged. Do you know that old joke about bears?"

Smith said, "Everyone knows it. You and your buddy are hiking and you walk between a sow and her cub. You say to your buddy, 'We can't outrun that bear.' Your buddy looks at you and says, 'I don't have to outrun the bear. I just have to outrun *you*.'"

"That's what we think Talbot did," Martin said. "He didn't try to deter the grizzly like he claimed. What he did was step behind Jim at the last second so Jim took the full force of the attack. Then Talbot ran away while Jim was fighting for his life. We don't think he even looked back until he was on top of the hill. It might be true that Talbot didn't shoot because he was afraid he'd hit Jim. But I'd bet Jim would have urged him to take that shot anyway—given the circumstances."

Joe moaned and shook his head. "Can you charge Talbot with anything?" he asked, knowing the answer.

"Nope," Martin said. "We can't even prove that he lied to us. He can claim he just remembered it differently in the heat of the moment. There's nothing we can do to the man."

Smith said, "The FBI can charge you with lying to them. The Game and Fish Department can't."

"I know all about that," Joe said, recalling his encounter with Jeremiah Sandburg months before.

"Tell him about the PR firm," Smith urged Martin.

"Yeah," Martin said to Joe. "So when he got back to Florida, Talbot hired a crisis management firm of some kind to salvage his reputation. Down there, he's being described as a hero who put his own life in danger to save his rube of a guide. You can find the articles online. This is another first for me."

He went on. "Not only that, but the Predator Attack Team is being savaged online for killing those bears. They say we're a bunch of trigger-happy rednecks. Social media is all over me—by name. We're talking people from around the world, not just the U.S. I'm now a bloodthirsty killer of endangered species. The social media mob is going after me, our team, and even my kids. They've posted wanted posters of me with my face on them. I've become one of those what-do-you-call-them?" he asked Smith.

"A meme," Smith said. "You're a meme."

"I'm a meme," Martin said. "Talbot's even gotten himself quoted as saying he wished the bears no harm and he thinks it's a tragedy what we did. He claims he begged us not to go after them, which as you know is a damned lie. Of course, the report will dispute his version of things when it ever comes out, but by then it'll all look really murky."

"I didn't see that one coming," Joe remarked.

"Neither did I," Martin said. "I'm still wrapping my head around it all. My wife won't even look at Facebook anymore."

"That's a good policy all around," Smith added.

Joe said, "Maybe the governor will go to bat for you."

All three men laughed at that.

Martin said, "This has turned out to be a real clusterfuck. But what really bothers me is trying to figure out why those grizzlies charged like that. Was it an anomaly? Will it happen again? Are other bears changing their behavior?"

"And will it be policy now just to let them?" Smith asked rhetorically.

"The department did a necropsy on both bears," Martin said. "I was hoping they'd find out there was something wrong with them, like if she had a brain tumor or she was so sick she was acting irrationally. But our people found nothing wrong with either bear. They were fit and healthy. They just decided to turn killer. No other explanation than that."

The explanation sent a chill through Joe's body.

"I missed all this," Joe confessed. "I've been bogged down over here with that shooting. And without my pickup, I haven't heard anything over the radio."

"Probably for the best," Smith said.

"Meanwhile," Martin said, "Jim Trenary's funeral is next week. It seems like half the town will be there. Several of the wealthy locals started a college fund for Jim's kids, and they're taking care of Jim's wife. It's been great to see. Heartwarming, in fact."

"Guess who didn't contribute," Smith said.

"Julius Talbot," Martin spat.

Joe's intrinsic faith in his fellow man took another hit.

MARTIN LEANED BACK from the pickup and held his arm up to the light of the pole lamp so he could read his wristwatch. "Well, I guess we better get going. We're late already and it's getting cold."

"Thanks again for bringing it over," Joe said, patting the bed wall of his pickup. "And thanks for catching me up."

Martin nodded and started to follow Smith to his vehicle. Before he got there, he stopped and turned around and pointed toward the bullet hole in Joe's door.

"That bullet wasn't meant for me," Martin said. "Is somebody gunning for you, Joe?"

"I'm not sure," Joe said. "But I think I'm getting closer to finding out."

"Take care of yourself," Martin said.

"You too."

JOE CALLED DAISY over from the WYDOT vehicle and opened the pickup door for her as Smith's truck vanished with receding red taillights.

He climbed in, adjusted the seat to fit him again, and texted Marybeth to say he was on the way.

About time, she replied. *Don't forget the pizza.*

As he drove toward Saddlestring, wind whistled through the cab from the new hole in his door. He tried to plug it with a ball of Kleenex, but it didn't solve the problem.

The denouement of the grizzly attack left him depressed and angry.

The hole in his door meant something else entirely.

TWENTY-TWO

JOE HAD TO STOP, ONCE AGAIN, FOR THE COW MOOSE ON his road to inspect his familiar pickup and let him pass. He noted that Nate and Liv's Yarak, Inc. van was parked on the side of the garage when he arrived home. Next to it was a black Cadillac Escalade with county two Wyoming plates. Cheyenne.

He paused for a moment after he turned the engine off and simply sat there. It had been a very long day, and he'd yet to put it all in perspective. Sue Hewitt had died of her wounds. Judge Hewitt *and* Duane Patterson were distraught and on the sidelines. Nate was in the county jail charged with murder and attempted murder. And now there was a bullet hole in the pickup near his elbow.

The aroma of the pizzas he'd picked up filled the cab and made Daisy drool from the seat to the floor in long strings of saliva.

"C'mon, girl," he said. "It's dog food for you."

Daisy bounded out and loped toward the house. It was hours past her dinnertime. Joe wished his life was as simple as his dog's.

LONG RANGE

———

KINK BERAN ROSE quickly from the couch and thrust out his hand to Joe and introduced himself as Nate's lawyer. He had an extremely strong grip Joe wasn't ready for.

"*Ow,*" Joe said. "Nice to meet you."

"And it's a pleasure to meet you," Beran said. "Governor Rulon thinks highly of you. He says you're one of the good guys."

"Appreciated," Joe replied as his cheeks flushed.

Marybeth took the pizza boxes and placed them on the table. Liv opened them and used a butter knife to rescore the wedges.

"I'm starving," she said with a nod to Joe as she pulled a slice from the pie. "I haven't eaten anything all day." Liv sat back down and Joe noticed the baby monitor on the tabletop. He could see an image of Kestrel asleep on her back. The baby was obviously in one of the empty bedrooms.

"It's good you've got an appetite," Marybeth said to her.

Liv gestured with the point of her slice toward Joe. "I'm finally optimistic. I may be getting angrier by the minute at the sheriff's department and this entire stupid situation, but I'm optimistic."

Joe turned to Beran for an explanation, and the lawyer told him about the witness who had contacted them. Joe fixed a light bourbon over ice and listened to Beran. Marybeth prepared plates for the three of them.

When Beran took a breath, Joe said, "Orlando Panfile? I've never heard of him. Where did he come from?"

"Don't know," Beran said. "My impression is he's an illegal who was trespassing on the Romanowski property when he saw the county vehicle. Like he was just passing through."

279

"And why would he come to Nate's defense?" Joe asked.

Beran shrugged. "He came forward like a good citizen even though he isn't, technically at least. Look, let's not look a gift horse in the mouth. As we speak, Governor Rulon is meeting with Panfile south of town at a rest area near Kaycee. The plan is to get the man's statement and the best description we can get of the county vehicle he saw. We forwarded photos of Sheriff Kapelow and Deputies Woods and Steck. If Panfile can identify the man who planted the rifle, well, the shit will really hit the fan, but my client will be free. That's what we're here for, isn't it?"

"My money's on Kapelow," Liv said from the table. "He's the only one who benefits from making this big case against my husband."

Joe didn't respond. Kapelow had shocked him with his recent behavior and grandstanding, but planting evidence? Joe wasn't sure he could go that far.

"Can you keep Panfile on ice?" Joe asked Beran.

"That's the question," Beran replied. "It's up to Rulon's persuasive powers to convince the man to stick around and testify at the preliminary hearing. You know how good Rulon is. He's very persuasive. He can sell cheeseburgers to vegans. But we'll see after they've met. If nothing else, the statement will help. It might even result in the dirty cop confessing to what he did before the hearing and the judge may vacate all the charges against Nate."

"Lots of ifs, ands, or buts," Joe said.

"You know how the system works," Beran said. "All in all, I like our chances of a quick acquittal."

They discussed where Beran could find a judge to hear the case. Joe winced when he mentioned Judge Hartsook-Carver.

"I've worked with her," Joe said. "My experience with her wasn't very good."

"How so?" Beran asked.

"She's a little like Kapelow. She's a politico with her eyes on higher office. In my estimation, she'd only hear the case if she saw how it would advance her career."

"Then leave that up to me." Beran beamed. "I'll frame it so she can shine when she takes down a corrupt cop."

Joe nodded. "That might work," he said.

He ate pizza and continued to listen while Beran discussed strategies and possibilities with Liv at the table. The lawyer was confident as well as thorough. It was obvious to Joe that Beran knew his way around a courtroom, but even more important he knew his way around a *Wyoming* courtroom, where long-standing relationships and connections often undergirded the outcome.

While Beran spoke to Liv, Marybeth sat next to Joe and pressed her lips against his ear.

"Beran showed up just as I was getting somewhere with the courthouse logs," she said. "I'll finish it when he's gone."

"So he doesn't know what we're working on?" Joe asked back.

"Not yet. One thing at a time."

Joe nodded. Marybeth was always better with strategy than he was, so he didn't argue with her.

ON HIS WAY to the bathroom, Joe paused and eased open the hall door to Lucy's old bedroom. Kestrel was asleep in the middle of the bed and she was hemmed in by walls of pillows so she couldn't roll off. Her eyes were closed and gentle ocean sounds played from a speaker Liv must have brought with her. The camera for the monitor was placed on Lucy's dresser.

Joe felt a pang. He missed a house full of girls.

AFTER HE RETURNED to the dining room, Joe didn't bring up the hole in his pickup door. Instead, he pretended to himself that the incident was just a strange coincidence, a random occurrence.

There was too much happening to add another item.

BERAN CONTINUED to check his phone for texts from Rulon while he consulted with Liv about Nate's defense. After an hour and two scotch and waters, Beran announced that he was tired and needed to get some rest.

"I've got a reservation at the Holiday Inn downtown," he said with a grimace. "Is there a better place to stay around here?"

"Unfortunately, no," Marybeth replied.

"Maybe I should invest in a luxury hotel in Saddlestring," Beran said. "It looks like you could use one."

"Please do," Marybeth said.

"Any word from Governor Rulon?" Liv asked Beran.

The lawyer nodded and scrolled through his texts. "They're still meeting right now," he said. "Rulon has Panfile's signed affadavit, although he doesn't yet have a commitment that the man will stay around for the preliminary hearing. Rulon thinks the best we can do is get the man's contact details and hope we can call him back when he's needed. We'll pay all his expenses, of course."

Beran grinned and gestured to Liv. "Actually, *you'll* pay for them."

"I can see why Nate loves lawyers the way he does," Liv said to Marybeth.

"What about the identification of the guy who planted the rifle?" Joe asked Beran.

The lawyer shook his head. He said, "Panfile says he doesn't recognize the culprit in any of the photos we sent. He told Rulon he was far away and he can't say for sure who he saw. He claims he *might* be able to identify the guy who planted the rifle if he saw his photo, but that these photos don't float his boat."

"What does that mean?" Joe asked, confused.

"I'm not sure," Beran said. "Right now, Rulon is texting me whenever they take a break. He's leaving out a lot of information and the man needs to learn how to text properly. He needs to go to a class, or sit down with any twelve-year-old out there. Rulon writes long sentences with proper punctuation and it takes him forever to get his point across."

Joe smiled at that. He couldn't actually visualize the ex-governor standing in a rest stop parking lot hunched over his cell phone.

"Anyway," Beran said, "I'll talk to Rulon after his meeting with Panfile and get clarification on everything. I'll try to convince him to drive all the way up here so we can talk."

"I'd like to see him," Joe said.

"So would Nate," Beran said with a sigh. "You people make me feel like sloppy seconds compared to Rulon."

"We go back," Joe said.

"So it's off to the Holiday Inn," Beran said with a frown.

"Keep me posted with any updates," Liv called after him.

"Absolutely," the lawyer said.

"Watch out for the moose in the road," Joe cautioned him.

"Moose in the road," Beran repeated as he went outside, shaking his head as if he'd never heard anything so insane. "You people live in a different world up here. *Moose in the road . . .*"

"City slicker," Liv observed after Beran had left. "But a good lawyer, I suppose."

AFTER A QUICK shower, Joe slipped into bed. His brain was foggy and overburdened with all that had gone on and he was too exhausted to put anything together in a logical sequence. His entire body ached with fatigue.

Marybeth was in her home office down the hall working on the courthouse logs. Liv had joined Kestrel in Lucy's old bedroom. If Beran or Rulon called with further news, they'd be the first to be briefed. That was okay with Joe, but he hoped Marybeth would finish up soon. He longed to pull her to him beneath the sheets. He never slept well without her, but tonight, he thought, might be an exception.

JOE DIDN'T KNOW how long he'd been asleep when he was awakened by Marybeth jostling his shoulder.

He focused to find her standing over him with wide eyes. She seemed distressed and excited at the same time.

"I've found something that will blow your mind," she said rapidly. "You are *not* going to believe this . . ."

LONG RANGE

———

NOW WIDE AWAKE fifteen minutes later, Joe sat on the end of the bed in his underwear and scrolled though his cell phone until he found the home number for Dennis Sun.

The producer himself answered on the second ring.

"How did you know I'd be up?" Sun asked.

"I figured Hollywood types didn't turn in early," Joe said.

"And what can I do to help the local game warden?" Sun asked.

TWENTY-THREE

C<small>ANDY</small> C<small>ROSWELL SAT UP WITH A START AND PLACED</small> both of her hands to the sides of her face and tried to recall where she was and how she had gotten there. Her brain swam with alcohol and the room spun at first and she tried to determine what had awakened her so suddenly.

She looked around. The table was still set with three place settings, two of which had been used and shunted to the side while the third sat pristine and untouched. Two-and-a-half empty bottles of 2004 Joseph Phelps Insignia Cabernet—the last of Tom's exclusive stash—sat on the coffee table. Missy was asleep in an overstuffed lounge chair across from her. Even in a wine stupor, the woman looked annoyingly composed, Candy thought.

Then she recalled why Missy was still there: Tom had not yet come home with Missy's purchase of drugs.

Candy glanced at the clock above the fireplace. It was twelve-thirty in the morning. Tom's shift was supposed to be over at nine, although he was often late. They'd eaten dinner without him, she now recalled. It had been delicious. Baby carrots in butter sauce and chives, glazed poached salmon over angel hair pasta, greens from a can that didn't taste like they came from a can. Missy was an outstanding cook who could conjure up wonderful things from a poorly stocked pantry. Perhaps the wine had helped as well.

Then she heard what had awakened her—the automatic garage door was closing. He was back.

MISSY DIDN'T STIR when Candy struggled to her feet and padded across the room into the kitchen. As she approached the garage door, she heard jostling from the other side and voices. Men's voices.

No, she determined, not men. Just Tom. He seemed to be carrying on a conversation with himself.

Candy cracked the door a quarter of an inch so he wouldn't know she was there but she could hear him. On one hand, she was ready to confront him. Missy had filled her with righteous confidence. The woman had convinced Candy to be bold, to demand what she wanted from him, and to take it without regrets. He'd roll over, Missy assured him. All men did.

On the other hand, Candy wanted to know what it was he'd been up to.

She leaned closer to the doorframe and tried to see him through the crack. He was trying to keep his voice low, but he was emphatic as he spoke. When he passed briefly through her slivered field of vision, she realized he was speaking on a cell phone. It wasn't his iPhone. It was the burner she'd discovered in his tool bench.

"I know, I know," he said. "I should have talked with you first. But when you told me what he was doing, which direction he was going, I thought . . ."

She couldn't hear the voice on the other end clearly except to determine it was male as well. Whoever it was, he wasn't being as restrained as Tom. The man on the other end was shouting.

"You think I don't know that?" Tom said in response. "I thought I had a clear shot. I saw him get out; I saw the red uniform shirt. Trying to take that shot without a spotter was insane, I know. But I'm certain it was his truck . . ."

More shouting. The shouter went on for a long time.

Tom came back into her field of vision. This time, his voice rose and his free hand waved in the air.

Tom said, "Look, I've had it. I've just fucking had it. I told you already this was over as far as I was concerned. I know I acted irrationally tonight, but I couldn't think of another way of stopping this before it went too far, which would hurt us *both*, as you know.

"Do whatever you have to do," Tom said. "I'm clearing out for good. And if they catch me, I'm telling them everything. That's right, I'll throw you right under the fucking bus to get a better deal. You can count on that."

She'd never heard him talk with such conviction. She wondered if he'd start to cry next.

The voice on the other end of the phone was calmer than it had been. And whatever he was saying to Tom went on for a good long time. Tom paced around the garage as he listened, and his only utterances were "Hmmmmm" and "Okay, I get that."

While he paced, she shifted her hips so she could try to maintain an angle on him. That's when she saw that the back door of his pickup was open and the rifle case she'd seen earlier lay across the length of the seat.

Tom had, once again, gone shooting. This time at night.

In the dark.

AS TOM TALKED, listened, and paced throughout the garage, Candy waited until he got close to the door to see his reaction when she pushed it open.

"Who are you talking to?" she asked, setting her feet and crossing her arms across her breasts.

Tom was in mid-stride when he saw her. He looked both surprised and frightened.

"I asked who you are talking to," she repeated.

"Look," he stammered. "Look . . ."

She could hear the man Tom was talking to ask, "Who is there?"

"Nobody," Tom said into the phone. "Hey, can I call you back?"

"Nobody?" Candy hissed. "*Nobody?*"

"That's not what I meant," Tom said to her, his eyes imploring her to be quiet.

"It's what you said."

The tinny voice from the phone asked, "Who in the hell is there? Did they overhear our conversation?"

"Really," Tom said into the phone. Then he winced and said, "Just my girlfriend."

"How much did she hear?" the man asked. Candy could hear the man clearly. He was agitated.

"Just my girlfriend the nobody," Candy said.

"How much did she hear?" the man shouted.

Candy found herself being nudged to the side by Missy, who had obviously awakened due to the argument in the garage. Missy stepped in front of her and held out her hand to Tom and said, "Where the hell is my package?"

TWENTY-FOUR

FIFTEEN MINUTES BEFORE, ORLANDO PANFILE HAD walked silently toward the house from his camp in a pale blue wash of starlight and just a slice of moon. He could hear coyotes wailing in the timber behind him and that was the only sound other than the watery music of a breeze through the pine trees.

He'd carried a sawed-off double-barrel twelve-gauge shotgun and there was a snub-nosed .357 Magnum revolver in a shoulder holster under his jacket. A sheath knife hung from his belt and he wore the cowboy boots with razors hidden in the shafts. His trouser pockets bulged with shotgun shells.

Panfile was exhausted. The American lawyer had been relentless, peppering him with questions, asking the same thing over and over again, cajoling him to sign a document promising that he'd be available to testify in court. Panfile had refused. He'd given the lawyer—who claimed to be the ex-governor of Wyoming, as outlandish as that seemed to be to Panfile—only what he intended to give him: a statement that would eventually result in the release of

Nate Romanowski from jail. That's why he'd given his real name—
a fake name might have been found out, and then his affidavit
would have been worthless. He'd debated for quite a while about
doing any of this. His whole *life* had been about avoiding the law.
But this was too important. Romanowski had to pay for what he'd
done—and he couldn't do that from a jail cell.

Besides, Panfile was going to be gone very, very soon. It was too
cold here, too isolated. He missed his children. And he was nearly
out of the food Luna had packed for him.

It was time to go home.

But first he needed to carry out his plan.

THERE WAS A LIGHT on in the rear guest bedroom of the Romanowski house. It was always the last one to go out at night.
Panfile didn't know what the woman did alone in her room after
everyone else had gone to bed. Maybe she had a television in there,
or more likely she was staring at the screen on her phone. That's
what Americans did, he'd observed. They stared at their phones.

He walked around the back of the house and paused before going around to the front. He knew from his surveillance that, unlike most of the homes up here in the countryside, there were no
dogs to raise an alarm. Plenty of falcons and hawks out in the
mews, but no dogs.

Panfile froze when one of the hawks shrieked. The high-pitched
sound chilled him to his bones. Would the others join in?

Panfile didn't trust the man's falcons not to know what was
about to happen. They had unexplainable and mystical qualities as
well as a special connection to Romanowski himself. If the falcons

knew something, Panfile surmised, the falconer would know it at the same time.

But Romanowski wasn't there, was he?

Panfile knocked softly on the front door. When nothing happened, he knocked harder.

A light came on inside. He stepped back on the covered porch so he could be seen when the curtains were eased back from the front window. The porch light came on.

The young woman who opened the door was wrapped in a bathrobe. Her hair was down and she had bare feet.

"Loren Jean Hill?" he asked softly.

She nodded her head and said, "I was wondering when you'd show up."

"May I come inside and wait?"

She stepped aside so he could enter. The home itself was neat and warm. He moved through it tentatively. He didn't want to act like he owned the place.

She said, "My brother . . ."

"He'll be okay," Panfile said to her. "He'll be fine. As soon as my people hear from me that all went well, that you did everything we asked of you, he'll be released."

"I'm supposed to believe you, aren't I?" she asked. "I knew he should never have let himself get mixed up with you people."

"He'll be fine," Panfile said again. "You'll be fine. We'll all be fine."

"You won't hurt them, will you?" she asked him. "Kestrel is just a baby. I've grown fond of her."

"I don't hurt babies," Panfile said, shaking his head as if disappointed in the question. "My intention is to give him a reason to come after me on my soil. That's where I have the advantage. I want him away from here where he's comfortable."

He'd told her too much. He said again, "Everyone will be fine."

"So what do you want me to do?" Hill asked.

"Call the mama and ask her to come back first thing tomorrow morning. Make sure she brings the baby."

"What if she's suspicious?"

"She won't be if you're convincing," he said. "Your brother's life depends on it."

Hers did, too. But he didn't think he needed to say it, and he didn't.

TWENTY-FIVE

JOE HAD A VAST CHOICE OF PARKING SPACES ON MAIN Street in front of the hardware store. The only other vehicles on the block were by the Stockman's Bar a few hundred feet away. They would likely be there until the bar closed at 2:00 a.m., which was fifteen minutes from now. He got out and shut off the engine and looked up. Duane Patterson's apartment lights were still on, which didn't surprise him. The man never slept.

It was a cool, still night. Although no inclement weather had been predicted, Joe felt the bite of snow on the way in the air.

He'd changed into a fresh uniform shirt and he clamped on his Stetson and took the unusual step of undoing the safety strap on his .40 Glock sidearm before mounting the stairs to the second level of the building.

Joe paused for a beat outside Patterson's door. He could hear Duane talking inside. And not just talking but shouting: *"How much did she hear?"*

Was someone with Patterson inside? It was awfully late for visitors, Joe thought.

He rapped sharply on the door and it got suddenly quiet inside. The peephole darkened for a moment while Patterson looked to see who was on the landing. Joe heard Patterson say something urgent and then the knob twisted.

When Patterson opened the door and stepped aside, he looked both sheepish and terrified.

"I'm sorry it's so late," Joe said. "Do you have company?"

Patterson inadvertently answered the question by glancing to the side and behind him. The phone on which he'd been talking was tossed onto the back of a couch. It was a cheap convenience store burner.

"I guess you know why I'm here," Joe said.

Patterson's eyes betrayed that he did.

THEY SAT ACROSS from each other in threadbare chairs that Joe guessed Patterson had bought at a garage sale when he was in law school. The coffee table between them was littered with fast-food containers and empty cups. The apartment looked the same as when Joe had seen it last—like a bachelor hovel.

Patterson sat forward with his elbows on his knees. As he waited for Joe to speak, he ran his fingers through his hair. His breath came in short bursts, and Patterson looked everywhere in the room except at Joe's eyes. It was the same behavior a guilty hunter displayed when he knew he'd killed an elk in the wrong area.

Joe said, "Stovepipe said something to me right after Sue got shot. He was pretty upset. He said he'd really come to like Sue when she visited the courthouse—that she'd bring him cookies and brownies."

Patterson didn't respond.

"It got me to thinking," Joe said. "How often did Sue Hewitt visit the courthouse, anyway?"

It wasn't a question demanding an answer, and Patterson knew it.

"Marybeth did an analysis of the courtroom logs from the last six months," Joe said while slipping his notebook out of his breast pocket and flipping it open to the most recent entries. "She cross-referenced the log Stovepipe kept against the county calendar. You're familiar with the calendar, of course. We were both surprised to find out that Sue visited the courthouse twenty-six times in the last half year. This didn't jibe at all with what Judge Hewitt told me in his chambers after Sue got shot. He admitted he'd taken his wife for granted, and when she recovered—*if* she recovered— he wanted to try to spend more time with her. He said he felt guilty about neglecting her, leaving her out there at that house for seven months a year by herself.

"So it didn't make sense," Joe said. "Either they barely saw each other, like the judge claimed, or Sue made a habit of visiting him often in his chambers. But it makes sense now. Do you know what Marybeth found?"

Patterson shrugged and stared at the tops of his shoes.

"Of the twenty-six times she came to the courthouse, Judge Hewitt was away twenty-five of them. He was gone on one of his hunting or fishing trips or attending a conference somewhere. Which means she came to the building to see someone else."

Patterson once again ran his fingers through his hair and looked away.

"My wife also accessed the records of the Eagle Mountain Club with Judy's permission," Joe said. "They keep track of how often members come and go, even in the off-season. They've got a piece of equipment that reads the bar code on the sticker on every member's windshield. I don't know why they do that, but they do.

"Anyway," Joe said, glancing down at the figures he'd written in his notebook, "Sue passed through the gated entry two hundred and thirty-one times in the last six months. That's not a crazy number, since she'd go get her mail and groceries in town at least a couple of times a day. But the weird thing is that Sue used her membership code at the front gate another thirty-one times during that same period, meaning that instead of just driving through the gate she stopped at the key-code box and punched in her number so the gate would open. Now, why do you suppose she'd do that when all she had to do is drive up and let the gate open automatically?"

"Don't know," Patterson grumbled.

"There are two explanations," Joe said. "Either she drove a vehicle without a club bar code sticker, but I doubt that. I saw those stickers on both Judge Hewitt's SUV and Sue's BMW. There were no other cars in their garage."

"Okay."

"Or, more likely," Joe said, "she gave the code to someone else so they could come and go whenever they chose. And I'm sure it doesn't surprise you to know that those key-code accesses *also* corresponded to times the judge was out of town."

Patterson shifted uncomfortably in his chair. He looked toward the window as if there were something out there. Anything to avoid Joe.

"Then there's Dennis Sun," Joe said. "I thought he might be our suspect at one point, so I went out to his ranch and saw that state-of-the-art long-range shooting facility. At the time, I didn't even think to ask who else he let use it, so I asked him that question tonight.

"Mr. Sun said he only let a couple of locals use his range because he didn't want things to get out of hand. He knows what a big deal long-range shooting is and he didn't want folks knocking on his door all the time. I think you know what he told me."

Patterson cleared his throat and asked, "What?"

"Mr. Sun said he allowed his two local hunting guides to use the range. He said he did that because he wanted to keep them happy and sharp when they went on hunting trips. But there was one other: Dr. Thomas Arthur. Sun said he wanted to accommodate the new doctor and help keep him around, so he encouraged him to use his range whenever he wanted. He even gave Dr. Arthur the code to the front gate and a key to the facility so he could use it when Sun was in Albania shooting a horror movie, or something like that. I've never seen any of his movies.

"Then I asked Sun if Dr. Arthur arrived with a spotter. He said he did. And he said it was you."

Patterson sat back in his chair with his legs splayed out. He rubbed his face with both hands and moaned.

Joe leapt up from his chair and snatched the burner phone from the couch before Patterson could react. It had been used moments before and the screen had not yet gone to sleep, for which Joe was grateful. Getting the password out of Patterson at that point might be difficult.

"Give it back," Patterson pleaded.

Joe ignored him as he scrolled through the apps and found the one he was looking for.

"VoiceAlt," he said aloud. "This is the app Marybeth told me about. If you open it before you place a call, it alters your voice so it's unrecognizable. And here it is."

Then Joe opened the file for calls sent and received. All of the received calls were from a single number, 307-360-2247. All of the placed calls were to the same number except for one: 911.

"So you used this phone yesterday morning to call the emergency dispatcher," he said. "That's when you left the message about locating a rifle in Nate's mews. You knew they wouldn't recognize the number, but you made sure they didn't recognize your voice, either."

Patterson looked away.

Joe asked, "So the question is why the two of you took a shot at Judge Hewitt. Or was Sue the target?"

"God no," Patterson said sharply, as if offended by the question. "I loved her. I really loved her."

Joe tried to keep his face slack, but a chill ran over his skin beneath his clothing.

"Did she love you back?" Joe asked softly. "She must have thought highly of you to visit you at work all those times and give you her club access code."

"I think maybe she did," Patterson said. "At least, she almost said it a couple of times."

"Almost?"

"It wasn't like we were having some kind of torrid sexual affair," Patterson said. "Sue would never do something like that. But she was lonely and she said she loved my company. We had long talks, that's all. She was starved for friendship, is how she put it. I told her things I've never told anyone in my life, and I made it clear to her that she was the one for me.

"But she wouldn't leave him. He treated her like crap and ignored her, but she couldn't make herself leave him. It was like he had some kind of sick hold on her and she couldn't break it. As long as the judge was around . . ."

Patterson's voice trailed off.

Joe said, "So you figured if you killed him and pinned the blame on someone else that she'd eventually be with you."

Tears filled Patterson's eyes. His shoulders heaved with sobs. Joe judged the man to be genuinely remorseful. It wasn't an act. He was as upset as he was delusional, Joe thought.

"He just ignored her," Patterson said haltingly as he cried. "She was the loveliest person I've ever met. She genuinely cared for people—even *him*. She was so lonely, and she'd suffered a lifetime of neglect. You know how he can be. You've seen how he's treated me over the years."

"He also fought for you to be named county attorney," Joe said.

"That's just so he could manipulate me," Patterson said bitterly. "He knew that if I owed him, I'd do what he said. He liked to hold that over my head."

Joe knew it to be true.

"Was Sue aware of the plot?" Joe asked.

"Of course not," Patterson said. "She was a wonderful person. I never told her what I planned to do. I knew she wouldn't go along with it. But I did it for *her*, Joe. She needed someone to break the spell he had over her."

Patterson's face suddenly morphed into an ugly mask as he said, "She served him dinner every night. She told me that. He sat there at his table and stared out the picture window and waited for her to serve his dinner. This wonderful, beautiful woman . . . served him. So I knew where he would be that night. Waiting to be *served*."

"How did you convince the doctor to be involved?" Joe asked. "Or did you pull the trigger yourself?"

"No, no. I could never make a shot like that. I was the spotter."

"So why did he agree to kill him?"

"You know, it doesn't seem like murder when it's that far away," Patterson said. "When you kill something so far from you that you can't even see the target, it's more like a game than a crime. We had no idea Sue would be in the room with the judge at that time. I didn't know it until the next morning."

"Again, why did he agree to be the shooter?"

"I was tipped that our doctor is running a very lucrative side business in illicit prescription drugs," Patterson said. "He's got wealthy customers from all over the country. I could have brought a case against him that would have put him away for a lot of years."

Joe nodded. That explained the sudden arrival of Missy, but he didn't bring her up.

"Did you threaten him with prosecution unless he helped you?" Joe asked.

Patterson didn't want to admit it. But after a heavy half minute of silence, he whispered, "Yes.

"I promised him it would be just one shot," he added. "But it never works out that way, does it? Things just go to shit. I've had dozens of clients over the years who did something wrong that wasn't so bad but it led them on a spiral where everything got out of control. I should have known it could happen to me."

"What about the assault on you?" Joe asked. "Did you two have a falling-out?"

Patterson said, "No, like I said, things went to shit. When I found out Sue got hit instead of Judge Hewitt, I panicked. I had to steer the investigation away from me.

"It was a setup. I told Tom where to be that night and where I would park my car. I scrunched down under the steering wheel and let him take a shot through my windshield so it would look legit."

Joe nodded.

"I loved her," Patterson said again.

"That's why you've been so upset," Joe said, trying to appear empathetic, even though he wanted to draw his weapon and pistol-whip Patterson's head. "Your reaction to Sue's shooting and death seemed kind of over the top at the time. Especially during that press conference. Now it's clear why you were so emotional. You accidentally killed the woman you loved."

"I'll never meet anyone else like her," Patterson sobbed. "I mean, look at me. Look where I live. How I live."

"I'm sure you're right about that," Joe said. Then: "Is the sheriff in on it?"

"What? No. Of course not." Patterson wiped tears from his cheeks and cleared his throat. "He's just incompetent. I knew he wouldn't figure anything out. I've seen him bungle case after case since he got here. I wasn't worried. I had no idea Judge Hewitt would bring you in on the investigation."

Joe felt flattered, but he didn't react. "Is that why the two of you took a shot at my pickup tonight?"

"I knew nothing about that until a few minutes ago," Patterson said. "That was Dr. Arthur acting alone. He's losing it, I think. The pressure is getting to him."

"So that's who you were talking to on the phone when I knocked on the door?" Joe asked.

"Yes."

"Did you buy a couple of burner phones to communicate with each other?"

"Yes."

"You learned some things representing and prosecuting dirt-bags."

Patterson closed his eyes.

"THE PERSON WHO drove the county vehicle to plant the rifle at Nate's place," Joe said. "That was you, wasn't it? You have access to the county motor pool."

Patterson nodded meekly. "Arthur didn't want to hand over his rifle, but I made the case to him that it would keep us both in the clear."

"Was it your intention to blame Nate all along?"

He nodded again. "If necessary. You know his reputation," Patterson said. "Nobody would put it past him."

"I would."

Patterson seemed too exhausted to argue, so he simply looked away.

"Does Dr. Arthur know I'm here?" Joe asked. "I heard you say something into the phone when I knocked on your door and you looked through the peephole."

Patterson nodded. "I might have said something."

"Either you did or you didn't," Joe said.

"Yeah, I think I did."

Joe stood up and hovered over Patterson for a minute. The county attorney was still seated and sweating through his scalp.

"I think we should leave right now," Joe said.

"Where are we going?"

"County jail," Joe said. "I assume you know the way in."

"Is there any way—"

"Nope."

"My life is ruined," Patterson cried. "I *should* be in jail. I'll never have the woman I wanted because I fucked up everything."

"Yup," Joe said. "Now stand up, turn around, and let me cuff you."

"Jesus, you don't have to do *that*," Patterson said.

"I just want to."

"Really, Joe. I'll go willingly. Or better yet, just leave me here and go on your way. I've got a shotgun in the closet and I'll end it all before you get to the bottom of the stairs."

"Stand up and turn around," Joe said through gritted teeth.

When the cuffs were ratcheted tightly around Patterson's wrists, Joe said, "How well do you know Dr. Arthur?"

"What do you mean?"

"You coerced him into this, but do you know his heart?"

"Why?"

"Because I've been around game animals who were shot or poached with high-powered rounds all of my career," Joe said. "I've dug hundreds of slugs out of carcasses so they could be sent to the state lab. Never in my experience has a slug splintered into so many particles that it couldn't be recovered. Modern bullets aren't known to do that. Sue Hewitt's injury was the first time I'd ever heard of it happening, even though Dr. Arthur claimed that's what happened."

Because Joe had his hand on Patterson's shoulder to steer him toward the door, he could feel the man's muscles suddenly tense.

"Oh, Jesus," Patterson said. "He let her die."

"It might be hard to prove," Joe said, "but an autopsy might show that it wasn't even the bullet that killed her. Maybe it was really bad care. Or maybe it was a dose of the drugs he's selling to rich folks.

"Let me ask you a question," Joe said. "That morning I walked in on the two of you it seemed like you were having an argument. What was it about?"

"He was pissed at me," Patterson said.

"Why?"

The man sighed. "Because I told him Sue had briefly regained consciousness and I'd apologized to her for what happened. I hoped she'd find it in her heart to forgive me, but I'll never know. I'm not even sure she actually heard what I said, and she slipped back into sleep."

"Did you tell her Dr. Arthur was the shooter?"

"Yes. I confessed everything."

"So in a way," Joe said, "you killed her."

Patterson froze. "*What?*"

"Dr. Arthur didn't want Sue to recover if she had that knowledge. He knew that if she lived, he might go down for this. So he made sure she'd never talk."

"He should be next," Patterson hissed. "He should be the one going to prison. My God—if he's responsible for Sue's death . . ."

"You both are," Joe said.

Patterson turned his head and stared at Joe. His eyes were pleading. He was suddenly scared.

Joe drew his digital recorder out of his breast pocket and clicked it off. Patterson watched and said, "I forgot about that trick."

"It isn't a trick."

Joe checked to make sure the device had worked by scrolling through the recording file and turning the audio on.

Patterson could be heard saying, "You know, it doesn't seem like murder when it's that far away. When you kill something so far from you that you can't even see the target, it's more like a game than a crime."

Patterson winced. Then his eyebrows arched as he thought of something. "You didn't read me my Miranda rights," he said. "It isn't on the tape."

"I didn't officially arrest you, either," Joe said. "I'm simply detaining you for your safety and mine. I'm giving the arresting honors to Deputies Woods and Steck at the department. They'll Mirandize you, so you don't have to worry about that."

Patterson sighed. "Technically, that won't fly."

"I'll take my chances."

OUTSIDE ON THE SIDEWALK, Joe kept behind Patterson and prodded him on toward his pickup. The county attorney was sobbing again. Big, racking sobs.

It was getting colder. Joe looked down the length of Main Street until it vanished in darkness beyond the street lamps. He could hear the river flowing like liquid muscle beneath the bridge. Far beyond the river, the rise of the foothills blacked out the bottom of the starry night sky.

From within the distant hills, he saw a tiny yellow blink of light that almost didn't register at first. When it did, Joe had no more than a second to react. But when he reached out to shove Patterson aside, he was too late.

The bullet hit Patterson with a fleshy *thunk*. The man rocked back on his heels and stiffened, then fell hard to his side. His head hit the exterior brick wall of the hardware store on his way down.

Joe went down with him because he still had a grip on Patterson's collar. Joe's face was spattered with hot blood.

The crack of the rifle shot washed over them, the sound bouncing off the walls of downtown buildings. The crack was muted, likely because the shooter had used a suppressor.

Joe scrambled over Patterson, trying to see in the light of the street lamps where the man had been hit. Patterson's body jerked and his feet thrashed. He was unable to reach for the hole in his throat because his hands were bound behind his back. His eyes were panicked and wide.

"I'll get those off," Joe said, rolling Patterson to his side so he could get at his hands. He fumbled in his pocket for the cuff keys, but he was shaking too hard to locate them. The exit wound in the back of Patterson's neck pulsed blood.

By the time he found the keys, Duane Patterson was still and gone.

The second round smacked into the bricks inches above Joe's head and the debris from the wall stung the side of his face and neck. He scrambled away from Patterson's body and flattened himself facedown on the concrete of the sidewalk.

He lay there with his eyes wide open and his cheek bleeding while the muted crack of the second shot rolled over him. Joe didn't move for several minutes until he heard the wail of approaching sirens and he was convinced the shooter was gone.

TWENTY-SIX

Forty-five minutes later, Joe was third in a task force of law enforcement vehicles speeding out of town toward Dr. Tom Arthur's home on Buckbrush Road. The hastily organized strike force was led by Deputy Woods with Steck right behind him, then Joe, then Saddlestring chief of police Williamson, followed by two cruisers driven by town cops. Flashing light bars lit up the passing brush and trees in psychedelic colors, although only the lead SUV had turned on its siren.

After Woods had arrived on Main Street to find Patterson's lifeless body, they'd pulled it into an alcove next to the hardware store out of the line of fire. Joe and Woods had huddled together in the shadows between the buildings while Joe explained what had happened. Woods listened, then he'd called Deputy Steck on his cell phone at home and shouted that they needed him on scene immediately.

At first, Joe wondered why Woods hadn't made the request via county dispatch. Woods was rattled, he thought. Then he realized what Woods was up to and he agreed with the decision: keep Sheriff Kapelow in the dark, so their boss wouldn't show up at the scene. Woods then called Williamson at home, then the EMTs at the clinic on the remote possibility that Patterson was still alive, then Gary Norwood to secure the crime scene on the sidewalk and in the alcove.

"Where did the shots come from?" Woods asked.

Joe gestured to the east.

"From the hills?" Woods asked. "That far?"

"At least a thousand yards away, judging how long it took between the flash of the muzzle and the bullet hitting Patterson."

"Shit," Woods said. "That was a hell of a shot."

He raised his Maglite and thumbed it on.

"You need to get your face looked at," Woods said to Joe.

"I will. Eventually."

"If I were you, I'd go now."

"If I were you, I'd get that flashlight out of my eyes."

"Sorry."

The beam was squelched and Joe could see nothing but orange spangles in the dark.

"Steck's on his way," Woods said. "When he gets here, you can cut out and go get patched up."

Joe ignored him. He said, "Kapelow is going to find out what's going on soon enough. You know he's not going to be happy."

"Screw him," Woods said. "We don't want him anywhere near us right now if we've got an active shooter situation. Who knows what he'd do? He completely botched the investigation and let the shooter kick his feet up on his desk just down the hall from us.

Then he arrested the wrong man and crowed about it to the media. Now his terrific instincts have led to the murder of our county attorney."

Joe nodded, but didn't respond.

"Is the Game and Fish Department hiring these days?"

"Steck asked me the same thing. Nope. There's a hiring freeze."

"I think they'd take me over him, don't you?"

"Not my call," Joe said.

Woods shined his flashlight on Patterson's body and the beam lingered on the grotesque exit wound on the back of his neck. Joe felt his stomach convulse and he quickly turned away before he threw up.

"Poor guy," Woods said. Then: "Wait until the judge finds out."

AS HE DROVE, Joe winced when he raised his left arm and rubbed his uniform sleeve over his face. The numbness was wearing off and his cheek and neck were stinging with pain and oozing blood. He could feel the grit of the vaporized brick embedded in several large contusions. He was grateful his eyes had been spared of the debris.

Using Bluetooth, he called out, "River Home," and Marybeth answered the landline on the second ring. He wasn't sure the cell signal on the county road was strong enough to sustain both his cell phone and hers.

"Everything has busted open," he said to her. "You were right about Duane and Sue Hewitt, although it sounded pretty one-sided. He confessed the whole thing to me before he died. I've got him on tape."

"Oh my God," Marybeth said. "Did he kill himself?"

"He had help."

Joe briefed her as succinctly as he could about Dr. Tom Arthur's involvement.

"Was he the shooter?" she asked, incredulous. "Our doctor shot our county attorney in the street?"

"Yup. At least that's what it looks like."

"He tried to kill you at the same time?"

"He missed."

Joe chose not to tell her about his face and neck.

"This is insane," she said.

"Agreed. Like I said, we're going out to Arthur's house now. We've got him outmanned and outgunned. I don't know if we'll catch him there, but that's the plan."

"You need to be careful," she said. "He's shown he's desperate and he's proved he can kill from a long distance."

"I'm glad it's dark," Joe said. Despite Arthur's long-range skill, darkness would complicate an accurate shot. If it weren't for the illumation of the streetlights in town, Patterson would likely still be alive.

"We're getting close to Buckbrush Road," Joe said. "I'll let you know how it goes. But you can tell Liv when she wakes up that Nate will be free sooner than we'd hoped."

"I'll call her right now," Marybeth said.

"Call her? Isn't she there?"

Marybeth said Liv had received a text message from her nanny. Something about a big problem with Nate's Air Force.

"The falcons?" Joe asked.

"That's what Liv said. A mountain lion or a bear got into the

313

mews. Liv went out there to see what she could do. She took Kestrel with her."

"She took the baby? At two-thirty in the morning?"

"Kestrel was awake when the nanny called," Marybeth said. "Liv was feeding her. You remember those days. Time of day means nothing to a baby."

"I'll go out there as soon as I can shake free," Joe said.

"She'll appreciate that."

Joe left it there. He hoped, in fact, that a bear or mountain lion had somehow gotten into the mews and that it wasn't something— or someone—more sinister.

DR. ARTHUR'S HOME on Buckbrush Road was lit up like a riverboat when the law enforcement caravan swept under the archway and drove across a wide lawn toward it. The house was a New West three-story rustic mountain design built of prefab logs with a pitched metal roof and a massive river-rock chimney. Joe caught a glimpse of a massive elk-antler chandelier through the great room windows and he noted that the porchlights were on, there was light in nearly every window, and two of the three doors of the garage were open. Floodlights embedded beneath the eaves cast inverted Vs of light on the front of the house and a series of short lamps bordered pathways leading from the structure to various outbuildings. A dark barn sat next to it with a sign in front indicating there was a yoga studio inside.

The place looked strangely welcoming, Joe thought. Dr. Arthur obviously wasn't waiting inside in the dark with the purpose of ambushing them. Either that, or it was a trap.

Light up the exterior grounds as much as possible, Joe thought, and it would be easier for Arthur to pick his targets.

Woods's headlights lit up the interior of the garage as his SUV roared up into the driveway. Joe could see a bundle of what looked like clothing strewn beneath a workbench on the concrete floor at the far end of the garage.

Steck parked his SUV next to Woods and bailed out. He had a departmental AR-15 and he positioned himself behind the open door. The town police cars roared around Joe's pickup into the front lawn and stopped. Their headlights lit up the front of Arthur's house even more, and the multicolored wigwags from their light bars made the exterior of the home appear to be dancing in the dark. One of the town cops moved a car-mounted spotlight from window to window.

Joe stayed well behind the line of law enforcement vehicles. He pulled to the side, got out, and unlocked the large Kobalt gearbox in the bed of his pickup. He retrieved a tactical Kevlar ballistic vest and pulled it on over his uniform shirt. Then he dug his twelve-gauge Remington Wingmaster shotgun out from behind the front seat. It was loaded with double-aught buckshot and he racked a shell into the magazine as he walked across the pulsating lawn toward the back of Woods's vehicle. He kept his eyes on the windows of the house for movement, especially the top-floor bedroom on the south side, which was the only one that was dark. But he saw no blinds being pulled or windows opening.

He was well aware that while the vest offered some protection, it wouldn't stop a high-powered projectile fired from a high-tech long-range rifle. It was unsettling and terrifying, he thought. A bullet could be headed toward him at that second and there was no way he would know it was fired or to avoid getting hit. But at least, he thought darkly, Marybeth couldn't chide him about not taking any precautions, like the usual case when he was shot down like a dog.

Joe joined Woods, Williamson, and a town cop crouching behind the back of Woods's SUV. Steck was behind his vehicle next to them with a town cop of his own.

Woods said to Williamson, "Send two of your guys around the back so they're ready to intercept him if he comes out that way. I'll wait until they're in position and try to talk him out."

Williamson nodded eagerly. He turned to his officers and said, "You heard him."

The two town cops, who both looked to be in their early twenties and who both sported wispy cop mustaches, exchanged a baleful glance with each other before heading out. Joe guessed that they had the same contempt for the chief as Woods and Steck had with Sheriff Kapelow. Both, he thought, had the same fear he did: that they could be struck down at any moment by a sniper a long distance away.

When they were gone, the chief turned to Woods and Joe. He looked animated and gleeful, Joe thought. He was eager for a firefight.

"I wish you would have let me bring my MRAP," Williamson said to Woods. "This here situation is why we need it."

"You can go get it if we need it," Woods said. "But right now we don't know what we've got."

Joe was grateful their departure from Saddlestring had been

chaotic and rushed. He could envision the MRAP crashing through the front door of Arthur's home with a giggling Williamson at the wheel.

After a few moments, one of the town cops reported via Williamson's radio that they were in position.

Woods shinnied along the side of his SUV and reached in through the open driver's-side window for his PA microphone. After keying it, he said, *"Dr. Arthur, this is Deputy Justin Woods of the Twelve Sleep County Sheriff's Department. We have your house surrounded. There is no way out. I'm asking you to lay down any weapons you might have and step out through your front door with your hands on top of your head. We don't want anyone to get hurt."*

Joe peered around the back of the vehicle toward the house. He could see no movement inside.

Woods repeated his command. While he did, Joe saw Deputy Steck crabwalk toward the open garage. It was both a courageous and foolhardy action to take, Joe thought. He held his breath until he could see Steck enter the garage and sweep it with his rifle. Then Steck stood up, obviously relieved that there was no threat to him from inside.

Steck's voice came over Woods's handheld radio. "I'm inside the garage. Dr. Arthur's pickup is gone and there's a door into the house from here. I'll go inside, but I want to make sure you can cover me. Tell the cops to make sure all of our team knows what I'm doing, so they don't see movement inside and decide to shoot me."

"We don't want a friendly-fire incident," Williamson said to no one in particular. He was simply repeating what Steck had said.

Williamson continued: "And we don't want to shoot the doctor

317

if we can help it, either. I was on the search committee for a new doc for the clinic. Believe me when I tell you how hard it is to convince one to move here. Dr. Arthur was the only doc who would agree to come."

Joe and Woods simply stared at Williamson, and the chief seemed to realize he'd been thinking out loud. In his defense, he said, "It's gonna be hard to convince a new doc to come here if he knows we shot the last one."

"We hope to arrest him," Woods said. "Not shoot him."

"Either way, we'll have to find a new doctor," Williamson said.

"Then just tell your guys *not* to shoot Deputy Steck or the doctor unless he threatens anyone," Woods said to the chief. Joe could tell he was trying to keep his irritation out of his voice.

Williamson told his men to sit tight until Steck was inside and he gave the all-clear.

"Hey," Steck said through the radio, "there's somebody in here. Oh, fuck—there's a woman down in the garage."

Joe looked to see Steck gesturing toward the bundle of clothing by the workbench.

"What's her condition?" Woods asked Steck over the radio.

"She's breathing. I don't see any blood."

It was at that moment that Joe recognized a vehicle parked in the shadow of a grove of aspens on the side of the house. He hadn't seen it earlier because of the bright lights everywhere else.

County twenty-two plates. Missy's Range Rover.

Was she the person in the garage? Was she inside? Was she dead? Had she been forced to accompany Arthur as he fled?

Joe fought an urge to be okay with any of those outcomes. And he felt guilty about it.

LONG RANGE

——

BUT IT WASN'T Missy bound in duct tape and barely conscious on the garage floor. In a heavily slurred voice, she said her name was Candy Croswell.

Joe squatted down next to her as Steck cut through the tape on her wrists and ankles with a pocketknife. Woods, Williamson, and the town cops had stormed inside and were sweeping the house room to room.

The tension of the situation had largely lifted and faded away now that it was obvious Arthur had fled the scene before they got there. The sudden release of tension often resulted in giddy behavior and dark humor in cops on the scene, Joe knew. He felt it himself.

"Tom is gone," Croswell said while her eyes filled with tears. "He left me. The cheating son of a bitch left me."

Steck asked her, "Tom is Dr. Arthur?"

"*Yumm*," she said, nodding her head. She meant "Yes."

"Did he drug you?" Joe asked.

"Yeah, but I was already drunk," she said with no inflection.

"How long ago did he leave?"

"No idea. What time is it now?"

Joe looked at his watch. "It's three-twenty."

"In the morning?"

"Yes."

"Then I don't know when he left me here," she said. "Not long ago, I think. The cheating son of a bitch chose his stupid rifle over me."

Joe and Steck exchanged glances when she said it.

"Sounds like a bad country song," Steck said. "'The cheating son of a bitch chose his rifle over me.'"

Joe didn't want to smile, but he did.

At that moment, the door to the house opened and one of the town cops said, "We've got another one inside. Another woman. This one's much older."

"I think I know who she is. Is she all right?" Joe asked. The answer would be important one way or the other.

"She's a mean old bearcat," the cop said. "She cursed me when I cut her loose and she ran into the bathroom and locked the door. She won't come out."

"I'll see what I can do," Joe said wearily. To Steck, he said, "Better call the highway patrol and get an APB out on Arthur's pickup before he gets too far."

"On it," Steck said. "A gray Ford Raptor with vanity 'DR TOM' plates, right? It should be fairly easy to pick out."

"Yup."

"And we'll soon find out who out there is listening to the police band tonight," Steck added ruefully.

"I'm keeping my car," Croswell said, gesturing to the Mercedes parked in the garage. "I don't care what he says. Fuck him. I *deserve* that car."

"MISSY, YOU NEED to come out," Joe said as he leaned against the bathroom doorframe. "We've got to ask you some questions about what happened here tonight."

He could hear her gasp when she recognized his voice.

"Why are *you* here?" she said. "I don't want to talk to you."

"Sorry."

"Go away."

"I'm not going away," Joe said with a sigh. "If you don't come out, we'll break the door down and drag you out."

"Do not talk to me that way."

As she said it, Woods walked by and winked at Joe.

"She's my mother-in-law," Joe said to him.

"Do you want to leave her in there?" Woods asked.

"Yup."

Missy said, "Stop talking about me. I can hear you, you know."

Woods rolled his eyes. Then: "We found a stack of checks in his office from clients all over the country. Some of them even say 'medication' in the subject line. Our good doctor was a drug dealer, it seems."

Joe chinned toward the locked door. "That's why she was here."

"She's an addict?" Woods asked.

"*I am not a drug addict*," Missy hissed from inside.

"She's addicted to husbands," Joe said. Woods covered his mouth with his gloved hand so he wouldn't laugh out loud. Giddy, Joe thought.

"I'm trying to *save* my husband's life," Missy cried.

"Then come out and talk to us," Joe said to her.

There was a long beat. Then her voice, much more softly than before: "Joe, can you get me my handbag from the living room? It's on a chair or on the coffee table. I look terrible. I need to fix my face before I can come out. There was tape around my mouth and in my hair. It's embarrassing. I can't let anyone see me like this."

"No one cares what you look like," Joe said.

"You've never understood anything," Missy said. "Now go get

my bag and pass it through the door. I'll open it for you. But don't you dare look at me."

"Gladly," Joe said.

He found it next to a gallon ziplock bag filled with prescription drug containers of what looked like hundreds of pills.

TEN MINUTES LATER, while Missy was still reconstructing her appearance in the bathroom, the front door blew open and a short man in full camo stepped inside. He brandished a semiautomatic rifle.

Joe was slow to react, but Deputy Steck and two of the town cops raised their weapons and shouted for the intruder to drop his gun.

Judge Hewitt did as he was commanded, but with obvious disdain.

"Oh," Steck said to him, "I didn't know it was you. Sir, I'm not sure you should be here right now—"

"Where is the bastard who shot my wife?" Hewitt demanded as he cut Steck off. "I'm going to kill him."

The judge had not only brought his own AR-15, but he had a Colt .45 semiauto in a shoulder holster. No one asked him to toss the weapon aside.

"He's in the wind," Joe replied to the judge. "There's an APB out for him."

"I know, I know, I heard it on the police band," Hewitt said to everyone in the room. "I didn't realize you all were already here. I thought you were out chasing him and I could catch the son of a bitch in his lair and put a cap in his ass."

"No, sir, not yet," Steck said. "We're in the process of securing the home."

"Don't let him get away," Hewitt said, wagging his finger at all of the officers in the room.

"We'll get him," Williamson chimed in from where he'd ducked down behind the couch when the door opened.

The look Judge Hewitt gave the police chief was withering. "It's a good thing your officers were on the ball and not hiding behind furniture," he said to him.

Then: "Joe, what in the hell is going on here? Why did Sue's doctor shoot her and then let her die of neglect?"

Joe glanced at the locked door to the bathroom, wondering how long Missy would take, then at Judge Hewitt.

"Let's step outside for a minute," he said. He threw an arm around the judge's shoulders and guided him back though the front door. Joe could feel Hewitt trembling.

"IT WAS DUANE," Joe said to Judge Hewitt when they were on the front lawn. "Arthur was the shooter, but Duane was the spotter. The whole plot was cooked up by Duane."

Judge Hewitt listened with incredulity. Joe played the most revealing snippets of Patterson's confession on his digital recorder. Finally, the judge said, "I think Sue just felt sorry for him. I didn't think he was smart enough to plan and carry out something like this."

Which was part of his motivation, Joe thought but didn't say. Duane was, in his twisted way, striking back.

"And Dr. Arthur," Hewitt said, "he either let her die or he

helped it along. I kept wondering why he didn't do more, but I actually trusted his judgment."

"Yup," Joe said. "Or maybe he's just a really bad doctor."

"I want to kill him."

"I know you do. But we're not going to let you."

"Then go find the son of a bitch and keep him away from me."

"Yup."

TWENTY-SEVEN

FROM HIS BUNK IN THE COUNTY JAIL CELL, NATE LISTENED to the chaos over the radio down the short hallway from the empty sheriff's department lobby. He grew more and more anxious by what he heard, and his eyes felt hooded by a shroud of upcoming violence. His breathing became shallow and his hands tingled.

He was furious and desperate at the same time. All hell had broken loose out there: the county attorney had been shot and killed by an unknown assassin, the home of the local doctor had been raided, hostages had been found, and the suspect was on the run.

But his feelings of impotence and rage had begun fifteen minutes before the radio in the lobby had begun to squawk. They'd begun when he was awakened by a heavy *whump* against the frosted, wire-reinforced glass of the only window in his cell that faced outside. The blow to the window had a lot of force behind it; enough that it had cracked several of the glass panels.

The impact had awoken something primal inside him because

he somehow knew what had caused it. When it happened, he sat up in bed wanting to render his own particular kind of justice in the worst way. Starting with the incompetent and feckless sheriff who had caged him on bogus charges with bogus evidence, all the while Liv and Kestrel were vulnerable.

Nate wanted out of that jail and he wanted out *now*.

FIVE MINUTES LATER, Nate heard someone enter the lobby and clomp around. That got his full attention. Sheriff Kapelow sounded flummoxed when he called out, "Ryan? Justin? Is anybody here?"

"Back here," Nate answered.

In a moment, Kapelow made his way down the hallway and he stood on the other side of the bars. He carried what looked like a bundle of feathers in his hands.

"Where are they?" he asked Nate.

"Out doing your job," Nate said. "I heard about it all over the radio somebody forgot to mute."

Kapelow shook his head, not understanding.

"They've got one of the shooters of Sue Hewitt and they're looking for the other one."

"They can't do that."

"They deliberately cut you out," Nate said. "So did the chief of police and Joe Pickett."

"*They can't do that*," Kapelow protested. "I'm the sheriff."

"And a piss-poor one. Now, let me out of here."

Kapelow just stood there, stunned. The significance of what Nate had told him reflected in his slack face. He looked even more feckless and deflated than Nate had thought possible.

"You're holding one of my birds," Nate said, gesturing at the crumpled falcon Kapelow carried.

"What?"

"That's part of my Air Force."

"I found it outside. It looked like it crashed into the side of the building. I don't know what to do with it."

"Hand it over. It might still be alive."

The sheriff contemplated the request for a minute, then unlocked the upper half section of the door and opened it. He thrust the falcon toward Nate as if handing off a football.

Nate gathered up the bird and cradled it like a baby. It was one of his best performing peregrines, a bird that had worked with him for several years. It still wore the tooled leather hood Nate had placed on it before he was arrested. The falcon had flown blind from his mews through the night and it had broken its neck when it smashed into the jail cell window.

"Is it yours?" Kapelow asked. "Is it dead?"

Nate nodded. He couldn't speak.

"How did it know how to find you? Here, give it back to me," Kapelow said. "I'll go throw it in the dumpster. Then I'll go find my men and take charge of the operation. Oh, there will be hell to pay."

Nate looked up slowly from the peregrine through an opaque film of pure red. In a series of lightning-fast movements, he dropped the body of the falcon, shot out both of his hands, grasped the back of Kapelow's head, and pulled him over the bottom door into the cell.

While the sheriff thrashed and tried to fight back, Nate took the man's weapon out of the holster and tossed it out into the hallway. He did the same with the pepper spray and cuffs on the sheriff's belt. Then he pinned the man down on the floor by placing his knees on Kapelow's shoulders and leaning over until they were nose to nose.

"You're letting me out of here," Nate hissed.

"You don't know what you're doing," Kapelow said. There was panic in his eyes.

"I know exactly what I'm doing," Nate said as he reached down with his right hand and took a firm grasp of Kapelow's left ear.

"Where is your keycard?" Nate asked.

"You'll go to prison for this," Kapelow said. "You're assaulting a peace officer."

With a hard torque of his wrist, Nate twisted Kapelow's ear off and the man screamed. Twin pulses of blood sprayed across the concrete floor from the side of Kapelow's head. His detached ear hung uselessly by thin strings of sinew.

"That bird flew here to warn me," Nate said as he switched hands and grabbed Kaplow's right ear. "*Where is your keycard?*"

"Back pocket," the sheriff howled. "Back pocket."

Nate let the pressure off and rolled Kapelow over to his belly. He found the card for the cell door in the man's jeans. After he did, he stood up. The sheriff moaned and bent his knees into a fetal position while he covered his detached ear with his hands.

Nate reached over the open half door and inserted the card into the door lock. It released with a click and he pushed it open.

"You're lucky I let you off easy," he said to Kapelow.

Before he strode down the hallway into the lobby, Nate ducked back into the cell and retrieved the body of the peregrine. It deserved a dignified burial.

Nate detached a first-aid kit from the hallway wall and tossed it into the cell. Then he slammed the cell door shut on Kapelow, kicked the weapons aside, and found his .454 Casull in the evidence room.

NATE ROARED INTO the yard of his home in Kapelow's stolen SUV and he knew instantly that Liv and Kestrel had been taken.

Their Yarak, Inc. van was parked in the open garage and the lights were on inside. The front door gaped open.

When Loren Jean Hill tried to explain that she'd been forced to call Liv home or the man would have her brother killed, Nate swung his pistol through the air and hit her on the side of her head with the long barrel and she dropped like a sack of cement.

For good measure, he stormed through every room of the house to confirm that no one else was there. Then he filled a small canvas duffel with .454 ammunition, binoculars, rope, gloves, a jacket, and two skinning knives.

The man from the cartel who'd taken his wife and daughter had an hour head start on him, possibly two. There was no way the kidnapper could know Nate had broken out of jail and was coming after him.

Nate abandoned Kapelow's SUV and tossed the duffel bag onto the passenger seat of his old Jeep Wrangler that he'd kept in a shed. He knew it would start because even though he rarely drove it, he'd kept it maintained and ready to go.

As he sped up the gravel road away from his house toward the highway, Nate thumped the steering wheel angrily with the heel of his hand.

He'd let this happen, he thought. Against his better judgment, he'd gone along. He'd put his family in danger by trying to be more like Joe—to trust that the system would be fair.

No more.

Going back on the grid, marrying Liv, and fathering a daughter had not changed the facts on the ground. There were still more Sheriff Kapelows out there than Joe Picketts. Nate's mission had always been to even the odds. Now, though, there were more innocent lives at stake. And it was his responsibility to save them.

When he approached the highway, he knew which direction to turn:

South.

TWENTY-EIGHT

Two days later, Joe nudged Rojo through a stand of closely packed aspen as he worked his way up the mountain. Rojo's steel shoes crunched on the bed of fallen golden leaves as more leaves fluttered down through the air around them. It was a cold morning, the first freeze of the fall, although the intense midmorning sun was softening the ground as it rose behind him in the west.

Following Joe up the mountain on horseback were Mike Martin and Eddie Smith from the Jackson office. They'd responded immediately to Joe's call, dropped what they were doing, and driven through the night to Saddlestring towing a horse trailer.

The three horsemen were a truncated version of the newly maligned Predator Attack Team, although this time they weren't going after a killer grizzly. They were hunting a doctor.

AFTER THIRTY-SIX HOURS and alerts across the states of Wyoming, Montana, South Dakota, North Dakota, Idaho, Utah, and Colorado, there had been no sighting of Dr. Arthur's unique Ford

Raptor with the DR TOM plates. It wasn't until Candy Croswell revealed, almost as an aside, that he'd recently closed on a remote mountain cabin on the back side of Wolf Mountain a few weeks before, that they knew where to go. She hadn't been there, she said. Once she'd found out it didn't have plumbing or electricity, she'd been reminded of her time in Alaska and said she'd had no desire even to see it.

A quick title search by Marybeth of the Twelve Sleep County Assessor's Office provided the exact geographical coordinates of the place—known almost immediately to her and Joe as "Dr. Tom's Cabin"—and she located it on Google Earth.

Joe had been in the remote area a few times checking elk hunters, and he knew the cabin wasn't easy to get to or sneak up on. The only access was a weedy two-track that meandered through the pines and literally ended in a mountain meadow. On the edge of the meadow, with its back end in the wall of timber, was the cabin Tom Arthur had purchased.

Because it would be an all-day journey even to get there to check it out, Joe had asked Martin to send the Lifeseeker unit over the mountains to do a sweep. The pilot reported that he'd picked up a brief cell phone signal in the vicinity of the cabin location, but that it was just a few seconds long, as if the owner of the cell phone had turned it on just long enough to search for a cell signal— which was unavailable—before punching it off again.

Joe had notified both the FBI and Judge Hewitt that they had a lead. Hewitt begged to go along, but Joe refused to let him. The special agent he'd spoken to at the FBI in Cheyenne had instructed him to do no more than determine if the cabin was occupied. If it was, Joe was told, he should alert the feds and await a strike team.

"I hear you," Joe had said.

The special agent was reassured, unaware that Joe had meant exactly what he'd said. He'd heard the man. That didn't mean he'd comply with the order.

Joe hadn't bothered alerting the sheriff's department. Both Deputies Steck and Woods had been suspended and weren't in the building. Sheriff Kapelow was bunkered in his office with his door closed, refusing to take calls from the media, law enforcement, or his angry constituents.

MARYBETH ALSO DID a background check on Dr. Tom Arthur, which was something the local hiring committee—including Chief Williamson and other prominent local types—had apparently failed to do before offering him the job.

The community had been so desperate to land a new doctor, she'd surmised, that they'd take whomever they could get.

Arthur's medical degree was from a university on an obscure Caribbean island that she'd had to look up to verify. Although he claimed he'd done his residency at the University of Houston hospital, there was no record of him there. He had been on the staff of a Baptist hospital in Oklahoma City for a year, but had left under mysterious circumstances and the administrator there wouldn't elaborate except to say she was glad he was gone. When Marybeth asked her directly if he'd been accused of selling prescription drugs on the side, the administrator had said it was "something like that."

Dr. Arthur had been sued for malpractice in Fargo, North Dakota, but had vanished before the civil trial took place. There was a four-month gap between Fargo and Saddlestring, where no doubt he'd been grateful to land. Marybeth learned that Arthur had been passed along from hospital to hospital by unscrupulous adminis- trators who feared lawsuits from damaged patients or a wrongful termination suit from Arthur himself. None of them had raised a red flag about his incompetence or criminal behavior.

She was furious at those hospital administrators as well as the local hiring committee for not vetting Arthur and for welcoming him into their county.

JOE AND MARTIN had studied the Google Maps images while formulating a plan. Because of the wide mountain meadow that fronted Arthur's cabin, the man—if he was there—would have a 180-degree field of vision. If they approached the structure in ve- hicles, he'd be able to see them coming a mile away. For a suspect who likely had a second long-range rifle, it wasn't a viable option.

Instead, the Predator Attack Team transported their horses to a trailhead four miles south of the cabin. They saddled up the mounts in the dark and were deep into the timber by the time the sun nosed over the eastern mountains. Joe had his shotgun in a saddle scabbard as well as the .308 Smith & Wesson M&P strapped across his back. There was a satellite phone in his saddlebag as well as binoculars, a handheld radio, a field first-aid kit, and extra am- munition. Martin and Smith were similarly armed and equipped.

AS HE RODE through the trees to the north, Joe felt both excited and sick to his stomach. He thought there was a very good possibil- ity that they could locate and arrest Dr. Tom Arthur, that it made sense that he'd hole up in a cabin while every trooper and every cop in seven states was out looking for him on the highways. How it would play out if he actually was there was another thing entirely.

Dr. Arthur was undoubtedly a desperate man. He'd killed before and he'd likely have no hesitation to do it again. They'd need to assess the situation and go in—if they chose to go in—with their eyes open and every possible precaution in place. It would be Arthur's choice to give himself up without violence or go down shooting. Joe prayed it would be the former.

But it wasn't just the anticipation of what could go badly that made Joe feel nauseous. It was a stew of feelings and realizations. He still couldn't quite believe that the county prosecutor had bled out from a gunshot wound right in front of him, or that he'd been shot at all. It seemed like a bad dream. After Patterson had confessed and humiliated himself before Joe, the man had been cut down.

Then there was the disappearance of Nate, Liv, and Kestrel. They were simply gone. Cell phone calls to Nate and Liv went to voicemail. Joe had driven to their place to find the van sitting there with the keys in the ignition, all of the doors unlocked, and no indication that they'd packed up to flee. Even the nanny was gone.

Joe had fed Nate's Air Force, and assured them without confidence that Nate would be back soon.

WHEN THE DENSE timber ahead of them started to lighten up, Joe realized they had found the open meadow. He signaled to both Martin and Smith to stop their horses while he dismounted.

Although Rojo was as reliable a gelding as he'd ever ridden and

335

he'd been trained as a cutting horse mount, Joe didn't dare simply drop the reins and walk away. Instead, he tied the horse firmly to a tree trunk. There was never any way to predict what even the best horse might do if they caught a whiff of a bear or mountain lion.

Joe limped toward the opening because his legs and butt ached from the saddle. Although Marybeth rode whenever she could, Joe rode when he had to. And he was paying for it with sore knees and dull pain in his thighs.

He lowered his profile and crabwalked through knee-high dead grass as he got close to the meadow. He crawled on his hands and knees to the edge and parted the grass as if looking through a curtain. Raising his binoculars to his eyes, he focused the optics.

The cabin, about two hundred and fifty yards away, was simple, weathered, and boxy. It was constructed of heavy logs and it had a faded green metal roof. There was a covered porch on the front with what looked like two ancient Adirondack chairs on it. A gray woodpile was stacked on the west side of the cabin, and on the east side, Joe could see the nose of a vehicle parked alongside it.

He sharpened the focus on his optics to see the R and D of FORD on the grille, as well as the DR TOM license plate. A thin curl of woodsmoke wafted up from the chimney.

Before Joe could scuttle back to confirm what he'd found, the front door to the cabin opened. Joe froze in place with the binoculars pressed to his eyes.

Dr. Arthur walked out on the porch and paused to sweep the forest with his eyes. He appeared to be in no hurry. He wore jeans, a canvas coat, and a floppy, wide-brimmed hat. Joe had never seen him look so casual. Arthur also had a heavy high-tech long-range rifle over his shoulder on a sling.

Joe knew that if he had a similar weapon, he could end it all that moment. Dr. Arthur would never know what hit him. After all, that's how *he* liked it.

Arthur moved off the porch and took the two steps down to the grass. He continued to survey the surroundings as he did so. After gathering several lengths of cut and stacked pine, he turned back for his cabin. But before he went inside, he paused and turned around. Toward Joe.

Although it seemed practically impossible, Arthur seemed to stare directly at him. It was as if his gaze penetrated the twin barrels of the binoculars and pierced Joe's eyes.

Then Arthur quickly went inside and kicked the door shut behind him.

"WHAT DO YOU MEAN he might have seen you?" Martin asked Joe in a whisper.

"I know it's crazy, but it's like he looked right into my eyes."

The three men were gathered together at the base of a huge spruce. Martin and Smith had dismounted and secured their horses. They talked in low tones so their voices wouldn't carry.

"What do you think?" Smith asked. "Should we call the feds in like they asked us to?"

Joe shook his head. "I don't think so. Arthur's truck is right there by the cabin. He could get in and just drive away and we'd never intercept him on horseback. By the time the FBI got here, he could be a hundred miles away."

"Agreed," Martin said. "We need to take him down ourselves."

"Right," Smith said, "but he's got that rifle. If he knows we're out here, he could pick us off one by one. We'll never even see it coming."

"Should we wait until dark?" Martin asked Joe.

Joe thought about it and again shook his head. "Maybe. But I don't like it that he could drive away any time. I think the best odds for us taking him down are right now when we know exactly where he is. He might think he saw something, but he can't be certain."

"How do we do it?" Smith asked. "Tell him to throw down the rifle and come out with his hands up?"

"I don't think that would work," Joe said. "Arthur's a doctor. He thinks he's smarter than everyone else and he's never been held accountable for anything. He's already shown us he's capable of violence. I doubt after all of this he'll just walk out."

"So what do we do?" Martin asked.

"We rush him," Joe said.

Martin looked at Joe with skepticism. But he listened further.

FIFTEEN MINUTES LATER, Joe climbed into Rojo's saddle and nudged the horse forward through the trees toward the meadow. He lifted the handheld to his mouth and said, "Mike, are you in position?"

"Roger," Martin said.

"Eddie?"

"Roger."

"Keep your radios on and start yelling if anything goes wrong."

Mike Martin had ridden his horse in a wide arc through the trees to the west of the cabin. He'd tied up and was to advance on foot through the timber and brush until he could clearly see the side of the structure. Eddie Smith had ridden around to the west. Both were to find good cover where they had eyes on the front door of the cabin. There was no back door.

Joe took a deep breath and tried to calm his nerves. His plan was audacious and he was glad Marybeth had not been there to hear it. Even now, after persuading Martin and Smith to go along with it, Joe was having second thoughts. Maybe calling in the feds and hoping they'd get to the location before Arthur left it was the prudent thing to do after all?

The germ of his strategy was something Nate had said when they'd found the location of the shot fired at Sue Hewitt.

Joe had asked, "How long does it usually take for a high-tech range finder to determine the distance and all the variables for the shot?"

"On average, fifteen seconds," Nate had said.

Dr. Arthur was alone in his cabin and he didn't have a spotter to call out the calculations for an accurate long-range shot. Which meant he'd have to guess if he had a target, or spend precious time determining the logistics. The rifle wasn't meant or designed for close-in snap shots. It was heavy—a computer mounted on a syn- thetic stock.

If he'd figured correctly, time and distance were actually in Joe's favor in this scenario. The closer Joe got to Arthur and his weapon, the harder he'd be to hit.

He hoped.

"Here we go," Joe said into his radio.

He eased the safety off his shotgun and held it at his side in his left hand. After pulling on the compression straps of his GAME

339

WARDEN ballistic vest as tightly as he could, he grasped the reins in his right. He clicked his tongue and Rojo moved through the last of the brush into the open meadow. Joe spurred Rojo with his boot heels and the horse broke into a dead run. Joe held on. His hat flew off his head and landed somewhere behind him.

Rojo ran fifty yards straight at the cabin when Joe saw the front kitchen window slide up. Arthur had seen him coming. After a beat, a rifle barrel emerged from the opening and rested on the sill.

Joe was not the horseman Marybeth was, but he tried to re-create her cutting horse exercises with Rojo outside their house in the corral. He laid the reins across the left side of Rojo's neck and squeezed with his right leg. The horse responded and Rojo cut quickly to the right in full stride. So quickly, Joe nearly lost his balance and flew off.

Righting himself, Joe guided Rojo back toward the cabin at more of an angle. After fifty more yards, he cut the horse to the left. This time, Joe was ready for the sudden shift and he leaned into it and didn't have to recover from it as clumsily as he had the first cut.

Rojo seemed supercharged. He was a horse on a mission. It was as if the gelding could sense Joe's terror and trepidation through the close contact of seat, legs, and reins.

Joe could only imagine Arthur inside looking through his powerful rifle scope, trying to keep it steady and on a target that was filling his optics with blurred images as it zigzagged in front of him and got steadily closer.

Joe cut Rojo to the right again, then left, then right and right again. He was close enough to the cabin now that he could see Arthur inside the window holding the rifle stock to his cheek. The muzzle swung back and forth erratically. A glint of reflected sunlight flashed from the lens of the optics.

When Joe was twenty yards from the front porch, he dismounted on the fly with the intention of hitting the ground running. Instead, his boots got tangled up on the landing and he tumbled forward face-first. His shotgun flew out of his grasp.

He rolled to his side and looked up at the window. Arthur wasn't there. Joe shakily got to his feet.

Before he could scramble to recover his weapon, though, Arthur threw open the front door and emerged. Ignoring his big scope, he thrust the rifle toward Joe like a heavy lance.

"*Drop it,*" Joe ordered.

Arthur didn't. He pointed the rifle toward Joe without aiming and pulled the trigger.

BOOM.

The impact of the bullet spun Joe around and he lost all feeling in his lower body. It felt as though he'd been hit with a baseball bat. In slow motion, he fell again to the ground, accompanied by a fusillade of two .308 rifles firing multiple rounds into Arthur on the porch.

The last thing Joe Pickett saw was the wide blue sky and the underbelly of a fat cumulus cloud.

TWENTY-NINE

AT THE SAME TIME, NEARLY A THOUSAND MILES AWAY IN the tiny and eccentric lobby of the Flying Saucer Motel on the outskirts of Roswell, New Mexico, the desk clerk scrolled through his cell phone for a number he'd entered years before. As he did it, he was observed by dozens of pairs of oval black eyes from alien figurines that occupied the shelving behind him. Each figurine cost $29.99 and supposedly resembled the beings from outer space that had crashed their ship near the town in 1947, an incident that had allegedly been hushed up by the U.S. government but was still celebrated—only partly tongue-in-cheek—by local businesses and the chamber of commerce.

The desk clerk was named Arthur Youngberg, and he'd had the job at the inn for five months after moving south from Townsend, Montana.

Youngberg had vacated his home up north after receiving a tip that armed agents of the U.S. Fish and Wildlife Service were planning a dawn raid with the purpose of arresting him and confiscating golden and bald eagles, red-tailed and prairie falcons, and a magnificent goshawk. To Youngberg, Roswell seemed to be a good place for an outlaw falconer without official federal eagle permits to go off the grid. Thus far, he'd been correct.

Roswell, population 48,000 people, was located in the southeastern quarter of the state, 155 miles from Lubbock, Texas, and 162 miles from Ciudad Juárez, Mexico. It was warmer than Townsend, but just as arid, and the wind blew gritty and stiff.

Youngberg was stocky and he moved with the gait of a cautious black bear. He came from a family of Wyoming farriers, but he'd gone his own way. He had a long beard streaked with gray and black military-style horned-rim glasses. All of his hunting birds had been relocated to a mews he'd constructed behind his double-wide trailer twelve miles from town. The birds seemed to have taken to the harsh terrain, and Youngberg ventured deeper and deeper with them, hunting prairie chickens and grouse on federal lands that were once occupied by the Walker Air Force Base—the place where the recovered aliens were supposedly hidden away.

Youngberg had been suspicious about goings-on at the motel since he'd been hired. Rather than families on vacation, the overwhelming majority of guests at the motel had been single men from Mexico who exuded menace. Many didn't speak a word of English, but they had plenty of cash to pay the bill. They drove new cars and often partied hard while they were there. The owners of the business seemed to have an understanding with people south of the border, he thought. Recently, three men had stayed nearly a week before they simply vanished.

He was also a regular contributor to an unruly website devoted to falconry, although he didn't post items under his real name because he knew the feds were reading it, too. There had been items on the site over the years featuring the name and exploits of a fellow outlaw falconer in Wyoming with a Special Forces background and a legitimate new bird abatement service.

Members of this particular breed of falconer kept in touch via the website, although most members of the community had never met in person. They used it not only to discuss falcons and hunting, but also to alert others about strident local and federal law enforcement activities when it came to possession of eagles, which, although the ownership was technically legal for qualified master falconers, had all but dried up. The feds didn't want private master falconers to hunt with eagles, even though statutes allowed it. Master falconers, especially those with a *Don't tread on me* view of government in general, helped each other stay a few steps ahead of the federal bureaucrats who tried to shut them down.

Nate Romanowski, the legendary master falconer from Wyoming, rarely posted on the site. When he did, it caused a mild sensation within the tiny but fervent outlaw falconry community. But he'd done a post just the day before.

Youngberg found the number and punched it up. Someone answered on the third ring, and Youngberg could hear highway noise and wind rushing. The connection was poor.

"Is this Nate Romanowski?"

"Yes, it is. Who is this?"

Youngberg identified himself and said he'd seen the post on the website.

"Go on."

"I'm at a place called the Flying Saucer Motel in Roswell, New Mexico. I just rented a room to a fiftyish Mexican national named

Orlando Panfile. With him was a very attractive dark-skinned woman in her early thirties and a little baby. She got my attention when she called the baby Kestrel, like the hawk."

There was silence on the other end. Either the call had been dropped or Nate was forming his thoughts.

"I'm an hour away," Nate said to Youngberg. "I'll call when I get there."

"They're staying in unit number seven," Youngberg said. "It has two bedrooms."

"Good. Call me if they go somewhere."

"Will do."

"What is the man driving?"

"A white Toyota Land Cruiser with Texas plates."

"Thank you. I know you didn't have to do this."

"We watch out for our own," Youngberg said. "Someone has to."

AN HOUR LATER, Orlando Panfile sat primly on the edge of the mushy bed in his bedroom and kept a close eye on the closed bathroom door. There was a Colt Python .357 Magnum revolver in his lap. Despite the wind outside rattling the windows and the shower sounds from the bathroom, baby Kestrel slept soundly in her car seat near the headboard. When Kestrel sighed in her sleep, Panfile smiled. She was a good baby, he thought.

The trip south had taken longer than necessary because he'd made several detours onto the obscure county roads and even deliberately gone hundreds of miles out of his way to the east and west on the journey. No one, he was sure, could have followed them. The killer of Abriella was still in jail as far as he knew, although he expected him to be released soon as a result of Orlando's statement to the lawyer.

Panfile had kept Liv under control by separating her from her baby whenever they stopped for gas, restrooms, or food. As long as he had Kestrel next to him, he knew, she wouldn't make a break for it or say anything to strangers they encountered. He hadn't made an explicit threat, but he didn't need to.

When they crossed the border into Juárez, he wanted Liv Romanowski to look fresh, clean, and unharmed, because there would be photos taken and posted. He'd texted his colleagues to make sure they were ready for them. They were.

He'd come to like her very much, as well as the baby. Liv was a good mother, and she was very clever. Liv had engaged him and suggested ways he could let her and Kestrel go with no repercussions. Her husband wouldn't seek revenge, she'd assured him. She'd make sure of it, she'd said. She didn't cry, didn't plead, didn't offer herself in a deal to be set free. She seemed to realize it was simply a business transaction and that he was doing what he was doing for that reason. He didn't tell her that his people *wanted* Nate Romanowski to come for her so they could make a very public example of him. Still, though, she was at times very persuasive, he thought.

More than once she reminded Panfile of Abriella: beautiful, curious, resourceful, and possessing a ruthless streak. He had no doubt that if he'd given her an opportunity, she would have slit his throat and fled with her baby. He admired her, and he'd told her he would protect her and Kestrel from some of his more brutal colleagues.

He heard the shower stop, and a moment later the bathroom

door opened with a puff of steam. Liv had a white towel on her head and another wrapped around her body. She didn't even look at him. She checked on Kestrel sleeping in her car seat.

"She's fine," Panfile said.

Liv nodded. "Knock on the door if she wakes up. I don't want you holding her. No offense."

"I've got five kids of my own," Panfile said, wounded. "I've held them all. I've changed their diapers. I know what to do."

Liv turned her gaze on him and the effect was surprisingly chilling. It was as if *she* had the gun.

"Hurry, please," he said to her. "We'll leave as soon as you're dressed."

LIV LOOKED AT her reflection in the bathroom mirror. He'd let her fill a bag at a local Walgreens with makeup and other items while he waited for her out in the car with Kestrel. While inside, she'd eyed other customers who were in their own worlds and none of them paid much attention to her. Not that she would have told them her baby was outside next to a cartel killer, but she wished she could have communicated something. That she couldn't made her feel complicit in her own kidnapping.

Liv knew they were close to the border. Once they got there, she had no idea what would happen. But she couldn't think of any way to distract him, grab Kestrel, and run away without risking the life of her baby and herself. Orlando was careful and calm. He had no vices to exploit.

Liv opened the latch and shoved up on the bathroom window frame. For a second, she envisioned a scenario where she would claim that she needed to change Kestrel's diaper out of his view, then she'd slip through the window with her baby and run.

Unfortunately, the window opened only three inches before it hit a barrier.

She leaned down and looked out. Dust from the sill blew in her eyes from the wind. But she'd caught a glimpse of something she hoped was real and not wish fulfillment, like her previous scenario.

Then she saw it again: a battered Jeep looking much like Nate's passing through the opening between two motel units.

Liv held her breath and stood motionless. She didn't hear a car door slam.

A moment later, there he was. He moved from unit to unit with his elbow bent and his pistol pointed up near the side of his face. She didn't dare shout, but she implored him with her eyes to look her way.

He did. Their eyes locked. He didn't seem anxious in the least.

Nate mimed a knocking gesture with his free hand and followed it by holding his arm straight out, palm down, and lowering it to the ground.

She understood and she nodded that she did.

Liv quickly closed the window, threw her clothes on, and opened the bathroom door.

PANFILE WATCHED HER come out. She was naturally beautiful, but he was a little disappointed she hadn't made herself up into something more glamorous since he'd intentionally given her the time and opportunity.

She smiled nervously at him and went straight toward Kestrel on the bed. The baby's head had listed to the side while she slept and Liv gently tucked in her blankets and set her right.

The knock on the outside door was firm and insistent. "Housekeeping."

Panfile recognized the voice of the motel desk clerk. He quickly checked to confirm that the bolt and the door chain were in place, that the hotel staffer couldn't just walk in on them. "We're fine," he called. "We don't require anything now."

The knock again. "Housekeeping."

As he stood up, Panfile saw that Liv had gone around the foot of the bed and was still tending to Kestrel in her car seat. He approached the door.

"We don't need anything," he said.

Another series of sharp raps. "*Housekeeping.*"

Could the man not hear? Panfile asked himself.

ON THE THRESHOLD of unit number seven, Nate stood to the side and thumbed back the hammer of his .454. He intently watched the peephole.

To Youngberg, whom Nate had asked to come from the lobby with him, he chinned toward the office and mouthed, "*Go.*" Youngberg scrambled away. There was no need to talk further, he thought. No reason for a dramatic confrontation. He had no interest in Orlando Panfile or in why, how, or what could have happened. All he cared about was that his wife and daughter were inside. His plan driving south had been simple: to go to Sinaloa and pile up bodies until the cartel released Liv and Kestrel. Youngberg's call had made it even simpler.

When the peephole darkened, Nate raised his revolver and fitted the entire muzzle around it with one motion and squeezed the trigger.

BOOM.

Nate squared himself in front of the door and kicked it open. The doorjamb gave way and the chain snapped, but the door would only open a foot because Panfile's body blocked it. Nate put his shoulder to the door and shoved and the body slid along the cheap linoleum flooring leaving a swath of blood.

The wall opposite the doorway was spattered with blood and brain matter. Nate glanced down as he stepped over the body to make sure his job was complete. It was. Orlando Panfile had no head from the nose up.

Liv looked up from where she'd gone to ground behind the bed. Her grateful smile beamed. Kestrel was in her arms wailing from the sound of the shot.

"Don't look," Nate warned her. "And don't let Kestrel see anything."

He had an irrational fear that his baby would retain the image of the gore in the room for the rest of her life. In response, Liv draped Kestrel's blanket over the baby's head.

"Are you okay?" he asked Liv.

"We're fine," she replied. "He was a surprisingly kind man, actually. But we're ready to go home."

"Let's go now."

He stood to the side to let Liv and Kestrel step over the body of Orlando Panfile and pass through the door into the gritty wind.

"Don't forget the car seat," Liv called to him over her shoulder.

THIRTY

Two weeks later, Joe awoke from a nap in his hospital at Billings General to a commotion outside in the hallway. The matronly nurse he'd come to dislike said, "Sir, our visiting hours are over."

She was strict about enforcing the rules. She was strict about everything. Joe got the distinct impression that she felt she could really run an efficient hospital wing if it weren't for all the patients and visitors in it.

"We'll only be a minute," a male voice said. It was Nate. Joe smiled in anticipation.

Nate entered his room first, followed by Liv holding the baby and Marybeth behind her.

"Don't get up," Nate said to Joe.

"Very funny."

The .338 Lapua round Arthur had fired had hit Joe on the inside of his left thigh and exited out the back. It missed his thighbone, but it had nicked his femoral artery on the way through.

Although he was unconscious at the time, he learned later that Martin and Smith had performed field first aid on him by elevating the leg and applying a tourniquet above the wound so he wouldn't bleed out. Dr. Arthur had not been so fortunate. He'd been hit eight times by Martin and Smith and he'd likely died before he hit the ground.

Joe had been taken to Billings by a Life Flight helicopter straight into surgery and then the intensive care unit. He learned that despite his fellow game wardens' care, he'd lost so much blood that he'd been minutes away from death. For the first week, he and Marybeth had been warned by the doctors that he might lose his leg.

He was recovering, though, and ahead of schedule. A year of physical therapy lay ahead of him, he'd been told, and maybe more.

Marybeth had been with him every day. He felt embarrassed to be so weak and useless. When he was awake, she kept him abreast of developments in Twelve Sleep County via Facebook, the online Saddlestring *Roundup*, and texts from friends and library patrons.

An arrest warrant had been issued for Nate Romanowski by the sheriff's department for assaulting a peace officer, escaping from jail, and several other charges for good measure.

Deputies Woods and Steck had been reactivated, but when they'd refused to apprehend Nate, they'd both been suspended from duty again.

Sheriff Kapelow, who had cruelly been dubbed "Sheriff Van Gogh" because of his missing ear, castigated by the community for pursuing the wrong shooter and suspending his men, had quietly packed up his house and vanished.

Judge Hewitt had announced that he was retiring from the bench to found and administrate a Sue Hewitt Foundation to provide grants and mental health assistance to the families of violent crimes.

Wyoming governor Colter Allen had announced his intention to give commendation letters to game wardens Mike Martin, Eddie Smith, and Joe Pickett for their actions in apprehending the killer. He'd also had his office send a bill to the Game and Fish Department for the cost of the bodywork on Joe's pickup due to high caliber bullet holes.

Missy had slipped away back to Jackson with her illicit medication and she'd called Marybeth to say that Marcus Hand seemed to be recovering.

Candy Croswell was participating in a true-crime podcast about unscrupulous doctors who defrauded both patients and loved ones.

Martin and Smith had both been placed on administrative leave by the Game and Fish Department pending an investigation because of their roles in the officer-involved shooting of Dr. Arthur. They'd spent at least some of their leisure time telling others about Joe's foolhardy but effective horseback run at the cabin that was now dubbed "Pickett's Charge."

Loren Hill had turned herself in to authorities and admitted her role in the scheme in order to protect herself after her brother was found hanging by the neck from a bridge in South Dakota, left there by his cartel-associated captors.

Marybeth had been elected chair of a new search committee to find a legitimate doctor willing to move to Twelve Sleep County and take over at the clinic.

———

Joe had been deeply touched when he'd awakened during the first week to find April and Lucy in his room. They'd carpooled from Wyoming when they heard the news and had waited at his bedside. Seeing them and grasping their hands brought tears to his eyes.

"I don't know what's going on," he'd said to them. "I just feel very emotional right now. It's got something to do with getting hurt."

"Don't apologize," Lucy said, tearing up herself. "It's okay." She'd always been the most open with her feelings.

"Just don't get shot anymore," April said with faux-ferocity. She'd always been the most intense.

"I'll try not to."

"Try harder," April said. And for a second, her mask slipped.

He asked them about how things were going at their respective colleges and if they had plans to come home for Thanksgiving.

"Will you be home by then?" Lucy asked.

"Yes. But I won't be hopping around yet."

Nate and Liv approached Joe, and Liv handed Kestrel to him. Joe cradled the baby and nuzzled her head with his chin.

Nate said, "You probably heard. I'm going back off the grid for a while."

"*We're* going back off the grid," Liv corrected.

Joe nodded. "I'll do what I can to get the charges dropped when I'm up and around. Maybe Rulon can help."

"Just concentrate on getting up and around," Nate said. "Right now, there isn't a sheriff's office to arrest me."

"I heard what happened in New Mexico," Joe said. "I hope that ends it."

"I do, too," Nate said. "But I'm staying vigilant in case they decide to come after us again. I'm better when I'm vigilant."

Joe had to concede the point. He could tell by Nate's nervous movements that his friend had something more he wanted to say. Joe waited.

Nate said, "Liv and I need to keep the company going while we're out of sight for the time being."

"Yes?"

"So there needs to be a new public face for Yarak Inc. for a while."

"Okay."

"And here she is," Nate said, stepping aside and nodding to Marybeth, who in turn nodded toward someone out in the hall. Liv gently retrieved Kestrel.

Sheridan entered with a sheepish grin and walked over to Joe. She looked radiant and mature, he thought. His twenty-three-year-old daughter and Nate's apprentice in falconry was back for the time being, and he was both grateful and concerned.

"You're okay with this?" he asked her.

"I'm excited. I really didn't want to go to grad school right now anyway."

"Learn everything you can about falcons," Joe said, "and nothing about twisting people's ears off."

"She's going to live with us for a while until she can find a place of her own," Marybeth said. "I assume that's okay with you."

Joe nodded. "Of course. I was getting too used to having my own bathroom."

April and Lucy came into the now-crowded room from the hallway. Joe realized it had been a setup all along to break the news to him. His three daughters gathered around his bed.

"Maybe you'll all come back," he said.

"Maybe we never left," Lucy responded. Marybeth cried happily near the door.

April rolled her eyes at the sentiment and said again, "You need to quit getting shot."

ACKNOWLEDGMENTS

The author would like to thank the people who provided help, expertise, and information for this novel.

Landon Michaels and the staff and engineers at Gunwerks in Cody, Wyoming, who gave up their time and vast knowledge on the manufacture and ballistics of long-range rifles and shooting.

Brad Hovinga, regional wildlife supervisor for the Wyoming Game and Fish Department in Jackson, provided background information and technical details on recent actual grizzly bear–human fatalities he investigated.

Special kudos to my first readers, Laurie Box, Molly Box, Becky Reif, and Roxanne Woods.

A tip of the hat to Molly Box and Prairie Sage Creative for cjbox.net and social media assistance.

It's a sincere pleasure to work with the professionals at Putnam, including the legendary Neil Nyren, Mark Tavani, Ivan Held, Alexis Welby, Ashley McClay, and Katie Grinch.

And thanks once again to my terrific agent and friend, Ann Rittenberg.